SWEET ANTICIPATION

"No," Ellari said, her lips only inches from his. "We can't. It's wrong."

"We belong together," Trigg whispered. "We need and want each other. I can't deny it any longer. Can you?"

Her eyes bright with questions, she shook her head slowly and melted into his kiss, surrendering her entire essence to its power.

Yes, this was what she wanted.

She trailed her thumb over his lips, still moist from their kiss. The raw loneliness she saw in his eyes surprised her and a yearning to fulfill all his longings erased the last of her misgivings.

She had no desire to stop him, no desire to stop what she knew was going to happen—what she wanted to happen with every fiber of her existence. At last, the waiting was at an end . . .

HEART STOPPING ROMANCE BY ZEBRA BOOKS

MIDNIGHT BRIDE   (3265, $4.50)
by Kathleen Drymon

With her youth, beauty, and sizable dowry, Kellie McBride had her share of ardent suitors, but the headstrong miss was bewitched by the mysterious man called The Falcon, a dashing highwayman who risked life and limb for the American Colonies. Twice the Falcon had saved her from the hands of the British, then set her blood afire with a moonlit kiss.

No one knew the dangerous life The Falcon led—or of his secret identity as a British lord with a vengeful score to settle with the Crown. There was no way Kellie would discover his deception, so he would woo her by day as the foppish Lord Blakely Savage . . . and ravish her by night as The Falcon! But each kiss made him want more, until he vowed to make her his *Midnight Bride*.

SOUTHERN SEDUCTION   (3266, $4.50)
by Thea Devine

Cassandra knew her husband's will required her to hire a man to run her Georgia plantation, but the beautiful redhead was determined to handle her own affairs. To satisfy her lawyers, she invented Trane Taggart, her imaginary step-son. But her plans go awry when a handsome adventurer shows up and claims to *be* Trane Taggart!

After twenty years of roaming free, Trane was ready to come home and face the father who always treated him with such contempt. Instead he found a black wreath and a bewitching, sharp-tongued temptress trying to cheat him out of his inheritance. But he had no qualms about kissing that silken body into languid submission to get what he wanted. But he never dreamed that *he* would be the one to succumb to *her* charms.

SWEET OBSESSION   (3233, $4.50)
by Kathy Jones

From the moment rancher Jack Corbett kept her from capturing the wild white stallion, Kayley Ryan detested the man. That animal had almost killed her father, and since the accident Kayley had been in charge of the ranch. But with the tall, lean Corbett, it seemed she was *never* the boss. He made her blood run cold with rage one minute, and hot with desire the next.

Jack Corbett had only one thing on his mind: revenge against the man who had stolen his freedom, his ranch, and almost his very life. And what better way to get revenge than to ruin his mortal enemy's fiery red-haired daughter. He never expected to be captured by her charms, to long for her silken caresses and to thirst for her never-ending kisses.

Available wherever paperbacks are sold, or order direct from the Publisher. Send cover price plus 50¢ per copy for mailing and handling to Zebra Books, Dept. 3388, 475 Park Avenue South, New York, N.Y. 10016. Residents of New York, New Jersey and Pennsylvania must include sales tax. DO NOT SEND CASH.

MICHALANN PERRY

TOUCHED BY FIRE

ZEBRA BOOKS
KENSINGTON PUBLISHING CORP.

ZEBRA BOOKS

are published by

Kensington Publishing Corp.
475 Park Avenue South
New York, NY 10016

First printing: May, 1991

Printed in the United States of America

Through our great fortune, in our youth our hearts were touched with fire.

Oliver Wendell Holmes

Chapter One

Chicago, 1871

At the familiar jangle of the bells over the pharmacy door, Ellari Lochridge glanced up from her work, a welcoming smile on her face. "May I help . . . ?"

The rest of her question froze in her throat, her attention snared by a flash of metal in the hand of the shabbily dressed man approaching her.

Licking her lips in an attempt to wet a mouth suddenly gone dry, she set her pestle and mortar aside slowly, her gaze deliberately fixed on the laborer's bleary eyes.

"Why, Mr. Schmelzel, what a surprise," she forced herself to say, despite the panic that gripped her. "I haven't seen you in ages. I hope nothing is wrong. I trust Mrs. Schmelzel and the children are all in good health." Praying her concerned tone betrayed none of the deafening apprehension thundering in her ears, she refused to think about what he planned to do.

"Mein family is vell. No tanks to you und your meddling!" He whipped a large kitchen knife into full view and slammed it down on the counter.

At the sudden crack of metal against wood, Ellari sucked in a startled breath, her calm facade shattered. Everyone in the neighborhood knew that Schmelzel had a terrible temper that became more and more violent with each drink of whiskey he consumed. And if the offensive odor assaulting her nostrils was any indicator, Jon Schmelzel had already drunk enough liquor to be dangerous—even deadly.

She chanced a frantic glance past him toward the door to the street—as if she expected a rescuer to come bursting into the drugstore at any moment, simply because she had willed it to happen. No one was there. She was completely on her own.

"Thanks to me?" she asked, her voice a high-pitched quiver, despite her effort to keep it steady. "I—I—don't understand." She took a cautious step back from the counter.

Her retreat came to an abrupt halt as she felt her back bump the supply cabinets directly behind her. New alarm coursed searingly through her veins. Only moments before, the cupboard had been an aid because of its convenient proximity to her work area; now it was her enemy, trapping her helplessly between it and the work counter.

She swiveled her terrified gaze to the right in a frantic search for an escape. Perhaps, if she skirted around the nearest end of the counter and made a dash for the street . . .

No, that would never work. From where Schmelzel

was standing in the middle of the store's main aisle, he could easily block her way, even if his reflexes were slowed by the alcohol he had obviously consumed.

Her frightened eyes rolled to the left. On the other hand, if she kept the counter between them, she might be able to make it to the storeroom before Jon Schmelzel could get to her. Yes, that was what she had to do. Make a run for the safety of the storeroom.

As if sensing her thoughts, Schmelzel tightened his scarred hand on the knife handle and propelled his upper body across the counter to grab her arm before she could put her plan into action. "You are putting vicked lies in de heads off mein family, und I haf come to varn you, if you do not stop, I vill make sure dat you do." He swirled the knife in a meaningful circle, its point only inches from her chest. "Do you unerstant vat I am telling you, *fraulein?*"

The vaguely disguised threat triggered an indignation deep inside Ellari, filling her with fear-paling courage. Emboldened by her anger, she resisted the urge to strain against the powerful grip on her arm. Instead, she stood her ground and locked gazes with the drunken immigrant. "Am I to understand that you intend to *kill* me, Mr. Schmelzel?"

Hearing his warning stated so bluntly had the desired effect on the laborer. His shoulders slumped in defeat, and he seemed to deflate before her eyes, as if he were a punctured balloon.

Though he didn't lower his knife or release his hold on her arm, Ellari felt the danger to her person lessen perceptibly. Her tone softened, and she smiled sympathetically. "You don't really want to kill me, do you, Mr. Schmelzel?"

His tear-filled eyes displayed the same heartbreaking hopelessness Ellari saw every day in the faces of the customers who came into her drugstore, and her heart ached anew for the poor immigrants who had come to America to seek better lives and had found nothing but hardship and hunger—often worse than what they had left behind in Europe.

Schmelzel shook his head. "I do not vish to kill you, *fraulein*. But you vill leave me no choice if you do not stop der trouble you make for mein family ven you tell mein boys dey must not vork at der glass factory."

"Believe me, Mr. Schmelzel, I don't want to cause your family any more trouble than you already have, but I simply cannot keep silent when I see what working twelve to sixteen hours a day in the Nylander Glass Works is doing to all the children of this neighborhood, not only yours."

"Vat it ist *doing, fraulein*, ist putting food in dere bellies—food dey vill not haf if dey do not verk." He lowered the knife slightly, but continued to grip her arm. "Everyone in de family must verk to earn de money to keep a roof over our heads and food on our table. De glass factory is vat is keeping us alive!"

"Alive?" She spit out a bitter laugh, the last of her fear erased by resentment as her mind filled with ugly visions of the ten- and twelve-year-old children who, stooped and listless, looked like weary old people.

"Working in the factory isn't keeping your children alive. It's killing them, some of them more slowly than others, but killing them all the same. And you're helping, just as surely as if you're using that knife to cut their throats! Tell me, Mr. Schmelzel, what do you think when you see an eight-year-old boy who has been permanently disfigured or crippled because he was so exhausted from being overworked he got careless and stepped too close to the furnace or slipped on the glass-littered floor? Those children could be yours—will be yours—if something isn't done to stop factory owners like Nylander!"

Schmelzel winced at the mention of injured children and inadvertently shot a bleary gaze to the corner of the drugstore where Ellari Lochridge frequently administered emergency care to workers injured at the glass factories. His cheek twitched uneasily as he looked back at the pharmacist.

Ellari's expression hardened, and she swallowed with difficulty. Unable to stop her bottom lip from trembling, she bit the inside corner of her mouth and choked back the bile that rose in her throat. "One way or another, children are being killed every day in the glass factories, all for the few cents a week the family will lose if they don't work! Perhaps you can accept that kind of thinking, Mr. Schmelzel, but I can't. And I won't! You can threaten me all you like, but I will not stop speaking out against a system that works children to death and creates fathers who care more for a child's earning ability than for that child's life!"

Ellari drew in a deep breath, straightened her

11

shoulders and met Jon Schmelzel's red-rimmed eyes with unyielding resolution. "So, you may as well kill me right now, because you will never silence me any other way."

His expression twisted with indecision, Schmelzel tightened his hold on her arm and put the knife point to her chin. "I'm varning you, *fraulein*. You vill stop making trouble, or I vill haf no choice."

"Then do it, Mr. Schmelzel," she ordered, gambling that underneath the immigrant's drunken, desperate exterior there was still a man who valued human life and would not be able to take hers.

After what seemed an eternity, Schmelzel's eyes grew dull with resignation, transmitting his decision an instant before he loosened his grip on her arm and started to lower the knife.

Relief washed over Ellari with a force that weakened the muscles in her legs. She sagged forward against the counter to stop herself from falling.

Like the startling crash of an explosion, the sounds of jangling bells and a door opening shattered the tense atmosphere. Their eyes equally round with surprise, Ellari and Jon Schmelzel turned to see the tall, nattily dressed man filling the doorway.

"Hey! What're you doing?" Trigg Hanahan yelled, instinctively lunging toward the knife-wielding man before him, all the while cursing himself for bad timing and a lack of good sense for not just turning and leaving the moment he had realized he had walked in on a robbery. After all, where was it written that he had to be a "knight in shining armor" to every "damsel" he found in distress?

But it was too late to change his mind now. Everything was happening at once: the robber spinning around to face him, the woman screaming, "No, Mr. Schmelzel!", and the sting of a knife point slicing across his own middle as the frightened immigrant squeezed past him to flee from the drugstore.

Stunned, Trigg looked down his torso. His buttoned yellow vest and the white shirt he wore beneath his plaid jacket were slit in a leering diagonal slash, from several inches above the left watch pocket to an equal distance below the righthand pocket. Already the raw material edges were collecting blood from the shallow cut that traversed his exposed belly. "Why, you son-of-a . . ." he snarled, bolting for the door to give chase.

"Let him go!" a female voice ordered from behind him.

"Like hell I will!" He yanked open the door, setting off the bells in a new flurry of jingles.

"Or I'll fire." The familiar click of a gun hammer being cocked reverberated through the air, bringing Trigg's departure to an abrupt halt.

"What the hell?" he asked, releasing the door and turning to face the woman. He briefly dropped his gaze to the pistol she fought to steady with shaking hands, which bolstered his confidence. She didn't have it in her to shoot him. That was obvious.

His mouth stretched into a deliberately amused grin. He looked to the side, then back at the woman in the somber gray dress. He wished he could see her face better. "Now, let me get this straight. That bum came here to rob you — maybe worse — and you're going to shoot *me* if I go after him? Do you mind if I ask why?"

"He's not a bum and he didn't come here to rob me," Ellari answered, her words hoarse and uneven.

"Oh?" Trigg raised his eyebrows in surprise, his curiosity increasing. "He sure had me fooled. But that doesn't change the fact that he ruined my only decent vest and shirt, and he owes me new ones." He turned again to leave, reaching for the doorknob as he did. "And I'm going to collect."

"You can't. He doesn't have any money."

"Then I'll take it out of his —"

A loud *thunk,* followed by the crack of a revolver being fired, cut him off. Instinctively, Trigg dove into the aisle to his left, amid a shower of broken medicine bottles raining to the floor.

Breathing heavily, he raised his head and waited. When a second shot didn't follow, he gingerly hauled himself to a crouch and waddled toward the wider aisle that centered the drugstore and led to the exit — which he intended to use just as fast as he could.

Slowly he eased an eye around the corner of the shelves until he had a view of the spot where he'd last seen the "gun-toting" female. His attention was immediately drawn to the revolver on the plank floor in front of the counter. He relaxed slightly. At least the lunatic woman was no longer armed, unless . . .

With my luck, she probably has a shotgun back there, he told himself, as he conjured up the ugly picture of his dead body with his face shot-off.

14

He began to rethink his options for making a safe escape. Unfortunately, the center aisle was the only way out of the store—and in the direct line of fire from the counter. Making a run for the door was definitely out. There had to be a safer way.

"Lady," he called out. "You win. I won't go after your 'friend.' Just give me your word you won't fire again, and I'll get out of your life."

There was no answer. Curious, he rose from his crouch to a stoop, just enough to enable him to peer between the brown and green bottles that stocked the top shelf. "Lady? Did you hear what I said? I'm willing to forget what happened if you'll just promise you won't . . ."

He stopped speaking, a deep frown furrowing his brow. The woman was gone. His gaze inadvertently jumped to the curtained doorway the end of the counter, and a wave of relief washed through him. Evidently, she had sneaked out the back way while he'd been lying on the floor waiting for the second shot to be fired.

Cautiously, he straightened to a full stand, all the time ready to duck at the least provocation.

"Ohhh," a weak moan sounded from behind the counter.

"Lady?" he asked, a crazy idea beginning to form in his thoughts. "Is that you?"

No answer. *Stupid fool woman probably got knocked out by the jolt when she fired that revolver.* He waited a full minute longer, his head cocked to the side.

Unwanted thoughts bombarded his mind. Maybe

15

she was hurt. *So, whose fault is that? Sure as hell not mine!*

Continuing to focus on the counter, he slowly stepped out into the aisle, groping behind him for the doorknob as he did. *I don't owe that crazy woman anything. All I wanted was some shaving soap, and she tried to kill me!*

His decision made, he wrenched open the door to the street. "I've got enough problems of my own, without looking for more of them," he grumbled aloud.

Another tortured groan sounded from behind the counter, bringing his retreat to an abrupt halt. This one sounded even more pitiful than the first. Guilt squeezed at his chest. Maybe he should at least take a quick look to be sure she wasn't seriously hurt. *She might have hit her head when she fell and be bleeding. Or maybe the gun backfired and she shot herself.* He released a humorless laugh. *It would be just like a crazy woman to shoot herself in the process of trying to kill the man who probably just saved her life. It's no more than she deserves.*

Still, he couldn't just leave her there to bleed to death, could he? With a disgusted growl, he slammed the door shut and took a step toward the counter, then froze.

What the hell am I doing? This isn't my responsibility. If she'd had her way, I'd be the one bleeding on the floor right now!

He wheeled around to face the door, but made no move to open it, his instinct for self-preservation rearing its head.

16

Think, man. If she really is hurt and bleeds to death, who will be blamed?

Trigg glanced down at the gaping tear in the new clothes for which he'd hocked his watch the afternoon before—though he should have paid his rent with it. "Who do you think?" he answered himself with a disgusted sneer. "The man who was seen leaving her shop in a bloody, torn suit, just before her body was discovered by her next customer."

Congratulations, Hanahan, old man. You've done it again. Either you take a chance that a lunatic isn't behind that counter waiting to blow your head off with a shotgun, or you gamble that you're not going to be blamed for it if she dies before help comes.

"Stop!" Ellari choked, twisting her head from side to side to escape the overwhelming ammonia odor stinging her nostrils.

"It's about time you woke up," a decidedly masculine voice greeted her.

Ellari's eyes snapped open in surprise. Fully awake, she looked up into blue eyes that gleamed with something she couldn't quite identify. What was it? Anger? Anxiousness? Apprehension? Whatever it was she saw, she knew it was dangerous, and her instinct for survival told her she had to break the connection that held her gaze locked to his.

"What's the meaning of this?" she asked hoarsely, turning her head to the side. "Who are you? What are you doing here?"

An astounded grin stretched across the man's

17

mouth. "The name's Hanahan, and I'm the poor dolt you used for target practice before you fainted," he explained.

Ellari's eyes widened with disbelief, and she struggled to sit up. "That's ridiculous! I don't faint. And I certainly don't go around shooting at strangers for no rea—" Memory flooded into her mind. She slapped her fingers to her lips. "Oh!"

"Remember now?" he asked, scooping her up from the floor in one easy motion as he rose.

"What are you doing?" She squirmed to free herself from his grasp. "Put me down!"

"You're not the one giving the orders now, lady." He strode to the treatment corner of the store and unceremoniously deposited her on the couch with less than gentle force. Before she could regain her balance, he sat down beside her. "If you know what's good for you, you won't move."

The effort to escape sent a wave of lightheadedness rocking over her, and Ellari fell back against the pillow, unable to hold up her head. She just needed a minute to regain her strength.

"What are you going to do?" she asked watching apprehensively as he lifted the pitcher from the washstand and poured water over the small towel she had folded and placed in a bowl that morning—as she did every morning in preparation for emergencies.

"First of all, I'm going to clean the cut on your forehead," he said, wringing out the towel and dabbing her head with it. "Then, I'll—"

"Ouch!" she wailed, grabbing at his wrist to pull

18

his hand away from her face. "You're hurting me!"

"Believe me, lady, compared to what I'd like to do to you, this is nothing. You're lucky I'm not using kerosene!" He knocked her hands out of the way and wiped at the bleeding scrape. "And I still might if you don't hold still and tell me why in the hell you tried to kill me."

"I didn't try to kill you," she said, her eyes dropping closed as she gave in to the sweet luxury of being taken care of. It had been so long. Years. Since before she had gone away to pharmaceutical school eight years ago when she was only sixteen—a lifetime.

"Excuse me if I find that hard to believe." He removed the cloth and dipped it into the water again.

"I just wanted to stop you. I couldn't risk having you hurt Mr. Schmelzel," she explained, her eyes opening and closing lazily as he brought the cool cloth back to her face. She could get used to this. "He has a wife and family depending on him."

Trigg blew out a snort of disgust. "I don't suppose it occurred to you I could have a wife and family who depend on me every bit as much as his depend on him?"

Her eyes opened wide. "Do you?"

His blue eyes focusing on her green ones, Trigg's anger suddenly softened. The store clerk was much younger than he had thought at first sight. And she wasn't nearly as plain-looking as he had assumed. In fact, now that wisps of light strawberry-colored hair had worked their way free from the severe, "old maid's" bun at the nape of her neck to form a soft frame around her face, he concluded she might be considered rather pretty.

"Do I what?" he asked, finding it difficult to concentrate on anything other than the idea of how she would react if he loosened the pins and released the rest of her hair from the unflattering knot.

"H-have a wife and children?"

"No!" he spit out angrily, tearing his gaze from hers and rinsing the cloth again, with much more energy than necessary.

A ripple of pleasure tripped through Ellari's chest at his admission. But no sooner did she feel relieved, than she scoffed at her ridiculousness. What difference did it make to her if he were married or not? It wasn't as if she would ever see him again. For that matter, why would she even want to? He was definitely not her type. *Too handsome,* she told herself, taking in his near-perfect features, his wavy black hair, his piercing blue eyes, and that mouth. . . .

"Which proves my point," he went on. "You don't know anything about me, and you tried to kill me!" He slapped the cloth into the water and turned back to her.

His angry tone brought her back to reality, and she struggled to sit up. "I told you. I didn't intend to kill you. The revolver went off by accident."

His mouth split in that astonished grin she remembered from earlier, and a coil of helplessness curled deep in her belly. She couldn't help the sudden regret that in a few minutes this man and his bewitching smile would walk out of her life—just as suddenly as he had come into it.

"Accident?" he snorted. "Lady, where I come from, when a person aims a gun at a man, cocks the hammer, and fires it, it's a definite sign that person means for someone else to be dead."

Astonished by the way her thoughts kept drifting into such inappropriate channels, she tore her concentration away from his face. "The revolver must have fired when I fainted," she said, her tone embarrassingly breathless.

"I thought you 'never faint.' "

Ellari straightened her spine. "Evidently today was an exception," she answered stiffly, feeling somewhat safer now that she refused to look him in the eye.

"For both of us," he commented dryly. "I have to admit, this isn't the only time I've been shot at, but it sure as hell is the first time I ever almost got killed for saving someone else's life!"

"If you will refrain from swearing, sir, I will try to explain," she started, keeping her tone as level as she could manage with him still sitting on the couch beside her, his hip only inches from hers — so close she could feel his body's heat raging through her.

"Please do," he said, his eyebrows arched skeptically. "I can hardly wait to hear."

Ignoring his sarcastic tone, Ellari went on. "Before you came into the drug store, I'd had a terribly frightening experience."

"And that explains trying to blow my head off?"

"I remember being afraid you would hurt Mr. Schmelzel, and I knew I couldn't let that happen, so I grabbed for the revolver Papa left under the counter. The next thing I remember is waking up to find you bending over me and holding smelling salts under my nose." She wrinkled her nose in distaste at the thought.

Trigg eyed her suspiciously. She could be telling the truth. Actually, that made more sense than to think the kickback of the revolver had knocked her out. Still, he'd been around too long to be taken in by a convincing "act," no matter how sincere she seemed! Without thinking about what he was doing, he brushed a lock of hair back from her temple.

"In case I believe you—which I'm not saying I do—is pulling a gun on a man . . ." He directed a purposeful glance down at his ruined clothing. ". . . the way you usually repay someone who risks his life to save yours, whether it was warranted or not?"

"No, of cour—" Ellari's gaze inadvertently followed the direction his had taken. "Oh! You're injured!" she gasped. She pushed past him off the examination couch, her strength regaining rapidly as her thoughts returned to more familiar—and safer—ground. "Why didn't you say something?" Instinctively, she reached for the buttons on his vest. "Here, let me—"

"Hey!" He grabbed her wrists. "What're you doing?"

A tremor of warmth exploded up her arms from the flesh and bone manacles surrounding her wrists, and her fingers stilled on the top button. Her green eyes filling with surprise, she couldn't help looking into his. "I—I was just going to look at your wound. You might need a doctor."

"It's nothing," he protested, his voice hoarse. He cleared his throat. "It's just a little scratch."

"Even 'little scratches' can become infected if they aren't treated," she said, forcing herself to twist her hands from his grip to undo the first button on the bloody vest. "Now, let me—"

"All right!" He brushed her hands aside. "Look if you must, but I can certainly unbutton my own vest."

"Then do it," she said, hurt by his gruff reaction to her touch. Her back to him, she busied herself by emptying the washbowl into the slop jar beside the stand.

Uncomfortably aware of the sounds of rustling clothing behind her, she twisted open a large brown bottle and poured some of its contents into the bowl. "Your shirt, too."

"What's in that bottle? What are you going to do?"

Recognizing the childish apprehension in his voice, the sprite inside her leaped to life for the first time in years. Glancing back at him, she grinned mockingly. "Don't tell me the man who 'risked his life' to 'save' me is afraid of a little carbolic acid."

"I'm not afraid. It's just that . . ."

She couldn't resist chuckling as she tauntingly sloshed the liquid around in the bowl. "Just that what?"

"Uh—"

"Yes?"

"It's just that you're making too big a fuss over a little scratch."

"Well, you can relax. I'm only cleaning the bowl." With exaggerated casualness, she dumped the carbolic acid into the slop jar. Taking her time, she refilled the bowl with clean water from the pitcher, then turned back to face him.

"What are you doing?" she gasped, her gaze darting involuntarily over the most impressive male chest and shoulders she had ever seen in her years of treating patients in her pharmacy.

He shrugged. "You told me to take off my shirt."

"I asked you to unbutton it, not remove it altogether," she responded frostily, dropping her gaze to the injury that traversed his flat midriff.

The man's face split into that infuriating grin, sending a new wave of discomfort spiraling clear down to Ellari's toes.

"What's the matter? Haven't you ever seen a wounded man without his shirt?"

A hot flush colored her face, but she couldn't bring herself to look away. "Of course I have."

"Well, what do you think?"

Her rattled gaze flew up to meet his. The devilish challenge she saw in his eyes sent a new explosion of frustration, confusion and embarrassment gyrating through her blood. "What do I think?"

"About my injury," he responded glibly, the twinkle in his blue eyes telling her he knew exactly what she was thinking about. "That is what we're talking about, isn't it?" he added with a sly grin.

Refusing to give in to the desire to look away from the appealing display of masculinity, Ellari forced a knowing smile to her own face. "If you're trying to get out of having me take care of that cut by embarrassing me, you're strongly mistaken." A quiver of satisfaction washed over her as his cocky smile sagged. "Now, stop acting like a frightened little boy, and let me do my job." She gripped his shoulder and forced him to straighten his posture. Then, with sadistic retaliation for his deliberate taunting, she slapped the cold washcloth across his middle.

Chapter Two

"Damn!" the stranger yelped, leaping to his feet and flinging the wet rag to the side. "What's the big idea?"

Brought back to her senses by his justified outburst, Ellari grabbed a dry towel and instinctively reached out to blot at the water spot spreading below the waist of his trousers. "I'm sorry, I don't know what I was—"

The impropriety of the action she was on the verge of taking hit her with gale force. Her horrified gaze flew to the man's face as her hand on the towel froze in midair, scant inches from embarrassing disaster.

"Don't worry about it," he spit out acidly. He snatched the towel out of her hand and rubbed briskly at his wet pants front. "You didn't do it on purpose, did you? It was an accident."

Guilt for her uncustomary behavior pulsing in her head, Ellari nodded. "An accident," she repeated, unable to put the thought out of her mind that he knew her actions had been deliberate.

Suddenly, her "victim's" mouth twisted into an amazed grin and his eyes sparkled with the travesty of the situation. Shaking his head, he chuckled and reached for his torn shirt. "But frankly, this place is too dangerous for a person with my 'peaceloving' temperament. The next 'accident' will probably do me in."

His good mood, coupled with the fact that he had obviously pretended not to notice her blunder, made Ellari feel even more ashamed than before. So far, the poor man had been knifed, shot at, and now doused with cold water—all because he'd tried to help her.

She touched his hand on the shirt with her own. "Don't go. At least not until I clean and bandage your wound." Understanding the skepticism she saw in his expression, she grinned sheepishly and drew an "X" over her left breast with her forefinger. "No more accidents. Cross my heart."

He studied her warily, then glanced down at the cut that streaked across his belly. "I might as well," he conceded, sitting back down. "The way my luck's been running today, I'll probably have lockjaw by morning if I don't let you clean it. It may already be too late."

Smiling her relief, Ellari spun away from him to pick up a brown medicine jar. "Oh, I doubt that."

"All I wanted was some shaving soap and a razor," he mumbled, slicing a disgruntled glance toward his ruined clothing. "Not that it matters now

27

whether or not I shave, since—thanks to your friend—my clothing isn't exactly in any shape for my dinner appointment."

At the mention of a dinner appointment, Ellari's mind filled with a picture of the handsome stranger sitting at a table in a romantic restaurant and clicking wineglasses with a beautiful, sophisticated woman gowned in jewels and lace.

Surprised by the envy that caught her off guard, Ellari tried to blot the scene from her mind. What difference did it make to her who he had dinner with? It wasn't as if she had thought such a handsome rogue might be interested in a homely female pharmacist who'd didn't even own a dress-up gown, much less have anywhere to wear one. Not that she would go to dinner with him if she had the chance. His type probably had a woman in every neighborhood in Chicago.

"Naturally, I intend to cover the cost of replacing your things with new ones," she informed him stiffly. She opened the jar she held and dipped a clean handkerchief into the white cream it contained, then turned back to face him. "Just as soon as I'm through here, I'll get your money."

The man's nervous gaze focused on the salve-laden white cloth as she brought it toward his belly. "Is that going to sting?"

Ellari shook her head. "No, it's not going to sting. In fact . . ." Before he could think of another excuse, she touched the ointment to the wound. ". . . it will take the sting out of your cut."

The muscles of his flat midriff flinched defensively, setting off a whole new flutter of unfamiliar sensations inside Ellari.

Relaxing as the soothing effect of the medicine spread over the width of his belly, her patient seemed oblivious to the turmoil he was creating in her thoughts. "Hey, that feels pretty good."

Reaching for a roll of bandage, Ellari bit her lower lip to disguise her anxiousness. "Now, aren't you ashamed of making such a fuss?" She pressed a gauze pad across his middle. "Hold that," she ordered, snatching her unsteady hand back from the warmth of his flesh as soon as he steadied the bandage.

Knowing it would be necessary to wrap a bandage around the man's naked torso to secure the pad, Ellari took a deep breath and reached around him with one hand and caught the roll behind his back with the other. Big mistake. Huge mistake!

Hit with the realization that she had trapped the stranger in her unintentional embrace, her face not more than three inches from his collarbone, her mind dissolved into emotional mush. Her senses reeled. Her nostrils burned with the sweet masculine scent of his skin. Her mouth became dry, and her breathing all but stopped.

Unable to move, Ellari helplessly lifted her eyes up to his face, where she was imprisoned by his amused gaze.

"Do all your patients get such intimate care?"

His words breaking her paralyzed state, Ellari

whipped back from him, still able to feel the euphoric effects of his breath on the hair framing her forehead. "Tie the ends of the bandage together to hold the pad. I'll go get your money and you can be on your way."

Without waiting for him to answer, she bolted for the back of the store.

Clutching a bundle to her bosom, Ellari returned in a few minutes, her face still hot with discomfort. Unable to look into his eyes, she dropped a ten-dollar gold piece into the stranger's hand. "This should cover your loss. And I want you to take this too." She handed him a high-quality leather case, opened to reveal a shaving mug and brush, a mirror, a razor, a razor strop — and the soap he'd come into her store to purchase. "I really am sorry for any inconvenience I caused you."

"This is too much," Trigg said — before the predominant "anything-for-a-buck" side of his nature could calculate what this sudden gain might mean to a man who'd been almost penniless, as well as homeless, only minutes earlier.

He eyed the gold coin and leather shaving gear — the finest he'd ever owned — then looked up at the woman. Where would she have gotten a ten-dollar gold piece? From the looks of her clothing and this drugstore, she wasn't wealthy.

"I only wish it could be more," she was saying sincerely. "These days, not too many people are willing to risk their lives to help someone else. Unfortunately, it's all I can afford. The pharmacy business isn't very profitable in a neighborhood where people usually pay you for your services with a thank you and a promise."

Oh, great! She probably gave me all the money she has in the place and is having second thoughts about it. Well, it won't work! I earned that ten and I'm keeping it!

"No, I don't suppose it is," he said, pocketing the coin before he could give in to the scolding voice in the back of his mind. Filled with self-disgust at the thought of sinking so low he would take money she couldn't afford to give him, he told himself he would pay her back as soon as he was on his feet. Maybe tomorrow — *if* his business dinner went as planned.

Forcing his mind away from the unpleasant possibility that Phelps wouldn't help him, Trigg returned his attention to the drugstore clerk.

"But no more talk about money," she was saying. "You'd better hurry if you want to make your dinner engagement. There's a clothing store two blocks north of here that specializes in men's ready-mades, and I'm sure if you tell Mr. Drummond I sent you, he will let you dress and shave for your meeting there."

Trigg glanced down at his naked chest, then gave his eyebrows a sardonic lift as he redirected his attention to the young woman's face. "Two blocks? Do you think that's such a good idea?"

He studied the play of embarrassment on her face and was momentarily stunned by what he saw.

Damn! She wasn't just passably pretty as he had thought at first. She was actually quite pretty—or could be if she weren't hiding her attractiveness behind the old-maid coiffure and clothing. Again, he wondered how she would look with her hair loose.

Furious with the turn his thinking had taken, Trigg quickly rebuffed the thought. *Watch it, Hanahan. This is one kind of trouble you don't need right now!*

Blushing nervously under his scrutiny, the woman shoved the bundle she'd been clinging to toward him. "I forgot. I brought you a shirt and vest to wear to the clothing store."

He studied the neatly folded clothing she held out to him. "Won't your husband be needing these?" he asked, wanting to rid himself of the feeling that this girl needed his help.

"Oh, I'm not ma—" She caught herself and stopped. "They're my father's," she went on hurriedly, obviously more aware of his exposed flesh than before. "Of course they're not new, but . . ." Her hands now empty, she interlaced her fingers and twisted them nervously. ". . . they should suffice until you can replace your others."

Unexpected relief shot through Trigg at the knowledge that she wasn't married—though for the life of him, he couldn't imagine why it made any difference to him. He wasn't ever going to see her again—especially now that he knew she had a father who no doubt owned a shotgun and would come after anyone who messed with his daughter.

Hell, he didn't even know her name—or want to know it. The smartest thing he could do was take his gold piece and get out of there—fast!

"Thanks." In his hurry to leave the woman and her problems to her father, he shook out the shirt with more energy than necessary. He poked an arm into the first sleeve. "Tell your pop I'll get these back to him in the next couple of days."

"You don't have to bring them back. My father died four years ago," she answered, without having any idea what that unwanted bit of information did to Trigg's insides. She shrugged and smiled sadly. "I meant to give his things away ages ago, but I just never got around to it."

Don't ask! She's got to have someone! An uncle, an older brother. Someone. Anyone! Despite his resistance, a wave of gentleness flickered inside Trigg. "I'm sorry," he said, the sympathy in his words genuine. "I know how hard that is on a family. Mine walked out on my mother and me before I was born." There was a slight break in his voice. He cleared his throat and added, "Of course, in our case, we were probably better off without him."

Puzzled by the anger she had heard in the man's voice when he mentioned his father, Ellari frowned and studied him as he concentrated on buttoning the shirt she'd given him.

Taller than average, at least nine or ten inches over her own five-foot-four inch height, he looked to be in his late twenties. And judging by his flashy

33

plaid suit and yellow vest, she easily concluded that he was probably one of the thousands of pushy salesmen that abounded on the streets of Chicago, selling everything from counterfeit stock in goldmines out West to womens' corsets and safety pins—whatever they could get a supply of cheaply, legally or otherwise, and turn over for a fast profit. Her father had called them hucksters and crooks, and had repeatedly told his daughter never to trust a man who "wears sporty clothing, smiles too much, or tells you he's going to make you rich— 'with just a small investment on your part.'"

The man held out his arms to check the fit of the shirt. "Not too bad, is it?" Directing a questioning smile at her, he reached for the borrowed vest.

Her reaction to the dazzling grin was immediate, and Ellari averted her stare sharply to the side in a frantic attempt at escaping. *At least he didn't ask me for an investment.*

Then the humiliating truth hit her, and the knot of self-disgust tightened in her tummy. *He didn't have to ask for money, idiot! You just gave him ten dollars you can't spare to replace a shirt and vest that couldn't have cost more than two!*

Furious at her own lack of good sense, she attacked the washstand in a flurry of cleaning activity.

"So, who's this E. Lochridge?" The disturbing man angled his head toward the wall behind the pharmacy counter as he adjusted his own coat over the replacement shirt and vest. "A relative, or just

34

your employer?"

Ellari glanced over her shoulder to see what he saw. "Why would you . . . ?" Her eyes fixed on the framed document on the wall and she understood. She faced him again. "For your information, *I'm* E. Lochridge, and that is my degree."

His mouth stretched in a disbelieving grin. *"You're* 'E. Lochridge, Pharmacist'? That's impossible. You're a woman."

Ellari stiffened indignantly and hurried to the front door. "I assure you, it is not only possible, but it is a fact. I own this store, and I *am* the pharmacist here." She wrenched open the door and held it for him. "If you're going to get to Mr. Drummond's clothing store before it closes, you'd better go. Thank you again for your assistance."

"There's no need to get all huffy." He joined Ellari at the door, donning his bowler hat as he did—and grinning. "I didn't mean to offend you. You just took me by surprise. I never met a lady pharmacist before, and this neighborhood is one of the last places I ever expected to find a woman who'd been to college." His blue eyes glittered mischievously and his smile grew more devastating than before—if that were possible.

Determined not to be appeased by his explanation—or his deliberately charming demeanor—Ellari slammed the door. Fists balled on her hips, she took an angry step toward him. "The neighborhood has nothing to do with your reaction. Admit it! You wouldn't have been a bit surprised to find an

35

educated *man* in this neighborhood, would you? Even though *anyone* who can actually read is a rarity in this part of town. But because I'm a woman, the thought that I could be educated is inconceivable to your 'superior' masculine mind, isn't it?"

Trigg opened his mouth to rebut, then snapped it closed. He had more important things to do than to stand here and defend himself for having a perfectly normal reaction to learning the pharmacist was a female. He had tried to make amends, but she had made it quite clear what he could do with his apology. Anyway, she was probably one of those women who were always looking for a fight, and to allow himself to be baited into an argument with one was a definite no-win situation. To think he'd let himself believe for even a moment that she needed his help.

"My mistake." Clutching "E. Lochridge" by the upper arms, Trigg lifted her off her feet, intending to remove her from his path so he could leave. Without knowing why, he brought her face level with his. His focus was immediately arrested by her surprised green eyes, and he hesitated, holding her, their faces inches apart, for a long moment, before he reluctantly set her aside.

Before he could make good his retreat, the top half of the drugstore door exploded inward with a splintering crash, sending a shower of glass spraying into the store.

Instinctively, Trigg spun around and shoved Ellari to the floor, covering her with his body to shelter her. "What the hell was that?"

Her face pressed into the curve of the man's neck and shoulder, Ellari struggled to move her head in order to breathe. "I don't know," she managed breathlessly once her nose and mouth were free. "Probably some children pitching a ball. I'm sure it was an accident."

"Kids playing," Trigg mumbled. "An accident." Suddenly aware of the warm female body beneath his own, he lifted his head and stared down at the frightened face—and decidedly kissable mouth—beneath him.

Scrambling with the agility of a man running from a fire, he leapt to his feet. Without looking at her, he roughly drew her up from the floor, then dropped her hands and brushed energetically at his clothing. "You could have been cut to pieces if you'd still been standing in front of that door when the glass broke! Why do you stay in this neighborhood?"

Viewing the broken glass that covered her floor, Ellari shrugged her shoulders with pretended unconcern and started toward the back of the store for a broom. "Believe me, I'm fully aware of this neighborhood's shortcomings. However, there are a number of reasons to stay. For one, this is my home. And for another, I'm needed here." She disappeared into the storeroom.

"For what? To serve as target practice for knife-carrying laborers and window-breaking vandals?" he yelled after her.

37

"Not that it's any of your business, but this is the only place many of these people can come for medical care," she called from the back room. "And I have a responsibility to be here for them."

"That's the craziest thing I ever heard of," he shouted after her, kicking aside a large piece of glass and moving to follow her. "Why would you risk your life to take care of people who pull knives on you and 'accidentally' bust your store windows all in the course of an ordinary afternoon? It sure couldn't be for the money."

Ellari reappeared in the doorway leading from the storeroom. "There are more important things than money, Mr. . . ."

"Hanahan," he reminded her automatically. "Trigg Hanahan. Give me a for instance. What's more important than money?"

"For instance, honor and one's responsibility to one's fellow man," she said righteously. "Besides, it's usually very quiet here. This was not an ordinary day."

"I bet," he snarled in disgust. "Here, give me that." He snatched the broom and dustpan from her and stomped back toward the front of the store.

She ran after him. "I'm perfectly capable of—"

Trigg turned and glared down at Ellari, bringing her pursuit to an abrupt halt. "Quite frankly, Miss Lochridge, I'm in no mood to hear how capable you are of anything. I'll sweep. You'll get a box to put the broken glass in. And while you're getting that box, you better find something I can nail over the door until the glass can be replaced."

"What about your appointment?"

Trigg scowled at the reminder and directed an irritated glance at the clock behind the pharmacy counter, then down at his rumpled clothing. "Just get the box."

His determined tone convincing her that arguing would be a waste of time, Ellari hurried to do as he had asked.

After silently working side-by-side for twenty minutes, Ellari stooped to pick up an overlooked triangle of glass wedged under one of the end counters facing the center aisle.

As she reached for the shard, her attention was caught by a large wad of paper. Giving the crumpled piece of trash almost no notice, she whisked it up from the floor.

Startled by the unexpected weight of the discard, she tightened her grip on it and brought it to rest on her knees. On closer examination, she realized it was more than crumpled paper. Instead, it was a sheet of paper wrapped around a hard lump and tied with a string.

Ellari cast a quick glance over her shoulder at the man who was helping her. Seeing that he was concentrating on finishing with his sweeping, she hurriedly unwrapped the paper and string package to expose its contents.

A rock!

Her pulse accelerated and her mouth grew dry with the meaning of her discovery. The broken window hadn't been an accident at all! It hadn't been a child's ball as she had wanted to believe, but a deliberate act of destruction directed at her store.

Apprehension pelting her thoughts, she spread the sheet of paper on her knees to read the crudely scrawled letters on it: Mind your own business, or you will be sorry.

"Oh!"

"What is it?" Trigg asked, hurrying to her side. "Did you cut yourself?"

Crumpling the paper and rock in her fist, Ellari cannoned up from the floor and thrust her hand behind her back. "No, I'm fine," she answered breathlessly. "It's nothing. I had a cramp in my knee."

Trigg eyed her suspiciously. "Are you sure that's all it was?"

"Of course I'm sure."

"In that case, you won't mind telling me what you're hiding behind your back." He took a step toward her, a knowing smile on his face.

Ellari fought the temptation to tell him about the threatening message. But she had no right to involve him any further in her troubles. She would just have to take care of this herself. "I'm not hiding anything." She brought her hands to the front, exposing her possession. "Just a piece of paper I picked up." With exaggerated nonchalance, she dropped the paper-hidden rock into the box with the glass they had swept up.

With the tinkling of more breaking glass, Ellari

immediately realized the error of her decision. Her eyes flew to Trigg's, which had assumed a curious amusement.

"Paper heavy enough to shatter glass?" He hunkered down beside the trash box. "This I've got to see."

He gingerly lifted the note from the box, not bothering to read the message on it. His face lit with pseudo-surprise. "Well, well, well. What have we here?" He held up the rock, and smiled knowingly. "This really is a tough neighborhood, isn't it? Kids play catch with rocks instead of balls."

"They're very poor and have to use whatever they have on hand. In this case it was obviously a rock."

"That makes sense. But I can't help wondering why a bunch of kids would go to the trouble to wrap their makeshift balls in paper and string. Seems like they would've figured out the paper wouldn't hold together through more than one or two pitches."

Dropping the rock back into the waste box to the crackle of more breaking glass, he concentrated on the tangle of string and paper in his other hand. Pitching the string aside, he uncrumpled the message.

Ellari grabbed angrily for the note. "What difference does it make?"

"Not a bit," he said with a taunting grin as he whipped the paper out of her reach. "It just makes me wonder, that's all."

"I thought you had a dinner engagement."

"Mmm," Trigg muttered, turning the note over to read the letter on the other side. The humor melted off his mouth, replaced with an angry scowl. He looked up at her and jabbed the note toward her. "You really are in trouble, aren't you? Who's threatening you?"

"No one is threatening me," she protested, grabbing for the note again, succeeding this time. "Not really. This is no doubt someone's idea of a prank. Probably some children I caught stealing penny candy and had to put out of the store. You needn't concern yourself about it." Praying her worry didn't show in her expression, she glanced uneasily at the store clock. "Thank you again for your assistance." She moved to usher him out the door.

Trigg started to go, then stopped. "Why did you try to hide the note from me?"

"Why did I —? Oh, that. I simply didn't want my inconsequential little difficulties to delay you any longer." A forced smile plastered on her face, she opened the door and indicated he should leave.

"Are you sure that's all it is? A mischievous prank?" Trigg asked, not certain whether his uneasiness about leaving her alone was because he was truly concerned about her or because he was looking for a way to delay the meeting at which Phelps would destroy his last bit of hope by refusing to loan him the money he needed. "Maybe I should stay in case they come back."

"Nonsense, you've already done more than enough for me. Go and enjoy your dinner. I'll be

42

fine. Again, thank you for all you've done."

Realizing how dangerously close he was to doing something really stupid—like skipping his dinner with the man who could solve all his financial problems, to stay with a woman who made it quite clear she didn't need or want his protection—Trigg resolved to get out.

Deciding right then he wouldn't—couldn't—turn his back on any help Phelps was willing to give, Trigg slammed his bowler hat on his dark head and stepped through the doorway. "In that case, I'll be on my way. Nice meeting you, Miss Lochridge."

Chapter Three

From the doorway, Ellari watched Trigg Hanahan until he turned the corner at the end of the street. The instant his broad shoulders disappeared from view, her own shoulders sagged. All pretense at nonchalance was dropped.

With frantic motions, she slammed the door, locked it and wrenched the shade down over the hurriedly patched door. Trigg Hanahan had done his best to cover the gaping rectangle with scraps of lumber she'd brought in from the alley behind the store, but she knew it would be very easy for another troublemaker to knock the boards off and walk right in.

She slid an apprehensive glance over the empty store. Was that a noise she had heard? She frantically swiveled her head from side to side. Her heartbeat accelerated. Could someone have slipped inside unnoticed? Could an intruder be hiding between the shelves?

"Get control of yourself, Ellari Lochridge!" she commanded, forcing herself to step away from the door. "No one's in here but you and the mice." Her posture stiff with false bravado, she took another cautious step toward the back of the store. "If you're this jumpy in broad daylight, what're you going to do once the sun goes down?" She forced a derisive chuckle through her lips, but the tinny sound of her thready laugh only emphasized her inner fear. She couldn't escape the feeling that she wasn't alone.

"Onward Christian soldiers," she began to sing softly as she cautiously continued down the store's center aisle, her eyes swerving from left to right. "Marching—Aaagh!" She jumped back a full two steps to escape the grab made at her ankles.

"Who are you? What do you . . ." Ellari stopped, her eyes wide with shock as her gaze dropped to a large, gray-striped cat that seemed to have materialized out of thin air.

Obviously nonplussed by her horrified shriek, the cat ambled toward her, his tail swishing with arrogant unconcern. A scolding meow his only comment to her unwarranted reaction to his presence, he arched his back and slithered himself around her ankles.

Laughing for real this time, Ellari dropped to her knees. "What are you doing in my store? You scared the daylights out of me! How did you get in here?" She scratched the uninvited feline's head between his ears, one of which had the pointed tip missing. He began to purr. "Are you hungry?"

As if the aging tomcat had understood her, his

purr intensified to a loud rattle as he twisted his furry body for another pass at her shins.

"In that case, why don't we get you something to eat?" Relieved to have her concentration taken off the imaginary villains lurking outside her shop, Ellari didn't even consider putting her four-legged guest back outside. She picked him up and started for the storeroom. "To tell you the truth, I wasn't looking forward to eating supper alone. How does boiled chicken and dumplings sound to you?"

"Meow," the cat answered, nudging her hand with his head to get the most pleasure from her fingernails on his scalp.

Ellari smiled. "It sounds good to me too. We'll have to give Mrs. Leopold a double thank you in the morning, won't we?" She shifted the cat in her arms, noticing that the tom's long fur gave him the appearance of being heavier than he was. "Why you're just skin and bones, aren't you? When was the last time you ate? Some of Caroline O'Leary's cream with supper ought to help fatten you up."

The cat answered her with a squeaky little meow and continued to purr.

"Did anyone ever tell you that you're a wonderful conversationalist?" She started up the stairs that led from the storeroom to her apartment above the shop. "We'll have a lovely supper and keep each other company the rest of the evening. We won't think about broken windows or nasty notes anymore tonight!"

* * *

"Oh, Mr. Hanahan, you are so brave to have helped that poor shopkeeper," Ina Phelps crooned, as she crammed a large bite of creamy dessert into her mouth. Smacking her delight, the plump woman lifted the eclair-laden fork to her lips again. "I can only imagine what a less principled man would have done under the same circumstances."

Trigg hesitated. Why didn't Phelps just get on with it and tell him yes or no? Why was the banker toying with him by ignoring the subject they'd come here to discuss, forcing him instead to pretend to be enjoying his daughter's inane babbling? For that matter, why didn't he, Trigg, just get up and walk out? *Because you've got nowhere else to go,* he reminded himself. *If Phelps doesn't lend you enough money to get Boss Stahl's "collectors" to stop breathing down your neck, you're going to be six feet under.*

"It was nothing," he mumbled in response to Ina's gushing compliment, and doing his best to ignore the nagging desire to forget the whole thing and leave, despite what awaited him if Reed Phelps didn't come through for him.

"Oh, I disagree. Our streets would be much safer for decent individuals if there were more men of your caliber," Ina insisted, before taking another bite of dessert.

Trigg hid his disgruntled moan behind a cough and a hand over his mouth. He wished she would shut up about it. It was over and he just wanted to forget it. He hadn't even intended to tell Phelps about the encounter at the drugstore, but by the time he had left Ellari Lochridge, there hadn't been enough time to go by the clothing store to replace the borrowed clothes or to freshen up. He'd had no choice but to show up for dinner rumpled and wearing the borrowed clothing — and to explain the reason for his inappropriate appearance.

Reed Phelps cleared his throat and gave his daughter a meaningful glance.

Ina immediately caught her father's unspoken message and blushed. Tittering nervously, she placed her fork down on her plate, leaving the last gooey bite she had been on the verge of devouring. Giving the uneaten tidbit a longing glance, she lifted her napkin to her 'mouth and blotted her lips with dainty little girl actions that seemed rather ridiculous to Trigg for a woman of her age. "If you gentlemen will excuse me for a few minutes, I'd like to freshen up."

Knowing Ina's absence from the table meant Phelps was ready to talk business, Trigg winced with apprehension. If there was ever a need for a good pitch and some fast talking, it was now. He had the next five minutes, at the most, to convince Reed Phelps to lend him enough money to pay off Stahl and invest in a new business venture — a venture he had yet to come up with!

Caught up in his own thoughts, Trigg was slow to realize the banker and his daughter were watching him with expectant stares.

"Oh, I'm sorry!" he blurted out, bolting up from his own chair to help Ina with hers. "Allow me!"

"Why, thank you," Ina giggled, her full face growing splotchy with embarrassment before she hurried away.

Once Ina was out of earshot, Phelps leaned across the table. "That girl is everything to me. There's nothing I wouldn't do for her. I swear I'd kill anyone who hurt her. Can you understand that, Hanahan?"

"I—I believe I can, sir. A man and a daughter must have a very special—"

"I intend for her to have anything she wants. No matter what it costs."

Trigg glanced around nervously. Why was Phelps telling him this? "I can see how a father would feel that way about his only child, sir. I'm sure I'll feel the same way when I have children of my own."

Silently studying Trigg for several seconds, Phelps bit off the end of a cigar and lit it. "I like you, Hanahan," he finally said through a cloud of smoke. "In fact, you remind me of myself when I was younger—all ambition and willingness to do whatever it takes to make it to the top. And I think with the right kind of guidance, you could have a pretty good future ahead of you if you want it."

Trigg's heart beat faster with relief and excitement. Phelps was going to lend him the money! He just knew it. And it hadn't even been necessary to come up with a convincing lie to explain his need for investment capital. "Thank you sir. I consider that a compliment."

Phelps drew on his cigar and cast a regretful smile in Trigg's direction. "Unfortunately, you're in a helluva mess, aren't you?"

"Mess, sir? I'm not—" He could have sworn his heart skipped a beat.

"Come now, Hanahan." The banker gave Trigg a

humoring grin, then went on. "You're not going to waste time denying the fact that if you don't come up with a thousand dollars—and fast—you're going to spend that future floating facedown in the Chicago River, are you?"

Trigg thought better of protesting. Of course, Phelps would know how much money he owed—and who he owed it to. "I hardly think it's quite that serious," was the only thing he could think of to say in his own defense. "And once I—"

Phelps held up his hand to stop Trigg. "It is that serious, son, and we both know it. And my heart goes out to you," he continued, "but quite frankly, I didn't get rich lending money to men with reputations for not paying their debts—especially to men like Boss Stahl. Too good a chance the borrower won't live long enough to pay me back."

Trigg's hopes sank to the bottom of his belly, where they curled into a painful knot of despair. Phelps had been his last chance. "Then why did you ask me to dinner, if you had no intention of lending me the money?" he asked, unable to disguise the resentment he felt. "Why didn't you just tell me no when I was in the bank this morning, instead of making me waste valuable time I could have used to look for another backer?"

Phelps nodded. "I considered that. But as I told you, I saw something in you I liked. Then it came to me that I might be able to help you out after all— that is, if you're willing to help me in return."

Trigg could barely contain his excitement. "Of course! Anything!" A look of trepidation covered his face. "You don't want me to kill someone, do you?"

Phelps threw back his head and laughed. "Nothing quite so unpleasant, I assure you."

Trigg blew out a sigh of relief. Thank God, he wouldn't be put to that test. He was so desperate in that moment, that he wasn't certain he would have turned down even that heinous a deal. "What do I have to do?"

Phelps glanced at the curtain leading from the restaurant to the ladies' powder room, then back at Trigg. "I'll put my cards on the table. I want you to court my little Ina. Then after a few weeks, I'll expect you to ask for her hand in marriage."

At the thought, the doughy face of Ina Phelps filled his mind, and Trigg winced with disillusionment. Had he really been so naive to think a man like Phelps would even give the time of day, much less a loan, to a street hustler like he was, without expecting something in return?

"Surely, you don't mean—"

Phelps nodded his head. "I have to face it. I'm not going to live forever, and the one wish I have is to see my little girl happily settled with a family of her own."

"Uh—uh, your daughter doesn't even know me, sir," Trigg protested lamely. "We just met this evening. She might not even like me, much less want to marry me."

The banker shrugged indifferently. "She'll like you if I like you. Face it, son. I'm a very rich man; and my daughter is very rich in her own right. You could not only pay off Stahl, but you'll be set for life. Can you afford to refuse my offer so easily?"

Trigg swallowed deeply. There had to be something else he could do to raise the money to get his creditors off his back. Something not so drastic as promising to spend the rest of his life with Ina Phelps as a millstone around his neck. *But what? I've tried every scheme and dodge I can think of, and I just keep getting in deeper.*

Despite Ina Phelps's lack of appeal, Trigg couldn't help feeling sorry for her. What a shame all her father's money hadn't been able to buy her an instinct for style, instead of outfitting her in expensive pink ruffles that would have been perfect for a sweet sixteen birthday party, but were definitely wrong on a woman nearing thirty. In addition, she had styled her hair in large, unbecoming sausage curls, obviously meant to combine with the ruffles to make her seem younger than she was.

Ellari Lochridge's face flashed into his thoughts, and he couldn't help remembering how attractive she was, despite her severe hairstyle and conservative dress. He could only imagine how lovely she would be if she had the expensive clothing that Reed Phelps could afford for Ina's wardrobe.

Of course, though Reed Phelps was rich now, that hadn't always been the case. Orphaned at the age of six, the man had raised himself in the slums of Chicago—an upbringing not unlike Trigg's own. However, there was one big difference. Trigg's mother had lived long enough to teach him to read and write, as well as prepare him for the future with enough of the principles of good etiquette and good taste to get him by in polite society—if he ever got there. Obviously, Phelps hadn't been so fortunate.

The thought of Phelps not being fortunate brought an ironic grin to Trigg's mouth. What did Phelps or his daughter need with good taste in clothing? They had money—lots of money. So much money, in fact, that they were welcomed anywhere in Chicago—right clothes or not. If ever there was a fortunate man, it was Reed Phelps.

The story Trigg had heard was that he had connived and propelled himself out of poverty by marrying the thirty-eight-year-old spinster daughter of a wealthy clothing merchant, who died within weeks after the wedding. Because his new wife had been her father's only living relative, Reed had inherited his father-in-law's wealth when his wife of less than a year had died giving birth to Ina. *Yeah, he's really one unlucky man, isn't he? Marrying for money didn't make him suffer much, did it?*

"But I don't have a few weeks, Mr. Phelps. Stahl expects full payment day after tomorrow, and if I don't pay—"

"I've thought that all out!" Phelps retrieved a folded paper from his breast pocket. "I'll buy you some time with Stahl, and on the day you and my daughter marry, I'll pay off your debt, as well as set you up in your own business. It's all spelled out in these papers I had my attorney draw up this afternoon. All you need to do is sign them."

Torn, Trigg considered the document in Phelps's hand. Ina wasn't really all that bad looking, he told himself. Maybe if she lost a few pounds and got someone to advise her on her choice of clothes and hairstyles, she might even be pretty. And it wasn't as if he would be the first man to ever get his start by marrying a rich wife.

His supply of alternatives depleted, Trigg hesitated for a moment, then with a forced grin reached for the contract Phelps held out to him.

Ellari bolted up in bed. "Mr. Cat? Is that you?" she whispered tersely, her eyes wide with apprehension as she scoured the dark room.

Her only response was a contented purr from the corner where she had made a bed for the stray.

She rolled over and pulled back the window shade to peer down at the street below. In the city, there were all sorts of things to disturb a peaceful night of sleep. *All sorts of things,* she assured herself.

Staring down onto the gaslight-illuminated street, she felt a wave of disappointment. Any other night there would have been some sort of activity to explain the noise she'd heard and to ease her apprehension: a horse and buggy going past, a late-night worker making his way home from the factory, or maybe a dog rooting in the trash. But tonight there was nothing, absolutely nothing. The street was totally deserted and quiet. Even the two men she'd seen talking to each other across the street earlier had gone home for the night.

Doing her best to believe that the noise she had heard had only been part of a dream at the end of a very trying day and evening, she lay back down. Her eyes wide, she stared at the ceiling overhead, fully awake and frustrated. After tossing and turning for hours, she had finally fallen asleep for a few minutes. Now she was awake again; and she knew she wouldn't be able to sleep until she went downstairs and saw for herself that no one was there.

Irritated with her unfounded suspicions, she lifted the covers and swung her feet to the floor. Unerringly, she slid into the precisely positioned slippers she placed at her bedside each night upon retiring. Her concentration on the door and on listening for other noises, she retrieved her robe from the bedpost and slipped it on. She grabbed her father's pistol from the bedside table and stood up.

The gun gripped tightly in her hands, Ellari started toward the stairs. She didn't bother with a lamp—she didn't need light to find her way around the drugstore and apartment that had remained exactly the same for as far back as she could remember. As a matter of fact, as far as she knew, not one shelf or piece of furniture had been added to the rooms or moved since before she was born.

Intending to quickly check to see that the front door was still secure, she stepped into the darkened store. If she hurried, she still might be able to salvage a few hours of this night for much needed sleep.

Ellari stopped dead in her tracks, her horrified gaze frozen on the door, unable to believe what she saw. The noises hadn't been a product of her overactive imagination. Someone was breaking into the shop.

55

Terror bubbled and swelled in her throat, cutting off her breath. Frightened beyond belief, she shrank deeper into the shadows and stared at where the gaps between the slats Trigg had used to secure the broken window let in enough light from the gas street lamp to reveal the dark shape of a man on the other side of the door.

Relieved very little by the knowledge that the intruder didn't realize he was being observed from inside the shop, Ellari took a bead on the ominous form. "Get away from that door, or I'll shoot!" she shouted with as much bravado as she could muster.

The shadow straightened, then jumped to the side. "Don't shoot! It's me!"

Me? Ellari asked herself, searching her memory for where she'd heard the familiar voice before. "Do I know you?"

"Trigg Hanahan," the voice announced. "I was in earlier today. Remember?"

Relief rocked through Ellari, but she ignored her first impulse, which was to rush to the door, fling it open and hug Trigg Hanahan for coming back. Instead, her revolver still cocked, she crept toward the door. "How do I know you're who you say you are? And what are you doing back here?"

"Aw, hell, I should've known better than to waste my time worrying about you. You made it real clear this afternoon that you don't want my help, didn't you?"

"You were worried about me?"

"Yeah, but it won't happen again. Sorry I disturbed you!"

The scrape of retreating footsteps reached Ellari's ears.

She hesitated only a second before she dashed the remainder of the way to the front of the store to unbar and open the door. "Mr. Hanahan, wait!" She stepped outside onto the sidewalk. "Don't go."

Trigg Hanahan stopped in his tracks and turned to face Ellari, a half-grin on his face. "You're not going to start taking potshots at me again, are you?" He tipped his head toward the gun in her hand.

Ellari couldn't help the embarrassed smile that curved her mouth. She lowered the revolver to her side. "What are you doing here? I didn't expect to see you again."

"I told you. I wanted to make sure you were all right."

A pleasant, warm feeling seeped through Ellari. "Why? You don't owe me anything."

Trigg shrugged and stepped closer to where she stood in the doorway. He stopped, fascinated by the strawberry-colored hair cascading down her back to her waist in a wild disarray of curls turned gold by the light of the street lamp behind her. No longer restrained in the tight bun she'd worn earlier, it was even more beautiful than he'd imagined it would be. And she looked even younger and more vulnerable than she had before. "What if I told you, I just wanted an excuse to see a certain pretty lady pharmacist one more time?" His mouth spread in his winning grin.

Ellari felt the heat rise to her face. Of course, she knew Trigg Hanahan was teasing her. Obviously, he was an accomplished flirt. She wasn't pretty and didn't fool herself for a minute believing he thought she was. But that didn't stop his sweet words from bringing a smile to her own lips. "I'd say you're one Irishman who has kissed the Blarney stone one too many times. Now, tell me the truth. Why did you really come back here tonight?"

He knew she wouldn't like the truth: that he'd been evicted from his apartment and had no prospects for a place to spend the night until he had remembered the couch in the corner of her pharmacy. It should have been an easy thing to pry a couple of boards off the door, sneak into the shop, get a few hours sleep and sneak out again without her knowing he'd even been there. Unfortunately, he'd been caught, so he hurriedly made-up a new story.

"I was on my way home and figured, as long as I was in the neighborhood, I might as well check on you and make sure the boards on the door were secure."

"That was very kind of you, but as you can see, your concern was unwarranted. The door and I are fine."

"Yeah, I can see that—for now anyway. But if you're smart, you're going to keep an eye and your gun on that door until you get a new glass put in. You never can tell when some unsavory type might come along and decide to take off a few of those boards and help himself to what's inside." He turned to go. "Sorry I woke you, Miss Lochridge," he called over his shoulder.

"Uh—Mr. Hanahan!"

He faced her again, a questioning light in his eyes.

"I was—uh—You didn't wake me. I was awake."

"Trouble sleeping?"

"I suppose today's events made me a bit restless." She clutched her robe at the throat and swallowed deeply. "Would you like to come in and have a cup of tea before you go home?"

The instant the unexpected rush of words was out of her mouth, she regretted it. What was she thinking of? A lady didn't ask a virtual stranger in to have tea with her in the middle of the night—especially when she was wearing nothing but her robe and nightgown! She cringed at what her parents would say if they had been alive to hear her invitation. And her neighbors! What would the neighbors say if they found out?

"Nice of you to offer, but it's pretty late. I guess I should be on my way."

Ellari breathed a sigh of relief for her salvaged reputation. "Of course it is. I wasn't thinking." She stepped back in the doorway and started to close the door, trying to ignore the wave of regret that embraced her at the thought of never seeing Trigg Hanahan again. "Thank you again for your concern. Good night."

"On the other hand," Trigg interrupted, joining her in the doorway and forcing her to back inside. "Maybe I'd better stay. I wouldn't be much of an Irishman if I turned down a lady in distress, now would I?"

With a decisive slam, he closed the door and slid

the bolt into the lock, then brushed past her and headed for her treatment couch.

Ellari was too stunned by the sudden change in his actions to speak.

"We could use a little light though. Where's the lamp?" He glanced around, surprised to see that the shop wasn't as dark as he'd first assumed, thanks to the light of the street lamp that filtered through the shades on the door and the two display windows flanking it.

Ellari instinctively pointed toward the kerosene lamp on the washstand in the treatment area.

Trigg nodded his head and took a match from the holder on the wall. He flicked the phosphorous tip to life with his thumbnail and held the flame to the lamp. "That's better," he announced as the lamp brightened the room with a rosy glow. "Much better." He flopped down on the couch and bounced up and down to test it for comfort.

"What are you doing?" Ellari asked incredulously.

"It's obvious the reason you couldn't sleep was because you were afraid someone was going to break in." He dragged the pillow into his lap and socked it to plump it up. "So I'm going keep an eye on things until you can get the door fixed in the morning."

"You mean stay here all night?!"

"How else am I going to protect you so you can get some sleep?" He turned a deliberately guileless grin on her.

Ellari's insides curled right down to her toes, though her brain reminded her to beware. "I told you, I don't need your protection. There's nothing to protect me from."

"If that's the case, why couldn't you sleep?"

Ellari paused, annoyed with herself for giving him that information to use against her. "I had some things on my mind, that's all." Her words didn't sound very convincing, even to her own ears. "It has nothing to do with what happened this afternoon."

His infuriating grin widened, turning her insides to jelly and her brain to puree. Suddenly, the idea of spending the night under the same room with Trigg Hanahan was having a peculiar affect on her rational thinking.

"You're not fooling me, Miss Lochridge. And you're not fooling that knife-carrying thug or whoever threw that rock through your door. You might as well admit it. You're scared to death they'll be back. And that's why you couldn't sleep. But you can rest easy now. They won't come around as long as I'm here. Now, how about that tea?"

"You can't stay," Ellari protested. "What will people think if you spend the night?"

"What they think won't matter a whole lot if they find your store trashed in the morning and you with that laborer's knife in your back, will it?"

Chapter Four

Ellari glanced at the boarded front door. Though there was a shade over the area where the window was supposed to be, the light of the street lamp emphasized the gaps between the boards, and she realized some of the spaces would easily accommodate a man's hand. "I suppose you're right," she admitted briskly. "A man on the premises could help deter intruders."

Trigg Hanahan's mouth spread in a satisfied grin, and he relaxed back on the couch. "I knew you were a smart lady."

Ellari fixed her most intimidating glare on him, determined not to be charmed further by his disarming ways. "That remains to be seen," she answered. "But in case you have any ideas there is more to this than a simple matter of necessity and convenience, let me remind you my revolver is loaded and I won't hesitate to use it." She wheeled toward the back of the store. "I'll get you a blanket."

"You mean you don't trust me? I'm hurt."

Refusing to acknowledge the pseudo-wounded tone in his voice, she looked back over her shoulder, her own demeanor deliberately stern. "For the record, I am only allowing you stay because at the moment you appear to be the lesser of two evils. But that does not mean I trust you. For all I know, you're a wolf in sheep's clothing and every bit as dangerous as Mr. Schmelzel and the people who threw the rock through my window."

"Does this mean I don't get that cup of tea?" He arched his eyebrows in mock surprise, obviously undaunted by her scathing outburst — or at least what she had thought was a scathing outburst.

Fighting an unexpected urge to smile, Ellari turned away and started for her apartment. "I'll bring the tea when I bring the blanket."

"Miss Lochridge!" he called after her.

Ellari stopped. "Yes?" she ground out through her teeth.

"If it wouldn't be too much trouble, a couple of sandwiches would sure taste good with that tea."

"A couple of —?" Ellari spun around to face him again. "Do you think I'm running a restaurant here? Besides, didn't you just have dinner?"

Trigg shrugged and gave her that helpless little boy smile that made her want to not only fix the requested sandwiches, but a full course meal as well. She clenched her fists in an attempt to reinforce her determination not to be taken in.

"To tell the truth," he answered, "my meeting

63

wasn't exactly what I had hoped it would be, and I pretty much lost my appetite."

"Very well," Ellari agreed, her tone sounding to her own ears like that of a prudish spinster teacher she remembered from grammar school. A wave of depression washed over her at the memory. That teacher couldn't have been much older at the time than Ellari was now. At the thought, she was hit with a flash of herself a few years from now, still unmarried and living alone above the pharmacy. "I'll be back shortly."

True to her word, Ellari returned in a few minutes, a folded blanket under her arm and a tray in her hands. "I trust cold chicken is all right," she announced, setting the tray down on the washstand. "There's a glass of milk in addition to the tea. And since you didn't have dinner after all, I put a slice of apple pie on the tray."

His eyes twinkling with hunger, Trigg reached for a sandwich. "Chicken and apple pie are my favorites." He stuffed a bite of sandwich into his mouth.

Despite her apprehensions about letting him stay, Ellari smiled at the eager way Trigg attacked the supper she'd brought. She had promised herself that she would simply give him the tray and go back upstairs. But preparing a meal for a healthy man with a hardy appetite and watching him enjoy it was a pleasure she had never known, and she found it difficult to turn away. It made her feel as though her whole insides were smiling. What must it be like to be someone's wife and know this warm feeling every day?

Realizing the direction her thoughts had unwittingly taken, Ellari stiffened her posture. "If there's nothing else, I'll leave you to your supper."

"Didn't you invite me to have a cup of tea with you?"

Ellari looked at him self-consciously. "That was a mistake. After all, what—"

"—would people think?" he finished for her, his tone taunting.

"Exactly." Her reply was defensive. Was she so dull and predictable that a stranger could know what she was thinking before she said it?

"Who's going to know? I doubt either one of us would find drinking a cup of tea with an acquaintance such a momentous occasion that we would rush out and tell the world about it. Do you?"

"Perhaps it's not a 'momentous occasion,' but it would be quite improper." *Listen to yourself, Ellari Lochridge. You're sounding more and more like Miss Sedgefield. What are you afraid of? It's only a cup of tea.* "I don't know anything about you."

"What do you want to know?" He blessed her with his winsome smile. "My life's an open book."

Everything! her mind answered without warning as she basked in the warmth of his radiant grin. *I want to know everything about you!*

Shocked by her own reaction, Ellari took a frightened step back as if she'd touched a hot stove with her bare hand, then pivoted away from the treatment corner to make a speedy escape. At the storeroom doorway, she paused, but didn't look back. "Please don't misunderstand. I appreciate your kindness for watching the shop tonight, but that's all it is."

"Actually, it never crossed my mind to think otherwise."

An unexpected pain sliced into Ellari's heart. Of course, he hadn't thought anything else. What man would be interested in a plain and ordinary-looking woman such as herself? Certainly not a handsome rogue like Trigg Hanahan, who could no doubt have most any woman he wanted.

She laughed inwardly at herself. *I'm a fool. I could have thrown myself at him and he probably would have pushed me away.*

She took a deep breath and cleared her throat to remove the lump that had suddenly formed there. "If you leave by the rear entrance before the sun rises, no one will see you. The alley is fairly deserted at that time of day."

"By the back door," he confirmed, an odd break in his voice. "Sure thing. No one will see me. You have my word."

"Good night, Mr. Hanahan."

"Good night, Miss Lochridge."

Long after she left Trigg Hanahan for the night, Ellari lay awake, unable to stop thinking about the man downstairs. Not that she would ever be seriously interested in a man like that—any more than he would be interested in her. Still, she couldn't escape the undeniable fact that he had come back to check on her safety—and that he was the most handsome man she'd ever seen in her entire life. Surely, he had better things to do with his time. But if he hadn't come back because he was interested in her, why had he? And why would he volunteer to spend the night on the treatment couch if he wasn't concerned about her?

Scoffing at the incredible idea that anything about her would appeal to Trigg Hanahan, Ellari gave up on getting any sleep and sat up. *Whatever brought him back, I know it wasn't because he found me interesting. So what was it?*

"Oh, my goodness!" she gasped, hit with sudden realization. *How could I be so stupid?* She bolted up from the bed and hurried for the door. *He came back to rob me. He probably thinks I have a whole drawer full of those gold pieces. He has no way of knowing I gave him my last one and have nothing of real value in the shop.*

Cursing herself for a fool, Ellari crept down the stairs. *It's all so clear now. He assumed I was asleep and was breaking in when I caught him. That's why he came up with that ridiculous story about coming back to check on me.*

Fully expecting to find her storeroom wrecked from Trigg Hanahan's search for money—and him long gone—Ellari peeked into the room, then froze. *That doesn't make sense. Everything's as I left it!* She cast a furtive glance at the back door, quickly confirming that the chain and bolt were still in place. Puzzled, she crossed the storeroom floor and peered cautiously through the curtains leading to the pharmacy proper.

Maybe he decided to settle for the few dollars in

the store and leave by the front door, rather than take a chance on being shot while he searched for more gold pieces. Her attention flipped to the cash box under the counter in front of her. To her amazement, the box was exactly where it should be and the shackle of the padlock appeared to be in place.

Her curiosity piqued beyond caution, Ellari pushed through the curtains to examine the situation more thoroughly.

Grabbing the lock, she jiggled it and found to her surprise, it was secure. "This just doesn't make sense," she mumbled to herself, staring dumbfoundedly at the padlock in her hand. "Unless . . ."

Hit with an incredible idea, she jerked her head up and directed her attention toward the screen that provided privacy for the treatment corner. Could Trigg Hanahan have actually been telling the truth? Was there really no ulterior motive for coming back? No reason other than genuine concern for her safety?

Before she could dislodge her building hopes with logic, a soft snore echoed from the behind the screen. Her heart leaped.

A contented sigh, followed by the gentle groan of the treatment couch and the rustle of bedclothes confirmed his presence.

Excited for reasons she didn't dare pause to examine, Ellari rushed on tiptoes to the opposite side of the store.

A warm whisper of relief swept through her as she caught sight of the sleeping man. He was dead to the world, and whatever his reason for returning, it obviously wasn't to rob or take advantage of her.

Her hopes began to climb. Maybe, just maybe—

Afraid to allow her foolish optimism to go any further with the thought, she started to leave, but she couldn't. She was too enthralled by the way the shade-diffused light from the street lamp outside limned and defined his handsome features and the muscles of his bared chest.

Hypnotized by the gentle rise and fall of his chest that accompanied his breathing, she stared. Of all of the male torsos she had seen in her emergency treatment center, and on her infrequent trips to the museum, his was definitely the most perfectly sculpted. Even the white bandage she had used earlier to cover his knife wound did nothing to detract from the perfection.

For one thing, Trigg Hanahan wasn't burly like many of the factory workers she had daily contact with. In fact, he was on the lean side, despite his magnificent shoulders and chest. His waist and hips were unusually slim, his belly flat and rippled with a ladder of corded muscles. There was not a spare ounce of fat on him.

Another attractive difference she couldn't help but notice was that he wasn't overly hairy like many dark-haired men she'd seen. The hair on his chest fanned his pectoral muscles, then tapered to an alluring path that trailed down the center of his body into the bandage around his waist, then appeared for a scant few inches before finally disappearing into the partially unbuttoned fly of his trousers. *Just the right amount,* she thought, comparing him to some of the more furry men she had seen.

A sudden chill gripped her. Blaming it on the night temperature, she instinctively stepped closer and reached for the sheet he had evidently thrown off in his sleep.

In one unexpected motion, he grabbed her wrists and yanked her off her feet, flipping her onto her back as he did and pinning her to the couch beneath his own body. "Whadda you think you're doing?"

Her chest bursting as much with fear as with his weight, Ellari couldn't catch her breath enough to speak. Wide-eyed, all she could do was move her lips in a silent plea for air and shake her head.

As full alertness overtook Trigg, his own eyes widened in recognition and horror. "Miss Lochridge!"

Ellari nodded her head weakly, her heartbeat slowing slightly.

"Oh, my God! I didn't reali—I thought someone was—" He bounded off her. Wrapping his arm around her shoulders, he drew her to a sitting position. "Are you all right? Did I hurt you?" He searched her face for an answer.

Still shaken, Ellari nodded, then shook her head. "I-I'm f-fine," she lied. The strain from the two attacks that afternoon, a sleepless night, a mysterious midnight visitor and now Trigg Hanahan's unintentional assault was suddenly too much for her. "You d-di-didn't—h-hu-hurt—" Before she could finish her statement, her eyes filled and overflowed with uncharacteristic tears.

His expression rife with instant guilt, Trigg enveloped her in his strong arms. "Ahh, don't cry." Delving his fingers into her hair, he drew her face to his chest in a comforting embrace. "I didn't mean to scare you."

"Y-y-you l-lo-looked c-co-cold," Ellari sniffled into his chest. "I-I j-ju-just w-wa-wanted t-to p-pu-put the b-bl-blan-ket b-ba-back o-ov-over y-y-you. I di-didn't m-mean to s-st-startle y-you."

He tightened his hold. Rubbing her arm with one hand, he massaged her head with the other. "I know," he consoled her. "It wasn't your fault. It was mine." He blew out an ironic chuckle. "I guess I made my bed in an alley too many nights when I was a kid. I still feel like I've got to sleep with one eye open or everything I own will be gone in the morning—especially my shoes."

Shocked by his words, Ellari forgot some of her own fright. "Who would steal a child's shoes?"

He laughed harshly. "Another kid who lives on the streets."

She raised her head to study his face. "Why, that's terrible."

"You're telling me," he laughed, pretending to make light of what he had told her. "Especially in the win—" His voice broke. Unexpectedly, her compassionate, tear-stained face stirred something deep inside his chest. "—ter," he finished, his tone distracted.

"You slept in alleys in the winter?"

He hunched his shoulders, then relaxed them. "It wasn't so bad. They say lots of fresh air is good for a kid. And it beat the hell out of being treated like a criminal at the orphanage the authorities sent me to

71

when my mother died."

Ellari knew there were hundreds of ragged children roaming the city, especially in the business district of downtown. Dirty and destructive, they were considered a general nuisance by most citizens. They begged and stole and even attacked pedestrians mercilessly, but she had always assumed they were simply undisciplined ruffians whose parents didn't supervise them properly. For some reason, it had never occurred to her they were orphans or to wonder about where they slept at night. In fact, the gangs of young hoodlums with nothing to do but wreak havoc were one of the arguments used by the proponents of using child labor in the factories. "I find it hard to believe life in the orphanages could be as bleak as you say."

He dismissed her comments with a shrug. "Yeah, well, I guess you had to be there to know what I mean." His serious expression transformed into his usual selling grin. "Hey, what are we talking about that for? What I want to know is, why are you roaming around down here in the middle of the night?"

Ellari's face grew warm with embarrassment. How could she tell him the real reason she'd come back downstairs? She glanced down at her hands in her lap and cleared her throat self-consciously. "Uh—I couldn't remember if I had given you a pillow, so I thought I should come down to check."

He placed a curved forefinger under her chin and lifted it so she had no choice but to look at him. Arching his eyebrows knowingly, he nodded. "And to make sure I hadn't run off in the night with the family jewels?"

Ellari's eyes widened in surprise, then clouded with chagrin. "Am I that transparent?"

With a deliberately non-committal grin, he wobbled his head from side to side. "Let's just say, you wouldn't get very far as a poker player."

Ellari couldn't help returning his smile. "About as far as a thief who would think there was anything to steal in this shop, I imagine."

He feigned surprise and mock disappointment. "No family jewels?"

To her own surprise, Ellari laughed out loud. "Believe me, if there were, I wouldn't have them locked away."

"Oh? What would you do with them? Wear them?"

Her expression grew disbelieving. "Now, can't you picture me wearing fancy jewels in this neighborhood, Mr. Hanahan? No, I wouldn't wear them. I'd sell them and use the money to go to medical school."

"Medical school? You want to be a doctor?" For once, he sounded genuinely surprised.

"All my life," she answered wistfully. "For a while it seemed as if I might actually have a chance to become one of the few women physicians in the country. I was even accepted at the Chicago School of Medicine. But then—" She paused, suddenly feeling foolish. Tilting her head to the side, she hunched her shoulders and grinned sheepishly. "I can't imagine what possessed me to bring that up. I haven't thought about going to medical school in years."

His sympathetic expression told her he knew she was lying. "If you wanted to be a doctor so much — and you had the chance, how'd you wind up running a pharmacy in this neighborhood?"

Ellari smiled and shook her head. "It's a long story, and really quite dull." She stood to leave. "You don't want to hear it."

Trigg caught her hand to stop her. "Don't go. I'm wide awake now and won't be able to get back to sleep anyway." He smiled. "Besides, you've got me curious now. I haven't met many people smart enough to be accepted to medical school, and never a woman who was. Don't you think it would be downright unfair not to tell me what happened?"

Ellari's gaze inadvertently roamed over the shirt-less man's chest, then dropped in horror to her own modest nightgown. What in Heaven's name was wrong with her? Why was she standing here, giving herself excuses to spend just a while longer in the company of Trigg Hanahan — despite the inappropri-ateness of their state of dress and the lateness of the hour?

Doing her best to ignore the disconcerting feelings gyrating through her, she told herself it had simply been so long since she'd had a personal conversation with anyone — and that was what had brought on her peculiar behavior. Of course, that would explain it. The only people she talked with these days were the customers and patients who came into her shop every day. And they all had so many problems of their own, it would never occur to her to discuss her own life and dreams with them.

"You don't want to hear my boring story," she protested, wanting to stay, but unable to believe he was really interested.

"Sure I do." He reached for her hand and coaxed her back down onto the couch.

"Well . . ." Her voice quivered as she perched tentatively on the edge of the sofa. Conscious of the fact that he still retained his light hold on her hand — and of the fact that she couldn't quite muster the desire to reclaim it — she licked her lips nervously.

"All right, but if you're bored to death, don't say I didn't warn you!" she laughed. "I had just finished pharmacy school and been accepted to medical school when my father died five years ago of a sudden heart attack. Without my father, I didn't have the finances to go on with my education or to hire someone to take care of my mother who had been in bad health for several years. Of course, the only solution was to take over the pharmacy and care for her myself. And that was the end of my plans to attend medical school."

She looked up, surprised to see what appeared to be admiration in his expression. Embarrassed, she cast her eyes away from his face. "As I said, it's a very dull story."

Ignoring her comment, Trigg asked, "Is your mother still alive?"

"I buried my mother six months ago."

"I'm sorry."

"Don't be. She's better off now. The last three years of her life she was completely helpless. Most of the time, she didn't even know who I was." Self-consciously, she glanced down at her hand in his, finding a gentle comfort in the contact. "I suppose I should go now."

"What's stopping you from going to back medical school now?" he asked suddenly.

His question triggered a defensive reaction in Ellari. How many times had she asked herself the same question? She snatched her hand back and glared at him, her expression bitter. "Just go back? And how do you suggest I pay tuition and support myself? The trustees weren't exactly enthusiastic about admitting me before. They only agreed to it because right after the war there weren't as many male applicants as in other years. If there hadn't been a shortage of men applying that year, even the fact that I made the highest grades in my pharmacy school class wouldn't have gotten me in. I'm sure there is no shortage now, but even if there were, I can tell you they won't let me attend their college for free — just for the 'honor' of having me there."

"You could sell the shop. There's nothing keeping you here, is there?"

Ellari bristled. "Oh? And whom do you suggest I sell it to? Look around you, Mr. Hanahan, this pharmacy barely makes enough to support one person. People don't invest in businesses they know are going to lose money. Besides, just because my mother is gone doesn't mean I don't still have responsibilities."

"To who?"

"I may not be a real doctor, but the medical care I give the people in this neighborhood is better than none—which is what they would have if I left the pharmacy to go back to medical school. That may not seem like important work to you, but it is to me! And I have no intention of deserting them."

"I have to admit your loyalty to people who threaten you with rocks through your windows and knives is commendable, but pretty dumb, don't you think? What have they ever done for you?"

"It's obvious you and I will never agree on a human being's moral obligation to others." She spun away from him and started for the back of the store. "Goodnight, Mr. Hanahan!"

"Hey!" he called, springing off the couch and giving chase through the store. "I didn't mean to insult you." He caught her arm at the door to the back room, halting her flight. "I was only trying to help. After all you've given up, I just think you deserve something good for yourself."

Slowly turning to face him, she looked up into his eyes. Expecting to see the teasing glint that frequently lit his expression, she was surprised to find what looked like sincerity in their depths. "You do?"

"Sure I do. But I know from experience that if you don't look out for yourself, no one will. You've spent five years taking care of other people. Don't you think that's enough? Take my advice, Miss Lochridge. Go to medical school and open a practice as far away from this neighborhood as you can get. Do it before these 'responsibilities' bleed you dry of everything you've got to give, then turn their backs on you when you can't help them anymore."

Ellari leveled her glare on his face. "I didn't ask

for your advice, Mr. Hanahan. And whether or not I choose to dedicate my life to helping people less fortunate than I am, rather than pursuing my own selfish interests, is none of your concern."

His face broke into grin and he chuckled. "You know what? You're right. It's none of my business." His gaze dropped to her mouth.

"None," she agreed, her own focus suddenly fixed on his eyes in a questioning stare.

"But take my word for it . . ." He leaned closer to her.

"For what?" Through no conscious movement, her body gravitated toward his.

He reached up and brushed a lock of hair back from her temple. "If you want something to happen, you've got to make it happen for yourself. If you sit back and wait to be rewarded for your good deeds, you'll go to your deathbed still waiting."

The gentle touch sent electricity racing to Ellari's every extremity, as the pain and bitterness in his words sent a pang of sorrow to her heart. Was that what an orphan learned living on the streets? To worry about no one's survival but his own? She was hit with an overwhelming desire to touch his face and wipe away the sadness she could see behind his eyes, but of course she didn't. Instead she spoke. "There are all kinds of rewards, Mr. Hanahan. Seeing a child who was near death become healthy again; seeing gratitude in a mother's eyes . . ."

"Yeah, but those rewards don't pay the rent or put shoes on your feet."

She laughed, no longer able to muster the desire to

argue over their philosophical differences. There was no point. Neither of them were about to change. "I can see this conversation is getting us nowhere. Good night, Mr. Hanahan."

"Miss Lochridge?" He tilted his torso toward her.

"Yes?" she answered, raising up on her toes as if she were the marionette, Trigg Hanahan the puppeteer.

"Thanks."

"For what?" she asked. They swayed toward each other.

"For the supper," he returned, his mouth only inches from hers. "It was great."

Breathless with his nearness, she was barely able to speak. "Thank *you* for coming back to check on me." Oh, Lord, was he going to kiss her? Did she dare allow it?

"I'm glad I did."

"Me too."

His lips were so close to hers now she could feel his breath on her face. All she had to do was move her own head a fraction of an inch and her mouth would touch his.

A sudden rush of embarrassment at the knowledge she was actually hoping she was on the verge of receiving her first kiss—and from a virtual stranger—brought her to her senses. She couldn't let this happen.

Drawing on every fiber of strength she could muster, she dropped her chin and stepped back. "Good night, Mr. Hanahan," she gasped as she wheeled away from him to make a frightened dash up the stairs to the safety of her apartment.

Once inside, she slammed the door and sagged back against it, her mouth still tingling from the near brush with that of Trigg Hanahan's.

Chapter Five

Trigg woke with a start. He looked around, frantic to figure out where he was. "What the . . . ?" Then it all came back to him with enlightening clarity. He was on the treatment couch of the Lochridge Apothecary.

"Who said that?" he heard an unfamiliar female voice ask.

He froze. *Hell! I was supposed to be out of here before she opened up!* He looked around for a place to hide, unable to believe he'd slept so soundly he hadn't heard her open the shop to admit her first customer of the day. *She's going to be madder than a wet hen!*

"I didn't hear anything, Mrs. Presinger," a second woman responded, her voice high and quivering with an obvious effort to control her anger. He had no doubt who this was! "Perhaps you heard a snatch of conversation from passersby outside."

"You're probably right," the woman conceded.

"Those gaps in the door don't keep out many street noises, do they? How did you say your door window got broken?"

"It was an accident. Some children playing catch got too rambunctious with one of their pitches," Ellari answered, her tone indicating to Trigg that she was still straining to keep it level. "Of course, I plan to have it fixed just as soon as I can buy a new pane of glass."

"Tsk, tsk," Mrs. Presinger scolded. "Some people ought to be arrested for the way they allow their children to run wild."

"If there's nothing more, Mrs. Presinger," Ellari said pointedly, "I really must get back to my inventory in the storeroom."

"Are you sure it's all right if I don't pay you for the cough syrup for my little Mary until the end of the week when everyone gets paid?"

"That will be fine. Or if you want, you can give me a few cents then, and the rest later on."

The shuffle of footsteps on the plank floor made it possible for Trigg to audibly track the two women as the pharmacist ushered her customer toward the front door.

"God sent us an angel when he sent you to us, Miss Lochridge," Mrs. Presinger praised tearfully. "A real angel. I don't know how I'll ever repay you for all you've done for me and my family. Lord only knows what would have become of us when we first arrived in America if you hadn't been here."

"You just get Mary well," Ellari insisted, opening the door for the grateful woman. "I'm expecting to see both of you at the next society meeting."

The customer cleared her throat nervously. "We'll do our best," Trigg heard the woman mutter, unconvincingly he decided. "It will depend if we can spare the time off from work."

The instant he heard E. Lochridge's "Good day, Mrs. Presinger," followed by the rattle of the slamming door, Trigg grabbed his boots and shoved his feet into them.

"What are you still doing here?" Ellari hissed through her teeth as she rounded the screen. By her tone, it was obvious she hadn't forgotten that a raised voice would be heard outside the shop and that she was struggling to keep from screaming. "I told you to be gone before I opened this morning. What if she'd seen you?"

Leaning over his lap to adjust his pants legs over his boot tops, Trigg glanced up and smiled sheepishly. "I guess I overslept."

"Overslept?! What happened to all that talk about being a light sleeper? My reputation could have been totally ruined!"

Trigg still couldn't believe he'd slept so soundly. How long had it been? Usually, the slightest sound or the first hint of daylight woke him up. "From what I heard, it would take a lot more than finding a 'patient' sleeping on your couch to tarnish your halo in that woman's eyes."

He glanced down at the bandage across his midriff. "Now that I think of it, can you check on this before I finish dressing?" He grinned mischievously, making no secret of the fact that he was deliberately changing the subject.

Ellari paused, her irritated gaze turning to concern as she leveled it on the bandage. "I suppose it would be a good idea." She reached for the knot. "But then you've got to leave. Is that understood? Not everyone in this neighborhood thinks as highly of me as Mrs. Presinger does. There are a number of people who would take great delight in seeing me disgraced."

Trigg made an X on the left side of his chest with a forefinger. "Cross my heart." His pretense of seriousness was obvious.

"Hmph. Overslept, indeed." She quickly removed the bandage and surveyed his wound. "It looks good. It doesn't need to be rebandaged." She reached for his shirt and held it out to him. "Consider yourself free to leave."

Automatically, Trigg looked down at his middle to confirm her diagnosis. Disbelief wiped the grin from his face.

Except for a pale pink line that traversed his belly, the knife wound had completely disappeared. "I don't believe it! I've had mosquito bites that took longer than that to heal. What magic did you perform? Or was Mrs. Presinger right? Are you really an angel?"

Ellari laughed in spite of herself. "It was hardly magic, Mr. Hanahan. The salve I put on your wound is excellent for burns and cuts. And with David Nylander's—" she swallowed as though she'd tasted something foul—"glass factory right here in the neighborhood, a day rarely goes by that I don't have to treat one or two of each."

"Well, it's great stuff. Has it got a name? I'd like to pick up a jar of it to keep on hand. You never can tell when it would come in handy. I bet it would be great on shaving nicks." He took his shirt and slipped it on.

"Well . . . I suppose I could mix you up a small portion to take with you."

A light literally flashed in Trigg's head. "You mean it's not something you buy to use on cuts and burns?"

"Goodness me, no. No commercial preparation I know of works nearly as well as Papa's recipe does. Besides, they're all too expensive, and this costs very little to make. I just whip up a batch every day or two to use here in the treatment center."

And she thinks there are no family jewels here! God! If I could get my hands on that formula, I could make a fortune! No more Reed Phelps or Boss Stahl to worry about. They'd be coming to me for money!

"What's in it?" he asked, doing his absolute best to sound as if he was simply making idle conversation as he buttoned his shirt, when inside he was reeling with the magnitude of his discovery.

"Oh, a little of this and a little of that!" Ellari said, dismissing the subject with a wave of her hand. "You don't want to hear about it."

Oh, I do! Believe me I want nothing more! he yelled inside his head, but he kept his thoughts to himself. He didn't dare chance giving himself away. The minute she realized what a money-maker she had in her possession, she might decide to market it

85

herself and he would lose his chance of getting in on the profits. "Probably too many big science words for me to understand anyway."

"Not at all. The ingredients are pretty common things. Papa always said it was the combination of the different elements and the exact amounts called for that make the salve so effective. But no more shop talk. I'm glad you're better, but you really must leave. I have a lot to do."

"Like go out and buy a glass pane to fix the front door? I could watch the store while you're gone." That would be the perfect opportunity for him to search for the formula.

Ellari's face twisted into a trapped expression. "Actually, I'm going to need to wait on that. I can't leave the pharmacy today. Besides, I can't really afford to replace it right now."

Seeing his opportunity, Trigg seized it—despite the twinge of guilt that seized him with the realization he had evidently taken her last penny the day before. "You can't leave the door like that another night. It's not safe. It's got to be fixed today!"

"Of course, I intend to secure the door more thoroughly before dark. I'll nail additional boards across the opening. And as an added precaution, I'll block it with a heavy shelf. Don't worry, I'll be fine until I can afford to hire someone to replace the glass." She turned away.

"Wait a minute!"

Ellari faced him again. "Yes?"

Trigg dipped his hand into the pocket of his trousers. He whipped out the ten dollar gold piece she'd given him the day before. "Since I didn't get to the clothing store on time, and you did feed me and give me a place to sleep last night, we can buy the glass pane with this, and I'll put it in for you this afternoon."

Ellari looked surprised, then touched. "I couldn't. That money's yours. I wanted you to have it, or I wouldn't have given it to you. No, I'll wait. And who knows, maybe someone can bring me a free piece of glass from the glass factory. But thank you for offering."

Determined not to leave until he had a legitimate reason to come back, Trigg brushed past her to the door. "Do you have a yardstick?" He made a show of sizing up the window with his hands.

Ellari rushed after him. "But I told you—"

Trigg took hold of her upper arms and looked deeply into her puzzled green eyes. "Miss Lochridge, has anyone ever told you that you're too stubborn and independent? I'm going to fix your door, and that's all there is to it. Now, will you please get me the yardstick?"

"Why, Mr. Hanahan?"

Trigg shrugged and blessed her with one of his toecurling smiles. "Because I can't measure the size of the glass I need to purchase without a yardstick."

He could see she had to fight to keep from smiling, and he commended himself on taking one step closer to winning her confidence—and her magic formula.

"That's not what I mean, and you know it. I had the idea you don't believe in helping anyone unless there's something in it for you. What is it you expect to gain by fixing my door?"

"Maybe I'm just a nice guy, or maybe I just want a little piece of mind. Even a cad would find it hard to live with himself if something happened to a beautiful woman and he could have prevented it by repairing her door." Hit with surprising realization that the words he had spoken were true, Trigg had to force himself to smile.

Seeming to be satisfied with his answer, Ellari nodded her consent to work on the door. "I'll get the yardstick, but I'm going to at least fix your breakfast to partially repay you."

"Best offer I've had all day," Trigg laughed, saying a silent "Thanks" as he watched her bustled backside disappear into the storeroom. He could tell by the lilting tone of her voice it would only be a matter of a day—two at the most—until he wooed her into giving him the formula.

He ignored the guilt that gripped him. After all, what good was the salve doing her? If it were left up to her, no one would ever profit from the wonder ointment. Not her, not him, not even the people who would buy it by the case once they learned how effective it was. It was up to him to see that didn't happen!

"By the way, Miss Lochridge, what's the E. stand for?" he called after her.

"It's Ellari," she answered, appearing in the split between the curtains, an attractive smile on her face. "And I have a confession to make. I let my father's preconceived notions influence me to misjudge you,

Mr. Hanahan. You have been very kind to me, and I'm most appreciative." She held out a ruler. "Is this all right?"

Trigg stared at the ruler as if he'd never seen one before, the germ of guilt he'd been wrestling with exploding into fullfledged shame and self-disgust. Could he really take this generous innocent's formula? "It'll work," he finally said.

"Mr. Nylander will see you now," the perfectly turned-out secretary announced in clipped words.

Returning the effeminate young man's disapproving glance with a smirk, Trigg stood up. "Thanks," he muttered, giving the secretary's expensive clothing a knowing glance as he brushed past.

Spying the man studying papers spread on the enormous oak desk on the far side of the office, Trigg quickly dismissed his irritation with the snobbish clerk and assumed his best salesman's smile. "Mr. Nylander, so good of you to see me on such short notice." He offered his hand.

Nylander glanced up at Trigg's extended hand, then back down at his papers. "I can only spare five minutes so I trust you will be brief. I'm a very busy man."

Trigg dropped his hand to his side with a slight shrug. So much for the friendly approach. "I can see that you are, and I won't take any more of your time than necessary."

Possibly no more than five or six years older than Trigg, David Nylander was paunchy around the middle and totally bald with the exception of the mousy brown fringe of hair horseshoeing the base of his skull from sideburn to sideburn. "In that case, what is it you want to talk to me about?"

Already, he had decided not to share his real purpose for being here with Nylander. "In my travels farther west, one thing that stands out in my mind is the drabness of the existence out there, especially on the plains, like in Iowa, Kansas, Nebraska and South Dakota. Out there, everything is flat and the same color. They even build their houses out of the sod."

"Is there a point to this?" Nylander interrupted impatiently.

"I'm getting to that. I notice that in the city, women are able to buy their lotions and creams in attractive jars made of colored glass. But on the farms out west the women not only must make their own medicines and cosmetics, but they have to store them in colorless clay crocks or old canning jars. What I'm proposing to do is bring a little color into the lives of the women out west by providing them with the same colored glass containers the city women have, to use for their home preparations — at a price of course."

"And you want to purchase your jars at Nylander? But I don't take orders. The man you want to see is Ed Vigel in sales. He'll give you a good price. On your way out, would you tell my secretary I need to speak to him." Nylander resumed his perusal of the papers on the desk, obviously considering the meeting concluded.

Frustrated to realize he'd been dismissed, Trigg

didn't move.

Nylander looked up, his expression annoyed. "Is there something else?"

God, how he'd like to wipe that damned superior look off Nylander's face. But if he wanted to market Ellari Lochridge's "Magic Skin Formula"—he was already thinking of it in those terms—in the style he'd envisioned, he was going to have to forego that pleasure. He had to have those jars! "You don't understand, Mr. Nylander. I didn't come here to buy jars."

"I'm in business to sell glass. If you don't want to buy that glass, why are you here?"

"I have a proposal for you."

"A proposal?" Nylander repeated, his tone indicating an obvious disinterest. "Well, you might as well go on. What's your proposal?"

Damn! It was hot. Trigg felt wet all over. His palms, his forehead, his underarms, his upper lip. He could see it now. Nylander wasn't going to give him the jars; Ellari Lochridge would figure out what was going on and wouldn't give him the formula; and he was going to have to marry Ina Phelps to keep Boss Stahl's goons from breaking his legs and dumping him in Lake Michigan. He cleared his throat, hoping to erase the sound of desperation he knew Nylander would recognize.

"What I want to do is become your representative out west and sell your jars on commission. I'm sure this can be very lucrative for both of us."

"In other words, you have no money and want me to stake your venture."

"I wouldn't put it that way . . ."

"Well, that's exactly how I would put it. Good day, Mr. Hanahan."

No matter how desperate his situation, Trigg Hanahan had never lowered himself to begging, and he had no intention of starting now. He would just have to think of something else. His mouth stretched into a strained grin. "Yeah, well, thanks for listening."

His posture erect with false confidence, he turned on his heel and strode out. He gave the secretary entering from the outer office a nothing-ventured-nothing-gained shrug as they passed in the doorway.

Ellari had tackled her cleaning with a spirit she hadn't felt in years. It had started out simply enough. She had just intended to sweep and mop the area and shelves by the front door to check for any broken glass she and Trigg Hanahan might have missed the evening before. One thing had led to another, and she hadn't stopped before every aisle, shelf and item of merchandise in the store had been given a thorough cleaning.

It didn't occur to her to question where the sudden burst of enthusiasm had come from—especially after a night of almost no sleep.

Proudly surveying the results of her hard work, she smiled, then looked down at her hands. They were filthy, as was her dress, apron and no doubt her face.

"It's a good thing business has been slow today,"

she said to her feline companion. Mister Cat blinked one sleepy eye, then returned to his nap in a narrow space he had claimed on a bottom merchandise shelf between boxes of sulphate of copper and powdered capsicum.

She couldn't help laughing. She had fed the cat that morning and put him out the back door; but as soon as she had reopened the door to take out her trash, Mister Cat had shot back into the store.

Actually, she'd put him out several times, but each try had had the same results. Once a customer had let him in through the front door. Another time, he'd come in when she had gone out back to wring out her mop. It was uncanny how every time she put him out, he was at the next door to open—front or back—in time to sneak back in.

Finally, Ellari had given up and told the cat he could stay if he would keep out of her way. That was when he'd found his meager little cubby and settled in—as if to say, *See? I don't take much room. You won't even know I'm here.*

"You know what I think I'm going to do, Mister Cat? I'm going to do something I've never done in the five years I've been here. I'm going to close the shop in the middle of the day and go upstairs to bathe and change my clothes. What do you think of that?" She flipped over the closed sign in the window, then slid the door lock into place and drew the shade over the boarded door.

Before she reached the curtains to the back, the cat disappeared into the storeroom and was waiting for her at the bottom of the stairs.

"Mr. Hanahan!" the winded secretary from David Nylander's office wheezed. "Thank goodness I caught you." He held his hand to his rising and falling chest in a decidedly feminine gesture. "Mr. Nylander wants to talk to you again."

Caught completely by surprise, Trigg failed to come up with a sarcastic response for the man who'd evidently chased him for two blocks. "What for?"

"He says there may be a way the two of you can do business after all."

"Are you sure?"

"Of course, I'm sure." The secretary puffed up with indignation that anyone would even suggest otherwise. "I wouldn't last very long in my position if I couldn't correctly relay a message from one person to another. Now, are you coming, or shall I tell Mr. Nylander you are no longer interested?"

"Oh! I'm interested all right." He looked down at the brown paper-wrapped pane of glass he was carrying back to Ellari's store, then spotted a paper boy on the corner. "Hey, kid! You want to earn a couple of pennies?"

"Sure, mister. Whatcha want me to do?"

Trigg propped his package between the boy's stacks of newspapers. "Keep an eye on this for me. I'll be back for it in a while."

"That's all?"

Trigg grinned sadly, realizing a street kid would do a lot more for two cents than watch a pane of glass. "Just be careful. It's glass and I don't want it broken."

The boy grinned, showing decayed and broken teeth. "Whatever you say."

"I knew I picked the right man for the job." Trigg flipped the boy a penny and said, "You'll get the rest when I get back." He turned to the secretary and gave the frail-looking man an unnecessarily friendly slap on the back. "Let's go."

Ellari looked at herself in the mirror and shook her head doubtfully. What had possessed her to leave the back of her hair hanging in loose curls, rather than securing it in the tight bun she always wore? Suddenly feeling foolish, she twisted the thickness into a knot and reached for her hairpins.

An urgent knock on the locked front door halted her hurried repairs to her hairdo. "It's him!" she said to the cat, dropping her hold on her hair and taking off at a run.

At the door, she paused to gain her composure. She was behaving like a silly schoolgirl. After all, he was only replacing a pane of glass. Then he would be gone. He wouldn't even notice she had changed into a different dress. Still, she glanced down at herself, adjusting the front folds of her skirt that draped back into her bustle.

Reasonably certain she could disguise the fluttery feeling in her chest, she gave her hair a quick pat and unbolted the door and opened it. The smile slid from her face like butter off a warm plate. It wasn't Trigg Hanahan at all.

"Anything wrong, Miss Lochridge?" the small elderly man asked her, his wrinkled face filled with genuine concern. "I never known you to close up in the middle of the day before."

"No, nothing's wrong, Mr. Czurak. I had some things to take care of and had to leave the shop for a while. What can I do for you? Did that liniment and tonic I sent over help Mrs. Czurak?"

The old man grinned and nodded with his entire body. "That it did. She's doin' much better today, thanks to you. And like I promised, I brought you them flyers you was askin' about." He brought the canvas bag that hung from his bony shoulder around to show her. "They look pretty good, if I say so myself."

"Oh, Mr. Czurak, I don't have enough in the cash drawer to pay you for them today!" she told the printer.

He brushed past her and dropped the bag on the back counter. "We already discussed that. I told you this was to pay for all the times you've helped my Hilda and me. I don't want your money."

She followed him to the back. "But I want to at least pay for the paper and ink you used to print them. I didn't intend for you to pay for them."

The old man laughed. He leaned close and cupped his hand to his mouth. "Between you and me, Miss Lochridge. I didn't. Your friend, David Nylander, paid for them."

"What?!"

"He hired me to do a print job for him and I 'accidentally' ordered a bit too much paper and ink.

By coincidence, it was the exact same amount it took to print the two hundred flyers you wanted."

"Why, Mr. Czurak, you ought to be ashamed of yourself!"

"You're right. You think I better take 'em out back and burn 'em?" He started to hoist the bag onto his shoulder again.

Ellari grabbed his hand to stop him. "Don't you dare!"

She and the printer both burst out laughing.

"Are you sure?" he asked, his eyes twinkling with mischief.

"I'm sure—but only because they're already printed and I hate waste. But I want you to promise me you won't do anything like this again."

Czurak shook his head. "Oh, I won't. I've learned my lesson."

"In that case, thank you."

"I just hope they do some good, Miss Lochridge, and don't bring you to harm. You know people are pretty touchy when someone comes in tellin' them how to live their lives."

"I'm not telling them how to live their lives, Mr. Czurak. I'm only trying to help them save their children's lives."

"You just remember what I said, and be careful. There's some of us in this neighborhood who'd be real sorry if anything happened to you."

"But just as many who wouldn't miss me even a little bit?" she asked with a forced laugh. "Well, don't worry, nothing's going to happen to me. I'll be fine."

Her assurances had a hollow ring to them, even to her own ears, and her high spirits from earlier plunged.

Chapter Six

Determined not to seem anxious, Trigg sauntered back into David Nylander's office and took a seat without it being offered. "I hear you've changed your mind about my proposition." He casually propped an ankle on his other knee and flicked an imaginary piece of lint from his pants leg.

His elbows propped on the desk, Nylander thoughtfully studied Trigg over his interlocked fingers. "That depends."

Trigg's excitement took a sudden dip. Dropping his raised foot to the floor, he stiffened. He should have known there would be a catch. There always was. "On what?"

"On how serious you are about wanting to work for me."

"I thought I made that clear. I'm very serious. I believe we can both make a lot of money with these colored jars. The women will love them."

"I'm not talking about glass jars here, Hanahan."

"You're not? Then what are you talking about?"

"I'm talking about hiring you to work for me in a different capacity."

A feeling of dread forced his excitement to drop another notch. "What capacity is that?" he asked suspiciously.

Ignoring Trigg's question, Nylander asked one of his own. "What would you say if I told you I've decided to *give* you your colored glass jars—free and clear—including a wagon and team to transport them west, as well as five hundred dollars in cash to finance your trip?"

Trigg could feel himself practically salivate at the thought of what such a windfall could mean. He'd heard hundreds of stories about the many wealthy business men in Chicago who had started out with only a few dollars in their pockets. All it had taken was hard work and a lucky break. Could this finally be his lucky break? God, he hoped so.

Fortunately, his years on the street kept his rising hopes at bay. There was one lesson he had learned in his years of struggling for survival: when something sounded too good to be true, it usually was. And this deal definitely smacked of being too good to be true.

"I'd say that's pretty generous of you, Nylander, but you don't strike me as a man who gives anything away without expecting something in return. What's the catch?"

"It's really quite simple. There's a certain person who is causing me a great deal of trouble. All you have to do is get rid of that person, and we'll

100

be even."

Trigg's expectations dove to rock bottom. There were certain lines even a man of his questionable morals wouldn't cross. "You want me to *kill* somebody?"

Nylander and his secretary exchanged sly grins. "I hope it doesn't come to that, but I have no doubt a clever young man with your ingenuity can come up with a less violent means of disposal."

Trigg leaned forward in his chair and leveled his gaze on Nylander. "Let me get this straight. You'll give me five hundred dollars—*cash,* a team of horses, and a wagon loaded with colored glass jars, and all I've got to do is get someone to stop giving you trouble any way I can."

"Precisely." Nylander nodded and offered his hand. "Do we have a deal?"

It was Trigg's turn to ignore Nylander's gesture. He couldn't shake off the nagging thought: too good to be true! "Not so fast. I need more details. Who is this 'person' you want me to run out of town? What's his story?"

"Not his story, Mr. Hanahan. Hers. Which is why I particularly chose you for the job. I have no doubt this woman will be susceptible to your charms. I'll admit I had another man in mind for this job, but quite frankly, his methods tend to be a little barbaric. Of course, if you're not interested, I'll have no choice but to use him. One way or another, something has to be done about this woman before the situation gets any more out of hand. It's already gone on too long."

Great! If I turn him down, some poor unsuspecting woman could be murdered. On the other hand, if I take the job, I'll have my jars, the money to start producing my Magic Skin Formula *and get out of town—and the woman lives. How can I say no?*

He held out his hand to Nylander. "You've got a deal. Where do I find this woman?"

Nylander took Trigg's hand and grinned. "That should be easy enough. You spent last night in her bed."

Ellari glanced down at her lapel watch, then at the clock on the wall in the back of the store. Two o'clock. What was taking him so long? He'd said he had a few personal errands to run besides picking up the pane of glass for the door, but surely he should have been back by now.

If he planned on coming back at all, she reminded herself, her spirits plummeting as she admitted she had only been fooling herself. *Obviously, he found something better to do with his time and money.*

"Not that I can blame him," she said aloud, opening the front door and peering outside. Though she tried to tell herself he wasn't going to be there, she couldn't help the sinking feeling of disappointment that hit her when she didn't find him ambling toward her along the wooden sidewalk.

Closing the door, she paused. "Stop fooling your-

102

self. Why would he want to come back to this dreary pharmacy to help an equally dreary old-maid pharmacist?"

She turned around and faced the back of the store, her eyes roving dejectedly over the freshly dusted and straightened counters. Funny, earlier, when she had believed Trigg Hanahan was coming back, the store had had an almost cheery appearance to it. The morning sun dancing and glistening off all the glass bottles arranged on the shelves had given the whole scene a festive air.

Now with the sun no longer beaming through the windows and her hopes dashed, she could once more see the pharmacy for what it really was: old and dreary.

"That's us, old store. Even scrubbed and looking our best, we're beyond help. We're still just a couple of dreary old things no one in his right mind would have the time of day for."

She tried to smile bravely, but she couldn't quite manage it.

"Stop feeling sorry for yourself, Ellari Lochridge!" she scolded angrily. "Since you won't be getting a new door glass today, you'd better get some more lumber from the alley and cover up those gaps in the door if you want a decent night's sleep tonight."

She stepped away from the door and was halfway up the center aisle when the bell over the door signaled its opening.

Her expression expectant, despite her loss of

hope, she spun around in time to see a hand and black sleeve disappear from the door as a rough, ugly voice called out, "Mind your own business, girlie, or you'll be sorry!"

Before she could get to the door to jerk it open and confront whoever was there, a series of loud cracks and pops began exploding at her feet.

Screaming, she jumped back, her frightened gaze targeting on two strings of firecrackers, flaring and snapping and smoking.

Her fear of fire giving her the impetus to overcome her natural instinct to run, she began stamping the crackling firecrackers. In less than a minute all the sparks from the potential firestarters had been subdued. Only then did Ellari allow herself to give in to the full impact of this latest attack.

With knees no longer able to support her, she accordion-folded herself to the floor, her gaze held prisoner by the charred spots left on the planks of her freshly mopped floor. Who was doing this to her? Who wanted her to stop speaking out against child labor so badly that they tried to burn her out?

Her first thought was Jon Schmelzel, but she quickly discarded that possibility. He may have threatened her with a knife, or might have even been the guilty party who broke her window, but he wouldn't have risked a fire. No one who lived so close to her shop would have done that.

Fire was always a threat in the older part of the city where not only the buildings and sidewalks were built of wood, but the streets were paved with it as well. The newspapers were constantly warning that the wooden slums fanning out from downtown were doomed to go up in flames at any time if something wasn't done about them soon.

The critics of the unstable tinderbox neighborhoods had been especially vocal lately, because there had been so little rain and everything was even drier than usual. Fires had been more prevalent and likely than ever before.

In fact, to her knowledge, a day hadn't gone by in the past month that the peal of the alarm bell from the watchtower atop the huge domed courthouse downtown hadn't announced a fire somewhere in the city at least once. There had even been days when the rumble of the horse-drawn fire engines dispatched from one of the city's four firehouses had seemed continuous. And just the week before, less than a mile away, an entire block of slapped together wooden houses, sidewalks and streets had been destroyed before the firefighters could put out the fire.

No, whoever threw the firecrackers, she was sure it wasn't Jon Schmelzel—or anyone else who lived in this section of the city. It had to be someone from outside.

The only other possibility that came to her mind was David Nylander, owner of the Nylander Glass Works.

Of course! Why didn't she think of him immediately? Nylander was the obvious culprit, though he wouldn't be doing the actual harassing himself. He would have hired someone else to do his dirty work, someone who wouldn't care if he destroyed an entire neighborhood in the process of carrying out his duties, while David Nylander sat in his big office and kept his hands clean.

"Well," she growled, bolting up from the floor, "Mr. Nylander, you're not going to shut me up with a few firecrackers. It's time you and I met face to face and set a few things straight."

Without warning, the bells over the door jangled loudly, crashing into her concentration. Anger propelling her, she lunged at the door and wrenched it open wide. "Who are you? Why are you ha—?"

She stopped and stared, needing a full second for the truth to register in her disbelieving mind. "You're back!" she finally gasped as full realization hit her.

Ruled by relief and natural reflexes, Ellari slammed into the befuddled man and wrapped her arms tightly around his neck.

Trigg embraced her with his free hand and reared back his head. "To what do I owe this enthusiastic welcome?" he asked with a perplexed chuckle.

Embarrassed, Ellari tried to step back, but the warm comfort of his hand on her back stopped her. She searched his face to confirm the fact that he was truly there. "I didn't think you were coming back."

"I told you I would. My other business took me longer than I thought it would." He locked his gaze on her upturned face, surprised to find tears in her

106

eyes — and even more surprised at the alarm those tears caused to flare in his chest. "What is it? Have you been crying?"

Her expression trapped, Ellari removed her hands from his shoulders to wipe the backs of her wrists over her eyes. "Of course not," she said with a sniff. "I must have gotten something in my eyes."

"Well, something's wrong." Without releasing his hold on her, he turned her around and guided her the rest of the way into the store. "What is it? Did something happen while I was gone?"

Startled, her focus leaped to his face, then inadvertently turned to the charred floor at their feet.

Trigg's gaze followed the direction hers had taken, fixing on the firecracker-damaged planks. "What the hell?"

He dropped his arm from around her shoulders and propped the new glass pane he carried against a nearby shelf. Hunkering down to examine the scorched boards, he plucked up a piece of partially burned string and held it to his nose to confirm what he suspected. "Who did this?"

"I only saw a man's hand and sleeve," she admitted, her voice low. "He was gone by the time I stamped out the firecrackers. But I have my suspicions who is behind these attacks, and he's not going to get away with it!"

"Oh?" Trigg asked, glancing up at her. He couldn't help admiring the strength that had returned to her voice and posture. "Who do you think it is?"

"Yesterday, I wasn't sure, but today I'm absolutely positive David Nylander of Nylander Glass Works is responsible."

Trigg winced at the mention of the man he'd agreed to do business with not an hour earlier. "That's a pretty strong accusation. Surely a rich man like Nylander has better things to do than vandalize your shop."

"Oh, he wouldn't do it himself. But I'd wager my last cent, he's hired someone to drive me out of business."

"Why do you think Nylander wants to drive you out of business?"

Ellari released a bitter laugh. "Well, he's tried everything else to convince me to give up my fight against using children in the glass factories. He's sent lawyers to plead with me and convince me that the glass factories will shut down if they can't use child labor. Then, when I refused to back down, they tried to get my sympathy by pointing out that if the factories closed, I would be personally responsible for entire families starving because they were all out of work. When that didn't work, he tried to buy me out by offering me an exorbitant amount of money for my business."

"Those don't sound like the tactics of a man who would order your store vandalized."

Ellari shrugged. "Evidently he got tired of my resistance to more peaceful measures and decided to frighten me into leaving. He must be very desperate if he's willing to chance burning down a

108

whole neighborhood."

Or something worse than arson—like murder, Trigg said to himself, feeling the weight of his decision to deal with Nylander even more now. "So, why didn't you sell? It seems to me that would have been the answer to all your problems."

"Oh, I would have made enough money on the sale to go to medical school—if I could have gotten accepted again. But I could never have lived with myself if I'd accepted. Not only would he have kept employing children to work horrendously long hours under inhuman conditions in his factory, but he would have closed the pharmacy and left all these people with no medical care whatsoever. My conscience would never allow me to make a new life for myself with money I had earned at the cost of children's lives and health. I'll stay here the rest of my life before I'll leave under those circumstances."

Ellari watched from behind her pharmacy counter as Trigg Hanahan put the finishing touches on the repaired door window. Just this tiny taste of what it must be like to be married and have a man who could do those husbandly things around the home created a longing inside her so fierce she actually ached.

"Well, I guess that does it," Trigg announced as he stepped back to admire his work. He opened and slammed the door a couple of times to test the set of the glass in the frame. "I bought a thicker pane than you had before, so its good and tight. I think the extra thickness and the snug fit will make it a little more durable." He picked up his tools and walked toward her.

His usual smile was in place, but there was something different about it that Ellari couldn't quite put her finger on. Was it a little stress she hadn't seen before? A touch of sadness?

"It looks wonderful—and very secure," she said, puzzled. "I really appreciate your taking care of this today. I have to admit I wasn't looking forward to spending another night like last night."

"Anything else you need fixing?" he asked, glancing around the pharmacy. He held up his hammer and the sack of nails. "As long as I'm here I might as well do it all."

"Oh, I couldn't impose on you any more than I already have. You've done more for me than I had any right to expect."

"You're not imposing. What do you need done?"

Ellari opened her mouth to protest further. Then, with the force of a bolt of lightning, she was hit with the realization that it was apprehension she saw in his eyes. For some reason, known only to him, Trigg Hanahan was searching for an excuse not to leave! Her joy soared. Maybe he was blind, or maybe he felt sorry for her, or maybe he was just plain crazy, but it didn't matter why he wanted to stay, only that he did!

"Well, I have been meaning to hire someone to fix a few loose steps going upstairs to

110

my apartment."

"Consider it done." He started for the back room.

"Mr. Hanahan?" she called after him.

He stopped at the curtains and smiled back over his shoulder. "Yeah?"

Ellari felt herself warm under the heat of his gaze. "Thank you," she said shyly.

"You're welcome," he answered with a lingering look she felt all the way down to her boot-covered toes.

The remainder of the afternoon, Ellari worked with a new zest she had never felt since she had assumed responsibility for her father's pharmacy. Suddenly, nothing seemed as bad as it had the day before, and she could allow herself to believe that nothing was impossible.

"Here you are, Mrs. Knowles." She handed a brown medicine bottle over the counter to a haggard-looking woman who looked to be in her late fifties, but whom Ellari knew to be in her mid-thirties. "Give little Willie a hot tablespoon of this every few minutes until he's breathing more easily. After that, give him a dose several times a day until the asthma symptoms are gone."

"Thank you," the woman said softly, placing a large paper-wrapped loaf of bread on the counter as she took the medicine. "I hope this will cover the cost. It's all I have, but it's real fresh. I baked it

111

this morning when I got home from my shift at the mill."

"It will be fine," Ellari said, giving the sickly boy beside her a sympathetic smile. "Now you be sure and take your medicine like a good boy, Willie."

"Yes'm, I will," he wheezed. "I can't miss work or the foreman'll give my job to another boy—and my pa'll tan my hide."

"Hopefully, one day soon you won't have to worry about things like that." She handed Mrs. Knowles one of the flyers Mr. Czurak had brought by earlier. "Next week we're holding an organization meeting of mothers of working children to discuss what can be done to end this terrible practice. We'd love to have you join us."

The woman's eyes shifted regretfully to her son's cropped head. "I can't, Miss Lochridge. My husband would nev—well, I just can't." On a soft choking sound, she took her son's hand and spun around. "Thank you again." She ran out of the store, dragging Willie close behind her.

Ellari stared after the pair, her heart breaking for the two of them and every other mother and child in similar circumstances. There had to be a way to change things for them and others in the same deprived circumstances. But there was only so much she could do alone. If only there were someone on her side willing to help. Someone with a knack for swaying people, someone with the ability to get things done, someone so determined the answer "no" would never be a consideration, some-

112

one who. . . .

The *tap-tap-tap* of Trigg Hanahan's hammer working its way up the stairs on the other side of the wall behind her head had been a comforting accompaniment to her work the past few hours. But now it suddenly took on the magnificence and beauty of the "Hallelujah Chorus." Of course! That was the answer. Who better to help children who worked twelve to sixteen-hour days year round and often never saw the sun because they were slaving in dark factories, than a man who'd spent his life living in the freedom of the out-of-doors?

Elated, Ellari spent the final hour before closing waiting on customers and treating patients cheerfully, all the time going over in her head what she would say to convince him to help her.

No closer to knowing how to broach the subject than she had been when the idea of recruiting Trigg Hanahan had occurred to her, she closed the door on the last customer and drew the shade.

Now that the moment was at hand, second thoughts ran rampantly through her head. What was she thinking of? He didn't care about her cause, and despite the work he'd done for her today, he certainly wasn't the sort of man who would work for free. Dejectedly, she bolted the door, then dropped her head forward to lean her forehead against the frame.

"Hard day?" a deep voice crooned from the back of the store.

Startled, Ellari straightened and whipped around

113

to face him. "No more than usu—" She stopped and gaped.

A sympathetic grin on his face, Trigg stood between the curtains to the storeroom. Shirtless, he had his fingers hooked on the doorframe over his head, stretching his lean torso making it seem even leaner. "Didn't anyone tell you working too hard will make you old before your time?"

She had known that he'd shed his shirt earlier—the unventilated stairway where he'd been working was particularly warm this time of the year. But she was still unprepared for seeing him like this. Her eyes roved unchecked over the sinewy muscles of his arms and chest, helplessly touching every curve and hollow of his sweat-glistening flesh with her gaze.

Embarrassed by her blatant staring, she cleared her throat self-consciously and forced herself to look him straight in the eyes as she walked toward where he stood. "You've worked hard, too, and you don't look any older than you did this morning. But you do look like you could stand a good meal. Are you hungry? It won't take me long to whip up something . . ."

She caught herself. Now he was staring, an amused grin on his face. "That is if you'd like to stay," she added hastily.

When he didn't answer right away, she immediately assumed he was searching for a polite way to refuse her invitation. "What am I thinking? You probably already have plans for dinner."

"I do have plans, but . . ."

"In that case, I won't keep you any longer. Thank you again for repairing my door and stairs." Wishing she could melt into the floor, she studied her own hands. Had she really thought she was going to talk him into helping her with her cause?

"Hey," he said, dropping one hand from the doorframe to raise her chin with a curved forefinger so she had to look at him. "It was my pleasure. I liked doing it."

Her emotions had bounced from elation to disappointment to elation again so many times since Trigg Hanahan had walked into her life the day before that she felt like a rubber ball. But here she went again! "You did?"

"Sure. I've never had a place of my own to fix up, and it gave me a little peek at what it might be like if I ever have that place—" His eyes twinkled. "—and a special woman to share it with."

Only the support of his finger beneath her chin kept her mouth from dropping open. He had voiced the exact feelings she had experienced all afternoon as she had listened to the comforting pound of his hammer, had thought about what she would fix him for supper—and had allowed herself to imagine what it would be like to be held in his arms at the end of the day.

"I enjoyed it too," she admitted shyly, her heart thudding with such force it hurt. Unable to look away, she searched his smiling face for an understanding of what he was thinking. "And who knows when I would have gotten those stairs fixed?"

115

"Or broken your neck," he laughed softly. "I don't know what kept you from killing yourself before now. Every nail had worked loose on several of them."

She grinned sheepishly. "I knew which ones I had to be particularly careful on."

"You should do that more often."

"What's that?"

He brought his thumb up from where it rested at the tip of her chin and traced her lower lip with it. "That. You have a beautiful smile."

Oh, Lord. Could this be happening? Did he really say she had a beautiful smile? Was he really touching her mouth so intimately and looking at her as if he were going to kiss her? Her eyes closed and opened dreamily. "I do?"

He nodded and lowered his head as he drew her face closer to his. "Definitely one of the prettiest I've ever seen—and one of the most kissable."

Before she could question her own actions, his lips ghosted over hers in a kiss so light she could have imagined it—except that her entire body erupted into flame, melting her will and reason.

Trigg drew back his head and examined her enraptured face. Her eyes were closed, their golden tipped lashes quivering where they lay over her lower lids.

Guilt and self-disdain rocked through him. Damn! Why'd she have to be so sweet and trusting—and ripe for the picking? If he had a thread of decency in him, he'd turn around and leave right

116

now. He'd forget his plan to seduce her out of her formula, and he would settle for the wagon load of jars Nylander had given him and get out of the city before daybreak — before Nylander knew he had reneged on their agreement, before Phelps could figure out that he'd never had any intention of marrying his daughter, and before Boss Stahl traced him to collect the rest of what he was owed.

Then a reminder hit him of what Nylander had implied would be Ellari Lochridge's fate if another man had to be hired to get her to drop her fight against the glass factories.

Of course, the threat could have just been Nylander's way of getting him to agree to take the job, he told himself. After all, the factory owner had assumed Ellari Lochridge meant something to him and was a way to get to him — which of course wasn't true. In fact, now that he thought about it, Nylander probably didn't even have a man in mind like the one he had described. Only a fool would risk being connected to the murder of a woman who couldn't cause much more harm to a big company like Nylander Glass Works than a mosquito to an elephant.

On the other hand, what if Nylander's threat was real? Could he leave knowing that was a possibility? But if he stayed, who would protect Ellari Lochridge from Trigg Hanahan?

He was trapped, trapped by the unfamiliar feeling of responsibility for another human being, and he didn't know what to do. If he left, she could be in serious danger. If he stayed her formula wasn't going to be the only thing he stole from her.

He had to get outside where he could think. "I've got to go," he said, his voice hoarse. He dropped his hand from the doorframe overhead and placed it on her upper arm with every intention of pushing away from her, but he didn't, couldn't.

"I wish you wouldn't," she whispered, her green eyes diamond bright as they drilled into his.

That was all it took to destroy his brief try at selflessness. He'd given her a chance to put some distance between them, and she hadn't taken it.

With a need that had nothing to do with his hunger for monetary success, he slid his hand from her chin to the back of her neck and brought his mouth down hard onto hers.

Chapter Seven

Nothing in her wildest fantasies about being kissed had prepared Ellari for what she felt when her lips met Trigg's. It began with an explosion deep in the pit of her belly, as if her insides had splintered into a million fragments of glass, then reflected out to every limb, converting her bones to jelly, her blood to fire and her thoughts to incoherent flashes of light.

Unable to muster even the strength to lift arms that hung uselessly at her sides, she sagged against him, reveling in the phenomenal glory of the moment.

His hold tight on the back of her neck, Trigg dug the fingers of his other hand into her arm where he grasped her. Starving to taste all of her sweetness, he ground his mouth against her closed lips in a frenzied assault to gain entrance.

Trapping her between the doorjamb and his hard body, he thrust his hips forward and burrowed his hands into the thick hair at her nape.

Finally, he lifted his head to give them both a chance to catch their breath. "You taste like peppermint."

"I—" Before she could explain that she had eaten a piece of the penny candy she kept in a jar on her counter just before closing the shop, he took advantage of her parted lips and kissed her again, this time achieving the sweet-tasting reward his tongue sought so urgently.

Carried beyond reason by her newly discovered passion, Ellari experienced a daring she had not thought possible. Beyond thinking, her primal instincts took control of her actions.

The strength in her arms returned with a purpose of their own. She brought her hands up from her sides and splayed them on the warm, sweat-misted smoothness of his back. Instinctively, she returned the pressure of his pelvis with a gentle rocking as her body strove to relieve the throbbing ache between her thighs.

"Ohhh," she moaned into his mouth, clawing her hands up his back to grip his shoulders on either side of his neck.

Keeping one hand on her neck, he brought the other around to cup and caress her full breast.

Startled by the intimate touch, Ellari mercifully reclaimed a modicum of reason. "No," she groaned, twisting her mouth away from his.

As if he'd been caught stealing, Trigg froze, his

facial features stunned, hurt. Their gazes locked, he left his hand on her heaving breast for a full second before he dropped it to his side and stepped back. "Sorry," he said, his eyes filled with a mixture of anger and bitterness. "Guess I misread the signals. I'll get my things."

Shame washed through Ellari. She had behaved abominably. No wonder he had thought it was permissible to take such liberties. She'd brought it on herself. "Perhaps, that would be a good idea."

He started to turn away, then stopped, his eyes boring into hers. "I'll go, but in the future, you'd better remember the next fellow you kiss like you kissed me might not be so willing to stop." He disappeared into the storeroom where he'd left his shirt, vest, coat and the purchases he'd made when he'd been out earlier.

Her lips compressed tightly in an effort not to cry, Ellari stepped away from the curtained doorway and moved to her work counter. When she thought about what had almost happened, she thanked the Lord for giving her that single moment of strength to do the right thing.

Pressing her balled fists to the worn surface of the counter, she sagged forward, not at all certain "doing the right thing" was worth the price she was paying—an emptiness from regret that was almost unbearable.

Using every ounce of resistance she could muster, she fought the overwhelming urge to call him back. She stood that way until she heard the door to the alley click shut.

A series of urgent knocks at the front door broke into her thoughts. "Miss Lochridge!" a child's voice cried. "Are you there?"

Accustomed to having people come to her door for help at all hours, Ellari rushed forward, relieved to have something to take her mind off Trigg Hanahan.

She quickly unlocked the door and swung it open. "Willie! What are you doing here?"

"Come quick," the pale child panted between labored asthmatic breaths. "Ma . . . needs . . . you. She's . . . hurt." He took her hand and tugged on it. "Hurry," he wheezed, each breath sounding as if it could be his last.

Not wanting to try Willie's strength more than necessary, she didn't ask what had happened. "Wait here. I'll get my bag." She ran to the treatment corner and whisked her black emergency bag up onto the washstand and quickly checked its contents. Satisfied that she had supplies to handle most any emergency, she snapped the bag shut and hurried to where Willie leaned against the outside front wall of the pharmacy, his small face pale and gleaming with perspiration.

Seeing that she was ready, the boy opened his mouth to speak.

"Don't try to talk," Ellari ordered him, pulling the door to behind her and kneeling down beside

122

him. She held a white handkerchief which she had dabbed with spirits of camphor, out to the child. "Willie, I want you to breathe into this," she instructed him, taking care to appear unhurried and calm. "Can you do that for me?"

Still gasping for air, Willie nodded his hatless head and covered his mouth and nose with the handkerchief.

She waited a moment to give the strong smelling medicinal a chance to take effect. When it did, she stood up and took Willie's clammy hand in hers. "Good boy. Now take me to your mother."

Within minutes, Ellari and Willie walked up a wooden stairway at the back of a dilapidated two-story building in the next block. Like everything else in the southwest Chicago neighborhood, it was built of weathered, splintering wood.

Inside the small apartment, the air was pungent with the odor of cooked cabbage and onions, fabric dye and too many human beings in too close quarters; Ellari immediately recognized the room as one of the many home sweatshops that flourished all over the city.

"Do you live here?"

Willie nodded, indicating the women and children working in the room. "They're my aunts and sisters. They don't go to the factories like me 'n' ma, so they work at home 'n' watch the babies."

This wasn't the first time Ellari had been in a

sweatshop to give a woman or child emergency medical attention, but no matter how many times she saw the conditions these poor, desperate people worked under, she never failed to be shocked, though this one wasn't much different than the others she had visited—better than some, worse than others.

Three women and two young girls sat at a table, their heads bent as they concentrated on feeding dark fabric pieces into the sewing machines before them. At their feet, several grimy tots—the youngest appearing to be no more than two years old, the oldest maybe four—pulled basting threads from finished pieces as the sewers dropped their completed work onto piles on the floor between themselves and the thread pullers. Two undersized six- or seven-years-olds ran from pile to pile, gathering, folding and stacking the garments by the door after the threads were removed, evidently readying them for the "sweater"—the middle man between them and the garment manufacturers—when he came to pick them up and bring more work to do.

No one looked up as Ellari and Willie entered.

In the corner, Mrs. Knowles lay on a mattress on the floor, a damp compress on her face. "Mama, I brung Miss Lochridge."

Doing her best to ignore the subhuman conditions of the sweatshop and the eye-stinging fumes of the fabric dyes, Ellari rushed to the

124

woman's side.

"Miss Lochridge!" Mrs. Knowles kept the damp rag pressed over her left eye and cheek and her head turned so she didn't look at Ellari, and struggled to sit up. "There was no need for you to come. Willie, I told you not to bother Miss Lochridge."

Ellari waved her hand from side to side to stop the woman's protests. "Don't worry about it. Willie was right to come for me." She reached for the cloth Mrs. Knowles held to her face. "Now, let me take a look at this."

Resigning herself to being treated, Mrs. Knowles dropped the compress to her lap so Ellari could see the extent of her injury. "It's nothing."

An eye swollen shut and a bleeding cheek twice the size it had been that afternoon were revealed. Ellari was unable to hide her shock. "What happened?!" she gasped.

"I fell," the woman quickly answered, self-consciously covering her swollen mouth with her hand to hide bleeding gums where a tooth had been earlier.

"Pa hit 'er," Willie volunteered.

"He hit you?" Ellari repeated, struggling to hide her dismay as she began to clean the ugly cuts.

"It wasn't his fault," Mrs. Knowles said, her one open eye raised to Ellari in a plea for understanding.

That did it. Ellari couldn't hold back her anger. "Not his fault!? A man twice your size beats you and it's not his fault?! Then whose fault was it?"

"I should have been here when he got home from work."

"He hit you because you weren't here when he got home?"

"You've got to understand, Miss Lochridge. My husband's not a bad man. He works hard to take care of our family, but when he found out Willie lost a day's pay today because I kept him out sick, he just got very upset."

"That's no excuse for taking it out on you, Mrs. Knowles.

"It was that piece o' paper you give ma that made him go crazy. When he saw it, he started throwin' things an' slammin' her against the wall. He thought she was comin' to your meetin'." Willie hung his head and added softly, "I thought he was gonna kill her."

Pelted with guilt that Mrs. Knowles was suffering because of something she had done, Ellari ached anew with frustration. She had only wanted to help, and because of her. . . . "Oh, Mrs. Knowles. I'm so sorry. I had no idea."

Mrs. Knowles shook her head and placed her hand on Ellari's arm. "It's wasn't your fault. If it hadn't been for that paper, he would have found another reason."

126

"This isn't the first time?"

"Naw . . . he hits . . . her all . . . the . . . time."

Hearing that Willie's breathing was becoming labored and difficult again, Ellari bit back further comments that came to her mind. She wasn't going to solve anything by getting the child or his mother any more agitated than they already were.

Speaking calmly, she continued to work on the battered face of his mother. "Willie, I want you to go outside in the fresh air and breathe into the handkerchief I gave you again."

Willie looked to his mother for permission. She nodded, and he left, the handkerchief already in place over his mouth and nose.

"Mrs. Knowles, why don't you and Willie stay with me tonight? I'll be able to take better care of you both there."

The woman shook her head. "I'm due at the factory in an hour, and I can't afford to miss my shift—especially since Willie already lost a day's pay today."

"But you're in no condition to work tonight!"

"I'll be all right." Mrs. Knowles stood up, her legs obviously unsteady. "See? I'm better already. Thank you for coming, Miss Lochridge," she said, lifting her chin proudly.

Ellari stared compassionately at the brave woman, knowing by her stubborn stance that arguing with her would be useless. No matter what she could say, Mrs. Knowles wasn't going to take her advice and stay home from work. "At least let me take Willie for the night. The strong odors from the dyes in this room are only making his asthma worse, and a good night's sleep in fresh air could work wonders."

The woman thought for a minute, then relented. "All right. But he has to be at the glass factory at six in the morning—no matter what. He can't miss another day, or my husband will be furious."

"You won't be sorry," Ellari promised, quickly cramming her supplies into her bag before Mrs. Knowles could change her mind. "And if you decide you need a place to spend the night after all, you know where to find me."

"I won't, but thank you for offering."

Ellari and Willie maintained a thoughtful silence as they walked hand-in-hand back to the pharmacy, both of them oblivious to the descending nightfall. The ache of helplessness in her heart was so great she was close to tears, and her thoughts were too full of rage to trust herself to speak any way other than emotionally.

Was there nothing she could do?

She glanced down at Willie as he stumbled. Poor little fellow. He was practically asleep on his feet. She was tempted to offer to carry him—he was so frail and underweight she could have easily done it — but she had no doubt Willie's ten-year-old pride would refuse her help. Instead, she slowed her pace.

As they turned the corner on her street, she spied a man stomping toward her from the middle of the block.

"What're you doin' with my kid?" he snarled.

"Pa!" Willie gasped, instinctively tightening his hold on Ellari's hand and dropping back a step to shield himself behind her.

Her heart pounding with trepidation, Ellari gave Willie's tiny hand an encouraging squeeze and planted her feet squarely on the plank sidewalk. "I'm taking him to my place to try to do something for his asthma," she answered, her tone conveying more confidence than she was feeling.

"Well, we don't need your charity. He lost a day's wages 'cause o' your meddlin', an' he ain't gonna lose another. Git over here, boy. You're goin' home where you belong."

The wheezing sound of his breathing increased in volume as Willie started to move toward his father. Ellari blocked him with her body. "Stay where you are, Willie," she ordered, her challenging expression leveled on the father.

His surprise obvious at the fact that she refused to forfeit the child, Knowles hesitated. "Let 'im go, lady."

"Can't you see he's sick, Mr. Knowles? He needs medical care."

"No old maid busybody who's got nothin' better to do than meddle in other people's business is gonna tell me what my family needs. Now, gimme that kid, or I'll—"

"What, Mr. Knowles? Beat me? Like you did your wife?" She glanced purposefully around at the small gatherings of spectators their confrontation had attracted. "Go on and do it. But I warn you, if you lay one finger on me or try to stop me from treating this boy, you're going to lose a lot more than the pitiful few pennies this child would have earned if he'd been able to go to work today. Do *you* understand what *I'm* saying?"

Knowles cast an uncertain glance at the observers to determine whose side they were on. Seeing the obvious answer in the crowd's threatening expressions, he backed down. "All right, have it your way. But he'd better be able to work his shift in the mornin' or someone's gonna pay. Do you understand what I'm sayin', Miss Lochridge?"

"Perfectly, Mr. Knowles," she answered coldly, her tone not revealing any of the pounding fear that pulsed through her.

With a deliberate move meant to force her to step aside, Knowles brushed past Ellari and the trembling boy. "You an' me ain't finished," he snarled for her ears only as he passed.

130

Ellari stared after the man until he disappeared around the corner. Then, ignoring Willie's protests, she whisked him into her arms and hurried the rest of the way to her shop.

At the front door, she set him on his feet to dig in her bag for her key.

"You have a talent for getting people riled, don't you, Miss Lochridge," a deep, amused voice asked from behind her.

"Oh!" Ellari squealed, snapping her head around in startled response. Discovering Trigg Hanahan coming toward her from across the street, she frowned to disguise the immediate thrill and relief that surged through her at the sight of him. "I didn't expect to see you again."

"I was down the street and saw you having what looked like a pretty heated conversation with that man." He shrugged and grinned. "And having witnessed firsthand the knack you have for getting into trouble, I figured I'd better stick around in case you needed my help."

"Well, as you can see, I didn't. But thank you anyway." She aimed her key at the lock, but her hands were shaking so badly she couldn't hit her target.

"I can see that you don't." He covered her hand with his and guided the key into the keyhole. Before he could twist the key in the lock, the door swung ajar. "Oh? What's this?"

Ellari gave Trigg an indignant sideglance. "I

was in a hurry when I left," she explained weakly. "I must have forgotten to lock it." She shoved the door open the rest of the way.

The sight that greeted their eyes brought a scream to Ellari's lips and a curse to Trigg's.

Suspended from a pole barring the center aisle of the drugstore was a dead rat that had been killed and hung as one would a rabbit or squirrel to bleed it before cooking. One of the flyers she had given out that afternoon was clenched between the rat's teeth, a message crudely written across it in black crayon.

Despite her horror, Ellari remained lucid enough to instinctively clutch Willie to her and bury his face in the folds of her skirt to protect him from seeing the vile scene.

His response equally automatic, Trigg propelled himself in front of woman and child to block their view. "Stay back," he ordered.

For once, Ellari didn't argue.

"What's wrong?" Willie asked, his wheezing voice muffled.

Ellari patted his thin shoulder and caressed his head. "Not anything for you to worry about. Isn't that right, Mr. Hanahan?"

Trigg faced her, his expression hard to read. "Yeah," he answered, ruffling the boy's head. "That's right." He took her arm and directed her out of the doorway. "Just a little mess that needs cleaning up. I'll take care of it. You two stay out

132

here. I'll be back soon." Without waiting for her to agree or disagree, he reentered the pharmacy, closing the door behind him.

"See?" she said, as much to ease her own fears as Willie's. "I told you there was nothing to worry about." She guided the boy to the wooden bench her father had put in front of the store years ago. "We'll just sit here and wait for Mr. Hanahan."

It took Trigg only a few seconds to cut down the rat carcass and dispose of it. The blood stain on the bare wood floor took longer. The entire time he worked, he alternated between chiding himself for becoming involved in Ellari Lochridge's problems in the first place, and asking himself what it was about her that kept drawing him back to her and made it impossible to walk away when she needed him. How many women in his life had he ever scrubbed a floor for? Only one, his mother, and she was dead.

After several minutes of concentrated rubbing and scouring with lye soap and a stiff brush, Trigg stood up and checked his work. Satisfied that all of the evidence of the vicious prankster's handiwork was gone, he wrenched open the door, his anger still not spent, despite the energy with which he had attacked the bloodstain. If he ever got his hands on the bastard who'd pulled such a rotten stunt, he'd kill him. "It's all right to come in now," he snarled, not sure who he was mad at.

Seemingly out of nowhere, Mr. Cat appeared at the door and sauntered past Trigg's legs, an annoyed "meow" the only compromise to his feline nonchalance.

All three human beings stared in disbelief as the cat entered the pharmacy with aristocratic aplomb and headed for the back of the store, his tail fluffed and held high, his walk unhurried.

Trigg and Ellari directed questioning gazes at each other, then broke out laughing simultaneously, the tension of the past moments miraculously lightened by the cat's unexpected materialization.

"Friend of yours?" Trigg asked.

"More like a visitor who came for dinner and forgot to leave," Ellari admitted. Standing, she drew Willie to his feet and walked toward the smiling man. It was amazing how the sight of that smile had the power to dim even the most horrible of the evening's memories—temporarily at least.

The instant she stepped inside the pharmacy though, she stopped, the bloody vision of the dead rat as vivid as ever. "Why would anyone do something so terrible?" she asked, her eyes filling with tears as she gazed at the wet floor.

A strong arm circled her shoulders and guided her over the wet patch of floor. "Don't think about it now. Take care of the boy, and we'll talk about this when you're through. He's practically asleep on his feet."

Ellari glanced down at Willie and smiled. At least, he is breathing more easily now that he was out of the sweatshop. "You're right. I'll take him upstairs and put him to bed and be back down shortly."

"Do you suppose I could borrow some more of your father's old clothes?" He plucked his wet shirt front away from his skin. "Mine are a little damp."

Embarrassed that she hadn't even thanked him for cleaning up the nauseating mess, much less noticed his obvious discomfort, Ellari grew flustered. "Oh, I'm sorry! I should have said something. Of course! You're more than welcome to anything he left. They're in a trunk upstairs. You can go through it and find something that fits while I get Willie settled." She gave Willie a prod toward the back of the pharmacy.

Trigg hesitated. "Wouldn't you rather bring it down to me instead? After this afternoon, aren't you afraid that—" He stopped, remembering Willie. "Well, you know."

Ellari looked back over her shoulder, touched by his sudden uncertainty. "No," she said with a smile, "I'm not afraid. Not of you anyway. Don't forget, Mr. Hanahan, I've seen your true colors more than once. No matter how you try to hide it, you are really a nice man. Now, are you going to come upstairs with us, or are you going to stand there in those wet clothes the rest of the night?"

"How is he?" Trigg asked from behind her.

Ellari cast a quick look back over her shoulder. Her heart leaped at the sight of him, as it had every other first instant she had seen him over the past two days.

He was standing in the doorway, his shoulder propped against the doorjamb, his weight on one bare foot. His knee bent, he had his ankles crossed, using only his toes to support the other foot. The shirt he had found in the trunk was unbuttoned, its tails hanging outside his pants. He looked relaxed and at home—as if being here with her were the most natural thing in the world. As if he belonged here.

Embarrassed by her own thoughts, she returned her attention to the sleeping boy. The bed where he slept had been hers until she had taken over her parents' larger bedroom six months earlier. "He's breathing better."

"Do you do this kind of thing often?"

"What kind of thing is that?" she asked, setting aside the steaming pot of strong-smelling herbs she'd brewed to help Willie breathe.

"Bring home sick and homeless strays like the

136

kid there." He nodded his head toward the cat curled into a ball at the foot of the bed. "And that worthless old cat."

Able to hear and feel the warmth in his voice, Ellari wasn't offended. Besides, the cat was worthless. Smiling, she blew out the hurricane lamp on the bedside table and turned to face Trigg. Shrugging, she spared him a sheepish grin. "I have to admit, I don't usually 'bring' them home. They just seem to appear on my doorstep."

He stepped back into the combination kitchen and sitting area as she came out of the bedroom. She quietly pulled the door closed behind her to give Willie the full benefit of the medicated steam still rising from the pot. "He should sleep through the night now. I gave him something to help."

She proceeded to the kitchen sink to wash her hands.

"I'm glad to hear that." He followed her. "He's lucky he had you to take care of him."

"For tonight," she said dejectedly. "But what about tomorrow when he has to go to work? Or tomorrow night when he has to go back home? And what about the thousands of children I can't reach? Who's going to help them?"

"Ellari—"

She tensed. He had called her by her first name! Oh, how she longed to turn around and throw herself into his arms. But of course, she couldn't. "Yes?"

"We've got to talk about what happened tonight."

"Would you like a cup of tea and some bread and jam?" she asked as if she hadn't heard him, her tone artificially gay. "I didn't have supper."

"Avoiding the subject isn't going to make it go away, Ellari. You've got to talk about it and make some important decisions before it's too late."

"I know it. And I intend to. Just not tonight." She took a match from the metal container she kept beside her stove. "Maybe tomorrow." She struck the match and held the flame to the burner under her teakettle as she adjusted the control on her gas range.

He grabbed her by the upper arms and spun her around. Bending his knees, he brought his face down level with hers.

"Ellari! These people are serious. And they want you to stop interfering in their lives!"

Her eyes brimmed with tears as she searched his features for understanding. "And close my eyes to what's happening to their children? Well, I can't. Whether it makes them angry or not, I have to help the children."

He tightened his grip on her arms and shook her. "Didn't finding that dead rat teach you anything? You've made some really ugly enemies.

And if you don't drop this crusade of yours, you're not going to be able to help anyone, even yourself. And I can assure you they're not going to stop with dead rats!"

Despite her tears, she managed to jut her chin defensively. "You don't even know me. Why is this so important to you?"

Trigg straightened self-consciously. His lips turned down at the corners, he shrugged to show his indifference and scratched his head. "Damned if I know. I must be crazy. Why else would I keep trying to stop you from getting yourself killed—when you're doing such a great job without my help?"

Chapter Eight

Trigg scooped up his wet clothes from the back of a wooden chair. Who needed this kind of aggravation? He certainly didn't. He had five hundred dollars, a wagon, a team of horses and a load of fancy glass jars worth at least a thousand dollars.

"I should have known better than to waste my time trying to help someone who either wants to get herself killed or who's just too crazy or stupid to be afraid. But either way, I'm not stickin' around to find out. The next time you get in trouble, lady, you're on your own, 'cause I'll be long gone!" He stomped angrily toward the stairs.

"Mr. Hanahan . . ."

He stopped, but kept his back to her. "What?!"

When she didn't say anything else, his curiosity got the better of him, and he turned around.

The instant he saw her face, his anger dissolved into shame and self-disgust. She looked like a little girl who'd been kicked—and he felt as if he'd done the kicking.

Her bottom lip was trembling and tears streamed freely down her cheeks. Her normally erect shoulders slumped, and her arms hung limply at her sides as if it would take too much energy to lift them. Her thick strawberry-colored hair wild and disheveled, she looked totally beaten. And he felt like a bastard of the worst sort.

Overwhelmed with the need to take care of her, he dropped his clothes and covered the space separating them in three easy strides. "Hey, don't cry. I didn't mean—"

She raised her watery green eyes to meet his. "I *am* afraid," she admitted softly. "And I don't want to die. But I don't know what else to do. I couldn't live with myself if I deserted the children now."

"Deserting them is exactly what you'll be doing if you get yourself killed and there's no one to take care of them when they're sick and hurt."

"I know in my head that you're probably right, but in my heart I can't stop thinking that if there's a chance I can save even a few children from a life of slavery in the factories or the sweatshops, I have to take it."

"Even if it means your life?"

She studied her folded hands for several seconds, then looked back up at him. "Do you think—? I mean—I know it's a lot to ask, but would you consider—?" She dropped her gaze to her hands again and took a deep breath. After a long pause, she raised her chin, her expression determined. "Could you stay here a few more days?" she asked in a rush of words. She lowered her eyes again. "Just until things settle down. I can't pay you, but—"

"You want me to stay? Here at the pharmacy?"

She shook her head. "I'm sorry. I shouldn't have asked. I don't blame you for saying no. You've already done more than I had any right to expect."

"Whoa!" he said, placing his fingers over her mouth to shush her. "I didn't say I wouldn't do it."

Her head jerked up, her eyes round with disbelief. "You mean you will?"

He shrugged and grinned. "I guess you're not the only one who doesn't always listen to your brain." This was perfect. Surely with a little more time, he could convince her to drop her challenge of the glass factories, so he could fulfill his end of the bargain with Nylander. And even better, now he didn't have to give up on getting the salve formula and making enough money on it to pay off Boss Stahl and Reed Phelps.

Ellari's mouth spread into a wide smile, and new tears filled her eyes. She threw her arms around his neck in an exuberant hug. "Oh, Mr. Hanahan. How can I ever thank you?"

He fought the urge to take advantage of her gratitude and kiss her. He'd seen this afternoon what happened when he rushed her. He'd almost lost his chance at the formula and the fortune it could bring. He didn't intend to make that mistake again. He would take it slowly this time.

He enclosed her in his embrace and patted her as one would a child. "I'm sure we'll think of something. But you can start by calling me Trigg."

She inhaled a shuddering breath. "Thank you— Trigg."

Their gazes locked, hers questioning and glistening with tears, his hungry and gleaming with leashed desire.

For a full minute, time was frozen. Then, as if controlled by a master puppeteer, they came together, their bodies melding in urgent embrace. Mouths responding thirstily, hands grasping desperately, they were lifted onto a new plane of existence, one so exquisite that almost all sense of reality evaporated.

Fortunately, Trigg retained a thread of sanity that reminded him of the vow he'd made moments before. He wasn't going to spoil everything this time. She wasn't the only woman in the world, but there was only one formula. With that formula he could have them all.

"Damn, lady!" he gasped, tearing his mouth from hers. He locked his hands at the small of her back and rested his forehead against hers. "Are you trying to drive me crazy?"

Though their bodies remained pressed together, his hands at her waist, her fingers interlaced behind his neck, Ellari felt an immense sense of loss.

No longer knowing—or caring—what was right

or wrong, she only knew the pain would be unbearable if he stopped kissing her altogether. The
need to be loved by him was stronger than any
hunger she had ever felt. "Don't stop," she begged,
lifting up on her toes.

With a growl of surrender, Trigg resumed his
adoration of her mouth with new fervor. Their lips
sealed, he swept her into his arms and carried her
to the unoccupied bedroom.

Lowering her gently to the four-poster bed that
took up the majority of the space in the small,
unlit room, he settled himself over her and blazed
a trail of kisses down her face to her throat.

Arching her head back, she reveled in the ecstasy that washed through her body. Unaware of
the way her hips rocked gently upward, urging his
to respond, she burrowed her fingers into the dark
hair at his nape.

Covering her mouth and face and throat with
desperate kisses, he instinctively slid his hand
along her ribcage to catch her breast from the
underside.

The instant he palmed the exquisite weight and
fullness, he froze, cursing himself. So much for
using good sense. So much for not being forced to
sneak out of town with the wagon and jars and a
little bit of cash. Success had been within his
grasp, and he'd thrown it away—twice!

He waited, but the expected rejection didn't
come. She wasn't protesting at all. Instead, the
helpless little mewing sounds she made and her

sensual movements beneath him, communicated the fact that she wanted him as much as he wanted her!

With renewed zeal, he massaged one breast, as he lowered his mouth to the other. He drew her aching nipple into his mouth and kissed it through the light cotton blouse and camisole she wore. When he had worshipped and laved both tips to hard, thrusting points, he lifted himself up on one arm and gazed down into her face. "Sweet, sweet Ellari," he sighed.

Circling her chin with a gentle hand, he lowered his head and kissed her parted lips, almost reverently. With his other hand, he nimbly unbuttoned her shirtwaist blouse and opened it.

Before she could protest, he tore the camisole downward and took her exposed breast into his mouth. And she was lost. Writhing under his exquisite motions, she clutched him harder to her breast, urgently lifting her rocking hips to match the throbbing deep in her womb.

Primal instinct ruling her actions, she clawed his shirt from his shoulders, craving the feel of his flesh against hers, all concern with right and wrong dissipated.

Trigg reared back and quickly removed his shirt. Wasting no actions or time, he hurriedly sat her up and whisked the blouse from her arms and tossed it aside. Kissing her mouth to stay objections she might make, he slipped her arms from the camisole and lowered it to her waist.

145

Despite the darkness, Ellari tried to cover herself, but Trigg would not allow it. Gripping her arms behind her with one hand, he cupped a thrusting breast with the other and bent his head to suckle its taut nipple. His gentle tugging and pulling drained all resistance, leaving her with a need so great to ease the ache deep inside her that she could only moan her pleasure.

Sensing her surrender, Trigg released her wrists and lay her back down. With one fluid motion, he hurriedly undid the tapes on her skirt and petticoat. Grasping her waist, he smoothed his hands downward, taking everything, including drawers, stockings and slippers, with him.

Shocked, Ellari whipped the cotton bed cover over her.

Returning his mouth to hers to calm her, he lifted his body off her and quickly shed his own trousers, underwear, boots and socks. Not giving her an opportunity to resist, he ripped the protective cover aside and lowered himself onto her vulnerable body.

At the touch of his naked flesh on hers, she gasped. Ripples of ecstasy shrilled through her in a wild scream of pleasure. Splaying her hands on his back, she opened her mouth to cry out her plea for relief from the hunger consuming her.

Taking her mouth with his, he nudged her thighs apart and cradled himself between them. Smoothing his hands downward, he bent her knees on either side of his flanks.

In uncontrolled response, Ellari lifted her hips upward, and Trigg was unable to remember why carrying his need to fruition was a mistake.

With one greedy thrust, he sheathed himself deep inside her with a wild groan of pleasure.

Unprepared for the startled cry of pain she released, he tensed. His senses zapped with total recall, his feelings of guilt magnified tenfold.

Not only was he a bastard of the lowest sort, but he was a fool as well. But he couldn't stop now. Not when his own body was raging with fire. He covered her face with apologetic kisses.

The stab of pain she had experienced quickly subsided, forcing the moment of regret she'd had to the back of her mind. She was only aware of the healing ministrations of Trigg's mouth on her face. The mouth she couldn't get enough of. The mouth she wanted to feel on her own.

Giving herself over to the compelling drive inside her, she burrowed her fingers into his thick hair and drew his mouth back to hers.

His tongue caressed hers fervently, and she returned his kiss with equal passion. She was totally consumed by the magnificent glory illuninating her entire being.

Slowly, their bodies began to move in the age-old rhythm of desire, each of his downward thrusts met by an upward invitation for him to go deeper.

The intensity of their united movements carried them to magnificent heights, higher and higher, until the fall was eminent.

Ellari cried out her release, digging her fingernails into the tensing muscles of his back.

With the last ounce of decency he could muster, Trigg denied himself the full pleasure of his climax by withdrawing from the haven of her body and spilling his passion into the coverlet she had used to hide herself moments before. It was unforgivable that he'd been such a cad and opportunist and had taken her innocence, but what was done was done. He wouldn't add to his sins by leaving her with a bastard baby in her belly.

With one last shudder, he lifted himself off her and collapsed along her length. "Are you all right?" he asked into the pillow where he burrowed his perspiring brow.

"Yes," she whispered, her voice husky in the aftermath of their passion. "Are you?" She caressed the back of his dark head.

Unable to forgive himself for taking advantage of the sweet, giving woman, he rolled off the bed. "Sure, I'm fine." He disentangled his trousers from her things and stepped into them. "I'd better go down and check the locks. You ought to try to get some sleep. It's been a hard day, and you probably didn't get much last night." He whipped the stained coverlet off the bed. "I'll take this when I go."

Confused and hurt by his behavior, Elllari fought not to cry. She drew the top sheet over her to hide her nakedness and stared after him as he padded on bare feet from the room. For several minutes after he was gone, she didn't move. She couldn't. She was too stunned. What had changed him from the sweet loving man he'd been one minute, into the cold, unfeeling man who had left her the next? What had she done that had made him so angry? Was their lovemaking a disappointment to him? Did she do something wrong? Had she said something?

She searched her mind for the answers to her questions, but the only conclusion she could draw was that she had behaved like a woman of easy virtue—and that he was treating her accordingly. Evidently he thought giving her favors to men was her way of paying for services. And she hadn't given him a reason to think otherwise!

Self-revulsion and disgust propelled her from the mattress. She ripped the top sheet from the bed and hastily wrapped herself in it as she ran into the apartment's tiny bathroom. She slammed the door and locked it, more thankful than ever before for the indoor toilet, tub, and sink her father had installed the last year of his life. Of course, they only used the indoor bathroom at night, conserving water by continuing to use the outdoor facility during the daylight. But right now, conserving water was the last of her concerns. She stabbed the plug into the sink's drainhole and poured water from the pitcher into it.

By the time she finished scrubbing herself almost to the point of self-abuse, she began to feel better.

Somewhat revived and wearing only a light robe, she stepped out of the bathroom ten minutes later, determined to put what had happened out of her mind. At least that had been her intention, until she found Trigg sitting in the living area, his arms crossed, his black glower leveled at her.

She sucked in a shocked gasp and clutched the dressing gown to her throat and at the waist. Fighting the urge to turn around and run back into the bathroom to hide, she squared her shoulders and returned his stare with equal venom. "I didn't expect to see you again," she said coolly.

"Yeah, well, I thought about saving you the trouble of throwing me out—again. But I decided the least I could do—besides apologize—was give you the pleasure of telling me to my face what a low-life piece of scum I am." He leaned forward and balanced his elbows on his thighs. Interlocking his hands between his knees, he concentrated on the floor.

Confused, Ellari gaped at him. "You came back to apologize?"

He looked up at her, his demeanor totally miserable. "I know what I did is unforgivable, but I want you to know I never intended for it to happen."

"*You're* apologizing to *me?*" she repeated again, still unable to fathom what she was hearing.

"I know it's a poor substitute for what you lost. And if there were any way I could relive the last hour and undo it, I would. All I can do now is swear I won't lose control like that again." He hung his head. "That is, if you still want my protection and can see your way to giving me another chance."

"I don't believe this," Ellari chuckled, a wry half-smile on her face.

"I don't blame you. I haven't given you much reason to believe me. It's bad enough when you can't trust strangers, but when you can't trust—" He stood up as if to leave. "I won't bother you again."

Ellari shook her head and actually laughed out loud at the irony. "Wait!"

Trigg's confused stare told her that he thought she had lost her mind. And maybe he was right. What other explanation could there be for her to be standing in a room with a man she barely knew, wearing only a robe with nothing under it— and giggling? Insanity was the only answer, but she couldn't stop laughing.

"But, you said—"

Her own relief made her take mercy on his confusion. "You don't understand. When you rushed out of here, I thought it was because you were angry with me."

His expression didn't change as he took a second to absorb the meaning of her words. Then it split into an amazed, gaping grin. "Why would I be mad at *you?*"

Suddenly embarrassed, Ellari blushed and

looked down at her hands twisted into her dressing gown. She shrugged. "Maybe because you were disappointed in me, or maybe you regretted committing yourself to help a woman of loose virtue, or—"

He reached her in a single step and grasped her arms. "Stop that! You're not a woman of loose virtue! You're the most decent woman I've ever met. Much too good for me. And as for disappointing me, making love to you was wonderful."

She looked up, glassy-eyed. "It was?"

"You really don't know how special you are, do you?"

"Special?"

He nodded, his eyes filled with pain and self-loathing. "And beautiful. And too good to have anything to do with a street hustler who sees what he wants and takes it without a thought for anyone else."

"Aren't you being a bit hard on yourself?"

"How else should I be? The facts speak for themselves. I saw you, I wanted you, and I took you without a single qualm or consideration for what losing your innocence would do to you. If you ask me, I'm not being hard enough, and you have every right to use that pistol of yours on me! I deserve worse."

Maybe it was her relief at knowing she hadn't been to blame for his anger; or maybe it was hearing him say she was special and beautiful; or maybe it was the heat searing through her to have him standing so close; or maybe it was the pure and simple fact that the thought of being alone again was more unbearable than facing the memory of what she had done . . . whatever the reason, Ellari was overwhelmed with a need to comfort him and make him stay.

Acting on instinct, she sandwiched his face between her palms and held his head so he could see her eyes. "I'm as much to blame for what happened as you are. I could have—should have—stopped you."

"Still, it was my fault. I took advantage of your innocence, and there's no excuse for it."

Ellari studied his unhappy features for a long moment, then dropped her hands and stepped away from him. "Obviously, we both realize we made a mistake, but the only thing we can do now is put our mistake behind us and go forward with our lives from here."

"In other words, I get out and stay out this time."

So that was why he was so anxious to take the blame for what had happened. Just as she had suspected, he regretted his promise to help her, but didn't want to admit it. He wanted her to tell him to leave so he could do it with a clear conscience. Well, he wasn't going to get off so easily. If he left her now, it wouldn't be guilt free if she had anything to say about it.

"That's one possibility. But if you're sincerely sorry about what happened, I would think your guilt would triple if you left me here unprotected, and the men Nylander has hired to drive me away end up killing me—after you gave me your word."

Trigg's expression soured visibly. He looked like he was going to be sick. "You mean you don't want me to leave?"

Hurt by his reaction, Ellari bit her lip, hating herself for wanting him to stay. Still, she had to have some protection until she could discover who was actually after her and do something about it. Besides, Trigg Hanahan owed her.

"Don't worry. Our arrangement will be strictly business," she said stiffly. "The minute the danger is gone, I expect you to go as well."

"Strictly business, huh?"

"Strictly."

"I did say I'd help you, didn't I?"

"Does that mean we have an understanding?" she asked, holding out her hand to him.

Trigg looked down at her extended hand, then up into her eyes. His expression filled with pain and regret, he clasped her hand. "Looks like we do."

Having taken care of his personal needs in the outdoor facilities, Trigg reentered the pharmacy through the back door. He had spent a long, sleepless night on the couch in the treatment area examining his problems—problems that seemed to be multiplying by the hour.

And every line of possible solution he had thought of had led to the same conclusion. After what he'd done, he couldn't steal out of town and leave Ellari here at Nylander's mercy—and if he stayed he had to square things with Reed Phelps and Boss Stahl fast, or he wouldn't be much protection to her or anyone else. And there was only one way to do it: one way or another, he had to get his hands on the Lochridge skin formula—the untimely birth of his conscience be damned.

Just as he started to pull back the curtain separating the back room from the rest of the pharmacy, he heard voices and stopped.

"Willie's much better this morning, Mrs. Knowles," he heard Ellari say. "But he really shouldn't go to the factory today. And I'm afraid it will only get worse if you don't do something to permanently remove him and your other children from the unhealthy environment of the factories and sweatshops. Their lungs and young bodies are being destroyed—"

Damn! How was he going to protect her if she kept sticking her nose in where it was none of her business? Didn't last night teach her anything? Well, if fear for her life wasn't enough to make her stop churning up trouble, maybe the hint of scandal would do it.

"Ellari," he called cheerfully, bursting through the curtains, shirtless and grinning. "Is there any—" He paused, properly taken back to find Ellari was not alone. "—coffee?" he finished

155

sheepishly.

Ellari's head swiveled in horror at the sound of his voice. Mrs. Knowles' eyes widened with shock, then narrowed with disapproval as she shot Ellari a questioning glance.

"Perhaps you should concentrate on how you live your own life, Miss Lochridge, rather than telling me and my family how to live ours." She grabbed Willie's arm and whisked him toward the door.

"Please, Mrs. Knowles," Ellari pleaded, rushing to catch the retreating woman. "It's not what it looks like! He works for me!"

Mrs. Knowles paused at the door. "No doubt. Good day, Miss Lochridge. Thank you for taking care of Willie. I'll pay you as soon as I can."

"There's no—" Mrs. Knowles hurried outside, dragging the boy behind her. "—charge," Ellari finished to the closed door.

Anger like she had never known began deep inside her and rolled to a violent eruption. "How dare you do that to me!" she snarled, spinning around to face him. "Do you realize that right this minute she's telling every one of my neighbors she saw a half-naked man coming out of my living quarters?"

"Sorry, I thought you were alone." He grinned apologetically.

She stormed to where he stood in the curtained doorway, a pseudo-innocent smirk on his face.

"Liar!" she blasted, balling her fists and pum-

156

meling him on the chest. She was close to tears. "You embarrassed me deliberately and I want to know why!"

He caught her wrists in his grip and held them between them. "You ought to be thanking me. I just saved you from making a serious mistake. Sorry I embarrassed you, but it was the fastest way I could think of to stop you. After all, I am here to protect you, aren't I?"

"By destroying my reputation?"

"If I hadn't come in when I did, you could've had a lot more than that destroyed if Willie's dad got wind of what you were telling his wife."

"What are you talking about?"

"Somehow, I don't think he'd be too pleased to hear you were still butting into his business and trying to get his kid to stop bringing home a pay envelope every week."

"Hrrr!" Ellari growled in uncontrolled frustration. She struggled to free her hands so she could hit him again.

Trigg tightened his grip on her wrists and grinned. "Is that any way to treat someone who's just doing his job?"

"Your job is to protect me from attacks and vandals, but that doesn't give you the right to interfere in how I live my life."

"Doesn't it occur to you that's what Knowles and Nylander feel about you?"

A flash of uncertainty crossed her features. "It's not the same thing," she said, her anger wavering.

"They're working the children like slaves for a few cents a week."

Trigg looked down at her hands against his chest, then at her mouth only inches away. God, it would be so easy to lean forward and . . . No! Even one kiss would be dangerous.

He dropped his hold on her as if he'd been burned and wheeled toward the back room. "Do you think you can stay out of trouble long enough for me to bathe and shave—and finish dressing?"

An indignant intake of breath, followed by the opening and slamming of cupboards in her work area, brought a grin to his lips. He stopped at the curtains and smiled back at her. "By the way, what's for breakfast? I'm starved."

Chapter Nine

For the next several hours, Ellari worked with a furor, deliberately staying busy so she didn't have to decide what to do about Trigg Hanahan. She knew she couldn't let him stay. This morning had shown her that. But she couldn't bring herself to make him leave either — for reasons other than the protection he offered, if she were honest with herself.

She tried to convince herself that asking him to stay had been a mistake and that if she were going to salvage her reputation she couldn't allow him to spend another night in the pharmacy. But no matter how she tried, she was unable to dismiss the fear she felt at the thought of not having him nearby, ready to come to her rescue at a moment's notice.

Nor could she ignore the warmth that swelled in her heart each time she remembered the delight she'd experienced cooking his meals and sitting down to share them with him. Dining alone for so long, more often than not, she ate her meals directly from the pot, and standing at the stove rather than sitting down. Even though she had still been angry and had refused to respond with more than a few curt words when he had tried to make conversation, their meals together had been some of the most satisfying moments she had experienced in years.

Most of all, she couldn't stop reliving the pleasure she had known in his arms the night before. She tried to put it from her mind by chastising herself, but every time she thought of the touch of his lips on hers, she reexperienced the kiss, right down to the flipflops her stomach had done.

Even more disconcerting, when she tried to chide herself for wantonly allowing him to touch and kiss her in such shockingly intimate ways, she had recalled the exquisite passion in such vivid detail that her breasts had swelled with longing, triggering an ache deep in her groin.

Most painful of all, though, was when she tried to scold and hate herself for giving her virginity to a man who wasn't her husband. Instead of regretting her choice, she throbbed with the need to feel him inside her again.

So went her day: strict Victorian morals at war with a desire so basic she didn't dare put a name to it. She filled prescriptions for customers who could afford doctors. She treated and prescribed for those who could not. She even rearranged and straightened the cabinets where she kept her pharmacy supplies — even though she had done it the week before. Yet, no matter how occupied she kept her hands, every action and thought remained overshadowed by thoughts of Trigg Hanahan.

The only thing she hadn't done was pass out flyers and talk about her meeting to people who had come into the shop. Her mind had simply been too overrun by confusion to take on any but the most automatic concerns.

After a day of mental turmoil, she had made no decision when she closed the drugstore at seven that evening. A part of her she hadn't known existed before last night still wanted him to stay, whatever the cost to her reputation, but the sensible, thinking side of her nature knew she had to tell him to leave — immediately.

Resigned to what she had to do, she resolutely climbed the stairs to her apartment where he had insisted on doing some repairs as long as he was here. As she entered the living quarters, she was aware of a silence she hadn't expected.

"Mr. Hanahan?" she called, her eyes rapidly scanning the kitchen and sitting room. "Trigg?" Odd. She hadn't heard him leave by the rear door. Of course, he might have stepped out when she was helping a customer in the front of the store. "Trigg? Are you here?"

Surely he wouldn't have left without telling her he was going.

"Maybe he took some trash out to the alley!" she said optimistically, starting for downstairs to investigate.

"Meow," Mr. Cat whined, coming from the small

161

bedroom where Willie had slept the night before.

Ellari stopped and squatted down to pet the cat, who purred happily and twisted his body until she was scratching his favorite spot on his back at the base of his tail.

"You're right," she said to the cat. "If he's gone, he saved me the trouble of asking him to leave. And if he's not, there's no need for him to think his whereabouts make any difference to us, is there?"

Giving the cat's furry head and neck a quick scratch, she lifted him and stood up. "Besides, the more I think about it, he'll be back. Even if he's changed his mind about helping me, he'll wait until after supper to tell me. He's like you. Neither of you is going to pass up one more free meal, are you?"

She lowered the cat to the throw rug at her feet and picked up the empty dish from the floor.

Not questioning why the possibility she wouldn't see Trigg again hurt so much, or why she wanted so desperately to believe he would be back, she quickly fed Mr. Cat, washed her hands and started supper—fresh cornbread and warmed over lima beans with bits of ham and onions.

By the time she took the cornbread from the oven though, she had no appetite. She could no longer fool herself. Trigg had left and hadn't even had the decency to say good-bye. Like the scoundrel she should have recognized him to be, he had sneaked out the back door. "It's all for the good. At least I don't have to ask him to leave now," she said to the pot of lima beans.

Mr. Cat meowed, then disappeared into the extra bedroom, where she kept a window open so he could go in and out via the fire escape.

"That's right! You desert me too!"

There was no responding meow, as she had grown used to receiving in the short time since the cat had taken up residence in her shop. Instead, she heard a strange muffled snort, followed by a long, drawn-out sound of escaping air.

Her heart stopped. Those weren't cat noises. Immediately, she thought of Nylander's hirelings. They could have been watching the shop all day waiting for Trigg to leave. Could they have pulled down the fire escape and come in through the window?

"Mr. Cat?" she whispered, damning herself for leaving her pistol downstairs under the counter because she had thought Trigg would be here to protect her. She picked up a frying pan and crept to the door. "Mr. Cat?"

There was no answer, only that whispering sound she now had no doubt was someone lurking in the bedroom, ready to attack her. Holding the frying pan over her head with both hands, she warned, "Whoever you are, I know you're there. You'd better leave. I'm warning you, I have a gun." The breathing came to an abrupt halt.

Poised for attack, she waited. After a long pause, the telltale creak of bed ropes brought a sigh of relief to her lips. Crawling over the bed was the only way to get to the window. Whoever had come

163

here to attack her was leaving.

She gave the intruder enough time to be gone, then cautiously opened the door the rest of the way and peeked inside.

The light from the living area spilled into the tiny room, confirming the fact that it was empty—and that someone had been there, if the rumpled bed was any clue. Vowing never again to be caught without her pistol within easy reach, she rushed to the bed and crawled over it to lower the window and lock it. From now on, the cat would just have to use the door like everyone else.

Sitting on the edge of the bed, she leaned forward and held her head in her hands. What was she going to do? So far, they had only done things to frighten her into stopping her campaign against using child labor in the glass factories. But who knew how much longer before they resorted to more violent ways to convince, her? She couldn't go on waiting for someone to kill her. She had to get some dependable protection. In the meantime. . . .

Suddenly, a strange feeling that she was not alone washed over her. Her head jerked up.

Out of the shadows from behind the door, the silhouette of a man materialized.

"Stop! Or I'll shoot!" she screamed, aiming the pan handle toward the approaching intruder, and praying that in the dark it looked like a gun barrel.

"With a frying pan?" he asked, an ugly chuckle in his voice as he continued his predatory advance.

"Who are you? What are you doing here?"

"What do you think I'm doing here?"

She glanced over her shoulder at the locked window, wishing now she hadn't closed it. If anyone was in the alley, they would have heard her screams through an open window. But through the glass. . . .

She tightened her grip on the pan handle. It wasn't much but it was all she had. "If you're here to rob me, you've made a bad choice. I have nothing of value for you to steal."

The man laughed. "I didn't come to rob you. You and me are gonna have us a little talk."

"A talk? About what?"

"About you stickin' your nose in other folks' business. Though seein' you on that bed puts me of a mind to do more than talk. Maybe flat on your back, you'll remember your place and stop causin' trouble for everyone."

Ellari held up the frying pan to ward him off as one would use a cross to fend off a vampire. "You stay away from me! The man I hired to protect me will be back any minute and he'll kill you if he finds you here."

Standing directly in front of her, the man threw back his head and laughed. "What makes you think he's comin' back?"

Alarm raced through her. "What are you talking about? Where is he? What have you done with him?"

The man grinned secretively. "Last time I saw your boy friend, he was headin' off with a coupla friends of mine. 'Course, it took a lotta convincin' to get him to go, but my friends and me got our point across."

A wave of shame washed over her for all the terrible thoughts she'd had about Trigg. She should have known he wouldn't leave without telling her—unless his departure were out of his control.

Anger and worry firing her, Ellari lunged at the man with a wild growl. Putting all her strength into her actions, she brought the iron skillet up between his legs. However, she missed her mark and only grazed one thigh.

"Damn you, bitch!" he bellowed, wrenching the pan from her grip. Pitching it to the floor, he fell on her, knocking the air from her lungs. "I'll teach you."

Grunting, he fumbled to pull up her skirts. However, before he could complete the task, his attack was brought to a halt by a screeching yowl that sounded to Ellari as if the gates of Hell had been opened.

The man's shriek of horror joined the hellish scream, and he bolted off the bed, clawing at his own back as he did.

"Get it off me!" he wailed, spinning in a frantic circle and slapping at himself.

As the light from the living area illuminated the gyrating man's back, Ellari saw her savior.

Claws of all four feet firmly embedded in the flesh beneath the thin cotton shirt the attacker wore, Mr. Cat was flattened to the man's back, his own ungodly howl every bit as loud as the intruder's.

Her own strength revived by the cat's gallant efforts on her behalf, Ellari scrambled off the bed and retrieved her frying pan. Holding the skillet above her head, she waited until the wildly twirling man spun around to face her. With an aim as deadly as if the Lord himself were wielding the pan against the devil, she brought it down onto the man's head.

His eyes bulged in shock, then rolled back in his head as he dissolved into a shapeless lump on the floor. The instant he went down, Mr. Cat leaped off him and began to preen his ruffled fur with characteristic nonchalance.

"Thank God you were there," she told the cat, who meowed in response, then continued to lick his paw. "I've got to get help!"

Her insides still trembling with fright, she ran downstairs and out the front door of the drugstore. "Help me!" she screamed to two men across the street. "Someone help me."

The two men gave each other questioning looks, then crossed the wooden street to investigate. "What's the matter?" one asked.

"Hurry," Ellari ordered, turning back into the shop, obviously expecting them to follow her. "He's still upstairs. I hit him, but I don't know how long he'll stay unconscious."

By the time they were at the back of the store, Ellari had given the two samaritans a good idea of what had happened. "Why don't you stay down here, Miss Lochridge? He could be armed. We'll take care of this."

Glad to accept their offer, Ellari nodded breathlessly and collapsed onto her work stool, suddenly exhausted. "He's in the bedroom to the right of the living room."

"Don't worry, we'll find him." The two pulled pistols from under their coats and started up the stairs.

Minutes later they were back, their weapons reholstered. "He's gone," one reported.

"Guess he came to and left by the fire escape," the other explained. "The window was wide open. I shut and locked it."

"Sure looks like you must have given him one helluva a fight though. There's blood all over your floor. What'd you use on him? A meat cleaver?" The two laughed heartily.

Ellari didn't answer, knowing no one would ever believe her weapons had been a cat and a frying pan. "Are you sure he's not still hiding somewhere in the apartment?"

The men grew serious and shook their heads. "Yes, ma'am. We went over the whole place to be sure, and he's long gone. But if I was you, I'd . . ."

"What?" Ellari asked defensively. "Close my drugstore? Leave town?"

The man looked at her as if she'd lost her mind. "Well, that'd probably be the smartest thing, but what I was goin' to say is, if I was you, I'd keep the doors and windows locked real good. I'll wager you made that bloke mighty mad, and would bet next week's pay he'll be back."

"Say, didn't I hear you had a feller livin' here now? Where was he when this happened?"

Suddenly, an alarm went off in Ellari's slowly clearing head. She had never seen either of the two men in her life, yet one of them had called her by name, and the other had heard about Trigg. Who were they? They certainly weren't dressed like the men from this neighborhood.

Casually, she shifted her hand from her lap to the place beneath her work counter where she kept her pistol. They were probably all right, but the way things had been going lately, she couldn't be too careful. And she wasn't going to tell them Trigg may not be coming back! For all she knew, they were the "friends" who had "convinced" Trigg to leave with them. And Nylander's men!

Secretly pocketing the pistol, she stood up and started around the counter. "He should be back any minute. Now, if you gentlemen will excuse me . . ." She indicated they should leave. "I'll be all right. Thank you for your help."

"Glad to do it," they said in unison and tipped their hats. "Just wish we could have caught him. You sure you don't want us to stick around until your friend comes back?"

"No! Thank you. I'm fine."

As soon as they were out the door, Ellari locked it and tugged a shelf in front of it. She quickly

169

checked the bullets in her gun, then went back upstairs. She wasn't ready to take the men's word that the intruder was truly gone. She wouldn't relax until she had seen for herself. But when she reached the apartment, it was as the man had said. Whoever had attacked her was gone.

So was Mr. Cat. Evidently, he had left by the window as well. *He'll be back,* she told herself, wishing she were so sure about Trigg. If the things that man had implied were true, he could be lying hurt somewhere—maybe even dead.

Worried to the point of panic, she paced the floor, not sure what to do. She didn't dare go out looking for him before daylight. It could be dangerous. For that matter, where would she begin to look? On the other hand, if she waited until morning to do something, it might be too late.

She glanced at the clock on the mantel. Nine o'clock. If she hurried, maybe she could at least get to the police station house two blocks away to report what had happened and be back before it was too late.

After checking to be sure the window in the back bedroom was locked, she turned out the lamps and hurried downstairs. If she stayed on the sidewalk and gave a wide berth to alley entrances, she ought to be all right. There should still be people outside to come to her rescue if she needed assistance. But just in case, she would keep her hand on the gun in her pocket.

As she walked past the back door, she gave it a

quick glance to be sure it was locked. Her heart leaped with panic. The door she knew positively had been closed all the way, was ajar—and was opening.

Her heart pounding so hard she could barely hear her own thoughts, she stealthily drew the gun from her pocket and stepped back into the shadows. Holding it with both hands, she took aim on the opening door and waited.

A low moan broke the silence. Ellari shrank deeper into the shadows and tightened her grip on the trigger. There was another low moan, followed by several thuds and a grunt. Then nothing.

When no one appeared in the door, she rushed forward and threw herself against it, hoping to slam and lock it.

An agonizing cry split the air at the same time Ellari realized something was blocking the door from closing. She looked down and saw a broomstick wedged in the opening.

"Go away!" she screamed, putting all her strength into keeping the door from opening further. "Leave me alone!"

"Ella—ri," a man's voice called, obviously straining. "Le—me—in."

"Trigg?"

"Yes, damn—it!" he grunted.

Ellari flung open the door.

"Oh, Trigg!" She ran down the stairs to where he lay in the alley, with the other end of the stick under him. "Thank God! I was afraid they had killed you." She dropped to his side. "What happened?"

"Just h—elp me inside," he groaned irritably, trying to stand up, but failing.

Working her arm under his, she managed to help him stand up. Once inside, she locked the door and started to take him to the treatment corner. However, he insisted on going upstairs. So, together they made the laborious climb up to her apartment.

Once she got him safely settled in her bed—because the spare room was still a mess—she hurried to the kitchen for the cup of water he requested when she started to undress him to check for wounds.

Holding his head and shoulders, she gave him sips until he quenched his thirst. "Do you feel better now?" she asked, lowering his head to the pillow.

He nodded, opening and closing his eyes drowsily. "Mmm, better," he sighed.

"I'll be right back," she said, standing up.

With a strength she hadn't expected, he grabbed her wrist and pulled her back down beside him. "Don't go."

"I'll be right back. I have to go downstairs to get some things to clean you up and tend your wounds."

"Not hurt."

"Not hurt? Look at yourself. You can't even stand."

"Drugged," he moaned.

"You were drugged? By whom?"

He shook his head weakly. "Jumped me from behind when I took trash out 'bout six-thirty. Held rag over my face and I went down. Must be chloroform. Next thing—woke up tied up and gagged in that old barn out back."

"They must be the 'friends' the man who broke in here was talking about."

Trigg struggled to sit up, his features alarmed. "What? Somebody broke in here? Are you all right?"

Warmed by his concern, Ellari coaxed him to lie back down. "I'm fine. He didn't hurt me." She didn't want to upset him further by telling him the entire story. "I'll tell you about it when you feel better."

He nodded. "I'm still kinda groggy." He dropped back on the pillow, his eyes closed. "All that matters is you're okay," he mumbled, his speech almost incoherent as he drifted back to sleep. "Talk when wake up."

For the next two hours, Ellari watched over the sleeping man, never leaving his side for more than a few minutes—once to light the lamps in the other room so she could see for herself that he wasn't wounded and to clean him up, another to quickly bathe herself and change her clothes.

Satisfied that the only injuries on his body were rope burns on his wrists for which she had done everything she could, she sighed and sat down in the straightback wooden chair beside the bed. All

173

she could do now was wait for him to sleep off the effects of the drug.

Suddenly, she was exhausted. The past three days had taken their toll. How many nights had it been since she'd had a decent night's sleep? Only two? Lord, it seemed like many more.

Fighting to think about anything other than how tired she was, she studied the sleeping man. Her happiness at knowing he hadn't left her was in direct conflict with the guilt that assailed her for what had happened to him. This was her fault. If he hadn't stayed to protect her, he wouldn't have been hurt at all. She swore in her mind that she would find a way to make it up to him. And no matter what it did to her reputation, she wouldn't ask him to leave—ever.

Her head fell forward, then jerked up several times in quick succession as she fought to stay awake. When she almost fell out of the chair with the last nod, she shook her head and stood up. She had to get some sleep.

She could go into the other bedroom and sleep there. She would be able to hear him if he woke and needed her. The instant that idea occurred to her, a chill of dread shook through her. Even with the window locked and the shade drawn, she hadn't cleaned the room after the attack and she didn't feel easy about sleeping in there. Besides, with the window shut, it would be too hot to get any rest.

She longingly eyed the bed where Trigg slept. What she wanted was to sleep in her own bed, in her own room, in front of her own window that not only let in a cool night breeze from the lake, but had no fire escape for an unwanted intruder to use. If only. . . .

A scandalous idea began to form in her desperate, sleepy mind. What would it hurt if she lay down on the side of the bed he wasn't using? He was sleeping so soundly, he wouldn't even know she was there. And if he did wake up and need her, she would be right there.

Taking the pistol from her pocket, she placed it on the bedside chest and gingerly lowered herself to the mattress. Taking care not to touch or disturb Trigg, she fell asleep instantly.

Trigg awoke with a start. He looked around the semi-darkness that surrounded him, trying to determine what had awakened him.

A decidedly feminine sigh answered his question as the bed moved, and a shifting body snuggled up to his side.

Smiling, he lifted his arm and settled Ellari's head on his shoulder.

Unable to resist the intoxicating fragrance of her hair, he bent his head and buried his nose in its thickness. He drew in a long hungry breath. God, he loved that smell. Nothing artificial about her scent. Just soap. But for some reason, on her it was more powerful than the most exotic perfume. Maybe it was because most of the women he knew

175

used perfume in place of regular bathing, which was obviously not the case with Ellari Lochridge. He sucked in another deep draft through his nostrils. Ahh, this had to be what Heaven smelled like.

Damn! What the hell have I gotten myself into? If I don't get out of here soon. . . .

Ellari squirmed restlessly, uttering distressed little whimpers.

For all his attempts to deny his feelings, he tightened his arm around her and kissed her forehead. "Shh, shh," he soothed. "Everything's all right now."

"Trigg," she murmured, obviously still asleep. "Trigg, where are you?" Her movements became more agitated as she rolled her head from side to side on his shoulder.

He patted her arm reassuringly. "I'm right here, Ellari. Go back to sleep."

She didn't hear him. "Oh, don't be dead," she pleaded. "You can't be dead."

"Ellari! Wake up! You're having a bad dream. I'm not dead. I'm here. With you. Trigg's here, honey. He's right here with you, and he's not going to leave you."

Ellari's tossing calmed, and after a moment, she lifted her head and stared at him in sleepy confusion. "Trigg?"

"Were you expecting someone else?" he asked, smiling into her befuddled face.

"Oh, Trigg!" she wailed, throwing her arm around his neck and covering his cheek and neck

176

with thankful kisses. "I thought you were gone. He told me you were—"

"Hey, hey. I'm fine. It was just a dream."

"Just a dream," she repeated, laying her head back down on his shoulder and nuzzling her face into the curve of his neck. "Just a dr—"

She jerked out of his embrace and stared down at him, this time her expression wide awake and horrified. She opened her mouth to speak, but only managed a sputtering gasp.

"Good morning," he said, reaching up to wipe a tendril of hair from her cheek with the backs of his fingers.

Slowly, he moved his fingers around to the back of her neck and brought her face down to his.

"No," she said, her lips only inches from his. "We can't. It's wrong."

"It's what we both want and need, Ellari. You know it. I know it. For whatever reason we came into each other's lives, we belong together. We need and want each other. I can't deny it any longer. Can you?"

Her eyes bright with questions, she shook her head slowly. As if hypnotized, she lowered her mouth to his. . . .

Chapter Ten

Ellari melted into the kiss, surrendering her entire essence to its power. Yes, this was right; yes, this was where she belonged; yes, this was what she wanted. Putting all the love for which she had waited for years to share with someone into her kiss, she clung to him. She felt safe and loved.

A grateful tremor of well-being quivered through her. Reverently, she lifted her head and cupped his face in her hand. Thrilling to the rasp of his un-shaved cheek against her palm, she gazed down into his eyes. Were there words to describe what she was feeling right then? The only one that came to mind was love—though even that all-inclusive emotion seemed inadequate.

She trailed her thumb over his mouth, still moist from their kiss. The raw loneliness she saw in his eyes surprised her. It cried out a need as strong as her own to be loved and nurtured which she had never suspected was there. Desire to fulfill his long-ings erased the last of her misgivings.

She hesitated only slightly before she bent her head to kiss his eyes closed. Gathering courage with each kiss, she ghosted her lips over his face and neck, pausing a scant quarter inch above his partially open mouth. "I was afraid I would never see you again," she admitted.

He shuddered and dug his fingers into her hair, bringing her mouth the rest of the way to his as he rolled her over and covered her with his own body. "God help us both," he groaned, "I want you."

With no sense of time or place, Ellari smiled and wrapped her arms around his rapidly rising and falling torso. She had no desire to stop him, no desire to stop what she knew was going to happen— what she wanted to happen with every fiber of her existence.

At last, the waiting was at an end. His mouth came down on hers, crushing her lips against her teeth as his tongue filled her mouth with an erotic suggestion of what was to come.

Her boldness fired by hunger, she used her own tongue to coax his deeper into her mouth. Of their own accord, her hips began to rock suggestively, almost as if they moved to a heavenly rhythm only she could hear.

In response to her instinctive plea, Trigg pressed his hand to her belly. The ache inside her was already reaching unbearable proportions. She lifted her hips higher against his hand, seeking relief from the desire consuming her.

Trigg's practiced hand slid up under her gown

and cupped her intimately. Moving quickly, he removed her drawers and took the bud of her desire between his fingers, tugging and twisting until she was writhing helplessly against his hand.

As if she had been propelled into the sky, Ellari became one with all creation. *If only this could last forever* was her only thought.

The next moment, she was pitched over the stars, then sent hurling back through space, shaking and twitching with violent contractions.

Crying out her exquisite agony, she clutched Trigg to her. She never wanted to let him go. She wanted to stay like this forever.

When her explosive tremors subsided, Trigg removed his hand and quickly stripped off his trousers. Rolling onto her, he filled her in one determined motion as his tongue filled her mouth.

This time, there was no pain as he slid into her. She only knew pleasure, fulfillment and desire. She bent her knees so that she could lift her hips up to match Trigg's urgent thrusts, wanting to bring him deeper into her.

Raining kisses over her face and neck, he pressed her knees up to her shoulders so that her thighs lay against her breasts. He drove into the tight hollow of her body over and over until the tension of her own desire again carried her to the point of explosion. Though she fought to hang on to the glorious peak a moment longer, there was nothing she could do to stop the volcanic eruption that shook her entire body.

Together, they cried out their release as they careened wildly back to reality from the zenith to which their lovemaking had carried them.

With a final shudder, he gently lowered her legs and looked down into her face. "Are you all right?"

Ellari's dreamy feeling turned to panic. He had asked her the same question the first time. Was he going to run away again? "I'm fine," she answered tentatively, studying his face. "And you?"

His face broke into a relieved grin. "As a matter of fact, I'm better than fine. For the first time in a long, long time, I feel like things are going to go my way—and all because of you. You're the best thing that's ever happened to me." He kissed her several times in quick succession and started to roll away from her.

Her heart soared. She was the best thing that had ever happened to him! Was this really happening to her? To plain and dull Ellari Lochridge?

Hugging him tightly, she wrapped her calves over the backs of his thighs to keep him united with her a while longer. "You're the best thing that's ever happened to me, too," she admitted, still afraid to trust her joy. *Please, let this be real,* she begged silently, tears of happiness forming in her eyes. "When that man told me his friends had taken you off, I was afraid I would never see you again."

Trigg's manner grew serious. "You and I are a team now." With a quick kiss, he rolled off her, despite her protests. "And it's going to take more than a couple of hired goons to get rid of me," he said, drawing her into his embrace and settling her head on his shoulder. "Those thugs are one of the things we need to talk about and make some decisions on tomorrow. But right now, what do you say we get a little more sleep before you have to open the shop? It's been a rough couple of days for both of us."

"Mmm," Ellari agreed, smiling contentedly as she possessively draped her arm over his chest. Rough, yes, but definitely worth every minute!

Her eyes still closed, Ellari stretched lazily and grinned. Had she ever slept so well in her entire life? She didn't think so. She felt so good, she was tempted to pinch herself. She felt lighter than air, and the man she loved was in love with her.

Well, that might be assuming more than she had a right to assume, she regretfully forced herself to admit. After all, he hadn't actually said he loved her. For that matter, the word love hadn't come up. But he had said they were a "team" now and that she was the "best thing" that had ever happened to him. He had even implied he was going to stay. So, even if he didn't love her, whatever had made him say those things was close enough to love to make her happier than she had ever been in her life. At last, she belonged to someone.

It had been too hot to sleep in each other's arms, and some time in the night they had drifted to their own sides of the bed, but she was suddenly overwhelmed with a need to touch him.

Her heart soaring at the thought of Trigg's face being the first thing she would see this morning, she turned on her side to face him. Smiling, she stretched her arm across the mattress and opened her eyes.

At the same instant her hand contacted only rumpled sheets, her eyes focused on the impression Trigg's head had left in the pillow. She was alone in the bed.

Alarm, disappointment and hurt raged through her, destroying her happiness. She bolted upright in bed, her eyes roaming over the room in a frantic effort to prove herself wrong. Had she been a fool to believe he had meant the things he had said?

"Trigg?" she called, not really expecting an answer, but unable to give up hope.

"Good morning, sleepyhead," he answered, coming around the door, that bone-melting grin on his face.

Her heart swelled with disbelief. He was here! Just like he had told her he would be. Feeling silly for the panic she had felt at not finding him in the bed, she did her best to cover for herself. "You're up!"

Barefoot and barechested, he wore only a pair of her father's old trousers. His hair was wet, as if it had just been washed, and he was wiping his freshly shaved face with a towel. "For an hour. I thought maybe you were going to sleep all day."

"What time is it?" she asked, suddenly aware that

the bright glare in the room was real sunshine, not the glow in her heart that came with his presence.

"About ten o'clock."

"Ten o'clock?!" she shrieked, crashing out of her euphoric mood. "Why didn't you wake me up?" She leaped out of the bed and raced toward the door. "I've got to open the pharmacy! My customers will be frantic."

"Relax." He caught her by the arms. "Don't worry about the store. It's all taken care of."

"Taken care of? What are you talking about?"

"I closed the pharmacy for the day."

"You what?"

"You were sleeping so soundly, I didn't have the heart to wake you up, so I closed for the day."

"How could you do that?"

He shrugged and grinned. "It was easy. I just put a sign in the window that said, 'Closed for the day.' "

"Well, you'll have to take it out of the window. I can't close the pharmacy on a whim. People depend on me to be here."

"They can survive without you for one day. Besides, you do too much for other people. They take advantage of you. But that was before you had me to look out for you. And I say, for today why don't we forget everything and everyone else and concentrate on each other?"

Unable to be angry when he gave her that little boy smile and appealing offer, Ellari weakened. The idea of "playing hooky" for a day with Trigg was

184

awfully tempting, but—"I can't. What if there's an emergency?"

"They'll work it out. It might surprise you to know that people all over the world manage to take care of emergencies every day without your help. When there's no one there to do for them, people can do a lot more for themselves than you might think." He paused and lifted her chin. "What do you say? Shall we give them a chance to find out what they can do on their own?"

"I don't know. What if—"

"Come on," he coaxed. "How long since you took a day off?" He grinned mischievously and kissed her forehead. "Besides, I want you all to myself. I don't want to share you with anyone today."

That did it. She didn't want anyone or anything to burst this warm bubble of sunshine either. "I suppose it wouldn't hurt to close for one day," she conceded with a surrendering grin.

"Good," he exclaimed, prodding her toward the bathroom. "Go get dressed. I'll fix breakfast. Then we'll be on our way."

She stopped. "On our way? Where are we going?"

"It's a surprise," he called over his shoulder. "Trust me, you'll love it."

"If I don't know where we're going, how will I know what to wear?"

"Wear something bright!" he answered. "And fix your hair like you were wearing it the afternoon I repaired the door window—maybe put a colored

185

ribbon in it."

"I didn't think you noticed my hair that day."

He chuckled. "Believe me, I noticed. Now, stop dawdling. The day's already half gone." He started checking through her cupboards for breakfast fixings.

"Trigg?"

"Yes?"

"I don't have a colored ribbon or bright dress. I've never had any reason to wear anything like that. Papa always frowned on what he called frivolous clothing."

"It was just a thought," he said. "You'll be pretty in whatever you wear."

Forty-five minutes later, Ellari studied herself in the oval mirror on the door of her armoire, amazed at what she saw. She looked like a different person. Younger, happier and even prettier than she had ever imagined she could be.

Though her dress wasn't bright by any means, compared to the somber grays and browns she usually wore, it seemed more festive than the brightest red. Purchased in a "frivolous" moment to wear to a tea at the dean's home when she was in school, it was a light tan cotton with a white lace collar and white pearl buttons down the front of the bodice. She hadn't worn it since then and almost hadn't remembered she had it.

Though she hadn't discovered a forgotten hair

ribbon among her belongings, there had been a pair of pearl combs her mother had received as a wedding present. In her freshly washed and towel-dried hair, they were perfect. At least, she thought so. Trigg might not agree.

Taking a deep breath, she opened the door to the living area and stepped out of the bedroom. "Is this all right?"

A high pitched whistle sliced through the air. "Wow!"

Ellari felt her face grow hot. She had heard men whistle at women on the street, but no one had ever had that reaction to her. "My hair's not dry, but you said to hurry."

"Your hair's perfect."

"Are the combs too extravagant? They were my mother's."

"The combs are perfect," he said, crossing to her. "You're perfect." He wrapped his arms around her waist and drew her to him. "In fact, you look so good, I'm not sure I want to take you out now. Every man on the street will try to steal you."

The color in her face deepened. "Don't be silly. No one will even notice me."

"Believe me, they'll notice." He slanted his mouth over hers and told her without words what he thought.

Ellari wrapped her arms around his back and returned his kiss. If he thought she was perfect, it didn't matter that she knew in her heart she wasn't. His reaction almost made her believe she was.

"I hope you're hungry," he said, rearing his head back to smile down into her eyes. "I used the eggs I found in the cupboard to make something a French landlady I once had taught me to make. It's called an omelette. I think you'll like it."

"I'm sure I will." She giggled at his excitement and wouldn't have dreamed of spoiling it by telling him she'd been cooking omelettes for years. "I can hardly wait to try it."

"Right this way, my dear." He guided her to the kitchen table and held her chair.

When she had eaten all she could, Ellari held her hands up to stop him from putting more on her plate. "No, it was delicious, but I can't eat another bite. You eat it."

Trigg glanced down at the mass of eggs and the thick slices of buttered bread remaining on the platter he held. "I can't eat any more either. Guess I should've paid more attention when that landlady told me how to gauge the amount to fix. What're we going to do with what's left? I don't think it'll be all that good warmed over."

Ellari laughed at his dilemma. "Well, I definitely owe Mr. Cat a special treat after last night," she said, having told Trigg during breakfast the details of her attack and the cat's part in her rescue. "We'll give some to him and put the rest in the ice box. Mixed with chopped pickles, a little olive oil and egg yolk—that is, if you left me any eggs—it ought to be good on sandwiches for supper."

His expression conveying his doubts, Trigg said,

188

"Are you sure?"

"Trust me," she teased. "You'll love it! Now, go finish dressing, before I die of curiosity about where we're going today."

"What about the dishes?"

"You cooked. The least I can do is clean up." She picked up their empty plates and carried them to the sink.

"You'll ruin your dress."

She whisked an apron from a nail on the wall and shook her head. "No, I won't. I'm going to put everything in the dishpan to soak. I'll wash them when we get back. Now, hurry up and get changed."

"I won't be a minute," he promised, hurrying toward the bathroom.

"Trigg?" she called, stopping him at the door.

"What?"

"Thank you."

"For what?"

"For breakfast—for everything." She choked back the wave of emotion she felt. "No one has ever made me feel as special as you have."

A flash of sadness skittered across his face, or at least that was what she thought she had seen. It had come and gone so fast that his playful grin was back in place before she could be sure. He tipped an imaginary hat to her. "The pleasure was all mine, m'lady."

* * *

Ellari trailed her hand in the water of Lincoln Park's lagoon, as Trigg rowed their rented boat along the shady perimeter of the little lake. Located in the northeastern sector of the city on the shore of Lake Michigan, the park was Chicago's newest and largest park, and Ellari had never been here before.

Enjoying the relaxing companionship, she reflected on what had been a perfect afternoon. They had begun their outing by sneaking out the back door of her pharmacy like two mischievous children, rather than take a chance on getting stopped by some persistent customer. Two blocks from the drug store, Trigg had hailed a cab and had given the cabbie orders to take them to Lake Street, the city's main shopping avenue where a person could purchase most anything, from rare books to clothing to fine cigars.

For more than an hour, they had wandered in and out of the dozens of stores and shops that lined the street. It was said property values on this street were as much as two thousand dollars a foot along the front. Consequently, most of the businesses were unusually narrow, but were extremely deep; and all of them were crammed full of merchandise so the owners could gain the most benefit from the expensive space.

Trigg had insisted on buying her a pretty pink flowered shawl in one shop, a handful of bright colored hair ribbons in another. When she had protested that he couldn't afford such extravagances like cabs and buying her gifts, he had shrugged, saying a friend who had owed him money had paid him back, so she shouldn't worry about it.

When they tired of fighting the crowds, Trigg led her into a small little shop that Ellari decided was a combination of a market and a restaurant. Behind the counter, there were smoked meats, cheeses, jars of pickles and a dozen or so foods with unfamiliar sounding names, as well as different sized loaves of bread. On the customer's side of the shop, wooden tables and chairs were packed close together, all occupied by hungry customers eating enormous sandwiches.

Minutes later, they were back on the street, a sack filled with sandwiches and a jug of lemonade in their possession. "Aren't we going to eat here?" Ellari giggled, taking his arm again.

"I have a place you'll like much better in mind." He held up a hand to a passing buggy. "Cab!" he shouted.

From the teeming Lake Street business section, the cab had whisked them to Lincoln Park where they had eaten their picnic lunch and drunk lemonade on a grassy knoll below an old shade tree on the lagoon's edge.

When she had admitted to Trigg that she had never been on a picnic before, he had promised her that this would be the first of many, and she had thrilled to the promise. Could this be happening? She thought that she was dreaming.

As a couple in a boat drifted past their picnic

spot, he had asked her if she had ever taken a boat ride. She'd been embarrassed to admit that boating was another experience she had never had. In her own defense, she had explained that her Scottish father had come to the United States without a penny in his pockets, and he'd had to scrimp and save for everything he'd gotten. There had never been any time or money for things like picnics and boating — when she was a child or when she grew up. However, with hard work and conservative living, his thriftiness had paid off and he'd built his own business and sent her to college.

"I'll be right back," he had announced, bounding up from the ground and taking off at a sprint.

Puzzled, she stared after him. Her curiosity getting the better of her, she quickly gathered up their picnic supplies and packages, thinking she would follow him.

Before she could locate where he had disappeared to, she heard her name called from the direction of the lagoon. She turned in time to see a rowboat float into view.

"Come on," Trigg called from behind the oars. "It's time you found out there's more to life than hard work and no play."

Ellari laughed aloud. "You're crazy! I'm not getting into that thing. What if it sinks?"

That had been an hour ago. She had been hesitant to step into the rocky boat, but Trigg had refused to take no for an answer. And she was so glad he had. Floating in the little craft, the cool water at her fingertips, the warm sunshine on her face as they passed in and out of the shadows of the overhanging trees that lined the bank, she felt as if she were in a romantic fairy tale.

Her eyes opened and closed drowsily. This must be what Heaven was like. If she lived to be a hundred, she didn't think she'd ever have a better day than this one had been.

"Come on, lazy bones! Time to go," Trigg announced.

Ellari's eyes snapped open, and she glanced around to get her bearings. "Did I fall asleep?"

He grinned. "Doesn't say much for my company, does it?" he chuckled, offering her his hand to help her out of the rowboat.

"Oh, no!" she exclaimed, scrambling out of the boat with his assistance. "Your company is wonderful! It was floating in the water. It was so soothing, it just rocked me—"

"Hey," he laughed, cutting her off. He lifted her chin and smiled warmly down into her distressed eyes. "I was teasing you! The whole idea for today was to get you to relax for a few hours and forget all the problems you've been having the past few days. The fact that you felt so at ease tells me I must have succeeded."

Ellari's eyes watered emotionally. Unmindful that they were standing in a public place with people all around, she reached up to caress his cheek. "This has been the best day of my entire life, Trigg — breakfast, Lake Street, the cabs, the picnic, the boat ride, the shawl, the hair ribbons. All of it."

"It has been nice, hasn't it? I've been under a lot of tension lately also, and it did me good to get away for a day, too."

"I don't know what I did to deserve having you come into my life, but I'm so glad you did," she said sentimentally. "No one has ever been so good to me. You're the dearest man I've ever known."

Guilt twisted cruelly in Trigg's gut. Great! As if he didn't already feel like a total son-of-a-bitch. Now, she had to go and say something like that.

Forcing himself to assume a joking demeanor, he placed his hand on her forehead. "I've had you out in the heat too long. It's made you feverish," he laughed. "Otherwise, you'd never say that about a bum like me."

"You're not a bum!" she protested. "You're—"

He cut her off with a quick kiss on the lips. "Save that kind of talk for someone who deserves it."

He whisked up their packages, flipped a coin to the boat rental operator, grabbed her hand and took off at a run, dragging her behind him. "Whadda you say we take the trolley back? It could be a while before an available cab comes along."

Back at her apartment, Trigg silently watched as Ellari fed the crotchety cat, then quickly whipped

194

up an unlikely concoction of olive oil and egg yolks.

"It's called mayonnaise," she answered when he asked her what she was making. With a mischievous twinkle in her green eyes she told him, "A *French* immigrant taught me how to make it. He was a chef in France," she added with pretended haughtiness. "What do you think of that?"

"French chef, huh? Guess that out does my French landlady."

She giggled and quickly crumbled the leftover omelette into a bowl. "I don't remember who told me about combining the mayonnaise with eggs to make a sandwich spread," she said, adding chopped pickles, salt, pepper and a dash of vinegar. "But since a lot of my customers pay me with food instead of cash, I usually have more eggs than anything else on hand."

She stirred the mixture and eyed it suspiciously. "I have to admit though, I never tried it with cold omelette. I usually use chopped hardboiled eggs. So this could be a real disaster."

Trigg studied her, a pensive smile on his face as he listened to her happy chatter. Was this the same somber female pharmacist he'd met a few days ago? Was she the woman he had calculatingly set out to seduce in order to get her skin cream formula? Or had somewhere along the way she become the seducer, and he the one who had been seduced?

It didn't make any sense. His purpose for being here should have been the most important thing on his mind. Instead, he sat here watching her fix supper and listening to her lively little stories — loving every minute of it and feeling as if he never wanted to leave.

The only "homes" he'd ever known were rented rooms, alleys and secret hideaways belonging to rich married women. This was the first time in his life he had ever felt as if he really belonged — or that he wanted to stay.

With any other woman, he would have gotten the formula and would have been making excuses to leave by now. But with Ellari. . . .

Damn! What the hell was he going to do about Ellari?

Chapter Eleven

Trigg rolled over onto his back and settled Ellari's head on his shoulder. "We've got to talk about the future and decide where we're going from here."

Still glowing in the aftermath of their lovemaking, Ellari was sure her heart literally stopped, then accelerated to double its normal rate. Talk about the future? Where *we're* going from here? Oh, Lord. Was he going to ask her to marry him?

Yes! she silently answered the unspoken question, the question she had given up hope of ever being asked. *Yes, yes, yes!*

Fighting the tears of happiness threatening to spill down her cheeks, she raised her head and gazed into his eyes. Surprisingly, he looked worried, as if he were afraid she would refuse his proposal. Silly man. His obvious insecurity tugged tenderly at her emotions. How could he think that her answer could be anything other than yes?

"Do you have something in mind?"

"As a matter of fact, I do. It's been on my mind

all day."

"It?" she asked coyly, her confidence soaring.

The muscles in his jaw knotted, then relaxed. "I've been thinking that you and I—"

"Yes? You and I—?"

"Should go into business together," he blurted out.

Ellari's mouth dropped open in stunned amazement. "Business?"

"You know, a partnership. The way—"

"A business partnership," she said out loud, forcing herself to hear the truth. He didn't want to marry her. He had never even thought about marrying her. He wanted to go into business with her!

Angry and hurt, she twisted out of his arms and sat up on the edge of the bed, her back to him. She reached for her robe and stabbed her arms into the sleeves.

"So that's what today was all about. I should have known. It wasn't me you wanted, but my drugstore. You thought if you were attentive to the pitiful spinster, she'd be so grateful for your charity she would just hand over her business to you. Well, I have news for you, Mr. Hanahan. You've wasted your time—and your charms. Even if I would consider such a proposition—which I won't—this place doesn't make enough money to support me alone, much less two of us. So I don't need a partner. And I especially don't need you!"

She started to stand, but he caught her arm and jerked her back down to the bed. "Look, I don't know what you're so riled about, but you're not going anywhere until you hear me out."

She directed a cold glance down at his hand on her arm. "Do I have a choice?"

"No."

Refusing to look at him, she crossed her arms over her chest. "Go on and say what you have to say. Then I want you to leave—and this time, don't come back."

Trigg released an angry growl and dropped his hold on her arm. "First of all," he said, snatching his trousers from the bedpost. "I don't want your drugstore. In fact, like I told you, I still can't figure out why you want to stay here." He stepped into his pants and stood up to fasten them.

"Then what *do* you want?"

"Dammit, Ellari!" He spun around to glare at her. "Can't you see I'm trying to protect you from getting yourself killed?"

"Why?"

"Do you want to hear my idea for how you can save your hide *and* keep on helping people, or not?"

Anger made her want to answer, "Not." However, if he really did have a solution to her problems, didn't she owe it to herself to listen? "Go on."

"Your cut and burn cream."

She twisted her head around to shoot him a questioning glance over her shoulder. "My cut and burn cream? What are you talking about?"

"It doesn't surprise me that it's never occurred to you what a gold mine that ointment of yours could be if you produced it in large quantities and sold it."

Ellari started to explain how she felt about making a profit with the cream, but he cut her off.

"However," he went on pointedly, "it does strike me as pretty odd that someone who spends all her time *talking* about *helping* people would deliberately deprive all but a select few of the benefit of her ointment, because she's too stubborn and set in her ways to make it available to them."

"I'm not set in my ways! And I'm not depriving anyone! It's free to anyone who needs it."

He heaved an exasperated sigh and plowed his fingers through his hair.

"*If* they know about your pharmacy, and *if* they're able to come here to be treated. But what about the people who don't even know that you or your ointment exist? Aren't you depriving them? Can't you see what it would mean to them to have a jar of medicine as effective as yours that they can afford to buy and keep on hand without having to visit a doctor—a doctor you and I both know they don't have the money to see?"

In spite of her thwarted fantasy of receiving a marriage proposal, Ellari couldn't help being intrigued with the idea of actually making money and helping so many people at the same time. "If this is such a 'gold mine,' as you put it, why do I need you? What's to stop me from making the cream and selling it on my own?"

Trigg shrugged. "Nothing—if you have the cash

to invest for up front expenses like ingredients, jars, labels, salespeople, and a bookkeeper. Do you?"

He paused, giving her the opportunity to answer. When she didn't, he went on. "I didn't think so. But I do. Another thing I have that you don't have is a head for business and turning a profit."

"I have a head for business," she blurted out defensively.

"Is that why you can't even eke out a dependable living for one person from the same drugstore where your father earned enough to not only support his family but to send you to college?" He shook his head hopelessly.

"That's not fair!"

"No, but it's the truth, isn't it?" He arched his eyebrows and waited for her reply. "Face it, Ellari. Your heart's too big for you to run your own business. You don't like worrying with the everyday things like paying bills and making a profit. You'd rather do what you're best at, taking care of people's injuries and illness. It kills you to charge for your services."

"Only because times are difficult for everyone these days."

"Not for people who're smart enough to seize the right opportunities when they come along. There are a lot of very rich men in Chicago — and many of them were no better off ten years ago than you and I are today. But every one of them was willing to take a chance, which I'm prepared to do. That's how sure I am we can succeed, if we put my money and business ability, which you don't have, together with—"

"My formula—which *you* don't have," she finished for him in a snide tone.

"Exactly," he agreed, not a bit irritated with her grasp of the situation. "We each have something to bring into the partnership that the other is lacking. And we both want something we can't attain without what the other has."

"And what exactly is it you want—besides my cream?"

He winced. "I'm going to lay all my cards on the table, Ellari. I've had some serious financial setbacks lately, and I need to make a lot of money fast, or I've got to leave town. The people I owe aren't too nice when they don't get paid what's owed to them."

"What about the money you said you have to invest in the 'partnership'?"

"Not enough. Besides, if I give it to them, I'll be in the same situation when the next payment is due. But if I invest it in a sure thing like your ointment, I can pay them out of my share of the profits and still have something once they're paid off."

"That explains why you need this partnership, but not why I do. I could borrow the money at the bank and hire someone to run the business end for me."

"A bank charges interest, if you can find one willing to lend you money without collateral—a partner doesn't. An employee expects to be paid before the profits come in, and even if they don't come in—a partner doesn't. And more importantly, if the business fails, the bank still has to be repaid. A partner doesn't. He takes the loss."

"I hadn't thought of that."

"Besides, your main goal is to help people less fortunate than you are, and maybe even go back to medical school if that will enable you to do more for them. Can you do that if you get yourself bogged down in learning all the aspects of running a big business?"

"Probably not," she admitted, fighting to control the tremble in her voice when she thought of her other desire—to marry and have a family of her own. "I guess you think it's pretty foolish that I would be more interested in those things than in getting rich."

"I don't think it's foolish at all. I think it's commendable. It's too bad there aren't more people in the world like you. What I do think would be foolish, would be if I can show you a way to fulfill all your goals by going into business with me, and you turn me down."

"All my goals? Don't you think you're exaggerating?"

"I don't think so. Not only will you be helping thousands more people than you are now, by providing them with the ointment so they can treat their own cuts and burns, but if you decide to go back to medical school and can't find the right buyer for the drugstore, we could hire someone to run it exactly the way you want it run. For that matter, you could even afford to start a free medical clinic in the neighborhood and support it with your share of the profits. Think of all the children you could help with a free clinic."

Ellari knew he was playing her like a piano. He knew all the right keys to press to get the desired effect: help the children, free medical clinic, go to medical school, don't desert the neighborhood people who depend on her for medical care, don't compromise her ideals. But even though she knew what he was doing, she couldn't help being intrigued. "What makes you so sure the cream will be as successful as you think it will be? What if it isn't?"

"That's the risk I'm willing to take. But I don't see how we can fail. People pay all sorts of money for 'miracle cures' that are nothing more than perfumed lard or sugar water. Can you imagine what they would pay for a cream that is actually as effective as we claim it is? Once the word gets around how good this cream is, *and* that the price is actually low enough for even the poorest pocketbook to afford to buy a jar, I don't think we'll be able to keep up with the demand." He took a deep breath and shrugged.

"Of course, if you turn me down, we're not going to find out if I'm right, are we? And you're not going to get to do all the things you could do if you say yes. One, because you're barely making enough to take care of yourself, much less enough to help other people or finance medical school. You, yourself, said as much. And two, because you've made so many enemies you're probably not going to live that long if I'm not here to look out for you. And I won't be."

"You're just trying to frighten me."

"Dammit, lady. You should be frightened. Why do you think I've stayed this long? Can't you see I care about what happens to you? I could have been gone days ago. But I stayed because I wanted to find a way to help you!"

"By helping yourself?"

Trigg heaved a frustrated sigh, then went on as if she hadn't made her insinuating comment. "I don't know what else I can say. If I stay, everyone wins: you, me, the people who will benefit from having your ointment, and the kids you could help with your profits. Everyone. But if I leave, we all lose. It's that simple."

Tempted, Ellari couldn't bring herself to admit his proposition sounded like a perfect solution to her problems. If she could earn a lot of money, there would be no end to the good she could do with it. And the way things were going, it was certain she wasn't going to earn it with her drugstore. That had become apparent even before Nylander and his men had started trying to run her out of business. As much as she hated to admit it, Trigg was right. She didn't have a head for business.

If only she didn't feel so used and embarrassed, she would say yes in a minute. But how could she work with Trigg, knowing he had deliberately seduced her to get control of her cream? Every day she would be reminded that she had been so starved for a man's attention that she had fallen in love with a man who only wanted her for the money he could earn with her. If only he had been honest with her in the first place.

Still, who would be hurt the most if she didn't swallow her pride and accept his offer? Not Trigg. He would just leave town and find another business to invest in. She, on the other hand, would go on as before, either until she couldn't afford to keep the pharmacy open any longer, or until Nylander's men killed her.

"I'll have to think about this before I can give you an answer," she said, choking back the tears of humiliation that wanted to come.

"Sure," he said, walking toward the door. Catching himself on the doorframe, he turned back to face her. "But don't take too long. Neither one of us has any time to waste — you even less than me. The people looking for me don't know where I am yet. But the bastards who've been harassing you are still out there, just waiting to see if you've taken their warnings to heart. And by now, my 'pals' are probably getting itchy about when they're going to get their money. So if we're not going to go into business, I've got to move on."

He disappeared into the other room.

Ellari stared after Trigg, torn with indecision. Was she going to stand here and let him walk out of her life because her pride was hurt? With or without a marriage proposal, the few days she had been with him had made her feel more alive than any other time in her life. Could she really go back to living the dreary day-to-day existence she had been living before he entered her life?

"Trigg!" she cried, running into the living room.

"Yes?" he answered from the kitchen sink, where he stood, pumping himself a cup of water, his back to her.

"I've made a decision."

His bare shoulders tensed, but he didn't turn to face her. "Well?" he asked, his tone holding no emotion. "What is it? Do I go or stay?"

"I'd like for you to stay," she admitted softly. Then she hurried to add, "But *only* as my business partner and consultant."

"Oh?"

"I think if we're going into business together, it must be understood from the beginning that our relationship will be purely professional from now on."

He turned to face her, his expression hard to read in the dim light, but she could almost swear that he looked sad. "Are you sure that's what you want?"

No! I'm not! her mind screamed. *I want you to feel the same way about me that I feel about you! I want you to kiss me and hold me and tell me you love me!*

Aloud she said, "Quite sure."

"In that case, why don't you tie the sash on your

robe and we'll get down to 'business.'"

His words sounded indifferent, but there was something in his eyes that confused Ellari. It made her feel like the guilty one, as if she had kicked a puppy.

"Now?"

He sucked in a deep breath through his nostrils, expanding his chest, then let the air out slowly. "I don't know how I can make this any clearer to you. We're both in serious trouble, and if we're not totally committed to this we're going to wind up dead! Now! Are we going to do it or not?"

"I'll get dressed. Give me a minute."

Revived slightly by a quick sponge bath and a change of clothes, (she had decided working in a robe with nothing on under it definitely would be counter-productive to her vow to keep their future relationship impersonal), she came back into the living area to find him at the kitchen table. A pencil in his hand, he studied the pad of paper before him.

"I made a pot of coffee," he mumbled, too engrossed to even glance up when she approached him. "You'd better get yourself a cup. It's going to be a long night. We've got a lot of work to do before morning." His eyes fixed on the figures on the paper, he picked up his own cup and sucked a swallow of the strong brew into his mouth.

Stiffly, Ellari walked to the stove and took a mug

from the shelf beside it. What had she done to herself by insisting their relationship wouldn't be personal? He was the one who was supposed to be punished, not her. But if working with Trigg Hanahan day after day without being able to look forward to his wonderful smiles, his twinkling glances and his teasing remarks wouldn't be punishment, she didn't know what would.

"Okay," he said as soon as she had poured her coffee and had taken a chair next to his. "The first thing we need to settle is who will be responsible for what. Then we need to draw up an agreement for how to divide the profits. I'd like to set up a timetable for getting the cream produced and on the market," he went on, obviously reading from his list. "After that, we'd better figure an estimate on how much each jar will cost to make, how much we should charge for it, and how much we can afford to spend on the initial batch."

Stretching her neck to see the list, Ellari instinctively scooted her chair closer to his as she reached for the pad to see what he had written on it. "Can I see?"

As if he'd been touched with a hot coal, Trigg jumped, slapping at his bare shoulder as her hair accidentally brushed across it. "My writing's hard to read," he growled, moving the pad. "I'll start at the top and read it to you."

Ellari shrugged and said, "All right, what's first?"

"Division of responsibilities," he answered. "Who does what."

"I may not have a head for business, but I do know what division of responsibilities means, Trigg."

Trigg cleared his throat. "I'm sorry. Of course you know what it means."

He tore the list from the pad and set it aside, exposing a clean sheet of paper. He drew a line down the center of the sheet and put each of their names at the top of a column.

"I think we're pretty much agreed on this one." He started to write on her side of the paper. "You provide the formula." He moved his hand to his own side of the sheet. "I pay for the initial supplies you need to start out: jars, labels, ingredients. You'll need to give me a list for what to buy. You prepare the cream and put it into the jars. I can help if you need me to—at least at first, before we can afford to hire you an assistant. I'll take care of having the labels printed up and put on the jars, which we can design together if you want, or I'll do it. Then of course, I'll handle the sales. What do you think of, . . . 'The Lochridge Magic Skin Formula'?"

"I suppose it's all right . . . maybe a little misleading since it's not actually magic, and it sounds more like a beauty cream than a medical ointment."

"That's a point. But I do like the word magic. It's a good selling word. How about "The Lochridge Magic Cut and Burn Ointment."

"Too long."

"A lot of them are. 'Stonebraker's Nerve and

Bone Liniment,' 'Renne's Pain-Killing Magic Oil,' 'Morehead's Magnetic Plaster,' and what about 'Dubbel's Menthane Vermifuge.' " He shot her a sideways glance. "Now there's an idea. We could call it the Lochridge Magic Vermifuge. I've always liked the sound of the word 'vermifuge.' Wonder what it means."

Ellari fought the grin that threatened to curve her mouth in response to the impish glint in his eyes. "A vermifuge is a cure for *worms,* hardly a name for a skin salve."

Trigg made a face. "I guess you're right. Too bad. It does have a special ring to it."

This time Ellari couldn't keep from smiling, not only at his humor, but with relief to realize that at least that part of their relationship wouldn't change. He would still tease her. Pretending to cough, she covered her mouth and turned her head away.

"Tell you what," he went on, "maybe if we make a list of the ingredients in the cream, one of them will give us an idea for a catchy name."

"Well, there's eucalyptus oil and—" She stopped herself short and narrowed her eyes at him. "Wait a minute, if I tell you the ingredients, what's to keep you from creating and selling the cream on your own?"

He threw down the pencil and shot her a withering glance. "Do you want this to work or not?"

"Yes, I want it to work."

"Then you're going to have to trust me."

"I'll trust you if you say we're going to make a lot

211

of money with this business. I'll trust you to be honest in the keeping of our books. I'll trust in your judgment when it comes to choosing the best name for the cream. I'll even trust you to be honest when it comes to fairly dividing our profits. But the formula stays in my family's sole possession. And that's final. So it's up to you. Do we continue with that understanding, or do we end our discussion now?"

Knowing she had driven the final nail into the wall, blocking any chance of their relationship ever becoming close again, she waited for his answer.

Trigg studied her for a long moment, then switched his gaze back to the list. "That's okay with me. But if I don't have the formula as insurance, then I want it in writing that you'll stop your fight with the glass factories."

"You can't ask me to do that!"

"I don't have any choice. If I'm going to invest all my money in your cream, I can't afford to have you killed by some angry glass factory worker or owner for butting into his business. Either drop the fight or tell me the formula."

"I can't desert those children. They need me."

"Alive, Ellari. They need you alive. Just like I do. You're no good to them, or to me, if you're dead! Besides, if you back off, once you make lots of money, you can attack the problem from a different angle. Money is a great negotiator. You're not getting anywhere the way you're going now."

Ellari thought for a moment. He was right

again—though it galled her to admit it. Not only was she getting nowhere in her fight against using child labor in the glass factories, but she wouldn't accomplish anything if she were dead. Alive and rich, she could really do something to stop the terrible practice.

"I'll agree to stop until we have earned back your investment and we've started to show a profit. I can't promise any more than that."

Trigg gave her a guileless grin and shrugged. "Then I guess we have an agreement." He held out his hand.

Ellari looked down at his hand, then back into his eyes. Wishing they could seal their bargain with a kiss instead of a handshake, she took his offered hand regretfully. "I guess we do."

The instant their palms touched, Trigg's expression changed. His eyes boring indecisively into hers, he held her hand longer than necessary.

Their gazes locked helplessly, they didn't speak. Trigg was first to look away. "I'll have a lawyer draw up papers in the morning," he said, his voice husky.

"And I will make a list of supplies I'll be needing." She stood to leave. "If we're done, I'm going to bed."

He made an exaggerated show of studying his list. "Sure, I'm going to turn in myself in a minute."

"Then, goodnight."

"Goodnight."

She started for her bedroom.

"Ellari!"

"Yes?" she asked, unable to disguise the expectant tone in her voice as she turned around to face him.

"What do you think of calling the cream, 'Magicure'? We can put 'For Burns and Cuts' in dark, easy-to-read letters under the larger eye-catching 'Magicure.' Or we could call it 'The Lochridge Magicure' if you like."

Her heart sank again. "No. Magicure by itself is fine. I'm sure it will sell a lot of the cream."

"Then 'Magicure' it is!"

If only there were a magic cure for a broken heart, she lamented silently as she left the room. *If only he loved me.*

Chapter Twelve

"Okay, Nylander, you can call off your dogs," Trigg announced, storming into the factory owner's office. "She's agreed to stop."

Nylander looked up from the papers on his desk, his forehead pleated with annoyance. "I don't appreciate having you burst into my office unannounced, Hanahan."

"No more than I appreciate having your thugs jump me and drug me so they could rough up Ellari Lochridge," Trigg returned angrily. "You and I had a deal that I would handle her in my own way." He flopped down in a chair and propped his ankle on the opposite knee. "I deserve a bonus for the hours I spent tied up and sweating in that hot shed." He flicked a piece of lint off his pant leg.

"A bonus?"

"Another five hundred dollars ought to cover it."

"In the first place, you've already been more than generously paid for your services, Hanahan. And in the second place, my people didn't drug you or 'rough up' Miss Lochridge. Why would they? The whole point of hiring you was to avoid the necessity for that sort of action if at all possible, and to keep me and my people out of it."

Surprised, Trigg dropped his raised foot to the floor and leaned forward. For some reason, he believed Nylander was telling the truth. "It wasn't you?"

Nylander shrugged. "Sorry to disappoint you."

"Then who—"

"It could have been anyone. Though the major portion of her slanderous activities are directed against me, I'm not the only factory owner who resents her interference. Do-gooders like Ellari Lochridge should be thanking us instead of harassing us. We're doing a favor for those ignorant immigrants by hiring their kids. If it weren't for us, those no-good little bastards would be out on the streets robbing and murdering the decent people of this city."

Nylander shook his head vigorously. "But that's another subject. What I really want to talk about is why you're here. Did you say Ellari Lochridge had been taken care of? Are you sure? How'd you manage it?"

Trigg nodded, swallowing back the bitter taste of guilt he experienced for siding with Ellari's adversary. He tried to console himself with the fact that there hadn't been much choice. He'd had to protect her, and this was the only way—other than kidnapping her and whisking her out of town. Still, he felt dirty and ashamed. "I convinced her she needed a business partner, and as part of our agreement I got her to agree to drop her fight against you."

"This calls for a drink." Nylander tugged open a desk drawer and produced a half-full bottle of whiskey and two glasses. "When are you leaving town?"

"We're not."

His hand and the bottle suspended in midair, Nylander froze. "What did you say?"

"We're staying in Chicago after all."

Nylander's face reddened, and he slammed the bottle down on the desk, causing the two glasses to bounce upward. "I paid you to get her out of town!" he shouted.

Trigg made a special effort to keep his tone even. "You didn't pay me to get her out of town. You paid me to get rid of her for you. And that's what I did. I got her to agree to drop this child labor thing and put her efforts into something else."

"For now, maybe. But I know that nosy bitch. All it'll take to set her off again is for one kid who's been injured at my factory to show up at her drugstore."

Trigg clenched his fists, fighting the urge to bury one in Nylander's face for calling Ellari a bitch. "She won't, because I'll be there to see that she doesn't."

"For how long?"

"Indefinitely. I told you, we're business partners now. Believe me, she's not going to cause you any more trouble. You have my word."

"Words and partnerships can be broken. I need something more concrete than your word. Perhaps, if you were to marry her I'd feel better about this."

"Marry her?"

"You could do worse. I understand she's pretty enough, and you're already sleeping in her bed. It wouldn't be that big a change—except that as her husband, you could forbid her to give me trouble."

"There's one little problem. I don't want to get married."

"Then get Ellari Lochridge out of Chicago. One way or another, I want a guarantee I don't have to hear her name again. Now, take care of it, or I go back to my original plan, no matter how unpleasant my other man's tactics are. Which will it be?"

A sick feeling rolled through Trigg. Damn! He'd been so sure he'd at least rid himself of Nylander. Now, not only had he discovered Ellari had other enemies, but Nylander wasn't ready to let him off the hook. "What if I can't convince her to marry me?"

"Oh, I'm sure you'll think of a way," Nylander said with a conspiratorial grin. "My men told me about how you two were acting like lovebirds all over the city yesterday, so I don't think she'll take much convincing."

"Your men followed us?"

"Of course. You didn't think I'd hand over all the money and supplies I gave you without retaining a little insurance that you wouldn't skip town to keep from holding up your end of the bargain, did you?"

"No, I guess I didn't." Trigg stood up to leave. "I'll let you know what I decide." He started for the door.

"Two weeks, Hanahan. Either marry her or get her out of Chicago. Or I call back my other man. As it is, he wasn't too happy I removed him from the project in the first place, and I've no doubt he's standing by, anxious to get another chance."

Trigg's thoughts were a tempest of indecision as he walked along the board sidewalks leading back to Ellari's drugstore. He was so lost in his thoughts that he was totally oblivious to the unusually hot autumn sun beating down onto the city of Chicago. Usually, his heart would have gone out to the panting dogs he saw lying in any shade they could find, tongues hanging and too hot to even bark as he passed, but today he was unaware they even existed. Nor did he pay attention to the profusely sweating people who had taken refuge from their oven-hot shanties and stores to sit outside, hoping to catch a hint of a breeze. The closest he came to recognizing that he wasn't alone on the street was an unconscious nod of his head when someone spoke as he strode by.

He didn't even notice the almost constant clanging from the firebell tower downtown, nor did he pay attention to the frequent firewagons that sped past him as they had every day for weeks. Under ordinary circumstances, the deafening thunder created by the clacking wooden wheels rolling over the wood-paved streets was impossible to ignore.

But these were no ordinary circumstances. Actually, from the moment he had walked into Ellari Lochridge's shop a few days ago, nothing about his life had been ordinary. He'd been shot at, cut with a knife, drugged, beaten, threatened, had found the opportunity he'd been searching for all his life—and had two potential brides foisted on him by two wealthy and influential men. Of course, he had never seriously considered marrying Ina Phelps, and he intended to make that clear to her father—just as soon as he made enough money to repay Stahl.

But the situation with Ellari Lochridge was another matter altogether, and certainly not one he could ignore or settle by simply giving back Nylander's money. He had no intention of doing anything that dumb. He wasn't that far out of control. Besides, giving Nylander back his money and supplies wouldn't solve anything. He'd still be trying to stay a step ahead of his creditors, and Ellari Lochridge would still be in danger. They'd just be broke.

At the thought of Nylander's men laying a finger on Ellari, Trigg's insides coiled, his fists and teeth clenched, and his mouth stretched into a restraining grimace. If anything happened to her, he would personally tear Nylander apart with his bare hands.

God, listen to me! Where had this compelling need to protect anyone but himself come from? It wasn't as if she actually meant anything to him. She was just a way to make his dream of getting rich come true. A particularly pleasant way perhaps, but that was all she was. So went his justifying.

By protecting her, I'm protecting myself. That's all it is. I keep her safe, I win. I let anything happen to her, I lose.

"Damn! Just once, it'd be nice to have things turn out the way I planned them," he mumbled aloud.

If only he could convince her to leave the city with him and set up the business somewhere else, it would solve everything. Waukegan or Joliet wouldn't be too bad, and neither city was so far from Chicago that he couldn't come back to sell the ointment every few weeks.

He laughed bitterly. Who was he kidding? Ellari Lochridge wasn't willingly going anywhere with him. She was too attached to that old drugstore of hers to ever leave it. Besides, she could hardly bear the sight of him since she had found out his reason for staying hadn't been as selfless as he'd led her to believe.

It was a shame he hadn't asked her to leave with him *before* he suggested going into business together. He could have told her he was in trouble and had to leave, but that he couldn't bear to leave without her. She'd have gone with him in a minute. He knew she would have. It had been in her eyes.

Trigg released a disgusted snort. As usual, his timing stunk. He had been thinking he could get the formula without making any long-term commitment or being forced to assume responsibility for her if he took her from her home. But he'd waited too long.

Now, even suggesting she go with him would be futile. She would be just as willing to go off with Nylander! He figured that as far as Ellari Lochridge was concerned, her new business partner was lower than the rats that lived in the muck and garbage beneath the planks of the city sidewalks. And the really disgusting thing was that she was right.

The only reason she'd agreed to his business proposal was because she was desperate, and because her innocence had been no match for his sales pitch. But no matter how naive she'd been, even as late as last night, she was a lot smarter today, and she would never leave town with him unless they were married—and that was out of the question.

Years ago, he had vowed on his mother's grave never to marry and inflict on a woman the kind of pain his father had inflicted on her. He wouldn't wish on anyone the likes of the no-good bastard who'd fathered him, then deserted Trigg's mother before Trigg was even born. And from what he'd been told by his mother, he was like his own father in too many ways to chance that he wouldn't be the same sort of rotten husband and father. He liked to think he was different, but the possibility that he wasn't was too great to take the risk. Ellari deserved better than that.

Marriage was definitely not the answer.

Nylander's "You could do worse," sounded over and over in his head.

"Yeah, but she couldn't," he answered aloud.

Anyway, even if she could do worse, a beautiful, intelligent woman like Ellari Lochridge would never settle for a low-class street hustler like he was. Oh, he might be all right for a brief romantic encounter, or at least that was what he'd been told by any number of wealthy married women looking for a little excitement, but as far as marriage—Ellari could have her pick of rich and educated men. She would never want him.

The idea of another man knowing the sweet honesty of Ellari's innocent passion and generosity flashed unexpectedly into his consciousness, bringing with it a jarring and disturbing new self-knowledge.

Whether or not he was good enough for Ellari Lochridge, he couldn't bear the thought of her with anyone else.

"What do you mean, he hasn't come calling?" Reed Phelps asked his tearful daughter. Pounding his desk with both fists, he shouted, "Treens! Get in here."

"Yes sir?" the butler responded immediately, as if he'd been waiting outside the door for a summons.

"Miss Ina tells me there have been no callers while I was in Springfield. Is that true?"

"Yes sir."

"Think man! Are you sure a tall, good-looking young man didn't come by? Maybe when Miss Ina was resting or out and you forgot to mention it. Dark hair. Flashy dresser. Trigg Hanahan is his name."

The butler stiffened indignantly. "I did not forget, sir. There were no visitors in your absence. The bell rang only once, and it was not a gentleman. It was a young woman seeking employment. Of course, I sent her packing immediately. Imagine, a twit with no more sense than to come to the front door instead of the rear, expecting to be hired in a fine house such as yours."

"Treens," Phelps growled. "I don't have time for your useless prattle about proper servant etiquette. Send someone to find Will Keedy, and bring him to me as soon as he gets here."

"Very well, sir," Treens replied evenly, never giving up a shred of decorum, despite the verbal attack from his employer. His board-straight posture unwavering, he turned on his heel and hurried from the room.

"What do you want with Will Keedy?" Ina asked.

Reed wrapped his arm around his daughter's fleshy shoulder and gently guided her over to the divan. "There, there, sweetheart. Don't worry your pretty head about it anymore. Papa's home now. I'm going to take care of everything. No one's going to hurt my little girl's feelings and get away with it."

A grin on his face, Trigg burst into the drugstore, determined to get his relationship with Ellari back to what it had been. Once he did that, the rest should be easy. "Ellari! I'm back."

He stopped short, momentarily blinded by the change in lighting from the glaring sunlight to the dimmer store.

As he waited for his sight to be restored, he became aware of an almost tangible stillness inside the store.

"Ellari?" he called tentatively, ominous dread beginning to gnaw at his gut. The last time he had felt such emptiness in a room was when he was twelve years old, right after the mortician had removed his mother's dead body from the one-room

225

flat they had lived in.

"Ellari!!" he shouted, his tone growing desperate. "Where are you?"

His boots rooted to the plank floor by apprehension, he made a desperate sweep of the shop with his eyes. She had to be here. She wouldn't have left the front door unlocked if she had gone out of her own accord. "Ellari!"

His sight fully regained, he helplessly zipped his frantic gaze back and forth over the unoccupied store.

"Oh my God!" he groaned as his search came to a horrified halt at his own feet.

The floor was stained with bright patches of red. Blood! Large puddles of blood, smaller splatters of blood, even lines of blood, as if someone had poured red paint on the planks while running through the store.

"Ellari!" He charged forward to follow the grotesque trail leading toward the treatment corner.

At the screen divider, he paused and sucked in a sustaining gulp of air, then rounded the end of the screen.

Ellari looked up from where she sat slumped on the treatment couch, shivering and hugging herself tightly as if she were cold. Her eyes were blank, as though she didn't recognize him. There were garish red smears of blood on her face, streaked pink where tears had streamed down her face.

Frantic terror collided with relief at finding her

alive. "My God, Ellari! What happened?" He dropped to a crouch in front of her and lifted her chin so he could look into her eyes. He frantically looked around, not certain what he should do. "I'll get you to a doctor."

Shaking her head, she pressed one hand to his chest to stop him, then wiped her hair back off her forehead with the other, smearing even more stains on her skin and on his shirtfront. Fresh tears formed in her eyes. "It's too late."

Trigg's eyes opened wide with horror as he saw the blood on her hands and the blood-soaked waist and skirt of her dress exposed by her gesture. "No! It's not too late!"

His own eyes stinging with tears, he ignored her protests and shot up from the floor. He whisked her into his arms as he stood. Holding her tightly, he ran for the door. "Oh, God! Somebody get a doctor!"

The overwhelming fear in Trigg's voice reached deep into Ellari's subconscious and rescued her from the stunned daze holding her captive. "Trigg!" She gently cupped his cheek and brought his face around so he could see her face. "A doctor can't help me."

Confused, he stopped at the door and stared. His tear-filled eyes dropped to her bodice.

Her own gaze followed the direction his had taken. Seeing the gory mess of her clothing, she released an anguished sob. "The blood's not mine."

His questioning stare leaped back to her face.

"It isn't mine, Trigg," she said, her voice small and trembling.

"Not yours?" He frowned. "Then who's?"

"They brought an injured boy to me from the glass factory, but—" She broke into fresh sobs and buried her face against his shirt, unable to go on. "Can we just go upstairs?"

Trigg hesitated, not sure he could believe her.

"Please."

Not certain he was making the right choice, Trigg did as she asked and raced up to her apartment. Upstairs, he took her to the spare bedroom, the closest to the top of the stairs, and gently lay her on the bed. "The first thing we need to do is get these clothes off and clean you up." His hands shaking, he reached for the buttons on her blouse front.

She didn't resist as he hurriedly undid the bodice and sat her up so that he could remove it. Working at a frantic pace, he whisked her camisole over her head, then lay her back down.

Relieved to see that she had been telling the truth about not being injured—at least in the heart, lung and midriff areas—he quickly got rid of her other clothes so he could check to be sure she hadn't been wounded in the belly, where the heaviest concentration of blood on her clothing had been.

His heart pounding in his ears with skull-splitting volume, Trigg shuddered violently as he revealed the rest of her body.

"Thank God!" Zapped of all his strength, he sagged forward and covered her face with kisses. "Thank God, you're all right!"

"He died, Trigg." Her voice was pitiful and small, like that of a child who had been violently betrayed.

Trigg raised his head. "Who died?"

"The boy," she whispered. "Willie."

"The child who spent the night here?" Trigg gasped, shocked by the feelings of sorrow that rocked through him at the news.

Ellari nodded, her mouth turned down at the corners, her bottom lip trembling. "I did everything I knew how to do, but I couldn't stop the bl—" She covered her face with her hands.

Guilt and blame worse than he'd already been feeling blasted through Trigg. If only he'd backed her up when she had wanted to refuse to let Willie go with his parents, the child might be alive today. "I'm sure you did all you could," he said consolingly, choking back his own tears at the thought of poor little Willie's wasted life.

"Oh, Lord, that sweet child bled to death in my arms, and I didn't save him. He deserved better than that. I'll never forgive myself. I should've done something.

"No, no," he soothed, pulling the spread over her and lying down beside her to take her in his arms. "It wasn't your fault."

She shook her head, burrowing her face into the hollow of his neck. "If only I'd—"

He tightened his embrace. "Shh. Don't think about it anymore. From what I saw, he had already lost too much blood before he got here for anybody to have saved him. Not even a doctor." His voice was husky. "You did all you could."

"It never should have happened. If only I had refused to let him leave, Willie wouldn't have been in that horrible factory today," she wept, her words muffled. "I knew he was sick, but I let him go."

"You didn't have a choice. His parents are the ones to blame, not you."

"But if I had stopped Nylander, he wouldn't have been at the factory. None of the children would be there."

For the first time, Trigg understood what Ellari had been trying to accomplish by fighting Nylander and his competitors. But even though he understood why it was so important to her, it didn't make it any less probable that the next time he found her covered in blood, it could be her own. And no matter how important ending child labor was to her, and to the children, he couldn't take that chance. He couldn't—wouldn't—lose Ellari.

"Don't you see, Trigg? We've got to stop Nylander and men like him from killing any more children. I can't back away. There's no time to wait. We've got to stop him now!"

"We'll talk about it later," Trigg mumbled non-

230

committally, as he disentangled himself from her grip and sat up.

"Where are you going?" she cried, her tone distressed, her eyes wide with fear.

"I'll be right back. I'm going to get some warm water and washcloths. You'll feel better once we get you washed up and in some clean clothes." He glanced down at his own blood-stained clothing and hands. "We both will."

"Promise you won't leave again," she begged.

He dropped back down and kissed her face. "I'm not going anywhere. And I'm going to see to it that nothing like this ever happens to you again."

When Ellari awoke she was in her own bed and wearing a clean white cotton gown. The shades, kept down during the day, had been raised, as had the window, to let in the night breeze, which was almost nonexistent as far as she could tell. The papers were calling this year the hottest and dryest in Chicago's history, and she believed it. There was just no escaping the miserable heat. *If only it would rain,* she mused, tossing off the cover, in the hope of feeling cooler.

Suddenly, the sound of breathing interrupted her idle, half-awake musings. She bolted up in bed, all thoughts of the heat and rain erased from her mind. "Who's there?"

Her eyes wide with apprehension, she searched

the moonlit room, halting on the barechested figure slumped in the chair in the corner. "Trigg," she breathed in a relieved sigh. Memories of how sweet and gentle the handsome sleeping man could be collided violently with those of Willie Knowles' bloody, unnecessary death.

Her eyes filled with tears as she remembered the terrible event. What would she have done if Trigg hadn't come back only moments after Mr. Knowles had torn his son's lifeless body from her arms and stormed from the store, cursing and blaming her as he went? She'd probably still be huddled in the treatment corner downstairs, in shock and alone and covered in blood.

She absently rubbed her hands on the thin nightgown she wore. The sweet, clean fragrance of soap sent a wave of pleasant sensations wafting through her mind. As if by magic, the nightmarish visions of Willie bleeding to death in her arms diffused and became slightly easier to bear. Instead, her thoughts were filled with memories of gentle hands dressing her, cleaning the blood from her face, strong arms holding her, softly spoken words consoling her and telling her that she was not to blame, his blue eyes filled with concern and shining with unshed tears.

The truth hit her. Every time she needed him, Trigg was there. When there was no one else to depend on, he was there. No matter how unpleasant she had been at their last meeting, and no

232

matter how unpleasant the task had been, he was there.

Yet in all the times he had taken care of her, she had never really thanked him with anything other than harsh, suspicious words. She had accused him of wanting to steal from her, when all the time he had been the giver, she the taker.

No one else who witnessed her fight to save Willie's life had even asked if she was all right, much less considered how hard Willie's death would be on her. Their only concern had been for the father and how he would pay for the funeral—especially now that the family had lost a weekly salary!

Sympathy and gratitude for the exhausted man sleeping in the chair mingled with regret and shame for the way she had misjudged him. No matter how it hurt to admit to herself that his reasons for helping her were no doubt selfish, the fact remained that over and over he had been there to take care of her when no one else had. Whatever his ulterior motives were, he was here, and she wanted him to stay.

She rolled off the bed and tiptoed over to the chair. "Trigg?" she whispered, tapping his arm gently.

"What!" he shouted, startled, his glassy eyes leaping to her face. "What's wrong? Are you okay?"

Ellari smiled reassuringly. "I'm fine. I just

233

thought you would be more comfortable in the bed. I spent more than one night in this chair when my mother was sick, and I know it's torture to sleep in."

Trigg squirmed in the chair to reposition himself. "I'm all right. Go on back to bed."

"Not unless you do." She put her hand on his back and tried to help him up. "I won't be able to sleep a wink if I know you're miserable."

Trigg resisted, obviously confused. "I'm fine here. Besides, the bed in the other room is a mess. I didn't get around to—"

"Who said anything about the other room?" Ellari asked, drawing him to his feet. "After all the sleep you've lost because of me, the least I owe you is a decent night's rest in the most comfortable bed in the house."

"You mean in here? In your—?" His gaze swerved uncertainly to her bed, then back to her face. "Where will you—?"

"I thought we would both sleep in this one." She ventured, suddenly self-conscious.

"Are you sure?"

"It's really the only practical thing to do if either of us is going to get a decent night's sleep," she babbled with pretended casualness, afraid she would burst into tears any minute. "After all, there's plenty of room, and the other room isn't made up, and it's not as if we haven't—" She stopped short, unable to go on.

234

"No, it isn't. But what about that 'purely business' relationship you wanted us to have?"

She raised her gaze to his, her pleading eyes stinging with tears. "I was a fool."

Trigg gulped loudly. "Then, what is it you do want, Ellari?"

She dropped her chin to her chest, unable to look at him. "I want to be held. Please. I don't want to be alone tonight."

Chapter Thirteen

Trigg held out his arms, and Ellari fell into them. He closed them around her and brought her deeper into his embrace.

With a contented sigh, Ellari twined her arms around his waist and pressed her cheek to his naked chest. Spreading her hands over his back, she reveled in the satiny feel of the hot, slightly clammy flesh beneath her fingers, the hair-roughened solidness of his chest against her cheek.

Magic relief flooded into her as she greedily inhaled the salty, musky scent of him into her nostrils. She wondered how it could be possible to see him and work with him every day, without knowing the comfort and security of being in his arms again. She had been a fool!

His mere presence in the same room made her feel safe and strong, as if anything were possible. But in his arms, she *knew* there was nothing she couldn't accomplish if she had him. In his arms, none of her goals were unattainable, none of her problems were unconquerable and none of her failures were insurmountable.

No, she wouldn't willingly give this up again. She owed him, she needed him, and she wanted him. She could live without a wedding ring. She could live without being a doctor. She could live without pretty clothes. She could live without many things. But she couldn't live without the way she felt in Trigg's arms.

She lifted her head and gazed up into his eyes, her look pleading with him to understand what she wanted.

Trigg hauled her against him, so hard it took her breath. The bulge he pressed against the softness of her belly left no doubt that he knew what she wanted and that he wanted the same thing. But instead of kissing her, he reared back his head and glared down at her.

"Be sure this time, Ellari. Either we'll be strictly business partners, or we'll be business partners who're also lovers. But it can't be both ways. There's not going to be any more wanting to be with me one minute, then changing your mind the next."

His fingers interlocked at the small of her back, he paused and inhaled deeply, his desire pressing forward. "It's up to you, and I'll go along with whatever you decide. But I'm warning you, the next time I share your bed, you're not kicking me out again. This time, I'm staying, so you'd better be real sure."

Her insides trembling with the enormity of what she was agreeing to, Ellari raised her hands to his face and sandwiched it between her palms. "I've never been more sure of anything in my life."

With a growl of relief, Trigg brought his mouth down on hers in an urgent kiss that exploded in every nerve ending and muscle and blood vessel in her body. Kneading and gripping the soft mounds of her bottom, he lifted her harder against his thrusting need, deepening his kiss with his tongue.

Seeking desperate respite from the explosive pressure between her thighs, Ellari tangled her fingers into Trigg's hair and ground her own hips forward.

Continuing to fondle her buttocks with one hand and kiss her, Trigg managed to unbutton the remaining buttons on his pants and clumsily start to shove them down his hips.

Just as anxious to be rid of the barrier between them as he was, Ellari gripped the waistband on either side and peeled the trousers downward, including his underwear.

Similar urgency ruling his actions, Trigg held the trousers tangled at his ankles to the floor with one bare foot, then the other, and wriggled out of them. His feet free, he kicked the pants aside, then ripped Ellari's gown up over her head and tossed it aside.

Both of them naked at last, Trigg cupped her bottom with his hands and lifted her off the floor, then brought her down onto his steely hardness.

Surprised, Ellari instinctively clung to him with

238

her arms and legs to keep from falling as he impaled her.

Their bodies rocking in united frenzy, Trigg clenched his fingers under her hips and lifted her almost off him. Then before she could cry out her protests, he brought her down on him again, slamming into her with his full power. Over and over he repeated the near withdrawal, then the violent thrust, each time seeming to go deeper than the time before.

She was helpless to do anything but hang on to him for the wild ride of passion. Gasping for air, she threw back her head and allowed herself to be whisked away on wings of ecstasy she hadn't imagined existed.

Then it was happening, that convulsive contraction in the heart of her sex, and she wailed out her explosive climax.

Still rigid with unfulfilled desire, Trigg carried her to the bed and lowered her to the mattress. Covering her passion moistened face and neck with kisses, he withdrew from the snug sheath of her body to trail his kisses down her body, over her heaving breasts and belly to the nest of moist curls at the apex of her thighs.

Before Ellari could grasp what was happening, he lifted her hips upward and caressed the swollen bud he found at the most private part of her body with his tongue and lips.

"Oh!" she squealed at the blistering, intimate touch. Instinctively, she raised her head and shoulders and tried to twist away from the searing strokes. But he persisted, quickly draining every bit of resistance from her. Writhing and sobbing with pleasure, she fell back onto the mattress and allowed herself to be whisked to the outer limits of sanity.

The explosion of her passion was unexpected and swift and violent, causing her to buck wildly against his mouth. Instead of ending her desire, her exquisite climax triggered an urgent need to have him inside her yet again.

This time when she pulled on his head and hair, he came away willingly, covering her body with frantic kisses as he slid back up her. In a hurry, he spread her thighs wide and rammed into the still quivering heat of her body, at last claiming his own release.

"Don't ever try to keep me out of your bed again, Ellari," he ground out, collapsing onto her, his body still jerking as the last of his tremors subsided. "I'm here to stay."

"I'm glad," she whispered, tightening her arms and legs around his sweat-misted body. "This is where I want you to be."

Ellari awoke early, with a new energy and optimism that she hadn't expected to feel again after Willie's death. She still had to fight to keep from crying each time she thought of the little boy's wasted life, and all the other children who were being brutalized in the glass factories, but now she had new hope for her cause. All because of Trigg. Together, they would see that Willie had not died in vain.

She rolled her head to the side to appreciate the man who slept there—and who took up more than his half of the bed, she noticed with a wry smile. Even with his black hair wild and tossed, and with the dark shadow of a day-old beard on his face, he was the most handsome man she had ever seen— and he was "here to stay." Those three words spoken in the aftermath of his spent passion sounded over and over in her head. He may not have said the other "three words" she longed to hear him say, but "here to stay" was almost as good. That knowledge gave her the strength to face anything, anyone—even every factory owner in the city of Chicago if she had to. Trigg was "here to stay."

Careful not to awaken Trigg, she sat up in bed and reached for her robe—which for the first time since she could remember was not on the bed post, but on the floor where it had been thrown. Grinning at her forgetfulness, she felt the floor for her slippers. They too were not where they always were. Obviously, when she had gotten up during the night to go into the bathroom, she had been in such a hurry to get back into bed and into Trigg's arms, that where she'd put the robe and slippers had been of no importance to her.

Bending to retrieve her scattered things, she smiled with satisfaction. Suddenly she felt very young. She mused that perhaps she wasn't quite the old maid so set in her ways, after all.

After taking a quick bath, she donned the dark dress she usually wore for cleaning, then loosely tied her hair back with one of the ribbons Trigg had bought her. Gathering the fortitude she knew would be necessary to face the bloody scene waiting for her downstairs, she took a last peek at the beautiful man sleeping in her bed. *I love you, Trigg Hanahan,* she silently told him. *And one day, I hope you will love me too.*

Downstairs, Ellari paused at the door leading from the back room into the store. Maybe she wasn't as ready for this as she had thought. Maybe she should wait until Trigg woke up and could go with her.

Stop it! Trigg's already cleaned up enough of your messes. Just keep telling yourself that he's here to stay and you can face anything. Taking a deep breath, she yanked back the curtain and stepped into the drugstore.

Surprise washed over her. Nothing looked any different than it had before Mr. Knowles had brought Willie into the store. She stared, dumbfounded. Whatever she had expected to find, this wasn't it. Of course the room was dim, only lit by the sun that had managed to filter through the white shades on the windows and door, which gave everything an eerie, unreal look. She feared that in the light it would be just as gruesome as she remembered.

She did not want to raise the shades until the evidence that Willie had died here was washed away, so she quickly lit two lamps. Her back to the front of the store, she closed her eyes, clenched her teeth, and wheeled around to face the horror. Determined not to back down, she took a deep breath and popped open her eyes.

What was this? The bloodstains on the floor of the center aisle were not there. She'd been so sure. Frowning, she followed the aisle to the treatment corner with her eyes. It was as if the blood she had remembered being there had been only a dream. *If only that were so,* she thought, moving woodenly toward the spot where Willie had bled to death in her arms.

Rounding the screen, Ellari stopped short. Everything was as it should be, spotless and in order.

"Trigg," she breathed. After taking care of her, he must have come back downstairs and cleaned up the grisly mess to protect her from having to face it in the morning. The love she had been certain must be the most complete love ever to exist increased tenfold in her heart. It was no wonder he'd fallen asleep in that chair. He must have been exhausted. Yet, he'd even sounded apologetic when he'd told her he hadn't cleaned the second bedroom!

Her immediate impulse was to thank him and tell him how glad she was he had come into her shop that first day. She turned and ran back upstairs. At the bedroom, though, she paused. What was she thinking? Waking him from a sound sleep he obviously needed was no way to show her gratitude, especially after all the trouble she had caused him.

Vowing to let him sleep until noon if he wanted to, she tiptoed across the room and drew down the shade, then gently pulled the door shut and went back into the main room. She quickly wrote him a note, telling him to come get her when he woke up and that she would close the shop and come up to cook his breakfast. Then she hurriedly changed into a dress more appropriate for waiting on customers, and filled Mr. Cat's bowls with food and clean water.

Back downstairs, she opened the backdoor to let in Mr. Cat, who growled impatiently and dashed past her on his way up to breakfast.

"Good morning to you, too," she called after the haughty cat as he disappeared from view. Apparently, missing dinner last night hadn't set too well with him, especially since he still hadn't forgiven her for locking the window upstairs so that he could no longer come and go at will.

Smiling, Ellari marveled at how the demanding glutton had survived before he'd come to her. She doubted seriously if the cat ever stooped to catching and killing his own dinner. In fact, it wouldn't have been surprising to learn that he'd sat outside her door all night long, waiting for someone to let him in, while rats and mice had paraded up and down the alley. Still, she couldn't help but be glad the lazy cat had come into her life. He had saved her from that attacker the other night, and he never had ceased to comfort her—even when things were at their worst.

A wave of sadness rolled through her as a vision of the scroungy old cat snuggled close to Willie flashed in her head. The elitist cat even had let the boy pet him, a privilege he reserved only for the person who fed him—when he was hungry. *Somehow, he must have known.*

Choking back her tears, Ellari hurried to the front of the drugstore. If it took the rest of her life, she wouldn't give up until the people responsible for Willie's death paid for what they had done. She would go on as usual, and one way or another she would stop them. "Who knows?" she mumbled to herself. "This may be the thing that finally wakes these people up and makes them fight Nylander."

She whisked up the blind on the door and flipped over the closed sign so that it read, "OPEN." Giving her eyes and nose a final wipe, she stuffed her handkerchief back into her pocket and unlocked the door. Taking a deep breath, she snatched open the door and stepped out onto the porch.

"There she is!" a gruff male voice shouted from across the street.

"Look at her! Opening up, like yesterday never even happened!" another screamed, joining the first man.

Totally taken aback by the men, Ellari couldn't speak. She could only stare at the angry band of factory workers approaching her.

"What have you got to say for yourself, Miss High-'n'-Mighty pharmacist?" a third voice yelled. "How's it feel to have that poor lad's blood on your hands?"

Stunned and confused, Ellari found her voice. "I didn't kill Willie."

"You might as well have. You let him die!"

"What gives you the right to play God and decide who lives and who dies?" yet another roared.

"No! I did everything I could to save him, but it was too late. By the time he got to me, he'd already lost too much blood. There was nothing else I could do. He severed an artery when he fell down at the glass factory. David Nylander is responsible for Willie Knowles' death. You know it, and I know it. I even told Willie's parents he was too sick and shouldn't go back into the factory, but they didn't believe me. No child should be forced to work in those conditions, especially one who was sick and could collapse on the glass that litters the floor at the factory, the way Willie did. Why aren't you up in arms against David Nylander? He's the one who killed Willie Knowles, not I."

"Give up lady. We're on to you. You thought if you let the boy die, it'd make us side with you an' blame the man who puts food on our tables and roofs over our heads by hirin' our kids to work for

246

him, didn't you? Well, you was wrong, and you ain't gettin' away with meddlin' in our affairs no more. Why don't you go somewhere else and peddle your advice? We don't want it."

"This is insanity!" Ellari cried. "Can't you see I'm on your side? I'm trying to save lives, not take them. I did everything I could to save Willie. I would never—"

A piece of rotten fruit from the back of the crowd whizzed past Ellari's head and splattered on the doorframe. "We don't need your kind o' help!"

More rotten fruit flew at her, several chunks hitting her this time, spraying juice and matter into her face and hair.

The shattering retort of a revolver brought the attack to an abrupt halt. Everyone froze, their surprised gazes fixed on the barefoot, bare-chested man who stood at Ellari's side, his firearm smoking. "All right! That's enough! You men go on home, or the next shot I fire won't be into the air." He leveled the barrel at the crowd.

Slowly, the angry gathering began to back away, but not without muttering and grumbling among themselves as they did. "Just remember what we told you, harlot!" a man yelled once the group reached the other side of the street.

"Why you—" Trigg lifted his gun as if he were going to fire, and the demonstrators took off running in every direction.

"Don't shoot," Ellari pleaded, placing a shaking hand on his arm. "Maybe they're right. I did think

247

Willie's death would make them see what Nylander and men like him are doing to their children, so maybe I let—"

"Stop that!" Trigg growled, grabbing her arm and backing into the store with her in tow. "You're not responsible for that boy's death, and I don't want to hear another word about it."

Inside, he dropped his hold on her, slammed and locked the door, then flipped over the "CLOSED" sign and pulled the shade, all in one agitated action.

"I want you to go upstairs and start packing your things," he snarled, jerking down the blind on the display window. "We're leaving here."

"What are you talking about? I can't go anywhere. I have to—"

Trigg whirled around to face her, his expression livid. "God dammit, Ellari. Are you totally dense? You're through here! You've done all you can for these people, and no one wants your help! Haven't they made that clear enough for you? NO ONE WANTS YOUR HELP!"

Each emphasized word hit Ellari with the force of a punch in the ribs. "That's not true," she whispered.

"Not anyone, Ellari," he repeated, his tone more gentle this time and filled with sympathy. "Not the factory owners, not the factory workers, not your neighbors, not the parents of the children you say you're trying to help. No one!"

Crossing her arms across her chest, she jutted

her chin. "I'm not leaving. I don't care about those other people. It's the children I'm trying to save, and no matter what you say, they still need me. Without me they have no voice."

His bare chest heaving with frustration, Trigg didn't speak for a moment. "We don't have to go far," he finally said. "And it doesn't have to be permanent. Just until things cool down here. We could go to Joliet. It's not more than thirty miles, but we could produce the Magicure there without worrying that the next person through the front door is going to shoot one of us, or burn us out. But it's close enough that I can make regular trips back to Chicago to sell the cream. Then after a year or so, when we've made enough money for you to open your clinic and afford to fight Nylander, we can move the whole operation back here if that's what you still want to do."

"I can't be gone for a year. Too much can happen in that long a time. Too many children can die in a year. I have to stay here, so that I'm ready when the opportunity to do something presents itself. Besides, I have to be here for the mothers and the children. I've no doubt they still need and want my help, whether or not the husbands and fathers do. We'll just have to run Magicure from here, as we agreed to do—that is if you still want to go into business with me."

Trigg shook his head. "You are one stubborn woman, Ellari Lochridge. Okay, I'll agree to stay here as planned, as long as you don't forget you agreed to back off this fight with Nylander until we've made enough profit to give me back my investment and pay off my creditors."

"I was hoping after what happened to Willie you'd release me from that part of our bargain, maybe even help me fight him."

Trigg's mouth dropped open in amazement. "You've got to be joking,. After what happened this morning, I'm more determined to hold you to our agreement than I was before." He stepped forward and put his arms around her, clasping his hands at the small of her back. "In case you don't realize it, I have more reasons for keeping you safe than just Magicure."

"You do?" Her eyes wide with wonder, she searched his face.

"I do. You mean a lot to me, Ellari, and I don't want anything—or anyone to ruin that."

"You don't?"

"I guess what I'm trying to say is, I—" He stopped speaking as if someone had cut his vocal cords. He looked embarrassed.

She couldn't believe her eyes and ears. Trigg was actually acting as if he were shy.

"I guess—I—uh—well, you know."

"No, I don't know."

"Well—it's like this. You're the first woman—except my mother—who ever got me to wondering what it would be like to settle down in one place and maybe even—hell, I just don't want anything to happen to you. Can we leave it at that?"

250

Ellari smiled, so touched by his confession that she didn't even care that he hadn't been able to say the actual words she so wanted to hear. The ones he had said were close enough for now. He had all but admitted he loved her, and she would hang onto that, find strength in it.

Her hands moving of their own volition, she caressed his rough, unshaven cheeks. "Of course, we can leave it at that."

Trigg studied her for a moment, as though there was something else he wanted to say. Finally, he said, "Seems like I remember a note about somebody promising to fix me breakfast. I hope that wasn't a dream. I'm starved."

Ellari laughed. "No, it wasn't a dream. But you're always starved."

Trigg bathed and shaved while Ellari cooked eggs, bacon and biscuits, served with fresh butter bought the day before from Mrs. O'Leary, and orange marmalade another customer had used to pay her bill earlier in the week.

"Mmm, that smells good," he said, coming up behind her at the stove and wrapping his arms around her waist. He ducked his head and kissed her on the side of the neck. "And so do you!" He took a pretend bite. "In fact—"

Giggling, Ellari picked up her spatula and swatted him on the back of the hand. "You'd better behave, or you're going to make me burn your breakfast—and if you're not going to let me open the drugstore so I can earn some money until we

251

get Magicure going, we can't afford to waste a bite."

She twisted out of his embrace and opened the oven. "Ah, perfect." She grabbed a thick towel and used it to remove a pan of lightly browned biscuits.

"Mmm, those look great." Trigg grabbed for a biscuit. "I'd better test them."

Ellari gave him a pseudo-stern glance and dipped the pan out of his reach. "Just wait!" she exclaimed, slapping at his outstretched hand. "Didn't your mother teach you it's not polite to−?"

She stopped herself, horrified by her own thoughtless words. "Oh, Trigg. I'm sorry. I shouldn't have−" She thrust the pan toward him. "Here, you don't have to wait."

Trigg flashed his winning grin at her. "Hey, don't worry about it," he chuckled. "I admit it. Manners were the last thing my mother and I worried about. Just keeping enough food in our bellies and a roof over our heads was our biggest concern. But now that I've got you to teach me those I didn't pick up along the way, it'll all even out. I'll teach you to have fun and you can teach me which fork to use."

With an exaggerated flourish, he pulled out her chair and waited for her to sit down. "My lady."

Am I? she asked him silently. *Am I really your lady? Oh, I hope so.* Flushed, she set the biscuits on the table and sat down.

All through breakfast, they kept their conversation light. They talked about the heat, the need for rain, the chance that the fires this year would out-number the record six hundred from the summer before—anything to keep from thinking about what was really on both their minds: Willie's death and the growing number of enemies they were collecting.

"That has to be the best breakfast I've ever had," Trigg finally said, popping the final bite of the last biscuit into his mouth. He leaned back in his chair and patted his stomach.

"Even better than your 'French landlady' could make?" Ellari teased mischievously. "You said she was the best cook you ever knew."

Trigg shrugged and picked up his plate. "That was before I met you. Her cooking was good, all right, but nothing she fixed compared to your bis-cuits. How do you get them so light?"

She cocked her head to the side and assumed a mysterious moue. "If I told you all my secrets, you wouldn't need me anymore."

He scooted his chair back on the plank floor and picked up her plate. He matched her taunt with a blatantly sexual grin. "I'm sure we could find something you'd be good for."

Blushing, Ellari gasped.

Chuckling, he carried the plates to the sink. "But as long as we're on the subject of your family secrets, we'd better get moving. I've got to pick up those jars and labels I ordered yesterday, and you need to go buy the ingredients you'll be needing—

unless you want me to pick up everything while I'm out." He glanced over his shoulder and gave her a deliberately testing grin. "I mean, it wouldn't be any trouble."

"It won't work, Trigg," she said, joining him at the sink with the rest of the dirty dishes in hand and giving him a look that said she knew what he was up to. "Even if you knew the ingredients I use in the emollient, it would do you no good. Half the secret is in the processing and the amounts I use of each ingredient. So I'm afraid you're stuck with me if you want to produce the Magicure."

Trigg grinned and took her into his arms. "I can't think of anywhere I'd rather be stuck."

Chapter Fourteen

With a sigh of satisfaction, Ellari spooned the remainder of the latest batch of Magicure into a pink two-ounce jar. Setting the cooking pot aside, she hurriedly began twisting lids onto the newly filled jars lined up on her kitchen table.

When she was through and had cleaned the utensils she used to prepare the emollient, she flopped down on the divan in the living room with a groan. What a couple of weeks it had been—actually it had been only twelve days, but it felt to her more like thirty!

It was a good thing she had let Trigg talk her into closing the drugstore for a while—not only to give the tempers of the people who blamed her for Willie's death time to cool down, but to give herself and Trigg a chance to establish a reserve of Magicure to sell once she opened the store again. Then she wouldn't have time to spend all day mixing the formula.

The big problem was, they could never get ahead.

It was taking all her energy and time to keep up with the demand. No matter how much Magicure she produced each day while Trigg was out selling what she had prepared the day before, he returned each evening sold out. In fact, the salve was selling so well, it had been necessary to replenish her initial supplies five times already in the twelve days since they had begun—six if she counted the trip she had to make to town tomorrow. In fact, he got rid of it so fast, she had accused Trigg of feeding what she had mixed to the pigs.

Of course, she had been teasing about the pigs, especially in view of the pockets full of dollar bills he'd returned to the drugstore with each evening. Not only was it obvious that he was really selling it, but the cream seemed to be every bit as popular as he had predicted it would be. Of course, she had no doubt, his winning smile and the appealing pink jars he'd chosen to use were definitely contributing factors in their immediate success. In a brown jar, she was sure it wouldn't have been nearly as appealing.

She wasn't complaining. She knew the more jars of Magicure they sold, the faster Trigg would be able to earn back his investment and pay off his debts, so they could begin to concentrate on a way to fight Nylander and his cronies. And the way things were going, that day wouldn't be long in coming.

"What's this?" Trigg boomed as he entered the apartment. "I'm out killing myself to make us rich, and I come home to find you lolling on the divan like a lady of leisure?"

Startled, Ellari sat up straight, an explanation on her lips. "I just that minute sat down! I ran out of ingredients again and—"

"Hey," Trigg laughed, taking hold of her hands and drawing her to her feet, "can't you tell by now when I'm kidding?"

Embarrassed, Ellari tried to cover for herself. "Of course I can. You just caught me by surprise."

He pulled her into his arms and pecked her forehead, her nose, then her lips. "Tell you what. To make up for how hard you've been working, what do you say I take you out to dinner tonight?"

"Out to dinner?" she repeated, excitement tripping in her chest. The closest she'd ever been to going out to dinner with a man was the picnic they'd had at Lincoln Park before. "You mean, in a nice restaurant?"

"A 'nice' restaurant isn't exactly what I had in mind."

"Oh." She didn't mean to let the disappointment show in her voice, but she knew it did. "Of course you didn't. I don't know what I was thinking. A nice restaurant would be entirely too expensive. After all, we're only getting our business started." She forced a bright smile, feeling guilty that she might have made Trigg feel bad because he couldn't afford to take her somewhere nice.

She hurried to make up for her thoughtless words. "We could go to that little place where you bought our picnic lunch—what did you call it? A delicatessen? I liked it there. Or, for that matter, we don't have to go out at all. I have some leftover boiled ham and—"

Trigg shook his head, his eyes twinkling with suppressed amusement. "I was thinking of somewhere a little fancier than sandwiches or leftovers. Actually, the place I have in mind is a lot fancier."

"Fancier? I don't understand. I thought you said we couldn't afford to go to a nice—"

Trigg put two fingers to her lips to shush her. "I didn't say we couldn't afford it. You did. When I said 'nice' wasn't what I had in mind, you assumed I meant less than nice, when what I meant was *better* than nice."

"Better than nice?"

"Fancy, elegant, luxurious, extravagant," he expounded. Taking a step back from her, he lifted her hand to his lips and kissed the back of it. "Miss Lochridge, will you do me the honor of joining me this evening for dinner in the Grand Dining Room of the Palmer House?"

Aghast, Ellari stared over her own hand into his mischievously sparkling eyes. "The Palmer House?! Really? You're teasing me, aren't you?"

He tilted his head and lifted his eyebrows in an expression that said, *What do you think?* "Well, which is it going be?" he asked aloud. "The Grand Dining Room, or leftover boiled ham?"

Unable to adjust to the idea of plain and ordinary Ellari Lochridge at the Palmer House, she didn't know what to say. She had dreamed of seeing the inside of the eight-story, mansard-roofed hotel since it had opened the past fall, but she had never dared to think she actually ever would have dinner there. "Oh, it sounds wonderful, but we really shouldn't. We can't afford such an extravagant evening out. We need to save our—"

"Shh! I don't want to hear any more of that. We've had a great start, all because of you, and you deserve a reward. I'm taking you to dinner at the Palmer House tonight, and that's all there is to it."

"But—"

He raised his eyebrows and cocked his head to the side. "What did I say?"

"But-I-can't-go-I-don't-have-anything-to-wear!" she said, running her words together to get them out before he could stop her.

He looked surprised. "You don't?"

Embarrassed, Ellari gave him an annoyed glance. "You know very well I don't have anything suitable to wear to a fine place like the Palmer House. I told you the most dressy gown I own was the one I wore on the picnic, and that would hardly be suitable for the Palmer House!"

"Then, I guess that evening dress I saw hanging down in the storeroom belongs to someone else. It's a shame though. It looked like it was just your size."

"What dress ha—" Her stunned eyes grew wide with understanding.

Trigg grinned. "Well, aren't you going to go see if

259

you can figure out who it belongs to?"

"You bought me a dress?" Ellari asked, taking a moment to let this latest surprise sink in. When it did, she threw her arms around his neck and kissed his face profusely. "You are the dearest, sweetest, most thoughtful man in the world. No one ever bought me a dress before, and I've never even had an evening dress on. I love—it."

"Hey, you haven't seen it yet. What if it's ugly? What if it's purple with green and orange dots on it? And what if one sleeve is longer than the other? Will you love it then?"

Her eyes filled with tears. "It won't matter. No matter what it looks like, I'm going to love it!"

"Whew!" He made an exaggerated wipe across his forehead with the back of his hand. "Then you won't mind if to get a really good price on it I had to take one with the bustle in the front, will you?"

With a giggle and a playful swat on his arm, she started to run. "Not if you won't mind being seen with me in it."

When Ellari stepped out of her bedroom an hour and a half later, her eyes shimmering, her uncertain smile trembling, Trigg felt the breath literally leave his lungs. Never, as long as he had lived, had he seen anything so beautiful as Ellari Lochridge in the pale green shot silk evening dress he had bought for her.

He took a step toward her. "I knew when I saw

260

this dress that it was pretty and would match your eyes. But I had no idea how truly exquisite it would be once you were in it."

Ellari blushed and put a hand to her chest above the low, scooped neckline. "Thank you. But are you sure the woman who sold you this dress knew what she was talking about when she said that low necklines and short, puffed sleeves are the style for evening gowns these days? It seems awfully risqué."

Suddenly her expression was stricken with horror. "I just had a terrible thought! Do you think she knew about us? Maybe this is the kind of dress a rich man would buy for his 'kept woman'!"

Trigg grinned. "I assure you, all the ladies in the very 'nice' restaurant where I had that unsuccessful dinner meeting the first day I met you wore dresses with the same kinds of necklines and sleeves—and very few of them looked like they would be *any-body's* 'kept woman.' " He lifted her chin and kissed her lips briefly. "Trust me. You're perfect for the occasion. Everyone will think you're a princess visiting Chicago from Europe."

Slightly appeased, Ellari blessed him with a hesitant smile. "I still don't feel right about showing my arms and—bosom—to strangers. I feel as if I'm flaunting the fact that you and I are lo—I think I'm going to get the shawl you gave me. Just in case you're wrong about what a decent woman wears out in the evening." She whirled back toward the bedroom.

"Maybe these will help," he said, reaching around

her and dangling a pair of very long white gloves in front of her face.

"You devil!" she squealed, snatching the satiny gloves out of his hand. "I knew there was something missing!" She hurriedly shoved her hands into the gloves and stretched them up over her elbows. "That's a little bit better."

"One more thing," he said, reaching into his pocket and producing a black velvet box.

"For me? What is it?"

"Why don't you open it and see? Maybe it's those family jewels you said you didn't have."

Gingerly, Ellari lifted the lid of the box. When she saw its contents, her mouth dropped open and her confused gaze shot up to Trigg's face. "I don't understand? How could you aff — I mean, the dress was extravagant enough. I shouldn't even take it. But I definitely can't accept such an expensive gift."

She slammed down the lid and shoved the box toward him. "How could you be so foolish? You're supposed to be spending all of our profits to pay off your creditors sooner, not buying me an emerald necklace and earrings!"

"Hey, relax! They're not real. I wish they were, and I plan to replace them with the genuine thing some day. But for now, I'm afraid the only family jewels I could afford to buy you are just glass. I got them for almost nothing from the woman who sold me the dress."

She looked stunned. "Glass? But they look so real."

"I thought so too. That's why I bought them. Besides, just because I can't afford to buy you the real thing—yet—doesn't mean you shouldn't start getting used to wearing nice things now. In case I haven't told you, lady, we're going to be rich. Now, turn around and let me put this necklace on you."

Turning her back to him, she lifted her hair off her neck so that he could clasp the necklace. A wave of sadness trembled through her as she tried to ignore the nagging voice inside her head that kept saying, *If you let him squander the profits on gifts and clothes and taking you places like the Palmer House for dinner, it will be forever before we pay off his creditors—and even longer until we can resume the fight against Nylander and child labor. You should tell him to take everything back and use the money the way we intended.*

"There you are!" he exclaimed. "Now turn around and let me see you."

Ellari glanced down at the emerald-colored drop resting just above the exposed shadow of cleavage of her breasts, and her eyes filled with tears. Just this once didn't she have a right to do something purely for own pleasure without feeling guilty.

She made her decision. Ignoring that pragmatic voice inside her head that had kept her a prisoner in her own home for the past five years. She spun around to face Trigg, her smile as bright as the stone shivering on her bosom.

Practicality be damned, tonight she was going to break out of her jail. She was going to the Palmer

House for dinner. She was going to wear the glass emeralds and the beautiful dress Trigg had given her. And she was going to love every minute of it. Tomorrow she would be sensible. But tonight . . . tonight was going to be hers.

A warm, satisfied glow tripped through Trigg as he looked down at the beautiful woman resting her head on his shoulder. Smiling, he tightened his hold on her so that she wouldn't be jostled too severely during the bumpy ride in the hack he'd hired to take them home.

Home. The very word sent an intense longing surging through him. All his life, he'd secretly wished for the right to use that word, but it had always escaped him. Of course, when his mother was alive, wherever she was had been "home" to him. But even then, there was never any real sense of the true meaning of the word home: a place where you were safe, a place where you could be yourself, a place where you belonged, a place where no matter what your faults were, you were accepted and lov—

Hold on there, old man! That kind of thinking is going to get you in trouble.

He glanced down at Ellari and smiled. The evening had been perfect: the dinner, the conversation, the pride he'd felt when every head in the Grand Dining Room had turned to admire Ellari when she had entered on his arm, the way her eyes had sparkled as she had taken in the lavish surroundings, the way she had giggled when the bubbles of her first champagne had pelted the tip of her nose. All of it.

For a while he'd even believed this feeling could go on indefinitely. That was until he had spotted a man he was sure looked familiar watching him from several tables away.

He wouldn't have thought anything of it if the man had been staring so openly at Ellari, but unlike everyone else in the room, this man hadn't been nearly so interested in Ellari as he was in Trigg himself. And while the men who were admiring Ellari lifted glasses in salute to Trigg's good fortune when he caught them staring, the instant Trigg made eye contact with this man, he had ducked his face behind the menu he was supposedly reading—but not before Trigg saw a hint of satisfaction pass over his features.

Of course, it could be one of Nylander's men, Trigg tried to convince himself, but he didn't think so. At least, he didn't recognize the man as one of the four men who had taken turns watching the drugstore and followed his every action since his last meeting with Nylander.

Besides, he'd already spied Nylander's evening man watching them from the bar. And Nylander's men dressed in nondescript suits and seemed to blend into any atmosphere, even the Grand Dining Room of the Palmer House. On the other hand, the roughly dressed man hiding behind his menu didn't.

No, he didn't work for Nylander. Still, Trigg couldn't escape the feeling that he'd seen him before. But where?

Trigg adjusted his arm around Ellari as he searched his mind for where he might recognize the man from. Could he be one of Boss Stahl's men? Trigg tossed out that idea. Stahl's men may be thugs, but even they could dress well enough to not stand out at the Palmer House. Who was he? And who was he working for?

Then it hit Trigg with a jolt. The time Nylander had given him was up day after tomorrow. Obviously, the man at the Palmer House was the man Nylander was saving to take care of Ellari if Trigg didn't marry her or get her to leave town. *Damn! This puts a whole new light on things. I could've sworn Nylander was bluffing!*

The hack came to an abrupt halt in front of Ellari's drugstore. "You sure this is where you want out, mister?" the driver called back over his shoulder. "This is a pretty rough neighborhood for a coupla swells to be out in at night."

"We'll be fine," Trigg growled. "How much do I owe you?"

"That'll be a dollar fifty. I charge extra to come to this part of town."

Trigg handed him two dollars. "Keep the change," he said, gently shaking Ellari. "Ellari, wake up. We're home."

Ellari lifted her head and glanced around groggily. "I must have fallen asleep," she giggled. Her head fell back to his shoulder and her eyes fluttered shut again.

Certain she was in no condition to walk, Trigg lifted her into his arms and stepped out of the hack. The instant they were clear of the wheels, the driver cracked his whip over his horse's back and drove off.

Glancing up the street, Trigg saw not one, but two more hacks stop and let passengers out at two different places and on opposite sides of the street in the next block. He couldn't see the face of the one man, but by the way he carried himself, Trigg was sure it was Nylander's evening watch.

However, the passenger from the second hack passed directly under a street lamp, and Trigg was able to make out clearly the swarthy features for a full two seconds before the man stepped into the shadows.

"Damn," he muttered, looking down at the sleeping woman in his arms. "We're a regular parade, aren't we?" Doing his best to look unrattled, he casually stepped into the alley that sided the pharmacy. Once he was sure the men following him couldn't see them, he took off at a run to the back alley—and door to the pharmacy.

Safely inside the shop, he fumbled with the lock to secure the door without dropping Ellari. That done, he sagged back against the door to catch his breath. His strength restored, he took the stairs up to the apartment two at a time and carried her straight through to her bedroom.

As he lowered her to the bed, Ellari opened her eyes and smiled. "Hello there," she cooed dreamily, reaching up to loop her arms around his neck. "Have I told you this is the most wonderful night of my life?"

Grinning, Trigg unhooked her fingers from behind his head and started to straighten up. "Only a dozen or so times—but who's counting?"

She frowned, then clasped her hands around his neck again. "In that case, did I tell you the dress you gave me is the most beautiful dress I've ever seen?"

"Yes, Ellari, you told me that too." Again he tried to disentangle her hands from his neck. "Now, why don't you—"

She tightened her hold. "Well, did I tell you I never tasted champagne before tonight?"

"Even that," he laughed. "Now, let's get you out of this dress and into bed."

Ellari grinned mischievously. "Are you planning on having your way with me, sir?" she asked, trying to sit up. "Because if you are—" she stopped, her forehead pleating as she obviously tried to remember what she'd been going to say.

Wanting nothing more than to pursue the entertaining conversation, Trigg regretfully shook his head. "Not tonight, love. I've got some—"

"Because if you intend to have your way with me, you need to get rid of some of these clothes." With surprising strength, she grabbed his lapels and tore his coat off his shoulders and flipped him over onto his back. Before he could react, she pinned him to the bed with her own body.

"Ellari!" He couldn't decide whether to laugh or to cry. This bawdy, aggressive Ellari was a side to her he would have enjoyed getting to know, but he couldn't. Not tonight.

He grabbed her hands, which were clumsily attempting to unfasten the buttons on his shirt, and tried to get her attention. "Ellari!"

"Mmm?" she asked, giving up her feat and laying her head down on his chest.

"I have to go downstairs and check the locks. Why don't you get ready for bed, and I'll be back in a few minutes. Okay? Ellari? Ellari?"

Her answer was a snort.

Great, she's passed out. Well, at least now she won't know I'm gone. Careful not to disturb her, he slid out from under Ellari. Standing up, he straightened his clothes and started to leave. Then he thought better of it. She would sleep more soundly in a nightgown. He'd better take the time to change her and get her settled in bed — in case this took longer than he thought it would.

Minutes later, Trigg crept down the dark stairway to the pharmacy. Lifting the shade, he peeked outside to make sure Nylander's man was across the street. There he was, just the way he'd been every night, but he wasn't the one who had Trigg worried. It was the other one, and he was nowhere in sight.

There's only one way to handle the situation. With a disgusted grunt, he moved the shelf blocking the door aside. A minute later, he crossed the street and approached Nylander's watchdog, who nervously glanced from side to side. Obviously, his orders didn't include what to do if Trigg spoke to him.

"Evening," Trigg said casually. "Where's your pal? Around back?"

"What pal's that?" the man asked in return.

"You know. Nylander's other man, the one who followed us from the Palmer House the same time you did."

"I don't know who you're talking about."

"One thing I don't get though," Trigg went on as if the other man hadn't spoken, "is why if you're working together didn't you share a cab? How does Nylander feel about you two wasting money like that?" Without warning, Trigg grabbed the smaller man by his coat front and slammed him up against a wall. "Who is he?"

"You're crazy, Hanahan," the man said with a forced laugh, but giving himself away with bulging, nervous eyes. "I swear to God I don't know who that fellow was. I didn't see him at the Palmer House, but I did see him when he got out of that hack. But from the way he was dressed, I just figured he was from the neighborhood, and it was a coincidence all our hacks got here 'bout the same time."

Trigg tightened his grip and pressed his fists harder against the man's neck. "A coincidence, huh?"

Now the man was really starting to look frightened. "I give you my word, he wasn't with me. I was working alone, like I been doing every evening since Mr. Nylander hired me to keep a eye on you and that pharmacist lady until my relief comes at three in the mornin'."

Trigg studied the man. Like all the men he knew to be working for Nylander, this one was young, nice-looking—if a bit on the effeminate side—and decently dressed. And as was the case with the others, none of them looked as though this was his regular line of work. In fact, now that he thought about it, this one looked as if he would spill his guts at a moment's notice, rather than chance being hit.

"Let's just suppose I believe you don't know who that fellow was," Trigg said, "did you 'happen' to see where he went after he got out of his cab?"

"Yeah. He came this way, walking sort of slow. But when he got to the corner there, he turned and took off running."

Trigg eyed the intersection half a block up. The alley behind Ellari's pharmacy crossed that same street. "About the same time Miss Lochridge and I—"

"—went into the alley beside the store," the man finished for him. "That's when I figured it was a coincidence we all arrived at the same time."

Trigg released his hold on the man's coat. "You'd better not be lying to me, friend." Without waiting for the other man to respond, Trigg made a dash

271

across the street and into the alley. He was more sure than ever that the man who'd been stalking them this evening was Nylander's other man, and that he was already preparing to act the instant Trigg's time was up.

Well, pal, you picked the wrong fellow to tangle with.

Once he was safely hidden in the shadows he crouched low and hurried toward the back alley. Because he and Ellari had used the rear entrance exclusively since they had closed the pharmacy, he had no doubt that was where he would find the would-be killer.

Pausing at the corner, Trigg peered cautiously around the building. Though he'd been sure the man would be there, when he actually saw him sitting on a wooden crate in front of the pharmacy's storage shed, his heart skipped a beat and he felt the sweat break out on his forehead and upper lip.

He'd never killed a man, but if it came to that he swore he would. If it meant saving Ellari's life, there was nothing he would not do. But hopefully, it wouldn't come to that!

Drawing his revolver from under his coat, Trigg aimed it and stepped out into the open. "You're trespassing, mister."

Startled, the man leaped up from the box, his eyes jumping from side to side in a desperate search for an escape. "Don't shoot, mister. I was just restin' for a bit. I didn't mean no harm."

"You can drop the act, pal. I know who you are,

and why you're here."

"You do?"

"And you can tell your boss I have everything in hand, so your services won't be required after all. You got that?"

The man nodded. "Everything in hand, services not needed. Yes sir, I'll tell 'im. Can I go now?"

Trigg eyed the man suspiciously for a long, indecisive moment. If he let him go, what assurance was there that he wouldn't come back? On the other hand, he couldn't very well shoot him. Nylander would only hire someone else; someone he wouldn't recognize when he came after them.

Deciding he had no choice but to take a chance, Trigg nodded. "Go on, but be sure you give your boss my message. And while you're at it, tell him I've decided to marry her, so he can stop worrying."

Chapter Fifteen

"We have to talk, Ellari," Trigg said, bringing the wagon to a halt in the alley behind the pharmacy.

Ellari felt a twinge of panic surge in her chest. Trigg had been unusually withdrawn and quiet throughout breakfast, the trip to Lake Street for supplies, and the drive back home, but she had assumed he was just tired from the night before, as was she. Now she wasn't so sure. "I didn't realize we haven't been."

"I mean really talk."

"You sound so serious," she said, fighting not to give in to the apprehension gripping her insides.

"I haven't made any secret of the fact that I've never been the sort who stays in one place for very long," he started, looking at his hands rather than at her.

The ache in her heart tightened. He was going to leave her. She could hear it in his voice. Despite the obvious success of Magicure, and despite the wonderful gifts and romantic evening at the Palmer

House, Trigg was going to leave her.

She wanted to squeeze her eyes closed and clamp her hands over her ears to block out what she knew was coming next. *Oh, Lord, don't let this be happening.*

Retaining the tentative grip on her composure, she stiffened her spine and stared straight ahead. She swore to herself that she wasn't going to cry. "No, I suppose you've been honest with me about your inability to settle down."

"And I didn't give you any reason to believe you'd be stuck with me permanently, but—"

Ellari struggled to swallow the strangling lump in her throat. "No. You didn't." *But I thought once you saw what it was like to have a real home with someone who loved you. . . .*

"The plain facts are, I'm a selfish, uneducated cad who's never called the same place home for more than a few months at a time; and I've done some things in the past I'm not too proud of. You deserve much better than me for a husband—"

The vice around her chest tightened. His words were squeezing the life out of her. *I don't want better! I want you!*

Not trusting herself to refrain from crying her frantic misery aloud, she bit her lip and remained silent. She focused her gaze on her hands twisting a fold of her skirt in her lap and waited for him to continue.

Trigg took a deep breath, then went on. "I know

this is sudden, but I—" He shifted on the wagon bench to face her and reached for her hand. "Ellari, will you marry me?"

Ellari's head shot up and snapped to the side, her eyes wide with unmitigated disbelief. "What did you say?"

"Will you marry me?" he asked again, his voice soft and rife with uncertainty.

When she didn't answer immediately, he nervously started talking again.

"I know I'm not the man your father would have chosen for you. I can't even promise you it's in me to change. But if you'll marry me, I'll do my damndest. I give you my word, I'll do everything in my power to make this marriage work and to make you happy. And I won't ever let anything or anyone hurt you."

"You want to marry me? I thought you—" Suddenly, the truth exploded inside her.

The dam on her tears burst, and she threw her arms around his neck. "Oh, Trigg! I thought you were trying to tell me you were going to leave. Yes, I'll marry you! Yes! Yes! Yes!" she cried between wet kisses.

"You mean you will?" he asked, his voice surprised, relieved.

"Of course I will. How could you ever doubt that I would? I love you."

He tightened his arms around her and hugged her to him. "You won't be sorry, Ellari. I swear to you, you won't be sorry."

A hint of misgiving tripped up her spine, but she hurriedly disregarded it. It did not matter that he hadn't *said* he loved her. He might not even realize it himself; but every day, he showed her in a dozen ways that he did. And one day he would be able to tell her. In the meantime, she had enough love in her heart to sustain them both until he found it in himself to say the actual words. "I know I won't be sorry, Trigg."

"I think we should get married as soon as possible. How does right now sound?"

Ellari laughed. "That's impossible. I want to wear my mother's dress, and I know I'll need to alter it. It could take hours. And—"

"Tomorrow then. I don't want to wait any longer than I have to." He hugged her and laughed. "Now that you've said yes, I don't intend to give you a chance to change your mind."

She giggled and returned his embrace. "That isn't going to happen in a million years. But tomorrow is perfect. I don't want to wait either."

Trigg glanced down at the pocket watch he had recently reclaimed from the pawnbroker with money he'd already earned with profits from Magicure.

Only one hour of freedom left. Damn, he hoped he was doing the right thing—not that he'd really had a hell of a lot of choice once he'd spotted Nylander's backup man closing in on Ellari the night before last at the Palmer House. It was marry her or lose her.

A pang of sorrow shot through him with the thought of Ellari no longer being a part of his life. Frowning, he told himself the reason he didn't want to lose her was because of Magicure, nothing else.

A disbelieving laugh echoed inside his head. *Who're you trying to convince, Hanahan? You like the idea of being married and having a real home and a wife, maybe even kids—like normal people. You're just afraid you can't handle it. You're afraid you're going to mess it up, like you do everything else.*

"That's crazy," he grumbled. "What've I got to be afraid of?"

Determined to see the marriage as nothing but practical, he ignored the part of him that insisted Ellari meant something to him, and that he was actually excited about their marriage and settling down.

It's the smart thing to do! That's all! Even if Nylander wasn't breathing down our necks, it would be the smart thing to do. As long as we're only business partners, there would always be the chance she could meet and marry someone else. And if she married someone else, her husband would have control of her half of Magicure and might try to crowd me out of it altogether. And

*that's one chance I'm not taking — not now that I
know firsthand what a true gold mine Magicure is
turning out to be.*

"Yep, this is definitely the smart thing to do," he
assured himself aloud, fighting the guilt that still
besieged him when he thought about how much
better Ellari deserved than a man like him.

*It's not as if I'm the only one who's going to
profit from this marriage. Even if I'm not the perfect husband for her, I'm going to be there to take
care of her and keep her out of trouble. Besides,
married to me, she's not going to have to worry
about what people are thinking about her any
more. Marriage is going to give her back the respectability she prizes so much, as well as give her
a protector and someone to fix things around the
house. She needs this marriage every bit as much
as I do.*

"I'm going down to make sure the horses and
wagon are secure in the shed," he called at the
closed bedroom door. "Then I'm going out front to
watch for the hack I ordered. I'd hate for him to
pass us by and make us late getting to the church.
I'll come up for you when he gets here."

"I'll be ready," she cheerfully returned from the
other side of the door.

The excitement and happiness in her voice triggered an unexpected joy in his chest, and he
frowned.

Damn! You'd think I was actually looking for-

ward to being tied down to one woman for the rest of my life!

Ellari made a final slow turn in front of the wardrobe mirror. She was entranced by the reflection of herself in her mother's wedding dress. It was amazing how much she looked like the young bride in the framed tintype picture on her dresser. Sewn in silky, cream-colored gauze and lovingly trimmed by Ellari's grandmother with handmade lace and tiny pearl beads, the dress was as beautiful today as it must have been on her parents' wedding day nearly thirty years before in Scotland.

"Oh, Mama," she said, smiling at the photograph, "I'd give anything to have you and Papa here with me today. I know you'd both be so happy for me." She paused and chuckled silently. "Well, Papa might have a problem accepting Trigg, but once he got to know him the way I do, I know he'd come around. And who knows, Trigg might have even been able to teach Papa not to take everything so seriously."

She picked up the treasured picture and held it to her heart, then gently replaced it on the dresser. She checked her hair a last time. She had let it fall loose down her back, the way Trigg liked it. She had adorned it only with her mother's pearl combs and a spray of white flowers Trigg had brought her.

"All I need now is the prayer book and the

handkerchief Mama carried and I'm ready to go," she told the mirror. "The next time you see me, I'll be Mrs. Trigg Hanahan!"

At the sound of a buggy and driver pulling up in front of the drugstore, she ran to the window to look out. The driver glanced around uncertainly. Realizing Trigg must not have finished in back, she called to the driver, "We'll be right down."

When the man waved to indicate that he'd heard her, she whisked up the bouquet of flowers Trigg had given her, the precious prayer book, and the treasured handkerchief, then hurried to the back bedroom.

She quickly unlocked the window and raised it to let Trigg know the hack was waiting. Before she saw him, she heard men's voices directly below.

Curious, she held her tongue and peered out the window. Directly below her, she spotted Trigg standing at the back door of the pharmacy with two other men. She started to call out to him, but caught herself. He was engrossed in what sounded like a heated argument with a well-dressed older gentleman. The other stranger was roughly-garbed and stood slightly off to the side, obviously absorbed in the conversation, but not taking part in it. None of the men noticed Ellari's presence.

Sensing that Trigg was in trouble, she resisted her impulse to interrupt. Maybe it was one of those creditors he was always talking about. Her mind racing with possibilities, she concentrated on the conversation below and on a way to help Trigg if he needed her.

"I swear to you, Mr. Phelps, I had every intention of calling on your daughter. I still do. I just thought it would be better if I waited until my new business got going and I had gotten a little bit ahead financially. I'd like to be able to afford to escort her to places a lady of her station deserves to be taken."

Confused, Ellari strained to hear better. What was he talking about? What did Trigg have to do with this man and his daughter? And why would he take her anywhere?

"Forget it, Hanahan. Mr. Keedy—" The man Trigg had called Mr. Phelps indicated the third man with his head. "—told me all about this 'new business' of yours. Don't forget, he saw you at the Palmer House Friday night. You were openly flaunting your disregard for our arrangement, as well as betraying your betrothal to my daughter with that 'new business' of yours, and you're not going to get away with it."

Ellari's heart sank with a sickening weight to the pit of her belly. Did he say "betrothal"? Was Trigg betrothed to another woman?

Trigg narrowed his eyes at Keedy, then looked back at Phelps. "I don't know what Mr. Keedy told you, Mr. Phelps. But if you'll let me explain, I'm sure we can straighten this out."

"This should be interesting."

"First of all, the other night was a business dinner. That's all it was. Miss Lochridge is my business partner. I wasn't betraying you or your daughter. We were there to discuss business."

Business? Ellari's stomach turned a violent somersault. She began to feel ill.

"What kind of business requires you to share the bed of a beautiful woman who isn't your wife?" Phelps spit out. "Or your betrothed?"

Trigg gave a forced chuckle. "I can see how you'd think that was what happened, but you're wrong. I've only been staying here to save money. I sleep downstairs on the examination couch."

"Come now, Mr. Hanahan. Do you take me for a total fool? You've been caught in your own lies, and I want to know what you intend to do about it. Are you going to break it off with this woman and marry my daughter, as we agreed? Or am I going to go to Boss Stahl and rescind my guarantee of the money you owe him at the same time I tell him where to find you and your 'business partner'? I'll give you until tomorrow noon to make your decision." Phelps turned to go.

Ellari had heard all she could bear. How could she have been such a fool. Trigg had never loved her. He had obviously promised to marry that man's daughter in exchange for financial help, then had decided it would be more profitable to marry her instead—in exchange for the unlimited profits he hoped to make with Magicure.

Hurt churned into anger, anger into wrath.

"Give him your answer now, Trigg!" she screamed out the window, hurling her bridal bouquet down onto the surprised men below. "Mr. Phelps, if your daughter wants this lying, cheating, womanizing scoundrel, she's more than welcome to him! I never want to see him again!"

Without waiting for a response, she slammed down the window and raced from the room, tearing flowers and combs from her hair as she went. Only taking time to bolt the apartment door, she ran for the safety of her own bedroom and threw herself onto her bed and sobbed. Never again, as long as she lived, would she trust a man.

"Ellari!" Trigg hollered, pounding on the door to her apartment. "You've got to let me explain."

"I don't want to hear any more of your explanations, Trigg Hanahan," she finally answered from the other side of the door he had pounded on for the past twenty minutes. "You're a liar and a cheat and an opportunist, and I don't want anything more to do with you. My father was right when he told me not to trust men like you. You only care about yourself. You'll do and say anything to get what you want. Even propose to a woman you don't love if the reward is big enough. Tell me, how many other women think they are betrothed to you?"

"No other women!" he protested. "You're the only woman I've ever asked to marry me. The only one I've ever wanted to marry."

She released a bitter, strangled laugh. "I'm sure that's what you told us all, including that Phelps woman when you proposed to her."

"I didn't propose to her, Ellari! Or to anyone else!" His hands splayed open on the door, he dropped his forehead forward and pressed it to the wood. "Please," he begged in a tortured groan, "you've got to believe me. I've only seen Phelps's daughter once in my life, and I didn't ask her to marry me!"

"You can't stop lying, can you? Are you going to try to tell me now that I didn't hear you tell that man I was nothing to you but a business partner?"

"I know what you heard, Ellari, but it was all a mistake. I was only putting him off until—"

"It was a mistake, all right. And you're the one who made it! You tried to make fools of us all; Mr. Phelps, his daughter and me. But you were found out. So you can crawl back under that rock of yours and leave me alone!"

"Please, Ellari. Let me in so I can explain."

"I told you, I don't want to hear any more of your lies. I want you to leave."

"I'm not leaving until you hear me out!"

"Go away, Trigg," she hollered. He could hear her walking away from the door.

"Ellari!" he shouted, resuming his pounding on

285

the door. A door slammed inside the apartment. Obviously, she was in her bedroom. He raised his voice. "I'm warning you, Ellari! Either you get back out here and listen to me, or I'm coming through this door."

There was a long silence in the apartment. "Ellari?" he bellowed. "I mean it! I'll break it down!"

After another long silence, he heard footsteps approaching the door. "If I listen, then will you leave?"

"After you've heard my side of this, I'll go, if you still want me to," he said reluctantly.

"All right." A sound as if someone were sliding down the other side of the door followed. "Go on, I'm listening."

Trigg took a deep breath and sat down on the top stair and leaned back on the door. He could imagine her sitting in the same position on the other side of the door, her back to his and her arms stubbornly crossed over her chest.

He felt like a bastard. She was the sweetest, most honest, most giving person he'd ever known, and he'd done this to her. He couldn't even blame her for the way she was feeling right now. He didn't deserve her forgiveness. But whether he deserved it or not, he didn't intend to give up until he got it.

"Well," she said impatiently. "What are you waiting for? If you've got something to say, say it!"

"I don't know where to start. It's all pretty complicated. You have to understand that I was really desperate when I agreed to court Phelps's daughter and—"

"—marry her," Ellari interrupted.

"No! You're wrong. I never told Phelps I would marry her. I only agreed to court her, in exchange for Phelps buying me some time with Boss Stahl—Stahl's the Levee saloon owner who was threatening to have me killed if I didn't pay him the thousand dollars I owed him by the next day."

"Come now, Trigg. If the subject of marriage never came up, what gave Mr. Phelps the idea his daughter was betrothed to you? And why didn't you point that out to him when he confronted you in the alley?"

"Of course, the subject came up. It was clear that was what he ultimately wanted to happen. He even said he would pay off all my debts and set me up in my own business the day I made his daughter my wife. But I swear to you, I only agreed to call on her and see what developed. I never promised I was going to marry her. Don't you see? I had to buy some time until I could find another way to pay off Stahl. I didn't have another choice."

"Until Magicure and I entered this heartbreaking story. From the very beginning, that's all I was to you—a way to get rich and pay off your creditors. I can't believe I was so naive. I actually thought you were helping me because you were a decent person under that self-seeking facade of yours. I believed you truly cared about me and wanted to protect me from Nylander, when all along it was only the formula for my cream you wanted to protect."

"That's not true. I do care about you. And I do want to protect you. Hell, I didn't know about the cream the first day I came into your drugstore, and I fought that worker to save you, didn't I?"

"Hmph. It wouldn't surprise me to learn that you'd heard about that cream and deliberately hired Mr. Schmelzel to frighten me so that you could be the great hero and save me—and worm your way into my favor."

Trigg cringed with guilt. She was right. That sounded exactly like something he'd have done if that was the only way to get his hands on the cream, but he didn't intend to admit it. "And I suppose I deliberately got myself knifed in the process? Even for me, that's a little extreme, don't you think?"

"I wouldn't put it past you. It wasn't that serious a wound, and it certainly helped to convince me you were genuine. But whether or not you knew about the cream that first day, it doesn't change the fact that you recognized its value the day after we met, or that everything you've done for me and with me since that day—including asking me to marry you—has been calculated to gain control of my formula. For all I know, you were behind everything bad that has happened since I've known you."

Trigg hung his head in defeat. "You're right about one thing. From the minute I saw how well that cream worked on my wound, I realized I could make a lot of money with it. But that doesn't mean I would deliberately hurt or threaten you. And it doesn't mean I didn't—don't—care about you or what happens to you. Because I want to be rich and successful doesn't mean I don't love you and want to ma—" He broke off, the delayed reaction to what he'd just said exploding in his head. Was it true? Did he love her?

A startled, choking gasp from the other side of the door echoed through the silence. "Just leave, Trigg. I don't want to hear any more of your lies. I told you I'd listen, and I have. Now I want you go away and never come back."

"Okay," he said with resignation. He stood up. "I'll leave for now, but I'll be back. We're still business partners, and you're not going to get rid of me so easily. You're stuck with me."

"We'll see what my lawyer has to say about that!"

Ellari lay in her bed and stared up at the dark ceiling above. Thank goodness, it was quiet at last. Hopefully, Trigg had finally given up and gone. Maybe now she could get some sleep without worrying that he would come crashing through the door into the apartment.

All through the afternoon and evening, her endurance had been strained to the limits as she'd been forced to listen to him moving around downstairs. He had dragged things across the floor, repeatedly opened and closed cupboards and slammed the back door. More than once, she'd even heard him pounding with a hammer. It had become increasingly obvious to her that he was either stealing everything she owned, or that he was deliberately trying to lure her out of the apartment with his mysterious actions.

Despite the severe test her curiosity had been put to, she had withstood the temptation to investigate. It was simply too dangerous. All it would take would be one look into his eyes or one smile from him, and she knew what would happen: her insides would turn to putty, her good senses would dissolve to mush, and she would start to believe him again. She would forget that he was a liar and a scoundrel, and that he had deliberately deceived her to get his hands on her burn and cut cream.

As much as it hurt her to cut him out of her life, she knew the only way to fight his magic over her was to never see him again. Even if he was downstairs stealing everything in her store, she would not give in and check on him.

She winced as she forced herself to add the word *"again"* to her thought. Actually, she had succumbed once to the urge to peek out the back bedroom window shortly before dusk. That was when she'd discovered that he had brought his wagon around to the back door and was loading it with the crates he had filled with jars of Magicure the day before after they had returned from their shopping trip to replenish their supplies—and after he had proposed.

Ellari burst into tears again as she remembered how happy she had been—and what an absolute fool she'd been! Oh, he'd been clever all right, and she had been vulnerable; but that was no excuse for her stupidity. *How could I have thought he was actually falling in love with me? Men like Trigg never fall in love with women like me!* For that matter, they probably never fell in love, period. They loved themselves too much.

She flopped her forearm over her eyes with a disgusted sigh. What hurt most was that she had only herself to blame. She should have known he couldn't be trusted. She should have known he wouldn't have stayed if he hadn't had something to gain. For that matter, what man would? She was plain as a church mouse to look at. She wasn't fun to be with. She had nothing to offer—

"Enough!" she demanded, bolting upright in the bed. "This wasn't my fault! And I did nothing to deserve being treated this way, and he had no right to do this to me. I've spent all day punishing and feeling sorry for myself, but now it's going to end!"

She stood up and put on her robe. "First thing tomorrow, I'm going to reopen the pharmacy and start distributing pamphlets against child labor again." She left the bedroom and entered the living room. "From this day forward, I'm—"

An instant of movement, followed by the familiar odor of ether, assaulted her senses as she stepped through the doorway, a frisson of a moment before a cloth was slapped over her mouth and nose. Instinctively, she sucked in a breath to scream, and total oblivion overtook her.

Chapter Sixteen

Ellari awoke with a start. Instantly aware she was not in her own bed, she struggled to prop herself up on her elbows and look around. Before she could make out any details in the darkness, her forehead collided with something solid above her, and she fell back, banging the hard surface beneath her with the back of her head—and a second thud.

Already, she felt as if the muscles of her body had been turned to water, and all her blood was rushing to her brain in a deafening frenzy to escape the overwhelming tide; the two blows hadn't helped. Maybe she should go back to sleep and solve the mystery of where she was later.

Unfortunately, the longer she lay there, the more awake she became, and the worse the throbbing in her head grew. With the awareness of the pain came increasing curiosity to know what had happened.

Still too groggy to be overly concerned, she lay

with her eyes closed and listened, hoping to find a clue or explanation without expending too much effort on her part.

Slowly, she realized she could hear the sounds of men's voices arguing in the distance, as if they were at the opposite end of a long tunnel. Becoming more confused with each second of growing consciousness, she forced herself to open her eyes, despite the pain and difficulty that simple action caused.

Tentatively, she patted the area beneath her, beside her and above her. Though there was a blanket directly under her, there was no doubt she was surrounded by wood. As if she were in some sort of long wooden box.

A box! *My God, I'm in a coffin!*

The panic she had felt when first waking and not knowing where she was returned with a rush of horror, dramatically intensified by a memory of the chloroform-soaked cloth over her nose and mouth. Someone planned to bury her alive.

The voices she heard seemed to get louder with each passing fraction of an instant. She could almost make out what they were saying.

Struggling to keep her panic at bay and not to scream, she pushed at the sides of the "box," determined to find a way out. That was when she discovered one side of the box was missing.

Frantic to get out, she rolled toward the open side, desperate for air. Free, she sucked in huge, relieved gulps and thanked the Lord for showing her the way out.

Once she had resumed her more normal breathing, she quickly realized she had not been in a box at all, but had been under the wooden bench seat of a wagon. But whose wagon? And why?

Her control only slightly restored by the knowledge that she wasn't in a coffin, she did her best to ignore the headache that was rapidly destroying her will to care what the answers were to those questions. Instead, she dragged herself to her hands and knees. Obviously, her kidnappers hadn't expected her to awaken so soon, or surely they would have bound her, she told herself. As it was, escaping should only be a matter of getting out of the wagon without being seen.

Peering cautiously over the rim into the darkness, she concentrated on locating the kidnappers. They were evidently the source of the argument she was finding it increasingly difficult to ignore as she struggled back from the unconscious void in which she'd been imprisoned.

Squinting to focus, she realized the wagon was parked in a dark, littered alley. There were three men about six feet ahead, beside the horses' heads. Thankfully, they were so intent on their disagreement that no one was paying any attention to the wagon.

It would be a simple enough thing to get out of the wagon and find a place to hide in the alley. Then when the kidnappers were through arguing, they probably wouldn't even notice she wasn't still sleeping under the seat when they drove off.

Wadding the blanket up under the seat to deter immediate attention that she was gone, Ellari scooted to the far side of the wagon from the kidnappers. She took one last glance back over her shoulder to make sure no one was looking, then started to slip over the side.

At the very moment when she would have made her escape good, one of the voices rose angrily, stopping her as surely as a hand on her shoulder would have. She froze. Her heart plummeted violently. Her eyes wide with disbelief, she swiveled her head toward the men again.

It couldn't be! Oh, Lord, it was. It was Trigg!

"Look, dammit! What good's it going to do anyone if you kill me? I swear to you I'm good for the money! All I need is one more week, and I'll have everything I owe Stahl, as well as a nice bonus for the two of you—to cover the cost of your trouble. I've got a really sweet deal going, but I need another week. On the other hand, if you kill me—Unnnh!" he grunted as one of the men lifted a pistol-wielding hand and whacked Trigg across the side of the head.

Trigg stumbled to his knees, and the sickening feeling inside Ellari grew worse. She not only had to find a way to get herself free of the kidnappers, but now she had to worry about Trigg as well.

Even as she told herself it would serve him right if she left him, she made a frantic search for a weapon to use against the men who had Trigg. Her gaze fell on the reins draped over the wagon edge. Elated by the obvious answer to her problem, she picked them up.

A moment of uncertainty swept through her. She'd never actually driven a wagon. But how hard could it be? She'd seen Trigg do it, and it had looked easy enough. All she had to do was yell at the horses and slap them with the reins. And they should take off running. She would only slow down long enough to pick up Trigg.

Gripping the reins tightly in one hand and keeping her head down, she walked on her knees to the center of driver's section of the wagon. Still not certain she could manage this, she peeked up over the wagon rim and a horse's rump.

"Tell you what, Hanahan." The man who'd hit Trigg gave an ugly laugh and raised his gun as if he intended to fire it directly into Trigg's face. "That wagon and team of yours'll more'n cover our troubles, not to mention the 'bonus' Mr. Stahl is giving us to kill you as a lesson to deadbeats who think Mr. Stahl's in the charity business." He pulled back the hammer on his gun.

"Trigg!" Ellari screamed, jiggling the reins over the horses' backs.

Everything happened at once. The horses bolted toward the three men, Trigg rolled to the left, the kidnapper's gun fired, and both of Stahl's men leaped to the right to get out of the path of the oncoming team.

As the horses charged between the three men,

Trigg bounded up from the ground. Grabbing a fistful of a horse's mane, he leaped onto his back, then collapsed over the animal's neck.

Relief coursed through Ellari, but it quickly died. If Trigg could do it, so could the kidnappers. Just as the thought occurred to her, one of Stahl's men appeared at the end of the seat, as he strained to pull himself up onto the bench.

Wielding the free end of the reins, she lashed at the grimacing face that glared at her from the side of the careening wagon. When that didn't make him release his hold on the wagon seat, she bent her head and bit down hard on the fingers gripping the side.

A tortured yowl ripped through the air as the kidnapper's face disappeared from view and he fell to the ground. Relieved by her success, she looked back to make sure she was truly rid of him, only to spot the second kidnapper crawling toward her over the crates in the back of the wagon.

Luckily, the ride was so wild, it was taking all the man's concentration to keep from being thrown off the wagon.

"Trigg!" Ellari screamed, frantically searching for something with which she could ward off the approaching man. Before she could find anything, Trigg lunged past her and grabbed the kidnapper's gun arm. With a strength she didn't know he possessed, he wrenched the gun from the other man and sent him tumbling off the back of the wagon.

Panting breathlessly, Trigg looked up from where

he had sprawled on top of the crates and grinned. "Thanks for the hel—Oh shit!" His expression dissolved into horror. "Turn the horses, Ellari! For God's sake, turn the horses!"

She swung back around, in time to see that the alley they were racing down ended in a T-intersection dead ahead, and the wild horses were mere yards from running headlong into a building.

"I don't know how!" she screamed back, dragging on the reins with all her might—but to no avail.

Lunging head first, Trigg dove for the front of the wagon, grabbing for the reins as he did. "Get down!" he ordered, wrenching the reins from her hands.

The strain obvious in the way the muscles in his neck stood out, he literally forced the horses' heads to turn to the sides by pulling on the reins.

Ellari did as he commanded and crouched down in the foot space in front of the wagon seat. For several tense seconds, the horses blindly continued their race toward the building ahead. Little by little, they started to veer—though it was the last instant before it was certain the horses weren't going to change their course back again and crash into the building after all.

Rounding the corner, the sweating, frothing horses slowed to a walk, then finally stopped halfway down the cross street. "Great!" Trigg mumbled, bounding out of the wagon, his head moving from left to right.

"What's wrong?" Ellari asked, straightening from her position on the floor.

"The horses are spent. They need rest before they can go on."

Ellari stood up and looked back over her shoulder. She was certain Stahl's men would be behind them in a matter of minutes. So far, they weren't in sight though, and she hurried to locate a way to get the horses and wagon out of sight.

"That alley over there!" she said, pointing excitedly. "There's bound to be a deserted shed or barn behind one of these houses. If those men are on foot, it'll give us time to find something. And if they have horses, it still ought to take them a few minutes before they can get them and come after us. By the time they do, we can get the wagon hidden, and they'll assume we kept going."

Giving her a nod, Trigg tugged the harness and clicked at the horses, encouraging them to move toward the alley. "Come on, fellas, just a little bit farther."

To Ellari's relief, the horses obeyed and followed Trigg into the alley, and in a matter of minutes, they were safely hidden inside a ramshackle barn. "What did I tell you?" she asked him, feeling strangely elated, in spite the seriousness of what had just happened, and could still happen if Stahl's men found them. And her headache was entirely gone. She glanced around, her eyes becoming accustomed to the darkness. "I guess now we just wait."

"I guess we do," he agreed, dropping a bar over the shed door and returning to the wagon. "Hand me that blanket under the seat. We might as well be comfortable while we do."

Doing as he said, Ellari passed him the blanket, then climbed down from the wagon, watching as he tossed the blanket onto a pile of old straw. "How long will we be here?"

"That depends on how fast the horses rally. Neither of them is used to doing much more than walking." He dropped down onto the blanket and lay back. "Ah, yeah, that's good."

"Shouldn't we find the horses some water or something?"

"Not 'til they cool down. They could colic."

"I see," she said, remembering suddenly that she had sworn to never speak to Trigg again. "If there's nothing to do but wait, suppose you tell me what this is all about, and why those men took me and your wagon." She sat down on the blanket too.

Trigg winced. "Actually, they didn't know you were there until you raised up and yelled. They thought I was alone when they jumped me. Keedy or Phelps must have tipped them off where I was and that I might try to skip town. That's the only thing I can figure out."

"They thought you were alone? Then that means—you! You're the one who drugged me? Why?"

He shrugged and gave her a humorless grin. "It was the only way to get you to come with me

301

without making a fuss."

"Come with you without a fuss? What are you talking about? Come with you where? I told you I never wanted to see you again!"

This time when he smiled, he gave her that familiar teasing, little-boy, you're-not-really-mad-are-you? grin she was helpless to resist. "I knew you didn't mean it."

"You knew I—?! Why you arrogant—! Who do you think—? I could have been kill—!" Every angry thought she was having was on her tongue at the same time, scrambling to be heard!

"Shh!" Trigg ordered her.

"Don't you shush me, you conceited, overbea—"

In one sure motion, he grabbed her and cut off her tirade with his mouth on hers.

Still angry, she tried to resist, but it was useless. Trigg's kiss was every bit as potent and incapacitating as the chloroform he had used to kidnap her, and like the chloroform, its insidious power seeped through her, spreading through her blood to every extremity and dissipating all resistance.

Continuing to kiss her, Trigg lowered her onto the blanket and covered her upper body with his own. Recognizing her compliance, he ended the kiss and smiled down into her face. "That's better."

"Why'd you do that?"

"I had to shut you up. If you'd kept up that yelling much longer, you would've led Stahl's goons right to us."

"I wasn't yelling!" Ellari protested indignantly,

302

her voice rising.

He kissed her again, this time even more thoroughly than the first.

Feeling herself start to dissolve into the exquisite euphoria his kiss never failed to produce, Ellari hurriedly began to list in her head every ugly description she could think of for Trigg Hanahan: loathsome, conniving, dishonest, womanizing, scoundrel, blackguard, rotter, cheater, liar. . . .

Unfortunately, it wasn't working. Despite her valiant efforts, she could feel her resistance evaporate like steam over a boiling kettle.

Trigg blazed a trail of fiery kisses down her neck as one hand slid upward to catch her breast and caress it.

"No," she begged as his mouth left hers. "We can't. Not here."

"Yes, here," he murmured against her neck as he brought a hand to her breast to caress and squeeze its firmness beneath her gown and robe. "I want you, and you want me."

Hating herself for being so weak, she rolled her head back to give his mouth better access. "But I hate you," she groaned, luxuriating in his lovemaking.

"No you don't. You should, but you don't, do you?"

Slowly, acting totally against her will, her hands rose to hold his head and riffle fingers through his hair. "No," she admitted reluctantly. "I don't hate you."

Hearing the compliance in her voice, he fumbled with the tie on her robe. Continuing to kiss her neck and upper chest and fondle her breast, he quickly opened her robe. "Don't you know by now, that we belong together, Ellari?" he asked softly.

Unable to lie to herself any longer or believe that she never wanted to see Trigg again, Ellari relaxed and gave up the last of her denial. Yes, she wanted him; yes, she belonged with him, if only for this brief moment in time. She would take whatever he wanted to give her, for however long he wanted to stay; and after he was gone, she would rejoice in her memories.

Giving herself up to total feeling, she shoved all her doubts and fears about betrayal and what the future would bring to the back of her mind. For now, she would be content to love and be loved.

Moving with frantic hands, they hurriedly helped each other undress. Their bodies pressed together, Trigg sought her mouth with his lips. His tongue caressed hers with gentle urgency, and she no longer fought her need to respond in kind. She surrendered herself to this one glorious moment. Nothing else mattered. Not the past, not the future. Only the glorious present.

When they had sated their thirst for each other's kisses, Trigg lowered his head to take a succulent, thrusting nipple into his mouth.

Her insides quickly fired to inferno temperatures, and the moisture between her legs became hot and creamy in anticipation. Tugging at his dark head, she brought his mouth back to hers to kiss him deeply and tell him with her body what she wanted.

Unable to resist her invitation, Trigg positioned his hips between her spread thighs and buried himself deep in the folds of her body.

Soon the only sounds in the shed were the rustle of the straw, the occasional snort of the weary horses, their soft moans and ragged breathing, and the slap of flesh against flesh as he drove relentlessly into her.

Together, they climbed to the zenith of the heavens, higher and higher, until they both knew the fall was inevitable. Clinging to each other with the intensity of a drowning man grabbing for a twig to save himself, they were hurled through the atmosphere to float back down to the dark, deserted shed.

With the return to reality came the return to sanity. Immediately ashamed and unable to believe her wanton behavior, Ellari struggled to get things back on an even footing.

"This doesn't change anything, you know," she said evenly. "And it certainly doesn't absolve you of telling me what this madness is all about and why I'm stranded here in this dusty shed with you and not at home alone in my own bed."

Trigg lifted his head and gaped at her, obviously surprised by her reaction.

*Good, s*he congratulated herself. *It's about time he realizes he can't charm and seduce his way out* *of every situation.* "Well, I'm waiting. Are you going to tell me the truth, or not?"

Heaving a sigh, Trigg rolled away from Ellari and lay next to her. "You're right, it's time you know everything that's going on."

Resisting the urge to align her body next to his, as she had done so many times when they had talked after making love, Ellari sat up and reached for her clothing with shaking hands. "I'm listening."

"It's all pretty simple—and complicated." He sat up and grabbed for his trousers. "I'm sure it's not too hard to see that between Boss Stahl and Reed Phelps, Chicago's gotten a little too hot for me right now."

When she didn't comment, he proceeded anyway. "So it's time to move on to a safer location. But—here's the complicated part—I didn't want to leave without you."

"Of course you didn't," she said, her tone sounding harpish even to her own ears. She jabbed her arms angrily into the sleeves of her robe. "Without me and the Magicure formula, you would be back where you started—in debt, being chased by creditors, and broke." She secured the tie on her robe with a double knot.

"That's not quite true. For one thing, I have enough Magicure on the wagon right now to earn the money I owe Stahl within the week—if I live that long. For another, the wagon and horses are worth something, and I still have money we earned this first two weeks that I didn't reinvest yet in supplies. So I wouldn't be in such bad shape."

"Half of all that is mine," she reminded him.

"True, but if I'm the unscrupulous bastard you think I am, a little thing like that wouldn't stop me from driving off with everything and leaving you with nothing. But I didn't." He hurriedly buttoned his shirt, then tucked it into his trousers.

She laughed bitterly. "Of course you didn't. Why would you settle for a mere wagonload of Magicure, when you could have half the whole business as long as you have me and I have the formula?"

Trigg looked hurt. "How many times do I have to tell you? I care about you, and I don't want anything or anyone to hurt you."

"No, that's a privilege you want to reserve for yourself."

Trigg shook his head helplessly. "Don't you realize we're not talking about hurt feelings here, or even about you realizing I'm a total son-of-a-bitch. We're talking about real, honest-to-goodness physical hurt. Whether or not you forgive me isn't going to change the fact that Nylander's pals're going to be all over you like flies on manure the minute you reopen the pharmacy and start causing trouble again—and that's exactly what you're planning to do the minute I'm not there to stop you. Isn't it?"

She jutted her skin defensively. "You don't know for a fact that Nylander is even behind the attacks on me or my store. You said yourself, some of the men in my neighborhood who resent my criticism of child labor are probably the ones responsible. For all I know, Nylander doesn't even know I exist."

Trigg shot her a look that said, *You're only fooling yourself if you believe that.* Aloud he said, "Believe me, I not only 'know for a fact' that Nylander knows who you are, but I also 'know for a fact' he's not going to let his flunkies stop at vandalism and harassment if you start up your campaign against his factory again."

"You're just saying that to frighten me into going with you so you won't lose the Magicure formula."

"Dammit, Ellari! I'm trying to save your life, not the damned formula. The simple fact is, if you open the pharmacy tomorrow morning, Nylander is going to have you killed!"

"You're lying."

Trigg breathed in deeply, then released a long, frustrated growl. "I wish I were, Ellari, but I'm not. Nylander told me himself that you're a dead woman if you don't stop. And that's why I can't leave Chicago without you."

Ellari felt the blood drain from her face. "I don't understand. This is insane. Why would Nylander tell—? You don't even know—When did you—?"

Suddenly, a thought hit her, and everything became clear. Clear and ugly. "You bought the Magicure jars from Nylander, didn't you? How could you, when you know how I feel about that factory? You swore to me they didn't come from there! You said you'd found a small factory called Jones Glass outside of Chicago that didn't use child labor."

Trigg felt sick. If he told her the rest of the story about his arrangement with Nylander, she would never believe he'd done it for her. But he didn't have a choice. He would rather have her lost to him and alive, than to let Nylander kill her.

"The truth is—"

"The truth!" she spit out. "You wouldn't know the truth if it walked in here and bit you!"

"The truth," he repeated pointedly, "is that all the glass factories use child labor. They truly believe they can't afford to stay in business if they can't hire kids to work in their factories. Nylander simply gave us the best price on the jars, so I got them from him. I made up the story about Jones to give you some peace of mind about using glass jars."

"And while you were buying the jars, I suppose Nylander just walked up to you and said, 'I'm going to have Ellari Lochridge killed if she doesn't stop speaking out against me and my factory.'"

Trigg shook his head and studied Ellari's tearful face. He'd really made a mess of things this time. She really hated him, and he couldn't blame her. "I went to him about buying the jars, and evidently one of the men he's had watching you for weeks now recognized me and told him about me staying with you. That's when he made his offer. He said he'd give me the jars free, if I would agree to get you to drop your fight against him and the other factory owners."

"Which you no doubt eagerly accepted," she snarled, "since you'd never turn down anything free, would you? Especially, when seducing women into doing what you want them to do is your special talent!"

"As a matter of fact, I didn't accept, eagerly or any other way. At least, not at first. But when he made it clear to me that if I didn't agree to help him, he had a man who was going to 'solve the problem permanently,' I realized I didn't have a choice."

She nodded her understanding. "Because you didn't want to risk losing the Magicure formula."

"Once and for all, it's not the formula I'm worried about losing."

"Now, why do you suppose I find that so difficult to believe!"

"Well, believe it or not, it's the truth." He stood up and walked over to the barred door. "I'd better find some water for these nags now. Then we can leave." His hand on the bar, he turned back to face her. "But before we go, there's one more thing you should know."

"What now? Don't tell me you have a wife and children you forgot to mention, and you want to get that lie off your conscience too."

"I guess I deserved that," he said with an ironic grin. "But no, there's no wife and children."

"No wife or children? Then what pray tell is this

310

last tidbit of knowledge I need to hear to make my day complete?"

"I doubt it will make your day complete, but it might at least convince you I've been telling the truth about the reason I stayed."

"I seriously doubt that."

"The reason I'm not worried about losing the formula, Ellari, is because I already have it."

Ellari sucked in an enormous, choking gulp of air. "What did you say?"

"I said, I have the formula. I had it even before we started Magicure. So, you see, I could have left any time. But I stayed to protect you."

"I don't believe you!" she finally said. "If you had the formula, why did you keep trying to yet the ingredients list from me? This is just another one of your lies."

"Think about all the times I had your apartment to myself to look for the formula, Ellari. I have to admit it took me several tries before I found the secret little compartment behind the spoon drawer in your kitchen, but I did. I found it the morning I fixed your breakfast and you slept late. I copied it and put it back in the drawer before you woke up."

He shrugged and gave her a regretful grin. "So you see, I not only didn't have to stay, but I didn't even have to suggest we form a partnership. I could have taken the formula, then manufactured and sold the cream myself, and you would have never known the difference. As for getting the list of ingredients from you, I was trying to cover up the fact that I already knew what was in it."

"Then why did you stay if not for the formula?"

"You're the one with the college degree, Ellari. Why don't you tell me?"

Chapter Seventeen

Ellari stared dumbfounded at the shed door through which Trigg had disappeared. Could it be? Could he love her?

No! she protested, refusing to allow herself to believe what her heart was telling her. *There has to be something else in it for him to gain.*

But what? He didn't want the drugstore, she didn't have any money and he'd had the formula all along. There was nothing else he could want from her. Yet he had stayed.

By the time Trigg returned with a milk bucket full of water for each horse, Ellari still hadn't figured out the answer to the puzzling mystery. "All right, I give up," she confessed, barring the door behind him. She turned to face him and leaned back on the doors. "Why didn't you leave once you got the formula?"

Trigg's shoulders tensed. Then he patted the neck of the horse he was watering. "If you'll remember, I tried more than once, but you keep needing my help."

She approached him. "Why?"

"What do you mean, why?" He crossed to the other horse. "Because every time I turned around, someone else was attacking or threatening you. That's why."

"That's not what I mean, and you know it," she persisted, closing the gap between them again. "I want to know why you kept helping me. What did you expect to gain by staying with me instead of leaving as soon as you found the formula?"

"Maybe I'm just the kind of man who can't turn his back on a woman in trouble," he answered quickly.

"Perhaps," she agreed. "But there must be hundreds of women who need help. Why me?"

"Maybe I felt guilty about stealing the formula from you and thought I owed you something." He set down the second bucket and watched the horse greedily dip into the water and suck.

"Chivalry and guilt," she said thoughtfully. "Definitely, two strong motivations. But for some reason, I still don't believe that's all there is to it. There's something you're not telling me, something else you expected to gain by staying. What is it?"

He looked away from her. "I've told you why I stayed. If you want to read something else into it, then go ahead. As for me, I'm going to get some sleep, so we can leave town in a couple of hours." He spun toward the blanket.

She caught him by the arm and stopped his evasive retreat. Reaching for his face, she turned it so she could look into his eyes. "What is it, Trigg? What's the real reason you stayed?"

Trigg stared at her, his expression stubborn and guarded. "I told you—"

"The truth, Trigg. For once, tell me the truth."

"All right, dammit. You want the truth? I stayed because for the first time in my life I felt what it must be like to have a real home and family, and I liked it." He looked down and released a bitter little laugh. "God, help me, I liked it a lot. Isn't that a joke?"

"I'm not laughing," she said, her compassion for the grown up boy from the streets wrenching at her heart. "There's nothing wrong with wanting to belong somewhere, and to someone. We all want that special place where we can feel safe and be ourselves and not worry that—" She smiled sympathetically. "—someone will 'steal our shoes' during the night."

He pursed his lips in a half-grin at the reminder of what he'd told her about his life on the streets. "You know what I liked most?"

"What?"

He gave her a reluctant grin. "Besides knowing I'd have my shoes in the morning, of course."

"Of course."

"I liked knowing you were waiting for me to come back whenever I left, and that you actually cared if I came back for no other reason than you wanted to be with me. I kept telling myself I was

315

like my father, and that being free and having no responsibilities was the only life for a man like me. I was sure the novelty of staying in one place would wear off. But the longer I stayed, the more I hated the idea of leaving."

He shook his head and chuckled. "Hell, I even liked putting out the trash and mucking out the shed and squabbling over who should get up and let the cat out—because it was our trash, our shed and our cat. From that day I first did all the repairs for you, I knew there was something special I'd been missing all my life. Of course, I convinced myself the only reason I wanted to stay was to find the formula." He shrugged. "But inside, I guess I knew there was more to it than that. So when I found the formula and realized I could leave, I suggested our partnership."

"So, in spite of the terrible things you said about my pharmacy and the neighborhood, that was really what you wanted," she accused, hurt despite her empathy for what having a home of his own must mean to a man who'd never had one.

"No!" he protested with an astonished grin. "It wasn't the pharmacy that made it feel like home. It was you!"

"Me?"

"It was knowing you were there and that you were depending on me. It was knowing you would worry about me if I didn't come back on time. It was the way your face lit up when you first saw me after a few hours apart. It was the way you watched me take the first bite of my supper to be sure I liked it before you started eating. It was all that and more. It was the way you made me feel. For the first time since my mother died, someone trusted me and believed in *me*. You made me feel like I had a right to the same kind of happiness other people had. But most of all, you made me realize I'm not my father, and that the things he wanted least are the things I want the most. Because of you, I knew I wanted a home and family more than anything else."

Ellari's eyes filled with tears. "But you could've had a home and family with Mr. Phelps's daughter. Why didn't you want to marry her?"

"Because I don't love Ina Phelps, Ellari. It's you I love. It's you I want to spend the rest of my life with. It's you I want to make a home with. It's you I want to marry. And it's you I want to take care of and come home to every night. It's always been you, Ellari. From the moment I pulled that dumb stunt of jumping Schmelzel to 'save' you and you pulled a gun on me, you've never been out of my thoughts—or my heart."

"Oh, Trigg!" she cried, unable to say anything else. Trigg loved her. He really loved her.

"I know it's too late to make up for all the lies I've told you, but you wanted the truth, and that's it. Once I get you somewhere where you're safe from Nylander, I'll get out of your life once and for all." He reached into his pocket and pulled out a scrap of paper. He held it out to her.

"What's this?"

"The formula."

"Keep it."

"I don't get it. You said—"

"—that I wanted the formula to stay in my immediate family," she finished for him. "And who's more immediate than a husband?" She smiled tearfully. "That is, if you haven't changed your mind about wanting to marry me."

His expression transformed from misery to disbelief to sheer elation. "Do you mean it? You're really willing to give me another chance?" Before she could answer, he whisked her feet off the ground and spun her around. "You won't be sorry," he vowed, covering her face with kisses.

"I know I won't." Laughing, she clung to him.

"The first thing we'll do once I get you safely out of Chicago is find a preacher to marry us."

"Do you really want to leave Chicago?" she asked, her tone obviously serious.

Eying her suspiciously, Trigg lowered her to her feet. "Of course not. Chicago's where the money is, but I don't have any choice until I pay off Stahl. You know that. And there's always Nylander."

"What if we could think of a way to convince Mr. Stahl to give you some more time, would you consider staying?"

Obviously curious, Trigg raised his eyebrows doubtfully. "Stahl's not going to settle for anything less than full payment—or seeing my head as an ornament on his hitching post as an example to anyone who owes him money and doesn't pay on time."

"What if we went to see him and put up the pharmacy as a guarantee that you would pay him within one week?"

Stunned, Trigg stared, his eyes strangely moist. "You'd risk your drugstore for me?"

"What risk? You said we have enough Magicure on the wagon to earn back what you owe him if we sell it in Chicago, didn't you? Anyway, if we go back to the pharmacy, I can continue mixing batches to sell in case we don't have enough after all."

He shook his head. "I couldn't let you do that for me. Besides—"

"It would be for *us,* Trigg."

"Besides, Stahl wouldn't go along with it. As much as you love that old drugstore of yours, it's not worth enough to cover what I owe Stahl. I do appreciate the thought, but we'd better go on like I planned, and come back after we have the money."

"But I can't go. I have no clothes."

"I packed some things in your trunk. They're on the wagon."

"And what about Mr. Cat? Who'll feed him?"

"He got by before you found him, and I'm sure he could again, but to ease your mind, he's in a cage on the wagon too."

Her gaze shot toward the back of the wagon. "I don't believe it! Why's he so quiet?"

"I gave him paregoric, just like I did you as soon as the chloroform started to wear off." He shrugged and winked. "There are some definite advantages to having a drugstore at your disposal."

His arm around her shoulder, he walked her to- ward the blanket. "Now, let's get a little bit of sleep. I'd like to be on our way around sunrise. Stahl's goons're like the rest of the lowlife who work on the Levee. They come out at night, and crawl back into their holes to sleep during the day."

"Well, it seems as if you've thought of every- thing," Ellari said, reluctantly allowing herself to be lowered to the blanket, "but I still think it would be a good idea to at least try to talk to Mr. Stahl before we go. If we leave the drugstore unattended for any amount of time, we could lose it anyway. It might as well be used for something good."

"Shh," he whispered, his eyes closing before his head even touched the blanket. "Trust me, this is the best way," he slurred, drawing her into his em- brace. "The fewer dealings we have with Nick Stahl, the better off we'll be. Don't worry, your store will be fine until we get back."

"It's not the store I'm—"

A soft snore, followed by a contented sigh cut her off. Smiling, she caressed Trigg's sleeping face and kissed him. "That's right, you go to sleep. You've had a very long day."

Wide awake, Ellari shifted over onto her back and studied the rafters of the shed for several min- utes, her mind swirling with thoughts. *I know I could convince Mr. Stahl to give Trigg a little more time if only I could talk to him. . . .*

* * *

Ellari hurried along Twelfth Street, her shawl-covered head filled with a flurry of second thoughts. Trigg would be furious when he realized she'd gone against his advice and come to the Levee anyway. Everyone in Chicago knew the Levee was the most lewd and wicked section of the entire city—a city known throughout the world to be one of the most corrupt cities anywhere.

It was said there was no entertainment or vice too depraved or perverted not to be found within the few square blocks bounded by State Street, Pacific Avenue, Twelfth Street and Van Buren. In fact, there were rumored to be a minimum of two hundred brothels alone within the area, not to mention the gambling palaces, dance halls, drug dens and exotic theaters that lined the few streets of the Levee.

At the intersection of Pacific, Ellari paused, not certain what she should do. When she'd gotten dressed and sneaked out of the shed, she hadn't given any thought to how she would find Boss Stahl once she got to the Levee district. She'd only been concerned with determining her whereabouts and how far she was from the Levee.

She had considered it a stroke of luck and a sign that she was doing the right thing when she found street signs near the shed, telling her she was only only a short distance from the pharmacy, and even closer to the Levee area. It had been a simple matter to cover the few blocks in a matter of minutes. But now she was stumped. Obviously, she was going to have to ask someone where she could find Boss Stahl.

Though it was evident the majority of the Levee's usual patrons and inhabitants must be sleeping off a night of lusty debauchery and heavy drinking, the streets were still well-occupied. All up and down Pacific and State people wandered, alone and in groups, into and out of a variety of gaudy, lighted establishments. Couples, their arms linked, disappeared into dark doorways, well-dressed gentlemen got into cabs and carriages, and drunken vagrants searched the sidewalks and gutters for discarded cigar butts.

From one saloon, came the voices of men and women raised in song and raucous laughter, and Ellari quickly discarded that as a place to ask questions. From another well-lit establishment, she could hear a piano tinkling out the familiar notes of a Stephen Foster melody.

At first sight, she thought that might be the best place to ask for information. However, on further consideration, she read the sign over the door: "Majestic Theatre—On Stage: Perverted Acts to Watch or Join In." She quickly discarded the Majestic as a possibility.

The longer she looked up and down the streets, the closer she came to the conclusion that she had made a very stupid mistake. Just as she was about to turn around and hurry back to the shed where she'd left Trigg sleeping, she spotted three scantily clad women talking to each other under a gas light and smoking long thin cigars.

Certain she had nothing to fear from her own sex, she hurried toward the three. "Excuse me," she said as she approached them. "I wonder if one of you could possibly tell me where I might find a man by the name of Boss Stahl."

The three, a blonde, a redhead and a brunette, turned as one and raked their drowsy-eyed glances up and down the length of Ellari. "Who wants to know?" the brunette asked.

"My name is El—uh—sie," she lied, "and I need to see Mr. Stahl on business. If you can direct me to his establishment, I'd be very grateful."

The redhead laughed. "Listen to her talk!" She wobbled her head and imitated Ellari. "I'd be very grateful." Her face grew hard and she shoved it close to Ellari's. "Firgit it, girlie. Boss don't use mousy little bitches in his place. 'Specially when they look like they'd faint dead away if they ever saw a man's cock, much less had to service one." She took a drag on her cigar and blew the smoke in Ellari's face. "Now git off our block, or I'm gonna scratch yer eyes out. Business is bad enough with this heat."

The blonde stepped between Ellari and the redhead and gave the other woman a dirty look. "Don't pay her any mind, honey. She's jest pissed 'cause a couple o' her regulars started visitin' a high-yellow over on Polk." The woman put her arm

323

around Ellari's shoulders and walked her away from the other two. "Now, why don't you tell me what you want with Boss?"

"I need to talk to him on a matter of a personal nature. Do you know where I can find him?"

The blonde looked dismayed. "You ain't knocked up, are you?"

"Knocked up?"

"You know, 'spectin' a kid!"

"Oh!" Ellari laughed nervously. "No, it's nothing like that. But I do need to see Mr. Stahl immediately. Do you know where I can find him?"

"Sure, everyone in the Levee district knows Boss Stahl." She looked from side to side. "Tell you what, I'm done for the night. Why don't I take you to him?"

"Would you? I would really appreciate that. Is it far?"

"Naw. Jest over there." She pointed a long, dirty finger toward the theater Ellari had seen earlier— the theater with the "perverted acts" on stage.

A frightening sense of foreboding shook through Ellari, and she took an unconscious step back.

"Come on," the blonde said, grabbing Ellari's arm and propelling her toward the theater. "I'll innerduce you. Boss'n me're real tight."

"On second thought," Ellari said, resisting the pull on her arm. "This can wait. It's awfully early. He's probably still sleeping, and I wouldn't want to disturb him. I'll come back later."

"Hell, no need to make another trip. Boss don't

never go to bed 'fore sunup." Her fingers dug into Ellari's arm and she jerked her forward. "Now's the best time to see him."

Short of simply dropping to the ground and being dragged, Ellari couldn't fight the powerful grip on her arm, so she was forced to run to keep pace with the prostitute's long-legged stride.

Before they reached the Majestic, a man stepped out of the shadows. "Well, well, well, Goldie, you waddn't thinkin' o' callin' it a night without turnin' in your take, was you?"

The blonde stopped short and looked around nervously. "No, 'course not, Sully. I was just bringin' it to you." She dug into her bodice and produced a thin wad of bills. She held it out to the man. "Things was real slow tonight. Guess it's even too hot to f—"

A backhanded slap across the mouth cut off the rest of her obscenity. "You 'spect me to live on this kind of take? I got expenses to meet. You're gonna have to do better or—"

"That's why I brought you this new girl," Goldie responded hurriedly, whipping Ellari forward before Ellari fully comprehended what was happening. "All she needs is some different clothes and she ought to earn you some extra. Or you might even sell her to one o' the fancy houses. She talks like a real lady."

"No!" Ellari screamed, the full horror hitting her at once. Catching Goldie off guard, she broke free and started running, the shawl sliding from over her hair to her shoulders as she did. She only got a few feet before she collided into the solid wall of another man.

Panic rancid in her mouth, she looked up into piercing black eyes as strong hands clasped her upper arms.

"Well, hello!" the dark-haired man crooned, a seductive smile on his handsome, mustached face. "What have we here?"

With Goldie in tow, Sully approached them. "Thanks for the help. Tonight was her first night on the job, and she's tryin' to hold out! I'll take her off your hands." He grabbed Ellari's arm.

"Get away from me, you vile man!" Ellari screamed, moving closer into the shelter of the arms of the man who still held her. "I don't work for him." She raised her pleading eyes to her rescuer. "I never saw him in my life!"

"I've got to admit she doesn't look like one of your regular girls, Sully," the handsome stranger said, not relinquishing his hold.

Sully's eyes narrowed threateningly. "Yeah, well, I decided my customers might like a change. Business has been a little slow this month. Now, give her here, or you can start payin' for her time."

"No!" Ellari cried. "I'm not a prostitute! I came here looking for someone, and that woman grabbed me and tried to give me to him. Please, you've got to believe me!"

"You lying bitch!" Sully snarled, lifting a hand as if to strike her.

The stranger caught the smaller man's wrist in midair and wrenched it backwards. "I don't think the lady wants to go with you, Sully, so why don't you go on back to the rest of your harem and leave this one to me?"

"The hell I will! I paid a hundred dollars for that slut, and I ain't leavin' without her."

"Johnny!" the stranger called, and an even larger man than he appeared at his side. "Give Sully here a couple hundred dollars to cover his loss. Then help him move his operation to a different location. I don't want to see him in this part of town again."

"Hey! You don't own the street!"

Johnny grabbed Sully under the chin and lifted him off the ground with one hand, while he stuffed bills into the smaller man's pocket with the other. "The boss says you move, you move. Now, you wanna walk or you want me to carry you?"

"I'll be in my office," Ellari's rescuer told Johnny, offering a crooked arm to Ellari. "Would you do me the honor of joining me for a cup of coffee, my dear?"

Still too shaken by her experience with Goldie and Sully to think with a totally clear mind, Ellari took the man's arm. "I think that would be a very good idea," she answered shakily, "because I think I'm about to faint."

Responding with speed and agility, the man swept Ellari up into his arms and hurried down the sidewalk.

"You don't have to carry me," she protested self-consciously as he whisked her past the Majestic Theatre. "I can walk."

"Nonsense. What kind of a gentleman would I be if you felt faint and I didn't take care of you?" He turned into the walkway on the other side of the theater and hurried up a flight of wooden stairs.

"Where are you taking me?" she asked, her frantically beating heart not helping her light-headedness.

"To my office," he responded, "so that you can regain your strength before I take you home." At the top of the stairs, he banged twice. The door was immediately opened by a sober-faced man in a black tailcoat. "The lady needs a brandy, Simms."

"Very good, sir!" The manservant walked across the lavishly decorated room to a marble and leather bar.

The man lay Ellari down on a plush red velvet settee and sat down beside her. He held out his hand without looking up as the valet approached and placed the brandy snifter in it. "That will be all Simms."

"Very good, sir." He immediately left the room.

The man moved close to Ellari and put one hand behind her head and lifted her head as he held the snifter to her lips. "Drink this. It will make you feel better."

Catching a whiff of the alcohol, Ellari wrinkled her nose. Turning her head to the side, she put her fingers to her lips. "No thank you. I couldn't possibly."

Feeling terribly uneasy in the opulent surroundings and with the handsome man studying her, she tried to rise. "But thank you for your assistance. I don't know what I would have done if you hadn't come along."

With a hand on her arm, the man stopped her from rising. "You can't leave yet."

Ellari swallowed deeply. "Really, I must."

"You do realize that if I hadn't come along when I did, no one would have seen or heard from you again, don't you?"

A violent chill shook her. "When I think about that terrible man—" She lifted her tear-filled eyes to the concerned face of the man. "I'm forever in your debt."

"In that case, don't you think I deserve an explanation for why a beautiful and obviously intelligent lady of your stature would come to the Levee in the middle of the night?"

"I came for my fiancé," she explained.

"Your fiancé let you come down here alone? He should be horsewhipped." He idly took the ends of the shawl that had slipped from her head to her shoulders earlier into his hands. "If you were my fiancée," he said, his voice soft and hypnotizing, "I wouldn't let you out of my sight." He gently tugged on the shawl and worked his hands up the length closer to her chest.

"He doesn't know I'm here," she said, her immediate desire to defend Trigg overruling her good sense. The instant the words were out of her mouth, she realized what she'd done.

The man arched his dark brows. "Oh. Then, he's the person you came to the Levee seeking? Perhaps I can help you find him."

Hope leaped in Ellari's chest. She wondered what she was afraid of — this man had been nothing but a gentleman, and maybe he could help her. "Actually, I was trying to find the man who *can* help him. His name is Boss Stahl. Do you by any chance know him or where I can find him? I believe he owns a gambling establishment."

The man's mouth spread in a lazy, amused grin. "It just so happens, I do know 'Boss.' His close friends call him Nick, though."

Excitement burst into a smile on Ellari's face. "You do? That's wonderful! Can you tell me where to find him? It's urgent that I talk to him right away. It's a matter of life or death!"

"I can do better than that. I know where he is right this minute." He stood up and lifted her hand to kiss it. "Wait right here, and I'll go get him."

He hurriedly exited the door through which they'd entered.

Unable to believe her good fortune, Ellari, scrambled to sit up and glanced around the lavishly decorated room. Everywhere she looked, the room smacked of riches and luxury. There were gold statues, exquisite dishes and vases on ornately carved tables. The rugs were tapestries, obviously expensive.

A knock at the door interrupted her thinking.

She looked up as the man who'd saved her came back into the room—alone.

Unable to hide her disappointment, she sagged back on the settee. "You couldn't find him."

"On the contrary." A smug grin on his face, he approached her and lifted her hand to his lips. "Nick Stahl at your service, beautiful lady. How can I help you?"

Chapter Eighteen

"You?" Ellari gasped. "You're Boss Stahl?"

Nick held out his hands in surrender. "Guilty as charged. But as I told you, my friends call me Nick."

"But you're so—" Astonished, she shook her head. "You're not at all what I expected!"

"Oh?" He sat down beside her on the settee again, much too close.

Ellari scooted nervously to the side, but was stopped by the upholstered arm of the sofa.

Smiling, Nick hooked his finger beneath her chin and lifted her face so he could look into her eyes. "And what exactly were you expecting?"

"I didn't think you'd be so—" She caught herself, horrified by the word that had first come to mind: handsome. "—young," she improvised. "I thought you would be much older, and not nearly so—"

He lifted his thumb and touched the fullness of her bottom lip. "Nearly so what?"

"So kind."

"Is that what your fiancé told you? That I was old and cruel?"

"No, of course not."

"Then what did he tell you?" He slipped his hand along her jaw line to the back of her head.

Ellari brushed nervously at her cheek where his fingers had touched the skin. She glanced away from him in an effort to escape his hypnotizing gaze. "Only that he owed you a great deal of money and that the loan is due now and he needs more time."

"And he sent you to plead his case for him? What kind of a scoundrel would do such a thing?"

"I told you, he doesn't know I'm here. I came of my own accord. Not to plead, but to offer you a business proposition of my own in return for an extension of my fiancé's loan."

"A business proposition? Now, I am disappointed." His hand cupped behind her neck, he trailed the pad of his thumb up and down the area behind her ear lobe. "Business is not exactly the type of proposition I had hoped to discuss with such a beautiful woman."

"Mr. Stahl!" Ellari said, twisting her head from side to side and placing her open hand on her neck to shield herself from his blatant caress.

"Nick," he corrected, his voice silky as he leaned forward and kissed the back of her hand.

"Mr. Stahl," she repeated pointedly, her insides

333

quivering with frantic apprehension. What had she been thinking to come here tonight? Nick Stahl was no less an opportunist than Sully; he was just less obvious.

With pretended unconcern, she stood up and moved away from him. "I'm perfectly serious. I came here to offer you a legitimate business proposition. If you're not willing to do me the courtesy of hearing what I have to offer, then I really must leave immediately."

An amused grin on his face, Nick took a gold case from his breast pocket and opened it to remove a slender, prerolled cigarette. Lighting the smoke, he leaned back on the settee. "My apologies. Pray, proceed."

Ellari wished she could just say, *This was a mistake. I shouldn't have come,* and walk out, but she knew she couldn't. She had to go through with this if there was any chance at all it would work. "My name is Ellari Lochridge. I'm a pharmacist, and I own a small pharmacy on Taylor Street on the West Side. I would like to put my shop up as collateral for a two-week extension on my fiancé's debt with you." She had decided to ask for an extra week, just in case Trigg had underestimated how long it would take to earn the money he owed Stahl, and in case she needed some time to negotiate with.

"We might be able to work something out—depending on the size of his debt, of course. I have to warn you, property in that part of the city doesn't have a very good value." He went to his desk and opened a drawer. "They say it's only a matter of time before the whole area goes up in flames." He pulled out a ledger book and began to thumb through it. "What's your fiancé's name?"

"Trigg Hanahan," she answered, certain he could hear the desperation in her voice. Trigg had already told her the drugstore wasn't worth nearly as much as he owed, but she had hoped Stahl wouldn't know that.

Nick's head jerked up in surprise, exposing his frighteningly angry black eyes for the briefest moment before he lowered them to his account book again. "Mmm, Trigg Hanahan. . . ." he mused, continuing to make a show of searching his ledger.

"Yes," she said shakily, pretending not to have noticed Stahl's first reaction to Trigg's name, or the fact that he was now pretending he wasn't sure who Trigg was. "I'm not certain how much he owes you, but I am sure my pharmacy will more than cover it—not that you will need to test that. Mr. Hanahan has a new business, and we're certain we'll be able to pay you in plenty of time."

"Ah, Trigg Hanahan," Nick said, thoughtfully examining the book a moment, before slamming it shut. He raised his head, a regretful smile on his face. "My dear, either you have been given a gravely disillusioning appraisal of your property's worth, or Mr. Hanahan has exaggerated the insigni-

335

ficance of his debt to me. Either way, I couldn't possibly go along with the terms of your offer."

"One week! Just give us one week!"

Nick shook his head, his expression seemingly regretful. "I wish I could help you, but it simply wouldn't be good business."

"But having Trigg killed would be?" she returned viciously.

Nick Stahl looked truly shocked and hurt. "I don't know what Hanahan told you about me, my dear, but do I look like a killer to you?"

"Obviously, looks can be deceiving, Mr. Stahl. But you're wasting your acting abilities on me. You see, I heard your men tell Trigg that you were going to give them a bonus for killing him, so that you can use him as an example."

Grinning, Nick pulled out another cigarette and lit it. "You must be the avenging angel who not only stole my boys' bonus, but tried to flatten them with a wagon at the same time. Now, it's my turn to say, you're nothing like I expected. You should have heard them describe you. Your hair was wild and streaking out behind you like flames from hell. Your teeth were fangs bared in a vicious snarl, and your white robes billowed like the wings of death." He shook his head and chuckled. "It must have been something to see. Wish I'd been there."

Ellari swallowed nervously. Digging her nails into the palms of her hands to keep from bolting from the room, she concentrated on keeping her voice level. "Isn't it worth waiting one more week to get your money, rather than losing it all, as well as the bonus you had planned to pay the two men you hired? After all, you can always have Trigg killed, but if he's dead, you'll never get your money."

He sauntered over to where she stood. Still smiling, he wrapped his fingers around the nape of her neck and jerked her close to him, bringing her mouth to within inches of his own. "I like a woman who knows what she wants and isn't afraid to go after it."

Refusing to let it show that she was every bit as intimidated as he obviously wanted her to be, Ellari narrowed her eyes glaringly and stood her ground. "And I like a man who doesn't force himself on a woman."

His mouth twisted in an amused grin, Stahl released his hold on her and returned to his desk. "You do have a point. Maybe we can work something out after all."

Shocked, Ellari was unable to keep up her facade for a moment.

"Oh, Mr. Stahl, thank you. I swear you won't regret this."

He sat down at his desk again. Leaning back in his chair, he laughed. "Before you get too excited, you might want to hear the terms of *my* proposition first."

An alarm went off in Ellari's head. "Your proposition?" she asked uneasily. "I don't understand. Aren't we talking about a one week extension in exchange for the deed to my pharmacy as collateral?"

"At best, your pharmacy can't be worth more than five hundred dollars, so I would need extra collateral before I could agree to the extension."

Ellari's heart sank. "But I have nothing else you would want."

"On the contrary, Miss Lochridge. You have something I want very much."

"What?"

"You have class and quality—something I see far too little of in my line of work. So, I will give Trigg Hanahan his one-week extension on the two thousand he owes me—"

"Two thousand? I thought it was closer to one thousand!"

"Originally, it was, but you mustn't forget the interest. And then there's the two hundred reimbursement for the cash spent rescuing you from Sully."

"I see," she said, not even trying to hide her sense of hopelessness. "I hadn't thought of that."

"Don't be so sad. As I started to say, I'm going to give you your extension."

Her head popped up. "You are?"

"In exchange for your services."

"Services?"

"Not what you're thinking—though if you choose

338

to honor me with such favors, I'll be most delighted. But that will be pure pleasure—on both our parts. I promise you that. This, however, is business. What I want from you is for you to stay with me for one week and act as my hostess at several important meetings I'm planning. A woman of your refined caliber will be just the thing to bring a little class to the sometimes shoddy world of business."

"What if Trigg doesn't pay in time?"

"Then you will continue to work for me until the debt is paid off."

"And if I refuse?"

Nick shrugged. "Then I will have my men take care of Trigg Hanahan as originally planned, and you'll work off his debt to me—if not as my companion, then either in my theater, or upstairs in my private dining rooms. Of course, if you can remember who is the boss and make an effort to please me, I might keep you for my own personal use—for a while at least. On the other hand, if none of those avenues work out, I'll be forced to sell you to the highest bidder to recoup my losses as best I can."

An explosive feeling of panic gripped Trigg's chest and woke him with a violent burst. He bolted upright. Filled with a frightening sense of loss, he frantically sliced his gaze through the early morning semi-darkness of the shed. Something was wrong. He was sure of it. Things were too quiet.

"Ellari!" he whispered, reaching for her as he continued to visually search the shed for an intruder and to listen for a sign that someone was outside.

Because of the sweltering daytime temperatures that were only slightly relieved at night, he wasn't surprised not to find her as close by as she'd been when they went to sleep. However, when he patted the blanket to its edge and she still wasn't there, his sense of foreboding intensified painfully. He jerked his head around, hoping to allay his fears and panic by finding she had rolled off the blanket in her sleep.

"Oh, my God, she's gone!" he gasped, leaping up from the blanket and bounding toward the door.

At the shed door, he immediately spotted the raised bar, and her whereabouts hit him full force. Shaking his head at his overreaction, he grinned and fell back against the wall. He didn't know whether to throttle her or to hug her when she returned from wherever she'd gone to relieve herself, but he definitely intended to give her a stern talking to. Modesty was all well and good, but in this case it would have been better to use a corner of the shed.

Whipping out his pocket watch, he held it near a crack between slats in the shed wall to check the time by the early morning light. Six-fifteen. If he hurried and fed the horses from the supply of grain he'd brought along, they would be able to leave as soon as Ellari got back.

"You're insane. People don't buy and sell other people." Ellari could hear the rising panic in her own voice, but she couldn't control it. "It's against the law!"

A smug smile stretched across Nick's face. Obviously, he could hear her fear too. "It's clear to me that you've led a rather sheltered existence, Miss Lochridge. The Levee is a world and law unto itself. The 'law' you're referring to is paid to look the other way. Young women are bought and sold down here all the time, and no one makes any attempt to stop it. It's not unusual for one female to change hands several times in a matter of weeks, each sale bringing a better price, especially for the fresher, more innocent ones. The more fortunate girls are purchased by the better brothels and may even stay there for years if their work is satisfactory. However, the less fortunate ladies wind up being passed from owner to owner and eventually working for someone like Sully, or worse."

He grabbed her at the small of her back and dragged her hard against him, so hard that she could feel his maleness pressing into her belly. "I'd say, so far, you've been one of the fortunate ones,

341

wouldn't you?"

She shoved at his chest. "If you call it fortunate to be held against my will and threatened and mauled by a man like you who pretends to be my friend, I suppose I am by your standards."

Nick dropped her so suddenly, she staggered backward. His handsome face grew ugly with anger. "I'll give you until noon to make your decision." He started to leave through the indoor entrance, but hesitated and turned back to face her, his charming demeanor restored. "Until twelve then, my dear."

"You won't get away with this. Trigg will come for me. You'll see!"

"Ah, so Mr. Hanahan knows you're here, after all. Well, all the better. I'll alert my men to be doubly on guard. They'll simply wait until he shows up and then remove him from the picture permanently." He paused and gave her a conciliatory grin. "Unless of course, he has my money with him or you have agreed to my proposition—in which case I will call off my boys."

He started to leave again, but stopped one more time. "And assuming one of the boys doesn't spot him and shoot him before he realizes he has the money he owes me with him!"

It hit Trigg with the sudden, heart-stopping clarity of a tornado. As surely as he knew he was standing in a deserted shed on the South Side of Chicago, he knew Ellari had gone to the Levee to try to talk to Boss Stahl.

Verbally castigating himself with every abusing term he could think of for not knowing immediately what she had done, he hurried into action. He had to get to her before it was too late, if it wasn't already.

Hands shaking, he hurriedly strapped on the new holster and revolver he had purchased for their sudden trip. Though he'd occasionally carried a revolver in the past, he had never worn one on a regular basis, but he was relieved now that he had decided it was time to start. *I should have worn it last night, instead of putting it behind the seat,* he berated himself. *If I'd been a little more concerned with safety, and less with my own comfort, none of this would be happening.*

Bending over, Trigg checked the knives he had hidden in secret sheaths in each of his boots, as well as the small pistol he always carried in his right boot.

"I never thought I'd say this," he mumbled to the still groggy Mr. Cat he had let out of the cage to feed. "But I just pray to God Nick has her, because if he doesn't—"

A shiver of dread twisted up his spine as he remembered hearing only the week before about a sixteen-year-old girl who'd wandered into the Levee looking for the real estate office where she was

343

supposed to take the mortgage payment on her family's home. That poor girl had simply disappeared and wasn't found until weeks later in a St. Louis whorehouse, her mind so muddled by drugs she couldn't remember how she got there.

Not certain what to do about the horses and wagon, but knowing he couldn't simply ride up in front of Stahl's place unless he wanted to be shot on sight, Trigg stepped outside into the alley. With the exception of two boys who looked to be about nine or ten years old and homeless, the alley was unoccupied. "Hey boys," he hollered, "how'd you like to make twenty bucks?"

The eyes of the two urchins grew round with greed. "Sure," they answered in unison, running to where he stood.

"Who we gotta kill?" the older boy asked.

Even under ordinary circumstances, Trigg wouldn't have smiled at the boy's question, because he knew the kid was serious. "No one," he said, digging in his pocket. "All you need to do is keep an eye on this shed and make sure no one goes inside. There's another twenty in it for you if everything's here when I get back."

The boys shot each other excited glances. "Sure, we'll keep a eye on it fer ya, mister. Whatcha got in there?"

Knowing the way the kids of the street thought even better than they did, Trigg grabbed them both by the shirt collars and brought his own face down to the same level as theirs. "In case you get any ideas about going inside yourselves, I'd better warn you, the whole place is booby trapped to blow up if anyone but me opens the doors or tries to so much as remove one slat. You got that?"

"Y-y-yes sir," they stuttered together.

Trigg nodded his approval and released them. "Good. I thought you looked like smart fellows." He handed them twenty dollars in bills. "Like I said, you'll get the rest when I get back."

The instant she heard Nick Stahl's retreating footsteps fade out of hearing, Ellari ran to the outside exit and wrenched open the door.

"Can I help you, miss?" the man who'd paid Sully asked, blocking the doorway like a heavy curtain drawn to keep out the sun.

"Oh! Johnny! Thank goodness you're here," she exclaimed, rallying with record speed from the shock of finding him there. "Come quickly. Mr. Stahl needs you. There's a fight in the hallway outside the room."

Without hesitation, the huge bulk of a man stormed past Ellari and across the apartment. The instant his back was to her, Ellari ran out the door and started down the outside staircase.

"Very smooth," a familiar voice crooned from the bottom of the stairs.

Ellari stopped short, her gaze coming to a frozen

stare on the smiling face of Nick Stahl.

"Tsk, tsk," he clicked with his tongue, climbing the stairs slowly, as a cat would stalk a bird. "I can see that taming you is going to present quite a challenge." He reached the step below hers and stopped, his face level with hers. "A challenge, I might add, that I'm looking forward to meeting with great relish."

Ellari narrowed her eyes threateningly, debating on the wisdom of trying to surprise him with a sudden shove. If she caught him off guard, he would lose his balance, and if she were really lucky, he would break his neck in the fall.

"Don't even think about it, Ellari," he said with a knowing grin. Without waiting for her to respond, he gripped her upper arms and turned her around, then prodded her up the stairs.

At the top, Johnny appeared in the doorway looking chagrined and embarrassed. "I'm sorry, Mr. Stahl. She said you was callin' for me."

"Don't worry about it, Johnny. You had no way of knowing Miss Lochridge would show us her gratitude for saving her life by tricking you."

Johnny stood aside to allow Ellari and Nick to pass. "No sir. I sure never woulda thought a lady'd do somethin' like that."

Nick gave him a consoling pat on the arm. "Well, now you do, so I want you to be doubly on guard. This is one stubborn lady."

"Oh, I'll do that, Mr. Stahl. You can depend on

me." He started to leave.

"By the way, Johnny," Nick called, stopping him. "Don't forget Sully's new location. I owe it to him to have first chance at buying her back if I decide to sell."

"Yes, sir. Anything else?"

"Yeah! Tell the others to be on the lookout for Trigg Hanahan. Something tells me he's going to be coming by in the next few hours."

"Same orders?"

Nick nodded. "If he's got the money he owes me, bring him to me alive. If not, get rid of him once and for all."

Disguised as an out-of-luck old man in rags he'd bought from a beggar an hour earlier, Trigg staggered into the alley beside the Majestic Theatre. "Jus' one whiskey," he mumbled to no one as he slid down the wall at the bottom of the stairs to Stahl's apartment. "That's all I need."

"Hey!" Johnny yelled from his post outside the door. "Go on, old-timer. Mr. Stahl don't want your kind hangin' 'round here pesterin' the customers."

Trigg made a show of lifting his head in response to Johnny's orders. Then he let it drop, chin to chest, as if he had passed out.

The sound of Johnny's weight lumbering down the wooden stairs set Trigg's heart pounding with anticipation. Stahl's bodyguard outweighed him by at least seventy-five pounds, so he knew what he was doing was dangerous to say the least. Unfortunately, getting past Johnny was the only way into Stahl's apartment to find out if he had Ellari. A pistol palmed in one hand, his other gripping the revolver, he waited.

"Come on, old man," Johnny coaxed, lifting Trigg from the ground by his coat collar. "You gotta go somewhere else."

Knowing his only allies against the larger man were speed and the element of surprise, Trigg hesitated only long enough to be sure of his footing.

Bringing the pistol forward, he jabbed it against Johnny's privates at the same time he pressed the revolver barrel at an upward angle into the man's mid-section.

"How've you been, Johnny?" he asked, raising his head to grin at the stunned man. "It's been a while, hasn't it? Where's Nick?"

Sweat broke out on Johnny's upper lip and forehead. "Mr. Stahl's in his apartment."

"Is Ellari Lochridge with him?"

"Who?"

Trigg shoved the pistol harder into the mass at the top of Johnny's thighs. "I've got no time for games, John. Unless, you want your balls blown all over this alley, you'd better tell me what I want to hear. Now, is she with him, or not?"

"He's with a woman, but I can't say if she's the one you're lookin' for. I didn't catch her name.

348

This one was dressed kinda like a old-maid school-teacher."

"Light red hair and about five-four or five."

"That's the one."

Trigg didn't know whether to cry or to be relieved. At least Ellari wasn't on the streets, and she hadn't been grabbed by some Levee pimp. On the other hand, if she'd been with Nick Stahl this long, he had probably already seduced her.

"All right, let's go." Trigg used the guns to turn Johnny back toward the stairs.

At the top of the stairs, Johnny paused. "You sure you wanna do this, Hanahan? Mr. Stahl's already put out a order to kill you on sight."

"Then I've got nothing to lose, do I?"

Johnny tilted his head and hunched his shoulders in resignation. "It's your funeral." He opened the apartment door.

Chapter Nineteen

Trigg stopped short, his stunned gaze fixing on the two people sitting close together on the settee. Looking very smug, Nick had his arm draped around a frightened and stiff-looking Ellari.

"Trigg, old friend. We've been expecting you," Nick greeted him with a grin. "Haven't we, my dear?"

"Are you all right?" Trigg asked anxiously. "So, help me, Nick, if you've laid a hand—"

"I'm fine," Ellari answered quickly. Her eyes shifted nervously to Nick, then returned to Trigg. "Mr. Stahl has been a perfect gentleman."

"I'm sure he has. He was always good at pretending to be what he wasn't." He prodded Johnny forward with the gun. "But you can drop the act now, Nick. The show's over. Come on, Ellari. Let's go."

"I'm afraid that's not possible," Nick said, seemingly unconcerned with the fact that Trigg had a gun on Johnny. "You see, Miss Lochridge has done me the honor of agreeing to stay here with me."

Trigg gave Ellari a fleeting look of confusion, then concentrated on Nick Stahl. "I guess you didn't understand me, Nick. Let her go, or Johnny's dead."

"No!" Ellari cried. "He's telling the truth. I'm staying here."

Trigg shot Ellari a hurt, questioning glance.

Nick grinned slyly. "The ladies always did prefer my company, didn't they?"

Trigg's expression filled with hatred. "Once you got them so full of drugs they didn't remember their own names, they did. But this is one woman you're not going to destroy. Ellari, get over here. Now!"

"I can't leave, Trigg. I've given him my word I'll stay and work for him in exchange for a one week extension on your loan. The best thing you can do is go and get the money he says you owe him and come back for me when you have it."

"That's crazy! I'm not leaving you with *him!*" He pulled back the hammer on the revolver.

"I'll be all right!" she exclaimed, her eyes growing round with fear.

"Maybe you didn't understand the lady, Hanahan," a new voice said from behind Trigg at the same time he felt the barrel of a gun dig into his back. "She said she wants to stay."

"No! Don't shoot him!" Ellari screamed. "He'll

351

leave peacefully!" She directed her pleading gaze to Trigg. "Please! It's the only way. I'll be fine. Mr. Stahl has promised me that as long as you're back in a week I'll be treated with total respect."

"And of course you believe him," Trigg said, the ache inside him threatening to explode. "Women always do."

"I have no choice, Trigg. And neither do you."

Her obvious struggle to be brave tore at Trigg's gut. Never had he felt so powerless and like such a failure. If only he could tell her everything would be all right and mean it. But he couldn't. He couldn't even convince himself that everything would be all right. If he tried to shoot their way out of Stahl's office, he'd be killed for certain, and then there would be no one to save Ellari from Nick. She'd never get out of here until Nick was through with her.

On the other hand, if he left peacefully, there was no guarantee she would be the same sweet, innocent woman when he got back, or even that she would still be here. But as she had said, he really had no choice. At least if he left and came back, there was a chance.

He narrowed his eyes at Nick Stahl. "I want your word, no one will give her any cocaine or morphine or any other drugs."

"The last thing I need is another air walker working for me," Nick laughed. "I simply want her to serve as my hostess at several business dinners I'd like to have. She'll lend a touch of respectability the girls who work for me wouldn't be able to carry off—if you know what I mean."

Trigg narrowed his eyes suspiciously.

Nick threw back his head and laughed. "No, she won't be asked to entertain my associates with anything other than polite conversation." He leveled a serious glare on Trigg. "Unless, you don't return with my money within the week—in which case, all promises are off."

"Very nicely done, my dear," Nick said as soon as Trigg was escorted out the door. "You learn quickly. I can see our relationship has excellent potential." He hugged her to him and kissed her on the cheek.

Her face twisted with revulsion, Ellari bounded out of his grasp and spun to face him. "You and I both know the only reason I pretended to be willing to go along with this disgusting scheme of yours was to protect Trigg. But he's not here now, and I expect you to live up to your end of our agreement and leave me alone. Is that understood?"

A bitterly amused smile snaked across Nick's face. "You'll change your mind. I think you'll see I can be quite convincing."

"Never! I'll die before I'll submit to being mauled by a man like you."

"Never is a long time, my dear Ellari. And I'm a very patient man. Before this is over, I'm willing to bet you will be begging me to touch you." He stood up and crossed to the inside door. "Because I doubt very seriously that your 'fiancé' is going to come to your rescue. He has a habit of disappearing when things get too dangerous."

Remembering that Trigg had been on the verge of leaving town sent fear and doubt racing through Ellari's veins. What if Nick Stahl was right about Trigg? What if the danger was too great and he just left her? Refusing to listen to or acknowledge the possibility that Trigg would desert her, she stiffened her spine and lifted her chin. "Trigg will be back, and he'll kill you if you lay a hand on me."

Nick smiled knowingly. "I'll send up someone with breakfast and to help you prepare for bed. Tonight will be your debut as my charming companion and hostess, and it wouldn't do to have you appear with circles under those beautiful green eyes of yours."

Before she could answer, he wrenched open the door and disappeared through it. She ran to the door and put her ear to it.

"No one's to enter or leave my apartment with the exception of myself and the maid I'll be sending up. Is that understood?"

"Yes sir, Mr. Stahl."

"And under no circumstances are you to leave

your post until someone comes to relieve you."

No! Ellari protested silently, realizing there was already a guard outside the door. Desperate to find a way out, she frantically looked around the large room, not doubting that Johnny or someone else was guarding the only other exit.

On either end of the room, she spotted windows. She ran to the one she anticipated to be at the back of the building. It would be her best chance for making an undetected escape.

Unfortunately, she quickly saw that the rear window of the room was not only a straight drop to another alleyway, but that there was a guard armed with a rifle watching the window. He grinned and tipped his hat when he saw her.

Panicked, she jumped back and pressed herself to the wall. That left only the front window facing the street.

Because people were on the street all hours of the day and night, she was certain the front window wouldn't be an option for escaping, but she dashed across the room to check it anyway.

Unfortunately, she'd been right. The front window was even worse than the back. With the exception of a six-inch ledge below the window that had obviously been put there for decorative purposes only, there was nothing to break a fall to the heavily traveled wooden sidewalk below.

Disappointed, she turned back to the room. She couldn't give up. There had to be a way out. A knock on the door startled her and she hurriedly scoured the room for something with which to defend herself. Her gaze zeroed on a silver letter opener on the desk. She dashed over and grabbed the weapon. Hiding it in her pocket, she flopped back down on the settee as the door opened.

"Mornin', Missy," an enormous black woman greeted her. "Mr. Nick said you'd be wantin' breakfast."

"Yes, thank you," Ellari said, out of breath, suddenly remembering she hadn't eaten since the morning before and that she was hungry.

"And while you eat, I'll draw up a hot bath for you. Nothin' like a hot bath to git rid o' your worries," the woman babbled cheerfully as she set up breakfast. "Then Mr. Nick says you're to get some rest. He's plannin' a nice welcomin' dinner for you tonight. Sez he wants to show you off. Oh, and he tole me you're not to worry 'bout losin' all your luggage on the train trip from Boston. He's havin' Madame Bordeaux, that fancy French seamstress all the rich ladies in Chicago go to, bring over some things for you to look at this afternoon. He says nothin's too good for you. And I know you're anxious to get into some decent clothes and outta that old maid disguise you traveled in so as no one'd be botherin' you on the train." The woman paused to take a breath and pull out a chair for Ellari.

Why would Nick Stahl tell this woman that

356

she'd come from Boston? Ellari wondered. For that matter, why would he say that her clothes were a disguise and that her luggage had been stolen to cover the fact that she needed new clothes? Surely a man in his line of business wouldn't worry about a woman's reputation, but that was exactly what he seemed to be doing.

Before Ellari could ask any questions, the woman went on chattering. "But I've got to tell you, chile. You're gonna have to do more than put on a plain dress and pull your hair back into a unbecomin' knot to keep folks from noticin' that pretty face o' yours. Now git yourself on over here and eat."

Unable to keep from responding to the woman's friendly conversation with a smile, Ellari sat down to breakfast. No one other than Trigg had ever told her she was pretty, and even in these trying circumstances, it sent a warm rush tearing through her blood. "Thank you—uh—what do I call you?"

"Everyone 'round here calls me Mammy, 'cause I'm the closest thing to a mammy most of 'em got, includin' Mr. Nick, hisself."

"Well, thank you, Mammy, this looks delicious," Ellari said, draping a cloth napkin across her lap and picking up her fork. An alternate idea for escaping had just occurred to her. If she could get Mammy to trust her, the woman might be the one to help her. "But tell me more about Mr. Stahl. I really know very little about him. I suppose you've

357

known him for a long time."

Mammy threw back her head and laughed. "Since he was a boy. I was workin' as a housekeeper for some rich folks over on Terrace Row on Michigan Avenue—bein' as how you're from outta town, you wouldn't know, but that's where some of Chicago's finest families live, 'ceptin' maybe the ones that moved to the North Division. Anyhow, I found him hidin' in the alley behind the house I was workin' in, and he'd been beat up somethin' fierce." She shook her head. "He couldn't have been more'n nine or ten, and he looked half-starved. Poor little street boy. So, I took him in and cleaned him up and fed him, then kept him hid in my room until he got better. And from that day to this, he never forgot his old Mammy. So when he growed up and won him this place in a poker game, he come got me and tole me, 'Mammy,' he says, 'from now on I'm takin' care o' you, and you don't never have to work again.' Course I tole that boy I worked all my life and didn't intend to stop now, so he give me the job o' overseeing the maids and cooks—for as long as I want it, and as long as I don't do no cleanin' myself. Only reason he 'lowed me to serve your breakfast was 'cause he knew I was dyin' to see you." She chuckled to herself. "An' to tell the truth, I think he wanted to show you off to ole Mammy, 'cause he knows I never 'prove o' them tarts he usually brings here."

358

"Did you find the people who hurt him?" Ellari asked, not certain she wanted to know about this other side of Nick Stahl, but curious in spite of herself. "Were they punished?"

Mammy opened her mouth to speak, then closed it again. She shook her head and started for the bathroom. She paused and looked regretfully back at Ellari. "There's wicked, ugly things goin' on in this world that a fine young lady like yourself's got no need to know 'bout. I'll jes tell you this. Young boys ain't no safer on the streets than young girls are if they wander into the wrong place at the wrong time. But that's all behind him now that you're here."

"Now that I'm—"

Mammy whipped open the bathroom door. "I'll start that bath now. Mr. Nick has the hot water pumped up here from the kitchen. You're gonna love it."

Accepting the not-too-subtle hint that Mammy had no more information she was willing to share at the moment, Ellari concentrated on eating her breakfast and trying to figure out how she was going to get away from Nick Stahl.

"You look lovely, my dear," Nick told Ellari, circling her as he spoke. "I've no doubt you will be a most delightful addition to my meeting this evening. The two gentlemen I've invited to join us for dinner are very important to my future, and I would hate to have anything spoil this opportunity for me."

Ellari glanced down at the tastefully exquisite white beaded evening dress Madame Bordeaux and Mammy had insisted was perfect for her. She was at least thankful that Nick apparently had meant it when he had said he wanted her for the look of respectability she could give him that his money couldn't buy, and nothing more.

"What if I do the wrong thing? I've told you, I've never been around rich people before, and I've certainly never worn clothes like these."

"All you have to do is smile a lot, pretend to be interested in what they are saying, and don't offer any opinions of your own. I have every faith you won't fail me." He trailed his finger from her temple to her shoulder, his smile frightening. "Because if you deliberately spoil this chance for me, Trigg Hanahan will be dead before morning."

Ellari fought the shiver of revulsion his touch caused her to feel. So much for the suspicion that there might be a decent human being hiding behind the hard veneer Nick Stahl wore for the world to see. She had let Mammy's blind love and devotion sway her, but that wouldn't happen again.

"In that case, I will do my best not to disappoint you."

Nick smiled. "I knew I could depend on you.

Now, before we leave, I should prepare you for any surprises. First of all, I'll be introducing you as Miss Elthea Wainwright of Boston. You're the daughter of the very rich Wilbur Wainwright, a close friend and business associate of mine. Your father made his money building ships, and he would be very happy if you and I decide to marry, hence your visit, so that we can get to know each other better. Do you think you can remember that information or do I need to go over it again?"

Ellari cast a withering look in his direction. "Elthea Wainwright of Boston, rich Wilbur Wainwright builds ships and wants his daughter to marry you—though don't you think it stretches the credibility of this little pretense to the limits to expect anyone to believe a rich man would allow his daughter to visit in a place like this for any reason whatsoever?"

Nick thought for a minute. "You're right. Thanks. I'd better think of a reason why he would go along with you coming here."

Darn! She'd meant her statement to be insulting and a put down, not a way to help him.

"I know!" he said. "How's this sound? I'm interested in getting out of this business and into a more respectable line of business. One business I'm considering investing in is Wainwright's. And knowing how smitten I was with you in Boston, he let you come here to convince me."

"Don't you th—"

"This is perfect. It goes right along with the reason I'm meeting with these gentlemen tonight. One's a businessman who wants me to invest in his company so that he can expand, and the other is his banker who wants to handle my business dealings. And both of them have the power to get me invited to join the most prestigious men's club in Chicago." He turned a sincere smile in her direction and kissed her cheek before she could stop him. "You really are going to be an asset." He held out an arm to her. "Shall we? I have a carriage waiting downstairs."

From the shadows of an alley across the street, Trigg watched as Ellari and Nick descended the stairs, he in black evening clothes, she in white sequins and silk. Her hair had been swirled up into a cascade of large curls, and even from this distance he could see the jewels that sparkled from her ears and at her throat.

"Damn you, Nick," he growled under his breath. "I don't know where you're taking her, but if anything happens to her, there aren't enough bodyguards in the world to save you."

He waited until the carriage drove off, then he loped down the alley in the opposite direction.

Willing her lips to form a smile, Ellari took a

362

deep breath as the two gentlemen rose to greet Nick and her in the dining room of the Tremont House Hotel.

"My dear," Nick said to her, "allow me to introduce my business associates, Mr. David Nylander and Mr. Reed Phelps."

As if she'd been socked in the chest and had all the breath knocked out of her lungs, Ellari stopped breathing, though for some peculiar reason, her artificial smile managed to remain intact.

"Gentlemen, I'd like for you to meet Miss Elthea Wainwright. She is the daughter of another business associate of mine. Perhaps you've heard of him. Wilbur Wainwright, the Boston shipbuilding magnate."

Nylander took Ellari's gloved hand and lifted it to his mouth, though his lips didn't actually touch. "My pleasure, Miss Wainwright. I trust you will find our city to your liking."

"Why — uh — yes, it is quite — uh — lovely," she stumbled through her speech, feeling light-headed. How was she going to sit through a meal with David Nylander without telling him what she thought of him?

"Are you all right, my dear?" Nick asked, squeezing her arm. "You look flushed."

"What?" she asked, forcing her attention away from Nylander and back to her escort. The unspoken message in his narrowed eyes gave her the strength to regain her aplomb. "I'm sorry." She fluttered her hand in front of her face. "I have not become accustomed to the warmer climate yet. I'll be fine once I sit down."

All three men scurried to pull out a chair for her. "Perhaps a glass of ice water will help," Reed Phelps suggested, holding up a hand to signal a waiter once they were all seated.

"That will be lovely," Ellari answered with a weak smile. "But please pardon me. I didn't mean to cause such a disturbance." She glanced around apprehensively. "Is everyone staring at us?"

"Nonsense, love," Nick said, picking up her hand and kissing it.

The men discussed the infernal heat for a few minutes, debating on whether or not this had been Chicago's hottest and dryest year ever, and on whether it would beat last year's six-hundred-fire record.

Ellari took the opportunity to try and determine how meeting David Nylander under these strange circumstances could be used to help her stop him from using child labor in his factory.

"I say, Miss Wainwright," Reed Phelps said, interrupting her thoughts. "I have the strangest feeling we've met before, but I can't think where. Is this your first trip to Chicago?"

"Yes!" Ellari answered, desperate to change the subject. "Have you been to Boston?"

"I haven't had the pleasure. Though I must say, it is one city I've always hoped to visit. Perhaps you will give me a tour when I do come."

"I'd be delighted," she said with a forced smile. "If I'm in the city at the time. I hope to do a great deal of traveling in the next year or two." She directed a side look at Nick, mentally ordering him to change the subject before she gave herself away. All she needed was for Phelps to ask her something specific about Boston, and she would be exposed.

Nick took her hint and leaned next to her to kiss her cheek. "I'm hoping to convince Miss Wainwright to stay in Chicago permanently. What do you say we order dinner now? I don't know about you gentlemen, but I'm famished." He held up a hand for the waiter, who hurried over to take their orders.

Much to Ellari's relief, talk about the weather, local and national politics and the general economy occupied the dinner conversation. Ellari did learn, to her surprise, that despite the ready availability of exquisite foreign cuisine and liquor at the best restaurants, rare roast beef and domestic champagne known as Mumm's Extra Dry were still the overwhelming favorites of rich Chicagoans. That wasn't any information, however, that would help her get the children out of Nylander's glass factory.

When they had finished eating, Nick sat back in his chair. "Has there been any news on my application to join the club?"

The two men glanced at each other uneasily. "We brought up your name at the last general meeting," Phelps began.

"And," Nick asked anxiously. "What did they say? Am I in?"

"Well," Nylander said hesitantly, "to be quite frank, old man, several of our members were hesitant to offer you membership to our club as long as your main source of income is the Majestic."

"Were they now?" Nick asked indignantly. "And who were these members who presume to judge me? Why don't we go talk to them? They're probably all over at my place right this minute."

Phelps patted Nick's arms. "Now there's no need to get riled up. It's only a few of the older members who are giving us trouble. The majority are ready to welcome you into our midst. It's just that some members don't think it's appropriate for one of our members to own a—" He glanced uncomfortably at Ellari, then back to Nick. "—*theater* in the Levee District when the rest of us are doctors, lawyers, politicians, bankers, hotel owners and such."

"That's a laugh. I happen to know most of your members have interests in businesses in the Levee, if they don't own them outright."

Phelps smiled understandingly. "That's true, but those connections to the Levee aren't flaunted. But don't worry, David and I have come up with a solution I think will appease the members who

366

blackballed you, and will make you even richer in the bargain."

"And what is that?" Nick gritted, struggling to keep from pounding his fists or dumping over the table or doing something equally violent.

"You know that David has been talking about expanding, and he has generously offered you the chance to buy as much as forty-five percent of Nylander Glass, in order to give you the legitimate business base you need from which to operate. He's even willing to change the name to Nylander-Stahl Glass. And of course, as the business partner of a man from one of Chicago's oldest and most successful families, no one will dare turn you down for membership. You'll be welcomed with open arms."

"What about the Majestic? I'll still own it."

Nylander shrugged. "You could sell it. I'm sure Reed could find you a buyer. Or we could hire a manager to run it for you. You could be a silent owner. All sorts of reputable businessmen own — uh —" Now it was Nylander's turn to glance nervously in Ellari's direction. "— businesses and rental property in the Levee. They just don't flaunt the fact by living above them or publicly participating in the operations."

"For that matter, I've acquired a number of places myself," Phelps volunteered. "So what do you say?"

"I say, I really appreciate you gentlemen being

willing to help me out like this."

"Then we have a deal?" Nylander asked, holding out his hand.

Unable to listen to any more of this conversation, Ellari bolted up from her chair. "If you gentlemen will excuse me, I'd like to powder my nose," she said with as much control as she could muster.

All three men stood instantly. "I'll show you the way, love," Nick offered, taking her arm and propelling her toward the curtained doorway at the back of the dining room.

Outside the doorway to the ladies' room, he stopped her. "I hope you weren't thinking of making a hasty retreat out the back way, Miss *Wainwright*. Because if you were, I think you should know you would not be alone." He nodded to the man who came through the curtains and took up a post near the back exit.

"Actually, it might surprise you to know that leaving never entered my mind. I'm finding it too fascinating watching you cow down to those two ignominious fakes who pass themselves off as gentlemen. They really do have you dancing on a string, don't they? You'd sell your soul for respectability, and they know it. But if you want respectability so much, I would think with your money and intelligence you could find much better ways to achieve it than to do business with an exploiter and murderer of children like David Nylander, who hides his crimes behind a family name, or with an opportunist like Reed Phelps— who evidently exploits anything he can get his hands on." She spun toward the powder room. "Now if you will excuse me, Mr. Stahl, I really must powder my nose, or we shall both be terribly embarrassed."

Obviously confused by her anger, Nick hesitated before he spoke. "Russell will escort you back to the table when you're ready."

Chapter Twenty

Flattened on the level roof of the Majestic Theatre, Trigg peered down on the street below to be sure no one was glancing in his direction. Deciding it was as safe as it was going to get, he took one last tug on the rope he had tied around himself and slithered feet first over the edge of the roof.

Quickly locating the window sill with his feet, he lowered himself into Boss Stahl's apartment with almost no effort. "You've still got it, Hanahan," he mumbled to himself, hurriedly removing the rope from around his waist and securing both the looped end and the other end behind the heavy drape on the window.

Glancing around the large room and at its expensive furnishings, Trigg shook his head in disgust. "Maybe you were right all along, Nicky," he muttered regretfully. "Maybe it really doesn't matter how you get there, only that you do. My way sure hasn't worked, has it?"

A sweet, smiling face, framed with wisps of

strawberry blonde hair popped into his mind, and his expression grew angry. "At least not until I found Ellari, and I'm not going to let you ruin this for me. This time, you've gone too far, Nick. You may be the 'Boss' of the whole Levee, the whole God damned city for all I care, but when you decided to take out your hate for me by destroying the only decent thing that's ever happened to me, you made a big mistake. A very big mistake."

Just then, he heard footsteps on the stairs outside, and he made an urgent dash for the bathroom.

"All right!" Nick Stahl snarled, slamming the door to the outside behind him and tossing his top hat onto a table. It was the first time he had spoken to her since they had left the Tremont. "I want to know what you meant about expecting more from someone with my background." He ripped off his tie and pitched it aside. "What do you know about me? What did Hanahan tell you?"

"Trigg didn't tell me anything. It was—" Ellari caught herself. Evidently, she had stumbled onto such a touchy subject that even his beloved Mammy might not be safe from Nick's wrath if he knew what the kindly woman had told her about him.

371

"Who then?" he growled.

"No one! It was simply a deduction on my part. Your desperation to be accepted by those men and into that club, as well as a few things you've said, led me to believe you may have had a pretty hard childhood and raised yourself on the streets. If so, I'm sure you've witnessed firsthand the terrible things adults can do to children to earn a profit. And what David Nylander does is one of the worst crimes. Under the guise of being a legitimate businessman and pillar of the community, he kills and maims children in his glass factory, where he treats them like slaves rather than children, and forces them to work long, crippling hours for pennies a day doing dangerous jobs—jobs that grown men should be doing."

"You don't know what you're talking about."

"Believe me, I do. I come in contact with those abused children every day in my pharmacy. I treat their injuries. I see their listless, unhealthy faces, deathly pale from never seeing the light of day because they go to work before sunrise and don't get out until after it sets. I've seen once perfect children dismembered and disfigured, their hands or fingers or legs missing because of accidents they have suffered working in the glass factories. I've even had them die in my arms." Her voice cracked. "Oh, yes, Mr. Stahl, I do know what I'm talking about."

He studied her for a moment, a play of emotion

on his face she didn't understand. "I meant about my background," he finally said. "And about what I want."

Assuming he was denying that he was raised on the streets, Ellari decided to drop the subject—for now—but if it took the rest of the week she was to be here, she was going to find a way to stop him from investing in Nylander's slaughterhouse for children. She knew she might not be able to stop David Nylander altogether, but she would try to at least put a kink in his plans for expansion.

"Perhaps you're right. But however you were raised, I'm sure you can still remember the helplessness of being a child. And I only hope you will consider what I've told you about Nylander Glass before you give him the money that will make it possible for him to brutalize even more children if he has the opportunity to enlarge his factory."

"If I don't invest, he'll get the money somewhere else. So why shouldn't it be me? Why should I turn down the chance to get what I want and make a profit at the same time?"

Ellari managed a pitying smile. "Knowing how they and their members feel about you, do you really believe they would have asked you for the money if they could have gotten it somewhere else? Come now, surely you're not that blind. I've been told I don't have any head for business whatsoever, but even I can see those men need you

373

more than you need them. And if promising you acceptance is the only way to get their hands on your money, then that's what they'll do. But after the papers have been signed and the money has changed hands and is under their control—remember they only offered you forty-five percent—don't be surprised to have them come back with another excuse to keep you out of their exclusive club."

Nick silently glared at Ellari long and hard. Then without speaking, he turned on his boot heel and strode angrily toward the door to the hallway. "When you wake in the morning, tell the guard. He'll have someone bring your breakfast. And don't get any ideas about leaving during the night. There are guards on both doors and watching the windows."

"But you haven't said what you're going to do about David Nylander's offer!" she protested, following him to the door. "Surely, you're not—"

"Good night, Miss Lochridge. I will see you tomorrow afternoon." He wrenched open the door and disappeared through it, slamming it behind him.

For several long seconds, Ellari didn't move. She couldn't. She was too annoyed with herself. Obviously, she had pushed him too far. Nick Stahl wasn't the sort of man who took well to having anyone second guess him, especially a woman. Right this minute, he was probably on his way to close the deal with Nylander and Phelps in the private meeting room he'd promised to join them in after he saw her back to the apartment. Out of habit, she slipped the bolt into the door.

"Now I've heard everything," a familiar voice muttered from behind her. "The prisoner giving her jailer financial advice."

Spinning around, Ellari found Trigg leaning on the doorjamb to the bathroom, his arms crossed over his chest.

"Trigg!" she whispered, running to him and hugging him. "What are you doing here?" She covered his face with kisses. "Thank God you're all right. He said they were following you and that you wouldn't be coming back. I was afraid he meant he was going to have you killed in spite of the extension."

She sandwiched his face between her palms and smiled. "I should have known you would outsmart them!" she told him, taking care to keep her voice low. "But how did you get past the guards? They're everywhere."

His face stern, Trigg removed her arms from around his neck and brushed past her. He walked to the outside entrance and put his ear up to the door to listen, then slid the lock into place. "He's gotten to you, hasn't he?" he said, turning back to face her.

"What?"

"Nick's got you thinking there's some decency in him after all, doesn't he?"

"No! Of course not."

"Then what was all that crap I heard you telling him?"

"If you heard, then you know. He's about to hand over a large sum of money to David Nylander so the glass factory can be expanded—and so Nylander will be able to hire and destroy even more children than he does now. Did you expect me not to try to stop him from helping Nylander anyway I could? Even if it means appealing to the most miniscule shred of decency he might possess. Besides, I found out he was a street orphan like you were. And that gives me hope that no matter what evil things he's done, he still might abhor the exploitation of children as much as I do."

Trigg's expression grew even more furious. He stormed past her. "Here I am going crazy—"

"Shh!" she warned in an urgent whisper. "Someone will hear you!"

He lowered his voice. "Here I was worrying about the woman I love being held prisoner by a man who hates my guts and wants me dead. And all the time, you were here having a nice social visit with Nick Stahl, discussing all the things you have in common."

"That's not true. I only meant that if I could arouse even an ounce of sympathy in him where children were concerned, maybe I could use that to hurt Nylander."

"Get into your own clothes," he ordered her.

"We're getting out of here."

"And how do you propose we do that when he has guards everywhere?"

"The same way I got in," he growled. "Out the window and over the roofs of the connecting buildings. So come on. Let's hustle."

Ellari didn't move. "I can't climb onto the roof!" she whispered disbelievingly. "The only thing I've ever climbed is a staircase, and I've been known to fall on them. I'd never make it. Besides, we'd be seen. You heard him say he has guards."

"Not out front." Trigg crossed to the window and looked outside. "I guess he figures he doesn't need one since passersby would see us. But folks on the street are too busy doing whatever they're doing to notice what goes on above their heads. No one looks up here. And as far as you climbing onto the roof, that's taken care of." He pulled the two rope ends out from behind the drape. "I won't let you fall."

"There's no way I intend to submit to being hauled onto the roof like a bale of cotton or a side of beef. Besides—"

"You're not going to be hauled like a side of beef!" He chuckled. "I'm going to use the rope to climb onto the roof. Then I'll lower it back to you to use only for a safety measure. Actually, once I'm on the roof, I'll reach down and take your hands and pull you up."

"Will you please stop talking so loudly?" she

asked, glancing nervously at the door. "If they find you in here, they'll kill us both!"

"Then get changed, and let's go," he hissed, putting pointed emphasis on each syllable.

"I can't."

"What do you mean, you can't? I told you I've got it all figured out. No one'll see us, and I won't let you fall; so what's the problem?" He narrowed his eyes suspiciously. "Or was all that talk about wanting to get out of here just an act?"

"Of course not. It's just that I can't leave yet."

"Why the hell not?"

She glanced at the door again. "How many times do I have to remind you to keep your voice down?"

"Why the hell not?" he repeated more quietly.

"Because I can't go until I know for certain if he's going to give the money to Nylander or not."

"Are you sure that's all it is, Ellari?" he asked bitterly. "Or is it that you've decided Nick's more your type with all his money and phony manners—and maybe even enough money to help you fight Nylander, without waiting for me to come up with it?"

"Don't be ridiculous. You know that's not true. There's no room in my heart for another man. I love you more than life itself, and there's nothing I wouldn't do for you."

"Then prove it. Leave with me right now."

Shaking her head, Ellari inhaled deeply. "You

378

still don't understand, do you, Trigg? And I don't know what I can say to make you understand. I have a moral obligation to help those children, a moral obligation that goes beyond us and what we feel for each other. I would love to go out that window with you right this minute. And if I don't go with you, I'm scared to death you'll stop loving me and will leave me. But as much it tears my heart out to think of never seeing you again, I still can't go. Not when I've been given this chance, maybe the only chance I'll ever have, to create a serious problem for Nylander Glass. No matter what the consequences, I simply have to stay and do my best to convince Nick Stahl not to help David Nylander."

He stared at her, shaking his head. "Obviously, your mind's made up."

The raw pain and anger in his expression shredded Ellari's emotions and certainty to pieces. How much good was she actually going to do by staying? The only thing she could realistically hope to accomplish was to create a delay for Nylander's plans.

On the other hand, if the desperation she had detected in the factory owner's demeanor meant he was on the verge of serious financial trouble, maybe even bankruptcy, there just might be a possibility that by staying she could create enough of an obstacle to shut him down altogether. Though the chances were slim to none, and Nylander was only one glass factory, she decided she couldn't turn her back on the possibility that she could do some good.

"Yes, my mind is made up," she agreed, conscious of the tears rolling down her cheeks, but too numb to lift her hand to wipe them away. "I have to stay."

"I guess there's nothing else to say," he murmured, turning toward the window as if to leave. "Except—"

He stopped in mid-step. "Except what?"

"Except maybe, 'I love you, Ellari, and even though I can't understand why you're doing this, I trust you, and I'll stand behind you,'" she said, her throat obviously clogged with tears.

With desperate speed, he whirled to face her and covered the space that separated them in two angry steps. "Damn you, Ellari Lochridge," he growled, capturing her in a ferocious, vicelike embrace. "You are the most stubborn, mule-headed, obstinate woman I've ever known in my life!"

His expression twisted with anger, he grabbed a fistful of her hair and jerked her head back so that her neck was arched, and her gaze locked with his. "I'll never understand you, but dammit, 'I do love you. And I'll stand behind you.'"

He sealed his vow with a hard, ravenous kiss. With one desperate tug, he tore her stylishly arranged coiffure asunder. Hairpins clicked to the floor like rain drops on a pane of glass as her thick hair spilled down her back.

"Trigg," she whispered, frantically kneading the hard muscles of his back and lolling her head from side to side as he bathed her neck with kisses. "We can't," she protested with a worried little giggle. At the same time, she stepped back to make the buttons of his shirt more accessible to her urgently fumbling fingers. "What if someone hears us?"

"We'll be very quiet." He ripped off his shirt and tossed it aside, then hurriedly removed his holster, boots and trousers as he continued to kiss her.

Clumsily, he tried to open the back fastenings of her dress, while covering her face, and eyes, and neck, and ears with kisses. When he couldn't manage them, he spun her around in his arms to work on them.

A small voice inside Ellari warned her that what they were doing could get them both killed. But her passion screamed out that it was right, screamed out not to be denied.

All she knew was that even if it meant her life would end this very night, she couldn't let Trigg leave without sharing the rapture of their lovemaking one last time.

The back fastenings unhooked at last, he peeled her dress and underthings down her slim body, following the trail of his hands with his lips. Hunkered down on his haunches, he turned her to face him again. Glancing up the length of her, he groaned, "God, I never thought there was anything on this earth as beautiful as you."

Gingerly, he lifted one of her feet, then the other, removing her slippers and the tangle of clothing from around her ankles with one quick sweep.

He wrapped his fingers around her calves and smoothed his hands up her legs until his thumbs met and burrowed into the hot division at the center of her body.

"Oh, Trigg," she moaned, helplessly rocking toward the pressing caresses. Bending forward, he grazed his kiss over the thrusting down of her mound, then slowly turned her, bathing her thighs and hips with his kisses as he did.

Continuing his assault on her bottom, he brought his fingers around from behind, trapping her hips between his mouth and the exquisite manipulations of the bud of her sex.

Stoked by his kisses, flames raged through her, bringing her to a rapid and fiery climax beyond her control. "Oh!" she cried, sinking to her knees, and catching her torso on the bed.

When he continued to twist and tug at the spasming heart of her sex, she lurched forward as if she were trying to get away.

Holding her prisoner with his hands, he situated his knees between hers. He covered her with his upper body, biting and kissing her shoulders and the back of her neck as he dug his fingers into the folds of her pelvis to drag the mounds of her buttocks into the curve of his hips.

Responding to the demand that pressed into her, Ellari instinctively widened the space between her knees and pushed back to welcome the power of his manliness.

He buried himself inside the hot sheath of her with a hard lunge. "Oh God!" he groaned. "It's so good!"

"Yes," she ground out between gritted teeth as he clutched her breast with one hand and brought her to another orgasm with the other, this one even more violent and shattering than the first.

Biting back the cry of ecstasy that surged in her throat, she buried her face in the bed linens to keep from screaming out her passion. Still, he didn't cease his mind-exploding caresses.

Deeper and deeper, he plunged into her heat. Again and again he brought her to the edge of sanity until she was so far removed from reality that all thoughts of caution were eradicated from her mind.

When the final explosion was imminent, she reared her head to cry out.

Acting quickly, Trigg covered her mouth with his hand. Absorbing the uncontrolled sounds of her ecstasy into his palm, he spilled his own passion into her as the muscles of her desire convulsed in spasm after spasm, to wring him dry.

After long, silent moments spent regaining his ability to move, Trigg gently withdrew from the slippery haven of her body. Standing, he lifted her onto the bed and lay down beside her.

"Trigg, you can't stay!" she whispered. "What if he comes back?"

"Just need to rest a coupla minutes," he murmured, dozing off in spite of her protests. "Haven't slept since I found you gone."

Smiling, she covered him up, then went into the bathroom to clean up. There would be no harm in letting him sleep for an hour or so before he left. They would still have plenty of time before dawn for him to slip unnoticed onto the roof. Then he could go sell the Magicure and be back in a few days with the money for Nick; by then, she would know if she'd been able to have any adverse effect on David Nylander or not.

Yes, things are going to work out all right, she congratulated herself, coming out of the bathroom wearing a nightgown Mammy had left for her.

Lying down beside Trigg, she concentrated on all the good things that were going to happen because she and Trigg had found each other. Together they would fulfill their dreams: his of being a successful businessman, hers of ending child labor—not to mention all the burn victims who were going to be helped by her Magicure. Yes, once they paid back Nick Stahl, there would be no stopping them.

384

* * *

A rapid knocking on the door jarred Ellari and Trigg awake. Hearts beating with panic, they bolted upright and stared at the door.

"Ellari," Nick called from the other side of the door. "I have some news."

Ellari and Trigg shot each other frantic glances. Then, simultaneously, as if someone had pushed a switch, they broke into action. He dove for the floor, gathering their scattered clothing as he made a beeline for the bathroom. She grabbed her robe and ran to the door, shoving her arms into the sleeves as she did.

"Ellari?" Nick's tone sounded anxious, agitated. He rattled the door as if he were on the verge of breaking in. "Answer me! Are you awake?"

Ellari sliced a worried look at Trigg, who peeked out of the bathroom and signaled that she should answer Nick, then closed the door all but about an inch.

"Y-yes," she answered, feigning grogginess, though she was fully awake. "Just a m-minute. I need—uh—to put on a robe." She took a last glance around to be sure there was nothing to give away Trigg's presence, then placed a shaking hand on the bolt and slid it open. She cracked open the door and peeked out. "What is it, Mr. Stahl? I didn't expect to see you before tomorrow."

Nick Stahl grinned sheepishly. "My apologies for

waking you. But from outside, I saw your light was on and I thought you were still awake."

"I must have dozed off," she hurried to explain. "But I'm awake now. What is it you wanted to see me about?"

"Aren't you going to let me in?"

Her eyes opened wide with apprehension. "Let you in?"

"You don't expect me to stand out here and carry on a conversation in the hallway, do you? And after all, it is my apartment."

"But I'm not dressed!" she protested. " 'Miss Wainwright' of Boston would never entertain in her bed clothes."

He chuckled. "I give you my word, your reputation and your chastity will remain untarnished. No one will think a thing of it. Now, please open the door, or I will be forced to open it myself."

Knowing she had no choice, Ellari made a hurried check of the room to be sure Trigg was hidden. "All right," she said, reluctantly opening the door. "What do you want to talk to me about that can't wait until morning?"

Nick strolled over the threshold, glancing casually around the room as if he were looking for something.

Oh, Lord! He knows Trigg's here. She closed the door behind him and followed him with her eyes.

Nick sat down on the settee and patted the cushion beside him. "Come sit down. I have some

386

news I think you may like to hear."

"I prefer to stand," she said, walking across the room so that to look at her he couldn't possibly see the bathroom door.

"Suit yourself," he said, removing a cigarette from his case.

"Have you come to tell me something about Nylander?" she asked him anxiously.

"As a matter of fact, I have. After thinking over what you said, I've decided to refuse his offer, and I thought you would want to know right away. It seemed important to you."

Her face broke into a wide grin. "Oh, yes! It is important!" She took a step toward him, her inclination being to hug him. Fortunately, she caught herself and stopped. "That's wonderful news," she said, her excitement only slightly contained. "I knew you couldn't be as unfeeling as you'd like everyone to believe you are! I knew you couldn't let the children down."

"I hate to burst your bubble, my dear, but I'm not doing it for any kids. I'm doing it for me," Nick said, studying her reaction with amused disdain.

"Oh?" She didn't know why she was surprised, but she was. It just didn't seem possible that she'd misjudged him so completely and that he would feel nothing for the children.

"Well, whoever you're doing it for, I'm glad," she said stiffly. "The more setbacks men like Nylander have, the more headway we can make in stopping them altogether. So I thank you, and I'm glad you told me right away." She moved toward the door, hoping he would catch the hint and leave, but he remained seated.

"Don't you want to know what made me change my mind?" he asked as if he didn't notice she wanted him to go. "It was something you said."

"It was? What?" She couldn't resist asking.

"When you pointed out that I would own almost half of Nylander's factory, but would in effect have no control over how things were run or even how my money was used, it got me to thinking. For as much money as I was going to hand over to them, I could establish my own legitimate business and start my own club—if theirs still doesn't want me. I'm considering selling the Majestic and buying a hotel in a better part of the city—something along the lines of the Tremont or Palmer House, or maybe even something really extravagant like the Grand Pacific they're building. What do you think?"

"Why, I think it's a fine idea," she answered. Her thoughts confused by his asking for her opinion, and she was amazed to learn how truly rich Nick Stahl must be.

"Good, because I can't do it alone. I need your help."

"My help?"

"You have an instinct for what is proper that

I'm lacking. I want this hotel to be the most elegant and stylish hotel in Chicago. First class, all the way. So of course I would especially want your advice on decorating." He chuckled. "It wouldn't serve much purpose to get rid of the Majestic, if I ended up on the other side of town with a hotel that looked like a fancy Levee bordello, would it?"

"I don't believe your gall!" Ellari gasped. "You've tried to kill my fiancé, and you're keeping me here against my will, yet you have the nerve to want me to decorate a hotel for you! You must be out of your mind."

"That's not the only thing I want from you, Miss Lochridge."

Unconsciously, Ellari gripped her robe at her throat and waist and shot a glance toward the bathroom door. "Oh?"

"Miss Lochridge," he said, standing, a smile on his handsome face. "There's no need to run and hide from me. I would never do anything to threaten the way my future bride feels about me."

"Y-your b-b-bride? You're engaged?"

He smiled secretly. "Miss Lochridge," he said taking her hand. "Will you do me the honor of becoming my wife?"

389

Chapter Twenty-one

You goddamn rotten son-of-a-bitch, Trigg swore silently, whipping the new revolver from his holster to check the bullets. He started to open the door, then froze. He wasn't thinking? He couldn't go in there shooting. The guards outside the doors would be inside in an instant, and Ellari would certainly be caught in the crossfire. He couldn't risk that. He'd have to wait and pick his moment when he could catch Nick off guard and stop him from yelling out.

"You want to marry *me?"* he heard Ellari ask Nick Stahl. "Why?"

Damn! She didn't sound nearly as outraged by Nick's proposal as Trigg would have expected her to be. Furious, he peered through the crack in the door.

"Don't be so surprised," Nick chuckled, stepping close in front of Ellari and tilting her chin upward so she had to look at him.

You bastard! Get your hands off her. It's not

enough you want me dead. You want the satisfaction one of knowing you stole her from me too.

"Why wouldn't I?" Nick answered Ellari. "You're beautiful, intelligent, and charming. I happen to think a union between us could prove quite pleasant, as well as beneficial to us both."

I'm going to kill him. I swear it.

"Beneficial!" Ellari gasped. "You want to marry me because it's beneficial? Beneficial to whom? Certainly not to me. I'd rather die than marry a man I don't love. Have you forgotten? I am engaged to marry Trigg Hanahan."

Now *that* was the indignation Trigg had expected to hear before. He relaxed slightly. Only slightly. He was beginning to be curious to see how Ellari would handle this. He wouldn't have dreamed of testing her love for him deliberately, but as long as the opportunity presented itself, it might be a good idea. Nick had always had a way with women, and if Ellari was susceptible to it, now was as good a time as any to find out.

Nick smiled. "Ah, yes. We mustn't forget the handsome and 'successful' Mr. Hanahan. However, I think once you've heard me out, you'll realize the advantages of marrying me far outweigh the 'love' you say you have for him."

"There's nothing you could say or do to make me choose you over Trigg. I love him with all my heart."

Atta girl. You tell the rotten son of a bitch.

"I don't believe that, and neither do you," Nick said in an obviously amused tone. "For one thing, Trigg Hanahan is a loser and always will be, while I always come out on top. Wouldn't you rather be married to a winner than to a loser, who's sure to spend the rest of his life hiding out from creditors and people he's bilked into investing in his get-rich schemes?"

"That's all in the past," Ellari said in Trigg's defense. "He's not a loser. In fact, he has a new business that is going to make him very rich."

Nick chuckled. "Trigg Hanahan always has a 'new business' that's going to make him 'very rich.' I've invested in several of them myself. Why do you think he owes me so much money? Face it, dear Ellari, even if by some extraordinary fluke he should enjoy a small amount of success, he'll never be able to support you or your children in the style a lady of your quality deserves."

Now it was Ellari's turn to laugh. "That shows how shallow you are—and how little you know about me. Being rich doesn't mean anything to me. It never has. So even if this new business isn't as big as we think it will be, we still have the drugstore, a roof over our heads and our love for each other. That's all I need or want."

"What will you do when the man you love so much mortgages your drugstore to pay off a creditor or gamble it away on one of his dealings, and you and your children are put out on the streets? Will

392

your 'love for each other' be enough to sustain you then?"

"That will never happen," Ellari said defensively.

"Oh, it will happen, all right. He's like his father; and like his father, he'll eventually move on. Just the way his dad did, he'll take everything you have to offer. Then he'll leave you alone to fend for yourself—possibly by begging or even walking the streets."

"You don't know what you're talking about. Trigg isn't like that at all."

Oh yes he does, Ellari, Trigg answered silently, suddenly feeling like the failure Nick was describing to her. Had he been fooling himself to think this time would be different?

Nick nodded his head, his expression almost sympathetic. "On the other hand, I have the means to not only give you and our children every luxury you ever dreamed of, but I also have something you may not have thought of. I can afford to pledge my financial backing to your fight against Nylander and the use of child labor, not to mention the connections I have."

So, the ultimate test, Trigg thought bitterly. *When it comes to money and luxury, I had a chance. But the kids in the factory. . . .*

Ellari twisted her chin out of Nick's grasp and walked away from him. "I feel sorry for you, Mr. Stahl. Don't you know you can't buy people any more than you can buy respectability?"

Trigg's mouth dropped opened in amazement. She had actually chosen him over the kids!

"You're turning me down?"

"Of course I am! I don't intend to marry anyone but Trigg Hanahan."

"We'll see how you feel at the end of the week when he still hasn't returned for you. Once you see firsthand what an undependable louse Trigg Hanahan is, you'll be only too glad to accept my offer."

"Don't hold your breath, Mr. Stahl. Trigg will be back, all right," she said with a disdainful chuckle. "And he'll have your money with him too. So you can stop worrying about it."

"I'm not worried in the least. You see, Trigg Hanahan and I go back a long way, to when we were kids on the street together. I know him well, and I can tell you from experience, he's probably in the next state by now. In fact, I'd be willing to make a wager that we've both seen the last of him."

"What sort of wager?" Ellari asked.

"Oh, I don't know—" Nick thought for a moment. "How about this? If Hanahan doesn't come back within the week, you agree to marry me, and—"

"And if he does come back for me," Ellari interrupted, "you give him a one-year extension on his note, with no additional interest, and he and I walk out of here free of the worry that your men are going to kill him."

My God, Ellari! You're a genius!

"If he comes back, why would you need the extension?"

Uh-oh. Why would you need it?

Ellari hesitated the briefest second, then continued. "Because until our business is fully established, we can use that two thousand dollars as operating capital to purchase materials."

Did I say you didn't have a head for business? Well, I was wrong!

Nick studied her for a long moment. "You'd willingly agree to marry me if you lose the bet?"

She nodded her head. "And to help you with your hotel, as well as dedicate myself to getting you accepted as a respectable member of Chicago society. But I don't think I'm going to lose. You see, I have faith in Trigg. I know he's not a loser, and I know there is nothing that would keep him from coming back for me."

She held out her hand the way she'd seen men in her neighborhood do when they gambled with each other. "Do we have a bet?"

Nick looked down at her hand, then grinned at her. "I always did like a woman who would put everything on the line for what she believed in. But I'm afraid this time you're in over your head, pretty lady."

Instead of taking her extended hand, he grabbed her upper arms and hauled her to him. "You have a bet. But I think a kiss to seal our bargain is

395

more appropriate than a handshake—since in effect you have just agreed to be my wife." He covered her mouth with his.

"Take your hands off of her, Nick!" Trigg growled, his tone low and menacing as he stepped into the room, his gun drawn and his expression filled with rage.

Startled, Nick looked up, his dark eyes locking with Trigg's. His upper lip twitched slightly, as if he couldn't find the words he wanted to say. He glanced back down at Ellari, his expression betrayed. "You set me up."

The hurt she saw in Nick Stahl's eyes tugged unexpectedly at Ellari's heart. "What did you expect? People in desperate circumstances must take desperate measures."

"You set me up!" he said again, this time shaking his head, a disbelieving grin on his face.

"Turnabout's fair play," Ellari said, torn with unexplainable guilt over what she'd done. "You thought you were setting me up, didn't you? You intended to make sure that if Trigg came back he never got to me, didn't you? I simply did it to you first."

Nick threw up his hands in surrender and looked back at Trigg. "You win."

He walked over to the bar and poured himself a shot of whiskey, which he tossed down quickly. Continuing to shake his head, he chuckled to himself and poured a second shot. "But we all know, in the long run, you're the real loser here, don't we?" he asked Ellari. "By next year, you'll be back here begging me for another extension for your loser husband. Or even more likely, you'll be asking me to give you another chance because he ran out on you and the kid he saddled you with—just like his pop ran out on him and his mother."

"Shut up, Nick," Trigg demanded. "Just put the extension in writing and tell your trained gorilla at the door that we've come to an agreement."

"Sure," Nick said, crossing to the desk. "The sooner you're out of here, the faster you can get to work on your next failure." He opened the ink bottle and dipped his pen into it. "October 3, 1871, Chicago, Illinois," he read aloud as he wrote. "I hereby agree to extend Mr. Trigg Hanahan's debt to me in the amount of two-thousand dollars for one year, due to be paid in full, on October 3, 1872, with no additional interest due. Nick Stahl, Esquire."

He finished signing his name with a flourish, lay down the pen and held out the paper to Ellari. "Congratulations on a game well played, Miss Lochridge. It's a pity all of your talents are going to be wasted. You and I would have made a fantastic team. We could have accomplished some great things with my money and your abilities."

Trigg grabbed the paper and said, "Ellari, go get dressed and let's get out of here."

"Not yet," Ellari said, standing firm where

397

she was.

"What?" Trigg and Nick asked in unison, their fours eyes wide as they gaped at her.

"None of us is leaving until I have some answers to a few questions."

"Answers?" they said together.

"You're beginning to sound like Siamese-twin parrots," she said angrily.

Nick was the first to recover. "Are you having second thoughts? Are you starting to realize you would be better off with me?" His tone was hopeful.

She shot him a withering glance. "No, I'm not having second thoughts. But I'm not leaving until one of you tells me what this is all about."

"What what is all about?" Trigg asked with a snarl. He stormed to the bar and helped himself to a whiskey. "That's a good idea," Nick said. "I think I'm going to need another one of those, myself." He joined Trigg at the bar and poured himself a double. "This night is beginning to be a little too full of surprises."

"Will you stop this ridiculous stalling and tell me what caused this feud between the two of you in the first place?"

"It's no mystery," Nick said. "He owes me money and tried to get out of paying it back."

"You're not fooling me, Nick Stahl. There's more to this than a simple debt, and you know it. You didn't get rich having people who owe you money

398

killed. It wouldn't be financially 'beneficial,' would it? So there has to be another reason you hate this one particular debtor so much that seeing him dead is worth losing two thousand dollars, *plus* the bonuses you promised the killers. What is it?"

"I have to admit, I'm curious to know the answer to that too, Nicky," Trigg said, sloshing more whiskey into his glass. "When we were kids, we were pretty tight."

Nick chuckled, though his laugh contained no mirth. "Yeah, we were tight, all right." He looked directly into Ellari's eyes. "So tight that he ran out on me at the first sign of trouble. And he'll do it to you. He'll always save his own ass—to hell with whoever he's promised to look out for."

"That's not true," Trigg protested. "I never ran out on you."

"No? Then what the hell would you call it when you said you'd take the first watch while I slept, then you left me to be grabbed by the hunters for a specialty bordello on Chicago Avenue?" Nick glared at Trigg, daring him to deny it. "How much did they pay you for me, Hanahan?"

The expression on Trigg's face grew sick. "Is that what you think? That I sold you out to a—"

"Well, didn't you?"

"No! How could you even think I'd do something like that? We were like brothers! You were the closest thing to a family I had."

Nick laughed bitterly. "Then why weren't you

there to warn me so I could get away?" He nodded his head, his expression showing the hurt he still felt from the betrayal. "I'll tell you why. Because you're a rotten, God damned Judas. That's why."

"It's not true," Trigg said, glancing helplessly from Nick to Ellari, then back to Nick again. "I never knew what happened to you. You've got to believe that. I was standing guard just like we took turns doing every night. You were hidden in a crate sleeping."

He took a sip of his whiskey. "I started to get groggy and thought a cigarette would wake me up, so I walked a way down the alley and lit up—the way we always did so the smoke wouldn't give away our hiding place. But, I stayed close enough to keep an eye on the crate you were sleeping in. The way we agreed to do. Remember?"

"Yeah, I remember."

"I had only taken a few puffs when a couple of older kids—maybe sixteen or seventeen—jumped me. I fought them, but it was useless. They were just too big."

"If that's true, why didn't you whistle for help like we agreed?"

Trigg shook his head. "At first, I thought I could handle them. You know how I always thought I could handle anything. Then by the time I realized I couldn't, it was too late. You were even younger and smaller than I was. And if I couldn't take one of them, what chance would you have had

400

against the other one?"

"So you left me there, sleeping and defenseless and feeling like I was safe?"

"I thought you were. Since I was alone and half-way down the alley from you, I was sure they didn't know about you. I figured the best way to protect you was to make them chase me somewhere else." He grinned sadly. "I may not have been as tough as I thought I was, but I was fast. You have to admit that I was fast."

"Yeah, but get on with the story. I'm beginning to enjoy this," Nick said sarcastically. "Maybe you should have been a writer. My curiosity is killing me."

Trigg gave him an angry glance, then went on. "I had dropped the cigarette when they jumped me, and I saw it lying on the ground next to me—still burning. I stopped fighting, and the guy holding me relaxed some. I deliberately stumbled so I could pickup the cigarette." He paused to pour himself another whiskey.

"When he hauled me back to my feet, I came up with the cigarette in my hand and buried the lit end in his cheek—I was going for the eye but I missed. Anyway, he dropped me to grab his face and I took off running. All I knew was I had to lead them away from that alley where you were sleeping."

Nick's complexion paled perceptibly. "You put out a cigarette on his cheek?" He looked as if he

401

were going to be sick.

"Mr. Stahl, are you all right?" Ellari asked, her natural concern for people overcoming her desire to dislike Nick Stahl. "Maybe you should sit down."

Nick shook his head, his eyes strangely moist. "One of the two who grabbed me had a burn on his cheek, and I heard him tell the other one that if he ever found the little bastard who'd done that to him, he was going to kill him." His expression hurt and forlorn, he stared at his drink. "All these years I believed you sold me out."

Trigg looked sick too. "They must have known I wasn't alone and gone back for you when I gave them the slip. I swear, Nicky, I didn't know. I always figured you were okay."

"But you didn't bother to find out for sure when you went back?"

"Sure I did, but it was a year before I got back and by then it was too late."

"A year? It took you a year to get around to wondering what happened to me?" Nick's tone was hurt and amazed.

"It wasn't like that. When I was getting away, I ran right into a policeman. I tried to tell him I was being chased, but he called me a little thief and dragged me into the station house anyway. Then, to make matters worse, he found some things in my pockets you and I had stolen that day on Lake Street, so he put me in a cell until the people from the boy's home came and got me." His eyes began

402

to water.

"All through the next year of beatings, maggot-filled food, and the solitary lockup room for weeks at a time, the only thing that kept me going was knowing that I'd been able to protect you. And now I realize it was all a lie. God, I'd give anything for another chance at those bastards who did this to us."

Nick laughed bitterly. "There's not too much chance of that happening in this life. They're dead."

"How do you know?"

"They came into my place a couple of years ago. Of course they didn't recognize me, but I'll never forget their ugly faces. Unfortunately, before I got to confront them myself, they started roughing up one of my girls, and Johnny put bullets between their eyes. They never knew what hit them."

He shrugged and held his hand out to Trigg. "So, I guess this brings the whole thing full circle, doesn't it?"

Trigg took Nick's hand with one of his own, and covered it warmly with the other. "I guess it does. But I do have one more question. When we met up after all those years, why did you act like the whole thing never happened? And if you hated me so much, why'd you lend me money instead of killing me on the spot?"

"Because I'd waited for my revenge for so long, killing you wasn't a good enough punishment for what I thought you deserved. I wanted you to suffer like I did. I wanted you to feel lower than outhouse slime like I had. So every time you came to me with a new scheme, I lent you money, then set out to make sure you failed. I wanted you so in debt to me that you'd be desperate enough to do anything."

"You almost succeeded."

"I know. When you agreed to marry Ina Phelps I was sure I had. I took great pleasure picturing you married to a pitiful woman like Ina with a protective father like Reed Phelps watching your every move like a jailer. Making you prostitute yourself to survive would have been an ironic punishment. Or so I thought. But you found a way out of the marriage, and I finally decided to quit toying with you and ordered you killed."

Nick cast a forlorn grin at Ellari. "But thanks to the loyal and persistent Miss Lochridge, the order will be cancelled now." He looked back at Trigg. "That's one smart lady, my friend. You'd better take good care of her. 'Cause if I ever hear you aren't treating her right, I'll string you up myself. Is that clear?"

The two men stared at each other for a long drawn out moment. Then, moving as one, they came together in a heartrending embrace.

Nick broke away first and directed a devilish grin at Ellari. "You realize of course that when I came here tonight, this isn't who I intended to end up hugging, don't you?"

"Do you suppose being the best man at my wedding would make up your loss?" Trigg asked.

Nick threw back his head and laughed. "I've been trying to convince your fiancée all night that I was the best man, but she wouldn't have any of it. How about I settle for second best—in this case only, of course."

"Are you sure you don't want to stay the rest of the night?" Nick asked an hour later. "You're welcome to use the apartment as long as you like."

"Thanks, but we've got to check on the drugstore, not to mention the horses and a mangy old cat of Ellari's, who's probably fit to be tied right about now," Trigg chuckled. "But we'll be in touch."

"Be sure you are. I'm still counting on that help when I start my hotel," he said to Ellari.

She stood on her toes and kissed Nick on the cheek. "You'll have it. And we're still hoping for your help with our fight against the glass factories."

"That reminds me," Nick said suddenly. "Phelps remembered where he'd seen you, and he told Nylander who you were. So you two be extra careful. That Nylander is a real serious enemy to have."

* * *

"Ellari?" Trigg called out when he awoke. He rolled over and fumbled groggily for his pocket-watch on the bedside table to check the time.

Smacking his lips to get rid of the sleepy taste in his mouth, and blinking his eyes to clear his vision, he snapped the timepiece open.

"Three-twenty! Damn! I've slept the whole day away!" He threw his feet over the side of the bed and grabbed his pants. "Ellari!"

A familiar sense of foreboding washed over him when she didn't answer. Drawing his pants up over his hips as he went, Trigg ran out of the bedroom.

He stopped, willing himself not to panic when he realized Ellari was not to be found anywhere in the apartment above her drugstore.

She's gone downstairs for something, he assured himself, remembering that when they had returned to the drugstore a bit before dawn that morning, they'd unloaded the wagon and just set everything inside the back door to keep it safe.

Still barefoot and shirtless, he ran down the stairs to the storeroom. He stopped short at the sound of voices on the other side of the curtained doorway. A sickening lump dropped to the bottom of his stomach like a stone in water, and he listened.

"Thank you, Mrs. Presinger," Ellari was saying. "It's good to be back. I'll be in touch about the meeting."

Stunned, he waited only long enough to be sure

the woman was gone. Then, livid, he tore open the curtain to find Ellari coming toward him.

Ellari's face lit up at the sight of him. "Well, good morning, sleepyhead. Or I suppose I should say afternoon?"

"What the hell do you think you're doing?" he snarled, storming past her toward the front door. "You promised you wouldn't open the shop again."

"Only until you had earned back your investment and we didn't have to worry about your creditors," she pointed out angrily, racing up the aisle after him. She caught his hand on the door to stop him from locking it. "But that's all behind us now, and it's time to open again."

"You can't. It's still too dangerous." He knocked her hand aside and slid the lock into place, then flipped the sign on the window over to show the store was closed. "Nylander's not going to let you get away with it—especially if he realizes you're the reason Nick withdrew from their deal."

"Well, that's just a chance I have to take. I've lost too much time already. People need me. I kept my end of our bargain by staying closed as long as I did. Now it's your turn to keep your part of the agreement. You said you'd help me fight Nylander once we got Magicure started and your creditors taken care of, and I'm going to hold you to it." She shoved the door lock open and returned the sign to its open side.

Trigg reached for the door to lock it again, his

407

unshaven face dark and scowling, but he stopped himself. "You're going to do this no matter what I say, aren't you?"

She smiled mischievously. "You know I am. Now, are you going to stand by your promise to support me or not?"

Trigg released a low, guttural sound of frustration. "I guess it'll be okay as long as you don't get any crazy ideas about doing anything else to antagonize Nylander."

He paused for a long moment. "And as long as you stick to taking care of sick people and dispensing medicine. Maybe once Nylander sees you're not going to cause him any more trouble—"

Ellari shot a nervous glance toward a pile of papers on the shelf nearest to the exit. "Uh—"

Trigg followed the direction of her averted gaze. "What's this?" he asked, his tone hiding none of the dread he was feeling. He whipped a flyer from the stack and gaped at it.

Ellari smiled sheepishly. "I've rescheduled my 'Save the Children' meeting for Sunday evening."

Chapter Twenty-two

His expression twisted with horror, Trigg read the flyer aloud, as if he had to hear it with his own ears to believe what his eyes were telling him:

"*SAVE THE CHILDREN!*. On Sunday, October 8, 1871, at 6:00 P.M. in the Jefferson Street Park, a group of citizens concerned for the safety and protection of children working in the factories will meet to discuss this problem. If you have ever known a child who was killed or injured while working in a factory, then you owe it to them to be there. E. Lochridge, Lochridge Pharmacy."

"Damn, Ellari!" He wadded the flyer and tossed it to the floor. "Do you realize what you've done?"

"Of course I do," she responded indignantly. She stooped to retrieve the flyer and smoothed it out. "Exactly what we agreed to do—go after Nylander once you were free to help me."

"But dammit, not like this!" He swept the stack of flyers up in his arms and started for the back of the store.

"Where are you taking those?" she cried, running after him.

"Outside to burn them—like I should have done weeks ago."

Ellari grabbed his arm. "Oh, no, you're not! I spent all morning changing the dates on those flyers, and I'm giving them out!"

"I don't care if you hand wrote every damned one of them. I'm burning them! I'm not going to stand by and let you deliberately set yourself up as a target for Nylander's hired killers."

Ellari dropped her hold on him. "Let me? You won't *let* me?!" she shrilled. "I don't need your permission. And you're mistaken if you think burning those flyers will stop me from having the meeting. By now, there's a flyer on every fence, in every store window, and in the hands of every woman within three blocks. These are just the ones I saved back to give out to customers who come into the pharmacy and might not have gotten one."

"You mean you went out and—"

"Not me personally. I paid three little boys to do it for me." She made a smug face. "Well, actually, *you* paid them, since I got the money to pay them out of your pants pocket."

"In that case, I'll just have to pay the same kids to pick 'em back up!"

"Now you're being ridiculous. Even if I would agree to that—which I won't—it's impossible. I gave each boy a hundred and fifty flyers to distribute. There's no way you could get even half of them back."

"Damn, Ellari!" Trigg cursed, slapping the stack of flyers down on the back counter. "How can anyone who's so smart be so stupid?"

"Stupid?!" she shrieked. "I was a genius earlier, and now I'm stupid?!"

"Maybe stupid was a poor choice of words. But you have to admit you don't think before you act. You have an idea one minute and are up to your neck in trouble in the next. Didn't your trip to the Levee teach you that you've got to think things through and consider all the possibilities before you do something? It's only luck, and by the grace of God, that you weren't killed—or worse. And now you go and do something crazy like this! I give up! Why don't we just send Nylander an invitation that says, 'Ellari Lochridge wants you to kill her. Come and get her. We'll leave the door unlocked!'?"

"You're exaggerating the situation."

"Oh, am I? I don't think so. Nylander told me himself, he was going to hire someone to get rid of you permanently if you didn't drop this thing. Why do you think I've worked so hard to get you to forget this crusade of yours?"

"That was before. But I think Nick did us a double favor by deciding not to invest in the factory. Now, because of him, David Nylander has bigger things on his mind than me. Compared to losing all that money, he probably hasn't given me a second thought. That's why this is the perfect time to strike—while his attention is occupied with other things." She smiled, confident she had made her point.

"Stop fooling yourself, Ellari," he said, his expression a dark scowl. "Men like Nylander always have time to do something about *anyone* who crosses them, no matter how small the offense. And believe me, he doesn't consider your offense small. You've challenged him publicly, and he's got to do something about you to set an example for others. Whether or not he believes you can cause him any real trouble, he's got to get rid of you to stop anyone else from trying to do the same."

"Does this mean you're reneging on your promise to help me?" She fought to hold back the disappointment and bitterness.

"No, I'm not 'reneging' on anything. I still intend to help you do something for these kids. But that doesn't include helping you get yourself killed in the process!"

"Well, all I can do is hope you're wrong. Because whether or not you like it, I'm going to be at that meeting on Sunday." She picked up the stack of remaining flyers and started for the front of the store. "And there's nothing you can do or say to stop me!"

"We'll see about that, Ellari." Swearing under

his breath, he angrily spun toward the back room. "We'll just damn well see about that."

She lay down the flyers and called back over her shoulder to his retreating back. "If you're thinking of kidnapping me again, you can forget it. I wouldn't forgive you this time. Either you can stay and fight Nylander with me as you promised, or you can leave alone."

He stopped in the doorway, his broad shoulders tensed, his head tilted back as if he were looking at the ceiling. "All my life I've wanted what we have a chance at," he said, his voice low and breaking. "A home, a family and someone who loves and needs me."

"Oh, Trigg!" she cried, making a dash for the back of the store. She wrapped her arms around his chest and lay her head on his bare back. "Don't you know how long I've dreamed of having the same things? I thought I never would have them. I was resigned to spending the rest of my life alone, taking care of other people's families, never my own. I had given up. But then you came into my life. And you gave me back my hope."

He turned in her arms and clasped his arms behind her waist. "If anything were to happen to you—" His face was contorted with pain, his eyes bright with tears.

Her own vision blurred with emotion, Ellari held his face in her hands. "Nothing can hurt me as long as I have you. Your love makes me strong.

413

You're my heart."

"And you're my soul," he said, burying his face in the curve of her neck and shoulder.

"Then stay and fight with me. Help me do what I have to do. You don't have to run anymore, Trigg. Together, we can stand up to Nylander and anyone else who threatens the things we believe in and value."

If only it would rain. Not that there was a chance in Hell it would, Trigg admitted to himself as he scanned the sky over Jefferson Street Park, his expression worried. There hadn't been a drop of rain since the first of July, and there was no reason to believe tonight would be any different. Still he searched the heavens, praying for a sign that this foolhardy meeting could be rained out.

The acrid smell of smoke hung in the air, as it had for several days now. Of course, what could they expect when there had been almost forty fires in the city in the past week alone? And most of them were here on the West Side.

Just the day before, a fire had destroyed four full blocks not more than half a mile north of the drugstore. After fifteen hours, the firemen had finally put it out, but it's odor still lingered in the air.

To make matters worse, the newspapers had been reporting that thousands of acres of Michigan and Wisconsin woods north of Chicago had been burning for days, and that the smoke and soot from those fires were being blown into the city as well.

No wonder every breath you take tastes like smoke, he thought regretfully, directing his attention back to Ellari.

He could tell she was disappointed by the meager turnout for her meeting: a few haggard, sad-looking women who kept glancing back over their shoulders, as if they were afraid someone would come up behind them and drag them off, and several pitiful, sad-eyed children who stood silently beside their mothers.

However, despite how badly he felt for her, he couldn't help but feel his own prayers had been answered in some way. Nylander hadn't tried to stop her from having the meeting, and there hadn't been any acts of vandalism since the flyers had gone out. Maybe she was right after all. Maybe Nylander hadn't heard about the meeting. Or maybe he'd decided threatening his workers into staying away was the best way to handle the situation.

But whatever the reason things had been so calm, Trigg was thankful. He hoped this would convince Ellari that they needed to come up with another way to fight Nylander, instead of setting herself up as a target.

"You might as well go on and start," he whispered to her. "I don't think any more will be here."

"I'll just give them a few more minutes," she answered, her gaze desperately searching the park for another gathering her people might have inadvertently joined.

"You're already twenty minutes late. These women don't look comfortable being here as it is. If you don't start, you're going to lose them too," he warned, anxious to get this over with.

"You're right." Stepping forward, she cleared her throat. "Ladies, if I may have your attention, we'll begin. I had hoped there would be more of us at this first meeting, but I'm certain once word gets out what we want to do, there will be more who join us each time we meet."

"I can't stay," one woman said suddenly, turning away and hurrying off across the park.

"Wait!" Ellari cried. "Don't leave yet! We haven't started."

Ignoring her, the woman broke into a half-run, as if the devil himself were chasing her.

Ellari directed a puzzled smile at the others. "Was it something I said?"

"You gotta understand," said a young woman with a baby in her arms, and a dirty two year old clinging to her skirt. "We're all takin' a big chance bein' here. If our men find out, there's goin' to be the dickens for us to pay."

"Then why did you come?" Ellari couldn't

416

help asking.

"Because we wanted to hear what you had to say," another answered.

"We see what the factories are doin' to our children, but we got no choice but to send them to work," yet another said.

"Me husband hasn't found work in a year. Our family'd starve if me boys didn't work at Nylander Glass, and me girls at the mill."

"I'm afraid I don't have any pat answers," Ellari admitted. "That's the reason for this meeting. I don't think there's anything just one of us can do. But if we unite, I firmly believe we can force the factories to stop using child labor and to start hiring grown men at fair wages to do the work. Children should be in school learning to read and write. One thing we might consider doing would be—"

"What do you think you're doin'?" a brawny man with a thick Irish brogue interrupted without warning. He rushed up and grabbed one of the women by the arm.

"Tim!" the woman gasped, her eyes round with horror. "I didn't—"

"Did ye think I wouldn't know what ye was up to, woman?" He dragged her off. "Now, git on home where ye belong."

Obviously dismayed, Ellari directed her forlorn gaze back to the small audience, momentarily at a loss for words. She quickly realized several more

417

women and children had simply faded away from the group when everyone's attention was on the other woman—as if they had never been there.

"One thing we could do is picket the factories and refuse to let the children go to work—"

"That's easy for you to say. You don't have anything to lose," a woman snarled angrily. "If we listen to you, we could lose everything." She grabbed her kids and hurried off, without giving Ellari a chance at rebuttal.

Another woman left, mumbling to her youngsters, "I should have known she wouldn't be able to help us either."

Ellari turned to the three remaining women. "If you want to leave, too, I'll understand."

"It ain't that we don't appreciate what you're tryin' to do, Miss Lochridge. It kills us mothers to send our babies into the factories to do work not fit for beasts, never knowin' if they'll come out alive and whole at the end of their shift. But we can't do nothin' else if we want to keep our families together and a roof over our heads. I guess we was hopin' you'd have some magic answer, but if it means puttin' our children in more danger than they're already in—like picketin' a factory—then I doubt there's any o' us willin' to do that."

"Not 'cause we wouldn't want to," a second inserted. "But 'cause we can't. It's jest too dangerous. Jest comin' here tonight was a big risk for us. If our husbands find out—"

"I'm sorry," Ellari said, her eyes filling with tears as she remembered the beating Willie's mother had taken simply for bringing home a flyer. "I guess I didn't think about that. I wanted so badly to help the children, it never occurred to me that I could be making things worse for them—and for you. Will you forgive me?"

One young pregnant woman who had remained silent throughout the brief meeting stepped forward and smiled. "Der is notink to forgif. You are a good voman. I only pray von day, mein baby vill be as brave as you." She cradled her distended belly and smiled apologetically.

As if acting on an unspoken command, the group broke apart, and each hurried back toward wherever she lived.

Trigg stepped forward and put his arm around Ellari's shoulders.

At his touch, Ellari turned and buried her face against his chest. "How could I have been so righteous and so egotistical to think I could make a difference?" she sobbed into the soft cotton of his shirt. "I never even gave a thought to what those poor women would be risking if they try to stand up to people like Nylander. What was I thinking?"

"Shh," Trigg soothed, smoothing her hair and rubbing her back as he tightened his hold on her. "You were thinking of Willie and all the other Willies in the world. And you were fighting for what you believe in the only way you know how to fight. Directly and honestly. That lady was right. You are brave, and I'm very proud of you."

"But I failed. I was so sure I knew everything. And all I did was bring more trouble to those women if anyone finds out they came. You were right before when you said I was stupid!"

"I shouldn't have said that. You know that's not what I think. You're the smartest person I know, and you didn't fail."

"Then, what do you call this fiasco, if not a failure?"

"The meeting might not have gone the way you expected, but whether or not it looks that way, I believe it was a success. You showed those women that they weren't alone, and that there was someone else who was worried about their children. You gave them hope, and you planted a seed in their minds they won't be able to deny." He kissed the top of her head.

"Tomorrow, or maybe the next day, when they think about tonight, they'll realize that the women who were daring enough to show up for this public meeting are only a fraction of the women who feel the way they do. They'll begin to talk among themselves about how to handle this, and mark my words, one of these days they'll come out into the open again. Only this time there will be hundreds of them who have united to fight Nylander and his cronies—maybe thousands."

"Do you really believe that?" she asked, lifting her face to gaze into his.

He blessed her with his magical, cure-all grin. "I really do. In fact, I think you may've started a revolution here tonight. Why, I wouldn't be a bit surprised to some day find a statue of you on this very spot. I can see it now. The inscription will read: Miss Ellari Lochridge. She gave birth to the army of women and children who ended child labor."

Smiling tearfully, she clasped his face and kissed him. "I love you, Trigg Hanahan. You're a dreamer and a madman, but I wouldn't change a thing about you."

"And I love you, Ellari Lochridge, with all my heart. And I wouldn't change a thing about you. Except maybe for you to—"

"Learn to think before I act," she finished good-naturedly. "Believe me, I intend to work on that."

He smiled mischievously. "Actually, I'm getting used to that unpredictable side of you. What I'd really change if I could wave a magic wand, would be to get you home and into bed right this minute. Because, quite frankly, Miss Lochridge, I'm suffering an undeniable need to make love to you, and I don't know how much longer I can control myself."

Their spirits much improved compared to what

421

they had been earlier, Ellari and Trigg half-ran, half-walked back to Taylor Street. Laughing and out of breath, they slowed down as they neared the drugstore.

At the front door, Trigg fumbled with the key. As he turned it in the lock, they heard a loud crash from inside the store. "Wait out here," he ordered her, shoving her aside as, revolver drawn, he raced inside to investigate.

With no intention of letting Trigg face alone whoever was inside, Ellari followed him into the store.

As she entered, the back door slammed, and Trigg sprinted toward it, obviously bent on catching the intruder.

Ellari stopped and stared, stunned and sick to her stomach. Her neat little drugstore was in shambles. The neatly arranged shelves were toppled over, broken glass bottles and torn cardboard boxes littered the floor, their liquid and powdered contents mingling in a gooey mess. The screen to the treatment corner was shredded, its wood frame splintered, and the stuffing from the treatment couch spilled through huge slashes in the upholstery. Everywhere she looked, thoughtless, indiscriminate destruction was evident.

Remembering the horses and wagon in the shed, she grabbed her father's revolver from under the permanent counter the vandal had been unable to topple and ran for the back door. She had no doubt that a person who would do anything this malicious wouldn't stop at hurting animals to make a point.

Inside the shed, she quickly determined that nothing had been touched. The horses shifted and snorted nervously. "It's me," she said, laying a hand on each of the velvety noses. "There's nothing to be afraid of."

The slam of the shed door pitched the small area into total darkness. Hearing the sound of running footsteps, she dragged her gun from her pocket and hurried outside. Spotting a running man halfway down the alley, she took off after him. She might not have been able to catch the man who had destroyed the inside of her father's drugstore, but she intended to see the face of her enemy once and for all.

Trigg tackled the man he had chased two blocks west on Taylor Street. Straddling the downed man, he clamped a strong hand around the vandal's neck and drew back the other fist, threatening to bludgeon his captive. "Who hired you?"

"No one!" the man gasped.

Trigg tightened his grip. He could feel the other man's frantic pulse pounding against his fingers and thumb. "Wrong answer. Who hired you?"

"A fella I never seen before today. I don't know his name."

"You're lying. Who is he?" He squeezed on the scrawny neck a bit harder.

"I ain't! I swear it," the man choked. "This prissy kinda feller come up to me in a bar near Nylander's an' asked if I wanted to earn ten dollars. I asked what he had in mind, an' he said he needed some clothes to make him look like a laborer and some help wreckin' this store on Taylor Street. So I said I'd do it."

"My God! You weren't alone!" Trigg ground out, realization hitting him full force.

The man shook his head weakly. "No. The other feller, he went out back to take care o' the horses while I finished up. I was 'bout to go upstairs when you two come in, so I lit outta there."

"Ellari! What have I done?" Trigg leaped to his feet, dragging his prisoner with him. Whipping the man's suspenders from his pants, he bound him to a lamp post and took off running toward the drugstore. "Please, Lord," he pleaded, accelerating his stride with each step, "don't let me be too late."

Fury supplying her with speed and stamina she'd never known she possessed, Ellari pursued the intruder a block and a half before he turned south on the alley between Jefferson and Clinton.

As determined as a starving dog who'd had his supper snatched from his mouth, Ellari stayed on

424

the intruder's heels. Her chest ached, but she found the strength to keep going in the knowledge that the man seemed to be slowing down and she was gaining on him. Though he was slender and had the build of a young man, it was obvious he wasn't used to running.

He made another turn up the alley that ran behind the ramshackle houses on the north side of DeKoven Street, disappearing from view.

Doing her best to quicken her step even more, she dashed around the corner, her eyes searching frantically for her quarry.

He was gone! He had simply evaporated into the darkness, as if he'd never been there at all.

Ellari stopped and concentrated on listening for the pound of running footsteps.

Besides her own gasping breathing and the sounds of a celebration and a fiddle playing, the alley was unusually quiet. Her gaze fell onto a two-story barn behind what she thought was Patrick O'Leary's house.

She knew he and his wife and five children lived in this block of DeKoven Street. She'd been here a couple of times to bring them medicine. Catherine O'Leary kept cows to supplement the family income, and provided Ellari and others in the neighborhood with fresh milk and cream. Surely, if Ellari knocked on the O'Learys' door and told them what had happened, they would be willing to help her search. Yes, that was the smart thing to do.

Making her way through the discarded boxes, papers and miscellaneous lumber that littered the alley and ground behind the barn, she started for the house, then hesitated. The back portion of the house where she knew the O'Learys lived was dark, and the front portion they rented out to the McLaughlins was the source of the music and laughing she heard. She hated to interrupt their party. Besides, what if the man she was chasing was in there? And what if it wasn't the O'Leary house after all?

Deciding she'd better sneak up to the house window and peek in to be sure before she knocked on the front door, Ellari cautiously crept past the shed.

Just when she was about to dash across the cluttered yard to the house, she heard a grunt inside the shed — a grunt that sounded suspiciously human. Of course, it could be lovers who had sneaked out of the party to spoon. On the other hand, it could be him!

Holding her breath, she pressed her ear to the plank wall to listen. It was a moment before she recognized the distinctive sounds of panting, the way a person who's been running struggles for air in short, rapid gasps.

Gripping her revolver with both hands, she crept around the barn and stepped just inside the open doors. "I know you're in here," she shouted.

"Come out or I'm going to start shooting," she warned, praying whoever was inside wouldn't realize that she would never blindly fire a gun into a barn full of live animals.

Ellari sensed the presence to her right before she heard or saw it, and still it was to late for her to react.

Whipping her head to the side, she saw the angry face of her attacker. In the frisson of a second it took her to assimilate what was happening, he brought a board down on her head with a skull-shattering crack that vibrated through her to her toes.

Her knees buckled and she went down, not quite unconscious.

"Damn fool woman," she heard the man curse through the half-conscious haze that filled her mind. Dragging her into the corner of the barn, he muttered, "You couldn't leave well enough alone, could you? You couldn't take the warnings and stop butting in where you've got no business butting in. Well, I'm going to end your meddling once and for all."

Chapter Twenty-three

Willing the quivering muscles in his legs to go even faster and his lungs not to explode, Trigg sprinted east on Taylor Street. *If anything's happened to her, Nylander, you're a dead man!* he vowed, his desire for vengeance refueling his strength. *I swear, you'll be in Hell before the night is over if she's not all right.*

Trigg was so engrossed in his own frantic thoughts, he didn't notice the laborer running toward the sidewalk until they collided and both tumbled into the street.

"Sorry," Trigg muttered breathlessly, dragging himself to his feet.

"My fault," the man panted, crawling to a stand. "I wasn't paying att—"

"You!" Trigg yelled, recognizing Nylander's secretary and grabbing him by the coat lapels. From the description the man he'd chased had given him, he had no doubt this was the Nylander flunky he was looking for. "Where is she? What have you done to her?"

His tongue evidently paralyzed by the shock of running into Trigg, the secretary gaped speechlessly, his mouth opening and closing as if he were trying to talk but couldn't.

Trigg ripped his revolver out and placed the barrel in the center of the man's heavily sweating forehead right between his eyes. "You've got 'til I count to three. One—"

The man's voice was miraculously restored. "She's in the barn back there," he admitted, pointing in the direction from which he'd come.

"Show me!" Trigg ordered, jerking the man into an about-face and prodding him forward with the gun barrel.

Behind the row of shanties and cottages on Taylor Street, the terrified secretary pointed out a barn at the back of a DeKoven Street lot.

"So help me, if you're lying, or if you've hurt her, you and your slimy boss will be roasting in Hell before morning."

Resisting the temptation to shoot the sniveling weakling then and there, Trigg lifted his revolver and brought the butt of the handle down on the man's head. The secretary collapsed into a heap.

Taking off at a run, Trigg sprinted toward the barn, his only thought to get to Ellari. "Ellari!" he yelled. "Answer me! Ellari!"

He grew aware of the smell of smoke only a second before he saw a billowy cloud escape from the back of the barn. "Oh, God! No!"

With a superhuman surge of speed, he raced to the front of the barn. He ripped open the doors that had been barred shut and burst into the smoke-filled chamber. "Ellari!" he yelled, coughing. "Answer me!"

"Help me," he heard her cry weakly from the back of the barn.

Tearing off his shirt, he dipped it in the watering trough and covered his mouth and nose with it. Running blindly into the thickening smoke, he found his way to where Ellari was tied to a support pillar in the back of the barn.

His eyes watering profusely, he put the wet shirt over Ellari's face and used a knife he took from his boot to cut her free. Once the ropes were undone, he picked her up and ran outside.

Just as they cleared the doors, whatever had been smoking in the barn suddenly exploded into flames. Fanned by a strong wind coming through the doors from the southwest, the blaze immediately grew, sending long fingers of fire reaching out through the slats at the back of the barn.

"Fire!" Trigg tried to yell as he ran toward Taylor Street, carrying Ellari, but all he managed was a hoarse, raspy whisper. "Fire!" he tried again, to no avail.

"Hey!" he heard someone cry at the house in front of the burning barn. "O'Leary! Wake up! Your barn's on fire!"

One by one, doors opened in the nearby homes, and people spilled out onto the lots and sidewalks to view the fire. No one seemed overly concerned. To them it was merely another fire in a season where fires were an everyday occurrence.

A safe distance from the barn, Trigg relaxed slightly now that someone had sounded the alarm. He collapsed onto the sidewalk and held his semiconscious burden across his lap. "Ellari?" He wiped the wet shirt over her face and neck. "Honey, please wake up."

"Trigg?" Ellari opened her eyes slowly. Reaching up she touched the top of her head and winced. "Ouch," she moaned, making a face. "That hurts."

"What happened?" Trigg asked, checking her head.

"I chased him into the O'Learys' barn, and he hit me with something." She closed her eyes. "I think he had a board."

"You've got quite a goose egg," he said, "but I don't think there's any serious damage. You're not bleeding."

She smiled weakly. "Maybe it even knocked some sense into me, huh?"

He grinned his relief and stood, lifting her as he did. "That might be too much to hope for!"

"Trigg! Look!" Ellari cried, pointing over his shoulder.

Holding her, he turned back toward the barn. The sight that met his gaze was a vision out of

431

Hell. What had been a small blaze moments before had completely engulfed the O'Leary barn in flames. Gigantic spears of fire shot into the sky, lighting the night with an eerie orange glow. The ground around the barn was alive with the spreading fire, as the flames consumed dried weeds, discarded shingles, and combustible rubbish—anything and everything in its path.

Frantic people in all degrees of dress and undress ran screaming toward them, carrying crying babies and whatever they had been able to save from their sap-laden pine-board shanties, before their tarred roofs had become food for the vicious wind-driven flames. Everything was on fire.

Trigg turned to run, determined to get Ellari out of harm's way.

"Put me down!" she screamed over the clamor of the people and the snapping and cracking of the fire bearing down on them like a train from Hell. "We've got to help that woman!" She pointed to an old woman who carried a baby on each hip, and had three young children clinging to her skirt. "She'll never make it alone."

"But your head!"

"I'm fine. Just help her."

Taking her at her word, Trigg put Ellari down, and together they ran to the struggling woman.

"Give me one of the babies!" Ellari ordered the woman as she snatched up the smaller of the three wailing toddlers from the ground. The woman

432

turned over a baby to Ellari without arguing as Trigg hefted the two larger children into his own arms.

Getting behind the two women, he herded the group forward. Her burden halved, and with no children clinging to her skirts, the old woman was able to move more rapidly. But every time Trigg looked back, he had the distinct sense that the fire was gaining on them. Shanties, barns, sheds, trash piles, cottages, sidewalks, streets were all being devoured with unbelievable speed.

The fires of Hell had been unleashed on the notorious city of Chicago, and there was no turning them back. They had no choice but to try to outrun the flames and get across the river into the South Side—or to sacrifice themselves to the ungodly holocaust descending on them.

Certain the fire would not cross the one-hundred-fifty-foot wide southern branch of the Chicago River into downtown, the panicked inhabitants from the West Side stampeded across the wooden bridges and through the tunnels into the South Side.

They carried bird cages, children, mattresses, pets, vases, blankets, books, clothing, large paintings, musical instruments, picture frames, boxes, valises, pots and pans—anything and everything they had been able to grab as they had fled from

433

their homes. They all believed if they could only make it to downtown, they would certainly be safe, since many of the buildings there were made of brick, and the streets of cobblestones.

Behind them, the ever-growing creature from Hell raged uncontrolled. Moving nearly as fast as a person could run, the fire lashed out long tongues of flame and sent blasts of iron-melting heat thundering along the wooden streets and sidewalks at a maniacal pace, while in the air the fiery breath of the demon rode gale-force winds from rooftop to rooftop.

Nothing was sacred, nothing taboo to the crazed beast, and there was no doubt that outrunning the holocaust was the only chance at survival.

Slowed by the woman they were helping, the growing mobs and the congested bridge, and because they had stopped several times to help other people, it was almost midnight by the time Ellari and Trigg and their group reached the Courthouse at the center of the city—nearly three hours since the fire had started.

None of the big fires had ever reached this far downtown, and Courthouse Square was packed with a solid mass of bewildered and exhausted people who stared in numb silence at the red-orange glow lighting up the entire southwestern end of the city from which they had escaped.

Feeling somewhat safe, and panting with fatigue, Trigg and the two women paused to regain their strength. However, their relief was shortlived.

"The fire's jumped the river!" someone yelled from an upstairs window of the Courthouse. "It's comin' this way!"

Renewed panic broke loose over the Square as the five-and-a-half ton bell in the two-story tower of the Courthouse clanged with more urgency.

The area erupted in a cacophony of hellish sounds and pandemonium. Desperate to escape the onslaught, everyone tried to run, but the streets were so congested it was difficult to do much but go with the mob—or be trampled underfoot.

Hysterical horses neighed and reared in wild-eyed terror; dogs howled and barked and ran in mindless circles; children cried and screamed; men cursed and whipped their horses mercilessly to push through the crowds; women wept and moaned as they searched for lost children and old people.

"I can't go on," the old woman wailed, stumbling over a huge brown rat that scurried across her path.

Trigg shifted the older of the two toddlers he carried to his back. "Hold on tight, boy," he told the child. "Give me the baby," he said to the woman, relieving her of her burden.

"Maybe that cartman has room for them on his wagon!" Ellari cried, pointing to a horse-and-wagon team.

Trigg nodded and sprinted toward the wagon,

leaving Ellari to hurry the woman along. By the time they reached the wagon, Trigg had come to an agreement with the driver. Together, they put the five children and the woman in the back of the wagon with several other women and children.

"You too," Trigg ordered Ellari. "I paid him to take you all over the bridge to the North Side."

"What about you?" Ellari asked, resisting his efforts to lift her into the wagon.

"I'd better stay here. It's going to get worse."

"I'm staying with you!" she screamed over the noise. "Give my place to someone else."

"I gotta go now, mister!" the driver yelled.

"Go on!" Ellari ordered the man. "I'll walk."

"Someone help me!" A woman in tattered night-clothes and large with child staggered toward them. "I can't go—" She pitched forward.

Working as one, Trigg and Ellari caught her before she went down. Trigg lifted her onto the wagon, and yelled to the driver. "You'd better go on."

Amid the churning turmoil, Trigg grinned at Ellari and shook his head. "You're some woman, Ellari Lochridge!"

She returned his smile. "We're a team. Remember?"

By one-thirty, flaming cinders were raining down on the roof of the Courthouse and onto the heads of the people who remained in the square. The roof began to smolder.

The home of Chicago's City Hall, the Cook County Courthouse, the mayor, the Board of Police, the chief fire marshall—and the county jail—the ungainly limestone structure was considered to be totally fireproof, despite the wooden tower at its center and cornices all around.

Streams of water were hosed on the Courthouse by exhausted firemen, but to no avail. It was not long before the roof of the building, made famous in postcards visitors sent back home from Chicago, burst into flame.

When the roof collapsed, the great fire bell crashed through five floors from the bell tower to the basement, pealing to the very end. The people in Courthouse Square scattered like frightened birds. At the same time, hundreds of beautiful white pigeons rose into the smoke-filled air. They circled a few times in wild confusion, then as if they had given up, they dove back into the flames.

The jails had been emptied when the fire had started to draw near, so now three hundred criminals were added to the swarm of good samaritans who'd stayed to help others, the doubters who hadn't believed the fire would actually reach this far, and the merchants who'd stayed to salvage records and merchandise.

Though many of the freed prisoners immediately stormed the deserted shops surrounding the Courthouse, looking for and stuffing their pockets with anything they thought was valuable, one jeweler on Randolph Street stood outside his shop giving out free bracelets, rings and watches to any who would take them.

By the time the throng reached Lake Street, the mayhem was in full swing. Looters made no pretense at being subtle, businessmen scrambled to save records and papers, people flagged down wagons at gunpoint, kindly old women became thieves, criminals became heroes. It was madness. There were even people lighting fires after they had ransacked stores.

And for many, this was truly the end of the world.

Monday afternoon, when Ellari and Trigg finally staggered into Lincoln Park along Lake Michigan on the North Side, the sight that welcomed them was as bizarre as any they had seen.

Many acres of the park were once an old cemetery, and the city had been in the process of moving the coffins to a new location farther north. Now, to Ellari's surprise, entire families huddled in the empty graves, doing their best to shield themselves from the continuous shower of sparks raining down on them by stacking grave stones around the graves.

In the beautiful lagoon where Ellari and Trigg

had picnicked only a few weeks before, people soaked themselves to keep the clothes from burning off their backs. Some used buckets and pans to ladle water over their bodies. Others chose to sit up to their necks in the water, seemingly oblivious to the drowned rats floating past their faces.

Others sat waist and chest deep in the waters of Lake Michigan, or buried themselves in the sand on the shore. One such family was in the process of dragging a couch into the lake to sit on. Others drove horses and wagons directly into the lake.

Everywhere, refugees sat on the ground in glassy-eyed despair, their meager belongings clutched to their bosoms—a bolt of material, a sack of silverware, a child's shoe.

Covered in soot, many were half-naked. Others were wrapped in tattered, sometimes smoldering blankets and nightshirts. Rich and poor alike all appeared to have suffered at least minor burns to their skin. Many people, especially the women, prayed aloud. More often, the men sought solace and oblivion from a more earthly power, a bottle of whiskey—probably pilfered from a liquor store during their flight from the fire.

For the rest of the day and evening, Ellari and Trigg helped wherever they could, fetching water for old and injured people, bandaging more serious burns and wounds with scraps of fine fabric they had found, consoling lost children and worried mothers, and even milking a goat to get enough milk for a tiny infant who'd been saved when his mother had died giving birth to it in one of the open graves.

At ten o'clock that evening, when Ellari felt the first drops of rain on her face, she couldn't believe it. "Did you feel that?" she asked excitedly, glancing up into the smoke-filled sky.

Trigg lowered an old man to the ground after helping him drink a few sips of water he'd brought him from the park's artesian well. "Feel what?" he asked, standing up. Cupping his hand behind his neck, he closed his eyes and wearily rotated his head.

"Rain," Ellari said, her eyes filling with emotion. "I could swear I felt—" Her face broke into a grin. "There it is again!" She looked down at her arm. "Look!" she squealed, indicating the rapidly multiplying water splotches on the back of her soot-blackened hand. "See. It's raining!"

"Rain!" someone yelled in the distance. "It's raining!"

"Praise God!" another person cried. "We're saved. Our prayers are answered."

It was two more days before Ellari and Trigg could think about making their way through the charred remains of what had been Chicago. It was estimated that more than seventeen thousand buildings had burned to the ground in less than a

440

four-mile square area, and though Monday night's miraculous rain had put out the blaze, the city continued to smoulder.

There was no hope of finding anything still standing that had been in the path of the fire, but Ellari knew she had to go back one last time and see the place where her father's drugstore had stood for so many years.

All along the way back to the southern West Side, they had seen evidence that despite the total devastation, Chicago would indeed rise again. Already, enterprising people were nailing stalls together to start up their businesses again, selling whatever they could find to sell. Churches had set up soup kitchens and shelters. Nearby cities had sent food and supplies and volunteers to help. The police department had been enlarged by using volunteers, and the United States Army had arrived to help keep law and order.

As they drew near the block where the Nylander Glass Works had been, they saw that it too had not escaped the fury of the fire.

"I have to admit, this is one place I'm not sorry to see burned to the ground," Ellari said, gazing over the vast desert of burned out rubble, fallen stone, and contorted metal pipes and machinery that had been fashioned into grotesque shapes by the intense heat of the fire. The only thing still standing on the enormous lot was the brick archway through which hundreds of children had passed each day to work in subhuman conditions.

The sounds of gunfire caught their attention.

"Get out of here, you filthy little vermin!" a man shrieked.

For the first time, Ellari and Trigg noticed signs of life in the factory's ruins. Like a frightened flock of blackbirds, small ghostly forms materialized and scampered across the charred remains. All of them were so covered with soot that they had been invisible at first glance.

A man loomed into view, his pistol sited on the fleeing youngsters. "If I catch you here again—"

"Hey!" Trigg yelled to divert the man's attention. "They're just kids!"

Obviously startled to hear another adult's voice, the man spun round to face Trigg and Ellari. "You!" the equally soot-covered man bellowed.

"Nylander?" Trigg asked uncertainly. "Is that you?" Black from head to toe, he looked thinner and older, and as if he hadn't slept in days.

Forgetting the young scavengers, Nylander leveled his revolver on Ellari. "You couldn't resist coming back to gloat, could you?" He indicated the destruction around him with his free hand. "Well, you got what you wanted. If you hadn't turned Stahl against me, I could have rebuilt, but thanks to you, I'm ruined. Does that make you happy?"

"I didn't come to gloat, Mr. Nylander, and I don't find happiness in any aspect of the destruction of our city, your factory included. But I have to say that I'm thankful for the fact that you won't be abusing and taking advantage of any more children in this place."

Nylander's face twisted with anger. "You think you've won, don't you, bitch? But you're wrong. I should have had you killed the first time you tried to turn people against me." He raised his gun to fire. "I'll see you in Hell for the misery you've caused me."

Moving quickly, Trigg knocked Ellari to the ground and fell on top of her, whipping his own gun out of the holster as he did.

Nylander's shot zipped over their heads.

Before Trigg could take aim and fire, a second shot rang out in quick succession to the first.

Before their eyes, Nylander clutched his chest and pitched forward, becoming one with the black rubble at his feet.

Staring in amazement, Trigg glanced around to see three grown men approaching. Though he didn't recognize them, he could tell by their dress that they were laborers from the neighborhood. "Thanks," he grunted, lumbering to his feet and helping Ellari to hers.

"Mr. Schmelzel?" Ellari asked, wiping her hands off on her own filthy clothing. She couldn't believe her eyes. The man who'd been ready to kill her not too long ago had just saved her life. "Is that you?"

"Ya, it ist me, Fraulein. Are you all right?"

"Yes, I'm fine. We're just thankful to have survived. What about you? Were you able to save any of your possessions?"

"Ve ver among der lucky vons in dat our house did not burn."

"It didn't?" Ellari asked, glancing around at the total destruction for as far as she could see.

"Der vind was blowink so hard dat nothink south of der fire burned. Even Patrick O'Leary's house is still standink."

"I can't believe it," she gasped, smiling her happiness for Schmelzel and his neighborhood. "I'm so glad you and your family were so fortunate."

Schmelzel's face saddened and his already drooping shoulders sagged. "But ve lost two of our boys in der fire."

"Oh, no! Are you sure? Maybe they just haven't been able to get back here yet. There are thousands of refugees still on the North Side, and on the upper West Side." Her heart ached for the poor man.

"I don't tink so. Dey vas verkink here in der factory on a special shift." He paused and glanced around at the heap that had been the factory, his eyes glistening with tears. "Ven vord reached dem dat der vas a big fire, Herr Nylander told dem der fire vouldn't burn der bricks und dat dey vould be docked for de whole shift if dey left der post before quittink time. Some of de boys left anyvay, but most were too afraid of vat der fathers vould do if dey lost der pay, so dey stayed. My two boys ver among dose boys."

"Oh, Mr. Schmelzel!" Ellari cried, tears running down her face. "I'm so sorry! If only there were something I could do."

"It ist mine fault. If I had listened to you, Fraulein, none of dis vould haf happened. My two boys vould be safe and alive, and I vould not haf dis emptiness inside me. Because dey ver afraid of me, dey are dead. I might as vell haf killed dem myself."

"No! You were only doing what you thought was right, because you loved them, Mr. Schmelzel. And they knew that."

Slowly, the children who'd been chased out of the ruins by Nylander began to materialize again. This time there were adults with them, both women and men. Automatically, they silently began to search through the charred rubble.

"What are they looking for?" Trigg asked.

"Ve search for our dead so ve can gif dem a proper burial."

"Would you like us to help?" Ellari asked, not really thinking there was much chance of finding the bodies, but feeling she should offer.

Schmelzel shook his head. "De livink are de ones who need you now, Fraulein. Der are many burns and injuries. You go take care of dem. Ve vill do dis ourselves."

445

"Very well, I'll try, but without medical supplies, I'm not sure there's much I can do but give emotional support."

"Your pharmacy vas one of de buildings dat survived, Fraulein," Schmelzel said with a sad smile.

"It did?" she and Trigg responded in unison. "But how?"

Schmelel shrugged. "God verks in strange and mysterious vays. Your whole block vas saved."

"Then that means—" Ellari caught herself. "Of course, I'm sure the looters have taken everything by now."

The man with Schmelzel who'd been silent until now spoke. "Ve tought, after de vay ve treated you, ve owed it to you to keep a eye on your store so no von vould take nothink till you come back. Ve even been feedink your horses."

"The horses are all right too! I can't believe it. I don't know how I'll ever make this up to you."

"Der is nothink to make up. Ve only hope you can forgif us for all der trouble ve caused you."

"We do have one little problem," Trigg interjected. He indicated Nylander's body with a nod of his head.

"Ve must report dis to the police and tell dem vat happened. Ya?"

"What did happen?" Trigg asked. "All I know is we found him like that when we were searching the grounds for survivors. I assume he killed him-

446

self when he found his factory was destroyed. Isn't that what you assume?"

The immigrant smiled gratefully. "Tank you, my friend. My family vill be forever in your debt."

Ellari and Trigg stepped inside the darkened pharmacy. It smelled like smoke, but otherwise it was as they had left it — wrecked and torn up by Nylander's men, but intact.

"Oh, Trigg, have you ever seen anything so beautiful?" Ellari asked tearfully, running from corner to corner. "I still can't believe how blessed we've been. We have the pharmacy, the horses, and each other. How much more fortunate can we be?"

Trigg watched her, smiling. "I love you Ellari Lochridge. You're all the blessing I'll ever need!"

Ellari paused and cupped his face in her hands. "What? Does this mean you've given up your plans to be the richest man in Chicago?"

"Not really. But now I know whether or not I'm a millionaire or dead broke, I'll be the richest man in the world as long as I have you."

A long drawn out meow scolded before Ellari could respond. They both looked down in surprise as a scruffy looking alley cat twisted lithely between their legs.

"Mr. Cat!" they laughed in unison as they dropped to their knees to hug the demanding feline.

"Where do you suppose he came from?" Trigg chuckled, scratching the cantankerous old-timer's back.

"I don't know, but now I know that all our dreams are going to come true. We're going to reopen the drugstore and make it nicer than ever, and we're going to help thousands of people with Magicure, and we're going to live happily ever after."

"How do you know that?"

"Because it was meant to be. You were meant to come into my life and turn it upside down, and I was meant to settle you down, and we were meant to live happily ever after—just like in the fairy tales. You just take my word for it."

"I guess I don't have much choice. This is one argument I'll be glad to see you win!"